MICHAEL ATAMANOV

EXTERNAL
THREAT

*Wishing you safe travels on
your fantasy journey,*

Michael Atamanov

REALITY BENDERS
BOOK TWO

MAGIC DOME BOOKS

External Threat
Reality Benders, Book Two
Copyright © Michael Atamanov 2018
Cover Art © Vladimir Manyukhin 2018
English Translation Copyright ©
Andrew Schmitt 2018
Published by Magic Dome Books, 2018
All Rights Reserved
ISBN: 978-80-88295-82-2

All books
by Michael Atamanov:

TABLE OF CONTENTS:

Introduction

Through
Enemy Eyes

PA-LIN-THU, CAPITAL OF THE FIRST DIRECTORY
PALACE OF THE RULING COUNCIL
SMALL COUNCIL CHAMBER

I N AN AUSTERE BLACK ceremonial toga, free of regalia or adornments, Thumor-Anhu La-Fin strode majestically up an illuminated path to a podium. From the corner of his eye, the old man could see rows of cold gazes radiating in the gloomy silent room. The Mage leader didn't even need his psionic abilities to sense the tension. He already knew how eagerly these lower-rank rulers would devour him if he slipped up or demonstrated so much as a hint of weakness or timidity. All these mages feared and respected only one thing: strength. So, as Coruler Thumor-Anhu La-Fin walked through the room, he couldn't allow a single muscle on his proud, majestic face to twitch.

And it was hard to maintain that composure because the high Mage had to leave his usual staff at the entrance to the palace. Though flawlessly polite and decorous, the guards at the front door were unflappable, insisting that he surrender his magical implement. They allowed him to take a similar-looking if powerless replacement, though. And now, as he walked, Thumor-Anhu La-Fin was putting a bit of weight on that toothless pretense, that mere cane. Being separated from his trusty wizarding utensil got under the old mage's skin and added fuel to the fire of anxiety inside him. It now seemed he was standing on the very edge of catastrophe. After all, never before in his forty years of power had he been asked to surrender his prized piece of knotted wood just to attend a meeting. Sometimes, when council sessions went on too long, its powerful magic provided much-needed support to his achy bones, so it wasn't purely a question of defense, either.

Any other day, Thumor-Anhu La-Fin would have made a huge scene, demanding he be treated with respect as a noble Coruler and elder. He was one of humanity's three highest overlords, so the insolent guards that dared make him part with his staff deserved nothing less. In fact, they should have been reduced to steaming puddles of protoplasm or carbonized statues. But today was not the day for stoking tensions. After all, this council session had been called to discuss Thumor-Anhu's fitness to lead a faction in the game that bends reality. And after a recent string of misfortunes, his faction really was in a rough position, a fact which cast his competency and wisdom into grave doubt...

Ever since it was introduced, the game that bends reality had captivated the minds of the ruling aristocracy. It offered truly limitless possibilities and learning opportunities. Furthermore, if one's magical power grew in the game, it increased in the real world as well. The game could also cure any disease and, with a few exceptions, grant absolute immortality. However, for now, the number of people that could enter and play the game was limited. In fact, there were so many more hopefuls than available openings that some had been contested by duels to the death. So, it came as no surprise that all three Corulers of humanity wanted to watch over and guide their society's progress in the game, and were even participating directly, each at the head of their own faction.

By now, the virtual world had provided a good deal of astonishing discoveries and advanced science by centuries, so the ruling council made it a top priority. Just one word from a faction leader, and high-value real-world resources would be requisitioned to exchange for alien technology in the game. Whole institutes of analysts and diviners were working nonstop to determine the most effective strategies both for growth and dispatching neighboring factions. If a faction leader needed someone of a particular profession, they could recruit straight from the top of that field regardless of the draftee's feelings on the matter. The need to dominate in the game had superseded all real-world problems. There was a famine in the Third Directory, for example, and an anti-mage uprising in the Sixth. Recently, the self-styled monarch of the Second Directory had even been allowed to join the ruling council. Sure, he was a successful and popular military commander, but he was the first person without magical abilities to sit on the council in eight hundred years.

Thumor-Anhu La-Fin was scheduled to speak third. The other two corulers had already finished their speeches, intelligently arguing their right to lead not only in the real world, but also in the game that bends reality. And now, the ruling council would hear from Leng Thumor-Anhu La-Fin. He knew they'd have lots of questions, so stepping up to the podium felt like going to the gallows.

Just before he reached the rostrum, Thumor-Anhu La-Fin slightly turned his head and glanced at the other two honorable Corulers. Anri-Huvi La-Shin was wearing a bright red ribbon on his toga, meaning he was going to chair this meeting. A good sign! Unlike Coruler Onuri-Unta La-Varrez, he did not harbor a personal disdain for Thumor-Anhu and would not try to make him look bad with trick questions and acrid remarks. Anri-Huvi La-Shin was almost a friend, at least, to the degree true camaraderie was possible between members of the upper aristocracy. And sure, Anri-Huvi La-Shin would probably want a political favor for his loyalty. Perhaps he would ask for his son to be put on the council, or for his newest wife to be handed a leadership position at the thermonuclear powerplant when it was up and running. None of that was impossible, though.

Just then, a huge screen lit up behind him, and the council went silent, hanging on his every word.

Thumor-Anhu La-Fin confidently spouted off numbers and performance metrics, not even looking at the presentation behind him, demonstrating an excellent memory and sharp mind. His colony was growing vigorously. He had five hexagons, all with high development, and a further two neighboring ones were being prepared for colonization. The capital hexagon had reached development level four. His faction now had over three thousand seven hundred players and a burgeoning manufacturing sector, and they were fully self-sufficient in everything from food to high-tech weaponry. What was more, trade had been established with the Geckho overlords and a high-speed road to the Geckho spaceport was under construction. His group did find itself in a somewhat rough neighborhood, though... The Leng figured this would be the lynchpin of his speech, so he spent the lion's share of his time on it. As an experienced politician, he knew not to try and sweep obvious problems under the rug. Much better to get out ahead of the issue, so the favorable framing would stick in the audience's mind. First impressions and all that...

So, as he put it, his faction had been saddled with troublesome neighbors. And that was not to say there were problems with the primitive NPC harpies or other mythical creatures. But the nearby player faction was a bit more of a challenge. The H3 Faction was very warlike, and they had around fifteen hundred players. What was more, the majority of the enemy faction was made up of professional soldiers with tons of real-world combat experience. So, despite Thumor-Anhu's superiority in numbers and technology, direct confrontation had not brought the desired result. Even still, after every skirmish, the factions just returned to their initial positions, so nothing was lost per se. But the H3 Faction had captured quite a bit of weaponry and equipment. And not only were they using it in battle, they were learning to reproduce it, which threatened to level out the technological imbalance.

But, Leng La-Fin had decided to change strategies, and was no longer trying to finish off his dangerous neighbors with a single decisive battle. All his projections showed that the H3 Faction was progressing slower than his. What was more, they didn't have any mages, and thus lacked the ability to detect mind control or implanted thoughts. So, he was now going to try and infiltrate the enemy with magic, using active propaganda to defeat them indirectly. And that tactic had already borne fruit. One of the top leaders of the H3 Faction had been working for Leng La-Fin for a long time, providing valuable information right from the enemy headquarters. And just yesterday, he was successfully evacuated to La-Fin's capital hexagon.

"And Coruler Thumor-Anhu La-Fin calls that a victory?" As the old mage feared, Coruler Onuri-Unta La-Varrez sunk his teeth into this weak spot. "Essentially, his most valuable agent has been neutralized. How is that something to celebrate??? I call it an abject failure! Also, considering his technological superiority and three-fold numerical advantage, I have a hard time comprehending how he could possibly lose!!!"

It took all Thumor-Anhu La-Fin's patience to

maintain a calm expression. In his report, he hadn't said he had three times more players. Three thousand seven hundred versus fifteen hundred was nowhere near that. But his opponent was probably not merely mistaken. He was almost certainly trying to draw attention to the numbers issue. He must have known about yesterday's bombardment of the grain hexagon. It had lost two development levels, forcing Thumor-Anhu La-Fin's faction to thin its ranks by seven hundred. Before the battle, he did have a three-fold advantage, and Onuri-Unta La-Varrez must have wanted to make sure everyone knew that.

Gathering his thoughts and emotions, the elderly mage started answering in an even and unexpressive tone:

"You mustn't underestimate our opponent. Despite their ignorance of the magical arts, the H3 Faction has a counterintelligence service that runs like clockwork, and they have exposed several of our spies already. And an agent as valuable as this one, with access to top-secret plans, can be exposed easily by giving him specific information, and waiting to see if it falls into our hands. Our man came under suspicion, so we pulled him out ASAP. He will be provided everything he needs and can be used as proof that we keep our word. What's more, after we established that players can move between our factions, entering one virtual reality pod and exiting another, it was time to test whether physical bodies can be brought from the parallel world into our own. Now we know they can, which will sway many hesitant H3 Faction members. And there will be more of them every day, because we have implanted thoughts to undermine their system of loyalty and mutual trust..."

Based on the buzz of approval, the council was mostly in agreement with Thumor-Anhu La-Fin. What was more, help came just in time from the chairman:

"Coruler Onuri-Unta La-Varrez is glossing over the geography and history of the parallel world, and so has neglected to mention that the H3 Faction is their largest country. On a number of occasions, they have defeated grand coalitions of the other factions we've encountered. And while Onuri-Unta wiped out the H11 Faction just after they entered the game, and vassalized the H8 Faction not long after, which were both campaigns of unquestioned valor, there is no comparison to what Thumor-Anhu is facing."

Such timely support would certainly have to be repaid... Honestly, Thumor-Anhu La-Fin himself didn't even know these details and made a mental note to look into the history of the parallel world. The report continued. Thumor-Anhu was particularly afraid of mentioning the significant ransoms he had paid, and the temporary ceasefire, but the ruling council had basically no comment. As a matter of fact, there were no problems right up until the end of the speech, which was about yesterday's battle.

"Aha, more evidence that Coruler Thumor-Anhu La-Fin has no aptitude as a military tactician or strategist!!!" Coruler Onuri-Unta La-Varrez said, taking the floor with statements that bordered on flagrantly insulting. "You'd have to be trying to fail with such a colossal advantage and the element of surprise! But fail you did, and now your whole faction is in dire straits!"

The council stayed silent in fear when the false staff in the great mage's hands suddenly began to glow with summoned energy. However, it went dim just as quickly. Thumor-Anhu La-Fin overcame his emotions and stopped any nasty curses from accidentally spilling out. His opponent was not suicidal so, if he was blatantly provoking Thumor-Anhu, he had surely tended to his defense. He must have had some friends who would have his back if it came to a wizarding showdown.

"Coruler Onuri-Unta La-Varrez should get his information from more reliable sources." Not a single hint of annoyance or any other feeling slipped through in the old mage's calm voice. "Because our attack achieved all its objectives. The enemy's oil well and refinery in the swamp hexagon were destroyed. That strikes a heavy blow to their mobility and military strength. You see, the H3 Faction is just now beginning to incorporate antigravs, while their native transportation technology requires petrochemicals as fuel. They were beginning to expand into the rocky coast, but that is now all up in the air because it's too hard to reach. Also, the H3 Faction currently cannot trade with the Geckho for the same reason. Restoring control over the swamp hexagon and repairing their citadel, demolished bridges, pontoons, dams, and defensive structures will take four days at least. And it will also take four days for them to rebuild their oil facilities. And ten days after that, the ceasefire will be over. Then we can just destroy it all over again..."

"But what about the heavy losses of manpower and forced retreat from the swamp hexagon? And the raiding party?" Onuri-Unta La-Varrez just wouldn't back down, but it was clear that was only still arguing out of inertia because his reasoning just kept getting weaker.

"We weren't trying to take control of the swamp hexagon. It is too hard to supply, and we'd have to place a disproportionately large garrison there because it's so near the enemy heartland. Were our losses significant...? Sure, thousands of our players went to respawn. But I already mentioned that we were up against trained professional soldiers, and the average level of the H3 Faction is higher than ours. What's more, we were facing the First Legion in the swamp hexagon. That's the enemy's highest-tier elite force, so it would be somewhat naive to expect our losses to be equal."

Before continuing his speech, Thumor-Anhu held a short pause and took a sip of an energy elixir. His old legs were shaking treacherously in exhaustion, and the mage even had to lean on the false staff so he wouldn't fall over in front of the whole council. What was more, he needed a pause to gather his thoughts because the biggest hump was now on the horizon. The enemy raiders had just waltzed into his territory! Then look at who they were led by! It was easy to see why this was a delicate topic. But he wouldn't exactly be able to cover it up now. After a moment of consideration, the experienced politician decided to tell them everything.

"So, the raiders... Yes, we were taken by complete surprise when they showed up behind our lines in the middle of pitched battles in the swamp hexagon and rocky coast. After all, we thought our spies would let us know about enemy combat operations in advance. But as our defector has already explained, even the H3 leadership was caught completely off guard. And the raid was more destructive than we ever could have imagined. It took some time to get forces back from the front, so the consequences were dire. The infrastructure of the grain hexagon was severely damaged, and it will take time to rebuild all they destroyed. What's more, the experimental *Sio-Mi-Dori* antigrav crashed while trying to pursue the raiders. We still haven't established the cause. There are qualified experts studying the wreckage now, but this accident will push back the timetable for putting such craft into serial production. As for the leader of the raid, it was a man named Gnat, a player I'm sure many of you have heard of..."

"The craftiest member of the H3 Faction? The one who has taken Coruler Thumor-Anhu La-Fin's granddaughter prisoner two times? He also sent you to respawn once if memory serves."

That question came from the chairman himself and, most likely, it was for the best. Thumor-Anhu La-Fin knew that there had been rumors swirling about this Gnat's behavior. They said he disrespected the Leng right to his face and had brought shame on the noble Minn-O La-Fin. He knew those facts were savored by his foes. But now, there was no incitement about "insulting a Leng," or even "dishonoring a noble lady." Coruler Anri-Huvi La-Shin was clearly formulating the question as delicately as possible and was probably hoping to reap the dividends of this in the future. And he deserved nothing less.

"Yes, Coruler Anri-Huvi La-Shin, that's the man. By the way, I advise all other rulers to look into this Gnat, because I am certain this won't be the last you hear of him. He's quite remarkable. I've had my eye on him for some time. He's still a new player, and he has no respect for the law or authorities. In his world, he was a criminal. The H3 Faction mostly hates him because he killed a beloved commander and is generally disobedient and defiant. That might make you think he's just some hoodlum, and the best he could hope for is a lifetime of hard labor. But strangely, despite all that, Gnat has already achieved the rank of Gerd. And our Geckho suzerains are crazy for him. They take him with them into space and even, despite all their assurances that they will not interfere in our conflicts, just one word from Gnat and they flew down from space to evacuate him in the middle of battle!"

At these words, a buzz came over the chamber. The council was discussing heatedly, unable to hide their astonishment. Thumor-Anhu La-Fin, very satisfied with the effect, made a brief pause, allowing the audience to say their fill, then continued his speech:

"And do you know what Gnat brought his scientists after his last voyage into outer space? An Annihilator of an ancient race, a functioning armored spacesuit of an unknown civilization and... this one's a real doozy! A highly detailed diagram of a Geckho starship!"

The audience started making a racket again. Some council members even jumped out of their seats.

But this time, the old mage gestured for silence, so he could continue.

"I see, honorable rulers, that you also appreciate the scale of the problem. Who knows what Gnat might bring back after his next journey into space? And who can guess what technologies that might provide our enemies? Potentially, this is a grave threat to our faction's technological advantage!"

"He must be stopped!" someone shouted, and Thumor-Anhu La-Fin was eager to agree:

"Precisely! Honorable rulers, I know perfectly well that you have dragged my name through the mud in private and laughed at my doddering foolishness. You say that I, a respected Leng and faction leader, am paying too much heed to a common player and you mock the five-thousand-crystal bounty I've placed on his head. Well, I'm doubling it. What is more, I officially promise sanctuary to any member of the H3 Faction who helps us take Gnat prisoner or neutralizes him in the real world! My agents will try to spread this information as widely as possible, so that every member of the H3 Faction knows! I want Gnat to be constantly on edge, so he cannot sleep, so he sees everyone he meets as a potential murderer. He cannot be allowed to trust any of his allies. Even if I don't ever pay that bounty, no person can live under constant stress for long. Gnat will be forced to choose: either leave his home planet forever or join us of his own accord! And my intuition tells me he'll choose the latter!"

The end of the great mage's speech was met with a standing ovation. From the corner of his eye, Thumor-Anhu La-Fin saw that both other Corulers were also applauding. Complete approval! He wouldn't be losing his rank, title or fortune today. Now, he just had to keep his promises.

.

Chapter One

Back to Space!

THE FIRST CHANGE I noticed back aboard the Shiamiru was that not all the bunk rooms were full anymore!

On my last flight, there were huge hairy Geckho sitting on every cot and pull-out seat. But now, walking down the corridor, I saw upper beds folded up and unoccupied. There were even a few empty ones down below.

"Gnat, six crew members decided not to renew their contracts," Uline Tar whispered when I remarked on the change. "That has Captain Uraz Tukhsh very worried, though he won't show it. But let's discuss that later. For now, buckle up. We're taking off."

"And what about my injured friend?" I asked, worried about Dmitry Zheltov. After all, this was his first time on this shuttle and he didn't understand a single word of Geckho. But Uline Tar reassured me:

"There's a medic working on him right now, so everything is fine. The human pilot was assigned to the second bunk, together with the Navigator and Senior Engineer. And, I'll have you know, that's a place of great honor!"

"And where are our bunkmates Vasha and Basha?"

The end of my question was drowned out by the roar of the engines, so she seemingly didn't hear.

However, I had already spotted the two big twin brothers in the neighboring bunk. Both of them bared their teeth at me in greeting and seemingly said something, based on the way their lips were moving. I waved back, but the extreme G-forces made it a real undertaking.

And that was just the beginning. We were still gradually accelerating.

After some time, it became totally unbearable... My back was pressed into the seat so hard I thought I heard my bones crack. On our last takeoff, it was somewhat less severe.

Seemingly, the blood was flowing out of my head because my eyes went dim. I was clinging to the edge of consciousness. The only sensory tether still holding me to reality was the sound of my heart pounding...

No, I couldn't die like that!

Before my faculties left me once and for all, I threw open the menu and brought up my statistics:

Gerd Gnat. Human. H3 Faction.	
Level-38 Prospector	
Statistics:	
Strength	13
Agility	15
Intelligence	19
Perception	21
Constitution	13
Luck modifier	+3
Parameters:	
Hitpoints	817 of 998
Endurance points	140 of 580
Magic points	0
Carrying capacity	58 lbs.
Fame	34
Skills:	
Electronics	24
Scanning	37
Cartography	39
Astrolinguistics	35
Break-in	15
Rifles	37
Mineralogy	13
Medium Armor	40
Eagle Eye	39
Sharpshooter	17
Targeting	11
Danger Sense	15

I needed to put one point into Constitution right away! I felt slight relief, but it didn't last long. I threw another point into Constitution, bringing it to 15.

The dizziness retreated. That was either my improved stats, or we reached our target velocity. I strained to catch my breath and turned my head to look at Uline, who was spitting mad:

"I guess our brainless captain forgot to turn on the gravity compensators! Or maybe something broke again. He's so inept, his arms might as well grow out of his ass!"

So, this was not normal. That put my mind slightly at ease. But, not wanting to think about stat and skill points anymore, I kept the window open and spent some time thinking over where to put my remaining points. What exactly did I need?

Strength? After raising Constitution, Strength had become my lowest statistic at just 13. It governed my carrying capacity, abil

ty to use heavy weaponry, throwing range and damage in hand-to-hand combat... On the other hand, did a Prospector or Listener really need high Strength? The answer was not apparent.

Agility? The only statistic I had never improved. I knew it could unlock higher-quality weapons from the Rifles group, though. And even if that was my only motivation, it was enough. The Krechet carbine and Annihilator both took all the Agility I had, so I couldn't ever wield a better one without improving it. Alright, I'd put one point there and bring it to sixteen. But I still had five of the eight stat points I'd gained from achieving the rank Gerd.

Intelligence? For a Prospector, working with complicated electronics, this was a very, very important statistic. I suspected my high Intelligence was a major factor in how quickly I was leveling Astrolinguistics and Cartography as well. I had no idea whether a Listener needed high Intelligence, though. But regardless, I was not planning to change class before the end of my contract with Captain Uraz Tukhsh. That could put me and my whole faction in an awkward position. After all, I wasn't sure if a Listener could use a Prospector Scanner, which is what I'd been hired to do. At any rate, I'd just become aware I could change class, so there was no rush.

In the end, I decided to add one point to Intelligence, raising it to 20. And then... I blinked in astonishment. Another parameter also changed:

Magic points	*114*

Just then, a blue bar came up below my life bar. Did I now have mana?! Cool, sure, but also a bit scary. What could I do with it? What could I spend Magic Points on, and from a technical standpoint, how did I use them? I hadn't gained any spells, so I was at a loss.

I was initially planning to invest just one point in Intelligence, but now I couldn't hold back and added another just out of curiosity. My magic points immediately grew to 119. But what good was that?

Alright, enough monkeying around. I still had Perception, a Prospector's most important stat. I was somewhat upset because, when I put on the new Listener suit, I had to remove my infantry helmet. And unfortunately the IR Lens, which raised my Perception by 2, was clipped to my old headgear. But that couldn't be helped. It was either the armor suit or the helmet and lens... Or was I wrong? I'd have to ask the ship's Mechanic if he could refit the IR Lens for the black Listener helmet. But that was for later. Now I had to spend my last three stat points.

I put another into Perception, bringing it from 21 to... why 23 not 22??? How? What made it go up by two? Luckily, a hint jumped in telling me that, for every point invested in a stat after 20, another was added as a specialization bonus. How nice!

But that put me at an impasse because I now wanted mutually exclusive things. What was best: invest the two remaining points in Perception, raising it to 26, or throw another into Intelligence, bringing it up to 23? But that would leave me with one more point... I thought for a long time, but concluded my main stat was Perception, not Intelligence, so I should improve that. So then, both remaining points into Perception, giving a mind-blowing 26!!! Now, I had freakish powers of observation! Nothing could hide from my all-seeing gaze!

I JUST HAPPENED to finish as Uline Tar undid her safety belts and stood up to her huge height:

"One of these days, the captain's bad piloting is gonna kill us... I wouldn't be surprised if we have only half a crew after this trip. Who wants to risk life and limb so some Aristocrat can play pilot?! The only plus is how much more room we've got. As the only woman on board, I even got my own bunk! Anyway, I need to get dressed!" With these words, the Trader lowered a metal curtain, closing the door and blocking off her bunk.

This was the first time I'd seen a bunk closed. Normally, they were all wide open. I thought I should probably leave, so I wouldn't embarrass the furry lady while she changed. But Uline kept me on the bench, placing a heavy hand on my shoulder:

"Gnat, you can stay. You're not a Geckho, so it doesn't matter if you see."

She was purposely speaking louder than necessary, clearly wanting the other Geckho to hear. At the same time, she showed me a familiar gesture, placing her hand to her lips. I used to think it meant, "we'll talk about this later," but it clearly had a somewhat different meaning: "keep mum."

Astrolinguistics skill increased to level thirty-six!

Intrigued, I waited to see what came next. Uline Tar pulled a folding table out of the wall and, one after the other, set out sixteen specially-cut large red crystals.

"Gnat, this is your share of the licensing royalties from the footage of the Relict base," she said barely audibly, just with her lips. "It's sixteen thousand. Put it in your inventory and show no one. It's a very hefty sum. Many in the galaxy would kill for less. Vasha and Basha got the same and, as far as I know, will be leaving the Shiamiru after the next voyage."

I followed her sage advice and stashed the crystals in my inventory. Meanwhile, I asked the experienced Trader if a person like me could put my savings in a Geckho bank.

"The civilization of Shiharsa has just one bank: The Bank of Shiharsa. That's all we need," she answered bizarrely. "I know for sure that Miyelonians, Trillians, Meleyephatians and other space races are forbidden from using the Bank of Shiharsa, to keep potential enemies from damaging the Geckho financial system. But maybe a member of a vassal race could have an account... I'll be honest, Gnat, I don't know. I'd have to check the law. But these synthetic crystals were invented for Geckho to pay our vassals, so it is probably not allowed. And now, Gnat, please turn around. I am going to get changed and also need to do my makeup."

I didn't argue, sat cross-legged on the edge of the bench, turned toward the wall and opened my inventory. I had plenty to do. During the raid into Dark Faction territory, I filled my backpack with plunder nearly at random. I knew for certain I had some decent Medium Armor in there, a Dark Faction chameleon cloak and a futuristic laser rifle, which I could not use due to class restrictions. There were some other strange artifacts from the crashed antigrav as well. I could not determine their properties, but I stuck them in my inventory anyway. Now was the time to sort through all this junk because I was on the verge of over-encumbrance and it was getting uncomfortable.

First of all, I checked the Prospector scanner. The enemy antigrav was very nearby during my scan, so there was a chance... my heart aflutter, I opened the diagram. Yes! I had a highly detailed three-dimensional model of the Dark Faction's *Sio-Mi-Dori* shock-landing antigrav. It would make an excellent gift for Gerd Ustinov and the other scientists!

After that, I got to the armor. It was a thick dark-colored jacket, made of two layers of dense synthetic fabric. It had protective inserts in the chest, back and shoulders, which were made of a material somewhere between ceramic and thick plastic. I had it at the site of the *Sio-Mi-Dori* crash for after I outgrew my kevlar jacket. Little did I know I would soon be receiving the Listener suit.

Dark Faction shock-division commander armor

Chemical defense +12, Radiation defense +12, Armor 34.

Statistic requirements: Constitution 14, Strength 14.

Skill requirements: Medium Armor 30.

Attention! Your character has insufficient Strength to equip this apparel.

The armor weighed nineteen pounds, which was a third of my carrying capacity. It was worse than the Listener armor in every way, so I had no reason to hold onto it. It would be a big shame to just throw it away, though, because it was superior to the armored jackets commonly used by my faction. But it was too bulky and heavy. Should I ask Zheltov if he wants it? I was sitting in thought when, just above my ear, I heard Uline Tar's voice:

"By the way, Gnat... no, no, don't turn around

yet! I just wanted to make a suggestion. You should ask the captain to store your crystals. He can keep them in his safe. You would have to explain where you got it all from, though, which is best avoided! The problem is that Vasha, Basha and I haven't told him about our little side hustle. I mean, it's none of his business. So obviously, we did not give him our crystals."

"But don't the Geckho all use an electronic payment system?" I asked in surprise, to which the trader answered with a smirk:

"Usually, yes. But your home planet... don't get offended... is such a backwater that half of the stuff available throughout the galaxy doesn't work there, including electronic banking. So, they just sent us a code to enter in an automatic terminal to withdraw the money in physical crystals. Well, what about the safe?"

I thanked Uline for the suggestion but refused. I didn't want to tangentially snitch on my friends, and I felt calmer knowing the money was with me. This way, I could use it at any time without having to ask permission.

"You know best. Anyway, you can turn around now! And help me hold the stencil on my shoulder. It's hard to dye with just one hand."

I turned around. Uline had removed her armored spacesuit and was now wearing a puffy robe with a tawdry picture on it. She was dying her thick black fur, holding geometric-patterned stencils tight against her body and dripping a liquid lightener from a little bottle, maybe even regular old hydrogen peroxide. So, this was how she made the fanciful patterns on her black fur.

Naturally, I helped Uline, and even did one stencil on her back all on my own. I didn't see anything unusual or shameful in it, although the fashion-conscious furball was clearly embarrassed. According to her, the Geckho female grooming process was considered very intimate, and most Geckho women only trusted their best friend with such private matters. But there were no women in our crew, so Uline decided to ask an alien. She wasn't sure I would agree, though. In return, Uline allowed me to store my things in her cabin and even use a few bags.

My conversation with the Geckho Trader was interrupted by the hall speaker blasting out a roar of dismay from Captain Uraz Tukhsh:

"Gnnnat, please come to the bridge! Your immediate assistance is required!!!"

Chapter Two

Copilot

THE SCENE ON THE captain's bridge was frighteningly surreal. The room was strewn with overturned chairs and broken glass, and the senior engineer was lying on the ground growling in pain and rubbing his bloodied jaw. Starship Pilot Dmitry Zheltov, stark naked and smeared with something green, had his back pressed into a corner. In his shaking right hand, he was pointing a pistol back and forth from the captain to the navigator, shouting hysterically and demanding to be brought back to Earth. In his left hand, raised high above his head, he was squeezing the lever of an already pin-less fragmentation grenade.

Eagle Eye skill increased to level forty.

"Zheltov, what are you doing?!" I shouted in a voice not my own.

The cornered Dmitry turned his head, then pointed the loaded pistol at me. It seemed he didn't recognize me in the new armor and was now only more riled up. I had no choice but to remove the helmet and show him my face.

"Gnat... uh... Gerd Gnat?!" Zheltov lowered his pistol and slid down the wall on his back, now totally incapacitated. I was afraid he might unclench his hand and drop the grenade, but Danger Sense wasn't triggering, so there must have been no risk. And in fact, the professional soldier slowly returned his pistol to its holster, picked the grenade pin up off the floor and put it back in place.

"Where were you, Gnat?! And where are we?" The pilot's voice was quavering, betraying an overpowering emotional tension.

Hmm... Weird questions, especially the second one. I asked Zheltov if he remembered being taken on as the Shiamiru's copilot.

"I was hired to fly a spaceship?! I don't remember that," the Starship Pilot admitted. "The last thing in my memory is leaving the Dark Faction tower. There were bodies all around, everything went blurry and I nearly fell over. I was bleeding, my Health Points were almost drained, there was no first aid kit, and our medic was dead... And after that... I'm not so sure... the starship landed, you told me to wait and left... Then I was dragged by the armpits for a while and saw a black screen saying, 'Your character is unconscious.' I just kept lying there, but nothing changed. I even left the game. I wanted to ask how the battle was going, but everyone was still busy. I got back into my virt pod and suddenly came to my senses with the high G Forces. It was just like summer training sessions at the academy.

So, I open my eyes and see that I'm lying on a table and some animal with big teeth is looking me over. In one hand, he's holding a little knife and, in the other, he's dripping some green sauce onto my body with a gravy boat. So of course, I kicked him away, jumped off the table and ran down the hallway. I couldn't find you, there were just... these things," Dmitry said, leading his hand over the captain, navigator and Geckho in the doorway. "And they're all growling and baring their fangs!"

I probably should have reassured Dmitry and patiently explained the situation, but I... couldn't hold back and broke down laughing! And I laughed until I cried, not able to stop for a long time, just falling victim to more and more fits of laughter. When I told the Geckho why the pilot was acting strange, the furballs all joined in and nearly rolled across the floor. I had never seen Geckho in such a state. The huge furry creatures were rumbling through tightly closed mouths, baring their teeth and contorting their faces into the most unbelievable grimaces.

If I didn't know that was what their laughter looked like, I would probably have been very scared. So just in case, I warned my friend that these Geckho were laughing their heads off, not trying to scare him. Seemingly, Dmitry Zheltov became embarrassed:

"Yeaaaah... I bet they all think I'm a psycho now. My Fame even grew to four... Gnat, you've gotta apologize to those two Geckho I punched out."

I walked up closer and reassuringly patted my friend on the shoulder:

"It's nothing, don't worry! The Geckho are

forgiving by nature and, as far as I can see, are not mad at you. Last trip, I accidentally cut off the electricity on the whole ship and it was no big deal. The furballs forgot eventually and even hired me for another voyage. The main thing now is to prove you're a good pilot and start learning Geckho. You have to at least be able to understand the captain's commands. There's no getting around that. And at level fifty, you should take Astrolinguistics. That way, there won't be any problems with understanding."

AND SO ZHELTOV, concentrating fully and wincing from the strain, was sitting in the copilot's seat. It was just a bit too big for him. I was standing next to him and translating all the explanations of the screens, levers, buttons and other equipment in the starship command center.

"Move this little lever to the left to kill inertia in the fourth cycle of the left maneuver thruster. It's used when turning the shuttle horizontally to the right to dock at a space station. The station's gravity cranes take over from there. You just need to give them your vector. And make sure to remember: the lever should go opposite the way you want to turn. Alright, that's almost it! Well, Dmitry, I sure hope you've learned something."

Astrolinguistics skill increased to level thirty-nine.
Electronics skill increased to level twenty-six.

The copilot placed his hand on the lever and

moved it into position, attempting to form a muscle memory. Then he nodded in confirmation, although he was somewhat unconfident and even seemed afraid. Uraz Tukhsh gave a growl of satisfaction and continued his explanation. I got straight back to translation:

"Alright, now turning left and right in low gravity conditions. You'll use this when flying near type-six satellites, comets and large asteroids. You push it up one from the fourth cycle to the fifth. Moving this stick gives turn direction, which also switches the second and first maneuver thrusters into neutral."

"Alright, Gnat, I can't take anymore," Zheltov groaned. "My head is bursting with all this new information. It's about to pop! First cycle, second, pull compensation, gravity thruster aberration... Too much new stuff! Tell the captain I need a break! I've leveled Starship Piloting to eight already!"

What a pity... After all, according to the captain's plan, we were about to get to the ship's scanners and radars. I was very interested in that because I was hoping to use the ship's scanning equipment for prospecting and figured that would quickly level Cartography and Electronics. And I was just a tiny bit before level thirty-nine. My progress bar was already ninety-seven percent full, so I needed just ten more minutes of studying terminology to level up. But apparently, it was time to end our class. Zheltov had been learning the spaceship controls for three hours and had just about scrambled his brains. I myself wasn't the least bit tired, just happy at the rare chance to absorb new information.

"Alright, Dmmmitry, get some rest!" Uraz

Tukhsh agreed, letting the copilot free. "We'll continue the lessons in half an ummi. And to give you a kick in the pants, let me warn you: you will be landing the Shiamiru on the asteroid yourself. If you are successful, you can join my crew!"

After I translated, true horror was reflected on Zheltov's face:

"Is this guy sick in the head?! This is the first time I've been at the helm of any spacecraft. I can't understand a single written word of their language, and he's trusting me to land?! What if I wreck the shuttle? I'd never be able to pay off a ship like this! Hell, all humanity working together would have a hard time!"

I understood perfectly that the captain could take control of the starship at any moment and correct an error, so the risk was not particularly grave. Zheltov also knew that, and was only so upset because the captain was springing a pop quiz on him... But seemingly, Uraz Tukhsh managed to pluck the right strings in the pilot's heart, because my friend asked me to tell the captain he would need only half as much break time.

"Now that's great news!" He bared his teeth in satisfaction and turned to me. "Dmmmitry is learning fast. He gained two levels in half an ummi, so he'll be ready when we get to the asteroid belt. But you, Gerd Gnat, must also prove yourself. The asteroid belt is massive and contains billions of objects. Most of them are just worthless specks of ice, stone and nickel-iron composite, though. We made thirty voyages and two hundred landings before we found anything even remotely interesting. Your job as a Prospector is to improve our ratio and, in a voyage or two, find us an asteroid with valuable minerals. If you can do that, I will offer you a permanent position."

Well, for the first time he was giving me a concrete set of conditions and, if I met them, an official promise of employment. I formulated the mission in my head. Considering the geological analyzers I'd bought at the space port, the ones given to me by Gerd Tamara, and the ones Uraz Tukhsh had purchased, I had a total of eight. And that gave me eight chances to find something of value and prove my worth.

I left the captain's bridge and ran into Dmitry Zheltov, waiting for me in the corridor:

"Gnat, here's what I'm worried about: we left the planet without getting approval, and leadership doesn't know what became of us! They might think we've been taken prisoner or, even worse, defected to the Dark Faction!"

I tried to reassure my friend and told him I had radioed Ivan Lozovsky to say we both left with the Geckho ship. But the Starship Pilot just kept panicking:

"That isn't how it's done! We need approval for this expedition, even if it is post-factum. We also need a clear mission. So, I'll exit the game right now and issue a report. One of us has to do things by the books!"

I realized it was pointless to argue. This rules-obsessed military man was accustomed to doing things as proscribed. To him, the very idea that one might act without orders was unthinkable and even blasphemous. I reminded Dmitry that he had just a quarter ummi before the captain wanted him back, one hour and twenty minutes. I asked him to also bring news about the cease-fire with the Dark Faction. What was the situation on the front? What were our losses? Did we manage to hold onto the Eastern Swamp? Did the Second Legion break the encirclement in Karelia? I wanted to know everything.

Dmitry nodded and... his character froze right in the corridor, blocking the already narrow passage. Ugh, damnit! Was it really so hard to realize he should go into his bunk before exiting the game??! Space was a red zone, so an avatar would never disappear here. But before the captain or anyone else got mad, I asked Vasha Tushihh to help me bring the heavy body into its bunk. The huge Geckho picked up the petrified body as if it were light as a feather and placed it on a free cot.

I was not about to leave the game to give some stupid report, though. Plus, it hadn't been very long since I'd reentered the game, just six hours. So, I was afraid I would still have broken bones and unhealed wounds, which might make it hard to move. Also, I had business to attend to here. Taking advantage of the brief respite, I headed to the ship's Mechanic.

AN HOUR LATER, my wallet was two thousand six hundred crystals lighter, and the lion's share of those expenses went to attaching the IR Lens to the Listener armor's helmet. I suspected the furry Mechanic had taken me for three times the going rate, because the job took ten minutes at most, and didn't require any materials. On the other hand, I had nothing to compare it with and any work with a unique item carried greater risks, which demanded high skill. At any rate, the IR Lens was now fixed tight onto the helmet. If needed, I could lower it over my right eye, and it worked the same as before.

The mechanic also threw in some weapon modification work as a bonus. The biggest change was to the Krechet. He expanded its magazine to fourteen rounds, increased its damage by 15% and reduced its weight by almost a third. The experienced mechanic also made a couple modifications to the Dark Faction laser rifle, which I was not able to use due to a class limitation against automatic weaponry. But now, it fired only single pulses. He also gave it a more powerful battery and made it shoot quieter.

Dark Faction laser pulse rifle (modified)
Range: 1800 feet.
Damage: 1300-2800 HP.
Firing speed: 11 shots per minute.
Silent*
Statistic requirements: Agility 15, Strength 13.
Skill requirements: Rifles 45, Sharpshooter 20.
  Battery charge: 100%
  Attention!!! Your character has insufficient Rifles and Sharpshooter skills to use this weapon.

Sure, I'd have to grow into it, but I'd taken a shine to this futuristic rifle, which could quietly fire over a third of a mile. A rifle like this could take down my character in two or three shots despite my Listener suit, so I was hoping I could frag similar-level enemies in two shots, maybe even one.

Finally, Dmitry Zheltov came back into the game and immediately found me. His alarmed expression led me to believe there was trouble. And I was right. I gave a shudder as the Starship Pilot began:

"Tyulenev defected to the Dark Faction! Once on enemy territory, he addressed our side over radio and said the whole mess in the Eastern Swamp was to distract our faction, so he could sneak across the border. He said our faction has already lost the war, and others should follow his example before it was too late. And that turncoat managed to get in their heads before our technicians figured out how to jam the signal."

The news was not merely worrying, it left me gasping. Apparently, for the last several months, the Dark Faction had been privy to all our plans. They knew our strong and weak points, our passwords and codes, and where we had our minefields, supply lines, firing positions and buildings. And that was not all.

"But there's good news, too. Three things, actually! The Eastern Swamp node held out, though it was tough going. When Gerd Tarasov reached the citadel with reinforcements, there were just five defenders left alive!!! Eventually, all the commanders died, and Nelly Svistunova led the defense. She is now celebrated as a hero! Also, in Karelia, the Second Legion wiped the floor with the Dark Faction. They took more than thirty darksiders prisoner! After interrogation, they're being exchanged for resources and four of ours, who were captured in the Eastern Swamp. And most importantly, our voyage with the

Geckho now has the official blessing of Radugin himself. He told me my mission is to gather intelligence about the mannerisms and culture of our suzerains, outer space in general, alien technology and so on. Also, Gnat, they really want you to go issue a report about the raid behind Dark Faction lines, becoming a Gerd, and your new armor."

"Why about the raid? Didn't you tell them?"

"Of course. But they want to hear your side." With these words, Zheltov started staring at the floor. "It bothered Ivan Lozovsky to see how easily we crossed the Dark Faction border. Dozens of experienced recon groups tried before us both in the west from the Graveyard and Golden Plain where we crossed, and in the east from the Great Caves. But every time, it ended in failure... Obviously it's bullshit to suspect us of working for the Dark Faction but I think that, since Tyulenev defected, the faction leaders are spooked and want to double check everyone..."

My mood collapsed. After all we'd done for the faction, I assumed us four raiders were immune to suspicion. What thanklessness! In many ways, we were the reason our faction hadn't lost control over the Eastern Swamp node. After all, who could say how the situation might have turned out if we hadn't diverted three hundred Dark Faction soldiers! Would the five last defenders of the citadel have managed to hold off an even stronger assault? I for one did not think so!

Chapter Three

Endless Asteroids

ANOTHER THREE and a half hours later, I was on the bridge of the Shiamiru hundreds of thousands of miles from a never-ending asteroid belt. On the screen, even the naked eye could see the plume of infinite dots. The ship's locator could detect millions or even billions of heavenly bodies ranging in size from grains of dust to dozens of miles wide.

"Your conclusions, Gnat!" Captain Uraz Tukhsh sat back in the pilot's seat looking stately with a glass of some bubbling purple drink in hand. His body language was very relaxed as if to say this was completely my call.

I spent a long time looking at the screen in thought, then asked the captain to filter out the dust particles and leave only the heavenly bodies large enough for our shuttle to land on. Uraz Tukhsh quickly changed the settings, but the image stayed roughly the same.

"Now run a gravity scan and overlay a density map."

"Why don't you do it, Gnat?" The Geckho unexpectedly suggested. "Just a bit ago, I explained all the locators and scanners for Dmmmitry, and you translated. Now, I want to see if you learned anything!"

Did he really think I had just been robotically translating without memorizing?! The scanners were of enormous interest to me and, over the captain's explanation, my Electronics skill leveled five times to thirty-one! And that was saying nothing of my two Astrolinguistics improvements. Plus, my character was now level thirty-nine!

What could I say? I wanted the captain to see what my high Intelligence could do! I chuckled, walked over to the control panel and quickly changed the settings. I overlaid density, which changed the picture completely. Now, two colors dominated the map, one for iron-nickel composite asteroids, and another for those made of iron-magnesium silicates like olivine.

Scanning skill increased to level thirty-eight!
Cartography skill increased to level forty!
Electronics skill increased to level thirty-two!
Mineralogy skill increased to level fourteen!
You have reached level forty!
You have received three skill points! (total points accumulated: seven)

I filtered out the unremarkable asteroids, then

zoomed in and showed Uraz Tukhsh the fifteen that remained:

"Here are the largest asteroids near the Shiamiru that have a somewhat unusual density. Some are too light, as if they have a hollow pocket and some are too heavy, which means they're probably made of something other than iron, silicon or nickel. We could further constrict the search by running a radioactivity test. That would show heavy metals like thorium, uranium, actinium..."

The captain picked his jaw up off the floor and turned to the navigator, who was just as shocked. He had a frog stuck in his throat, and it took him a long time to respond.

"Can you really do that?" Uraz Tukhsh finally asked, astonished. His black eyes were squinting comically, and he was breathing heavily through his nose.

Clearly, I had done something unusual, because the Geckho were staring at me. I had to explain:

"It seemed like a good idea to combine the results of various scans. That does require Scanning, Cartography and Electronics though. This scanner has pretty high requirements. But now, we have a new dilemma: there are fifteen potentially interesting bodies, but I have only eight geological analyzers."

Authority increased to negative 7.

Well, well, what an unusual message! For the first time since becoming a Gerd, I had impacted the authority parameter, raising it by one.

"And what do you suggest, Gerd Gnat?" Uraz Tukhsh set his glass aside and turned in my direction, listening attentively.

"If you don't have any objections, I would recommend checking the nearest asteroid first," I said, pointing at a large object just one hundred twenty thousand miles from the Shiamiru. "It is at the very edge of the asteroid belt, so it will be the fastest and easiest to reach. It has a suspiciously light core. It either contains a cavity, perhaps artificial, or water with heavy hydrogen isotopes. When we get closer, I could try and generate a 3D model of the asteroid with density gradients. Maybe that will clear things up. But failing that, one or two scans from the surface will be enough to determine the nature of the core. If there's nothing good, we can check that huge rock over there. But it's in a pretty dense cloud of small debris, so it might be hard to reach," I said, removing the size filter and pointing at the millions of treacherous stones hurtling through space.

"So, let's check the easy one first," the captain agreed and pointed at the copilot. He was listening carefully to our conversation, but I doubt he got the idea. "Let's just come right in for a landing, not stop to scan from space. I don't want to lose any momentum, and that will make Dmmmitry's first landing easier."

I wished my friend luck and gave him the light spacesuit and Dark Faction armor. The copilot's eyes went wide in astonishment, so I figured he appreciated my gifts. He even began mumbling something like, "I can't accept this, it's too expensive."

"Take it, take it, don't be shy!" I said, encouraging him. "The spacesuit doesn't even belong to me. I got it from the captain. And as long as you're working for Uraz Tukhsh, you can use it. Eventually, you might even be able to buy it off him."

I left Dmitry to prepare for landing, hurrying to my spot in the bunk. I was now twenty-five pounds under my carry weight and nearly jumping for joy. It felt so great to walk around unencumbered!

In the bunk, I warned Uline Tar that this landing would be our copilot's first ever, so she followed my example and buckled her safety belts. Ten minutes later, the engines changed tone and became louder but, much to my surprise, it was still quieter than past landings. And the thrusters weren't humming in overdrive with screeching whistles and ear-splitting creaks, either. My Danger Sense didn't even trigger. All that followed was a slight bump, and our shuttle touched down. It was actually the lightest landing I'd ever experienced.

"Everyone congratulate Dmmmitry on his first landing!" the captain's voice rang out on the loudspeaker, and the whole crew gave a happy rumble.

Uline Tar also bared her teeth in satisfaction and quickly unbuckled, changing instantly out of the colorful robe back into her spacesuit.

"Tell your friend he made a good first impression. If he keeps that up, he can join the crew! Hell, that was so good he could be main pilot!"

The captain's voice rang out on the loudspeaker:

"Technicians to the exit! Fasten down the shuttle, but do not open the cargo hold! Gnat and Uline come next! And Gnat, I hope you have enough sense not to run a scan right next to my ship! Take the third levitator and fly at least five hundred steps away, better a thousand! Everyone else, remain on board."

I checked the Listener suit's settings one more time. One tank of air would last six and a half hours, the magnetic soles could be turned on or off, and the miniature jet pack allowed me to pop over small crevasses in low gravity. I suspected this was nowhere near everything the Relict armor could do. There were complicated electronics in the chest and back, and I couldn't believe they were only for the energy shield. But I didn't have a clue how to activate the ancient suit's hidden functions.

"Gnat, don't sleep! The technicians have fastened down the shuttle. It's time for us to go!"

I hurried down the corridor after the huge Geckho woman. This time, I didn't mind being clipped to Uline Tar with the safety lash. It was nothing insulting, and I really shouldn't have gotten so mad before. It was just a precautionary measure. Then the external door slid aside, and I saw a true winter wonderland. Cliffs covered with compressed ice reflected millions of sparkles both from the sun and the Shiamiru's spotlights.

Without leaving the artificial gravitation zone around the shuttle, I crouched and pried loose a piece of ice with my knife, crumbling it between my gloved fingers. Just normal frozen water, even if it had borne millions of years of harsh radiation and thus contained a somewhat higher proportion of heavy hydrogen isotopes like deuterium and even trace amounts of tritium. Technically, it could be harvested for nuclear powerplants, but that would require heavy equipment, lots of time, and smooth logistics. We had none of that.

I found an exposed stone in a cliffside and broke it loose. On closer inspection, it was just chondrite. Composed of iron and magnesium silicates, it was the most common type of meteorite that fell on Earth. I already knew there wouldn't be much here, and we could just leave.

Mineralogy skill increased to level fifteen!

Mineralogy skill increased to level sixteen!

So, the game algorithms agreed. But Uline Tar had already taken out the levitator and was waiting for me with clear impatience. So, knowing the Geckho lady's passion for hoverboarding, I decided to indulge her. Also, flying through new areas on the levitator would quickly level my Cartography. It would have been dumb to pass that up.

I decided to tell Uline my conclusions anyway. With the tip of my boot, I wrote a phrase in Geckho on the crumbly ice: "There's nothing of value here. But if you want, we could just go for a ride." Uline spent a long time looking at the broken line, then silently erased it with her wide sole and pointed to the levitator.

"So, where are you gonna scan?" the Trader asked into the microphone, clearly for the captain and crew.

"Way over there, on top of that ice spire!" I said, pointing at a high peak of ice three miles away.

"Well Gnat, hold tight. Get ready to fly!" Uline warned me. Then she gunned it to breakneck speeds, making sharp turns and loops as she doubled around stones and spires of ice.

Cartography skill increased to level forty-one!

When we reached the summit, I could see the

spooky dark side of the asteroid. In the ghostly dim starlight, I could see only the barely visible contours of steep gloomy cliffs.

Cartography skill increased to level forty-two!
Eagle Eye skill increased to level forty-one!

Fortunately, the Geckho speed-demon was not foolhardy enough to ride in the dark, and she stopped. After making sure we couldn't be seen from the Shiamiru, Uline took the laser pistol off her belt, pointed it at the nearest stone surface and, setting it to constant beam, burned a bright red line reading:

"Thanks, Gnat! You're the only one in the crew that understands me. If you ever become captain of your own ship, call me up. I'd join you no questions asked!"

AS I FIRST GUESSED, scanning didn't reveal anything of value. It did confirm my observation about the stone and ice structure of the core, though. I also couldn't call it a total waste because I raised Scanning to thirty-nine, and Mineralogy twice to eighteen. Also, this trip with Uline finally broke the ice between us. I now had a true friend among the Geckho, and the Trader's unexpected confession made me think.

On the way back to the Shiamiru, to get a better idea of how this virtual Universe functioned, I asked Uline how much a starship would sell for. The Trader's answer made me bite my lip. Ancient jalopy ships with minimal equipment and nearly dead thrusters went for around four million crystals. No one would agree to insure a wreck like that, though. Our Shiamiru had run the captain six and a half million. A speedy interceptor went from twelve million on up, and that was without weaponry. And cruisers like Leng Waid Shishish had cost at least four hundred million, if not half a billion. So, even the cheapest spaceship required such an unbelievable amount that I could only give a heavy sigh and change topic.

We told the crew the scan hadn't turned anything up so, as soon as Uline and I were back inside, the shuttle started off from the asteroid and made for our next destination. It was four hundred thousand miles as the crow flies but trying to go straight through the asteroid belt would be suicidal. So, the captain was going to take a big dog-leg out into empty space, then return to the asteroid belt when we were closer. I explained the captain's route to Dmitry Zheltov, who had already changed into his new armor and was confidently piloting the shuttle.

We calculated that everyone who wasn't busy on the bridge had around an hour and a half of free time. Uline locked herself in her bunk. So, not wanting to bother her, I went to hang out with Vasha and Basha. The twin brothers confirmed their intention to leave Uraz Tukhsh's crew after the next voyage when their contracts were up. They didn't want to keep working for some loser and were hoping to find another captain to take them on.

All the while, the brothers were playing a three-dimensional board game called "Na-Tikh-U." It involved moving colored spaceship pieces around a glowing three-dimensional holographic board strewn with planets, minefields, space pirates and other hazards. What was more, they were playing for money. My interest was piqued, so after a round ended in Basha's victory and Vasha set thirty crystals on the table, I asked the huge Geckho to teach me the game.

An hour later, I had a grasp on the rules of Na-Tikh-U. In fact, I had even more or less learned all the common tactics. It was like a hybrid of three-dimensional chess, backgammon and dice. Na-Tikh-U could be played by two, three or even more players at once, and temporary alliances against a common enemy were just as common as their sudden implosion and backstabbing former allies.

I eventually learned to beat Basha and Vasha, even though the brothers joined forces against my space fleet almost from the very beginning. It was hard, but I intuitively realized how to make a very effective defense with my remaining pieces and, at the most critical moments, luck was on my side, handing me the exact roll I needed. The large audience that crowded the bunk by the end, entertained by our lively discussion and colorful commentary, greeted my victory with a roar of approval.

Fame increased to 35.

Authority increased to negative 6.

You have reached level forty-one!

You have received three skill points! (total points accumulated: ten)

"So, you beat our loaders. But they can't even count to four without their fingers! Let's see how you fare against me!" Uline cut in acridly, having stepped out of her bunk to see what all the commotion was about.

I wasn't opposed, but I didn't have time to play Uline. An alarm came on over the starship intercom, warning the crew we'd be landing soon. We all had to go back to our places and buckle in. And again, the landing went so smoothly I didn't even realize we'd set down. Dmitry Zheltov was beyond reproach and deserved all the applause coming his way.

Well, it was time for me to get to work. Unlike the last asteroid, this one gave me cause for hope. Its high density meant it probably contained something more interesting than iron or nickel. So, after placing three of my ten skill points into Sharpshooter, so I would at least meet the requirements for my pulse rifle, I put the remaining seven into Mineralogy, raising it to twenty-five.

Then, together with Uline, I left the Shiamiru. This asteroid looked utterly unlike the previous one. You might think two stones flying through space would be identical, all covered with glimmering ice, frozen plains and shooting spires. But this one was brownish red, and smooth like a huge piece of cast metal. It was shaped like a potato, and was two miles long, and one in diameter.

"That way!" I said, pointing at what looked like a crater formed by a meteorite slamming into the surface. I figured that would be the best place to scan the core.

Cartography skill increased to level forty-three!

Uline sped off on the levitator and was about to fly over the crater's lip when, suddenly, a blast of colorful electrical sparks erupted around us. Everything was swimming. I was totally disoriented, and so was Uline. The light show startled her, and she lost balance.

Danger Sense skill increased to level sixteen!

I cannot say how, but I twisted my body, unclipped my bindings from the somersaulting levitator and, after flying off the board, slid ninety feet on my stomach, leaving a long deep trail on the dark and surprisingly fine-grained surface. But I didn't bounce off and fly into open space. I just slid along the fine sand, as if this asteroid had its own gravity! I was even more surprised to see that everything abruptly grew brighter, as if there was suddenly artificial lighting!

I started getting up to look around the strange area, but the tether ran out of slack, giving me a sharp jerk and plonking me back onto my gut. Uline made a series of somersaults, then slammed into a building with her massive body... and it wasn't really a building but something like a vehicle on folding supports. Her high-pitched shriek rang out in my headphones and her words were mixed with groans:

"I think I broke my front right arm! And the levitator is smashed to bits... It won't even be good for parts now. Gnat, what is this place? Look up! I can't see the stars!!!"

Chapter Four

Mysterious Development

I HAD JUST NOTICED that, instead of a dark sky with millions of stars, there was an opaque white dome overhead, which occasionally sparkled with electricity. What the heck?

I ran a scan (not with a geological analyzer, just the icon), and looked with curiosity at the objects depicted on the mini-map: "Meleyephatian Automatic Processer," "Drill," "Meleyephatian Small Robot Loader," "Artificial Gravity Generator," "Automatic Ore Enricher," "Storage Containers," "Distortion Field Generator..." Seemingly, while searching for valuable resources, we had hit upon a place where someone else, hiding from prying eyes, had already mined all the ore. I wonder what they were extracting here in such secrecy?

"Gnat, Uline, what happened?" Our friends on

the Shiamiru were listening closely, so of course they noticed Uline shouting about the busted levitator and her broken arm.

The Trader wanted to answer and say what happened, but I gave an abrupt wave and placed my palm to my lips. Then I called her over to the automatic processor, went over to the nearest container, removed its lid and studied the contents.

Mineralogy skill increased to level twenty-six!

"What is that?" the Geckho woman asked in incomprehension and even disgust, seeing the gray powder that filled the small container almost to the top. "Gross... Is it radioactive?"

I fearlessly lowered my hand into the container and lifted out a handful of the fine gray powder. Even with the artificial gravity, which was just a fraction of what I was used to, I could feel how heavy it was. I practically immediately guessed what it was, and decided it was better not to share this news with the whole crew. Carefully pouring it back into the container, I took out my laser rifle and inscribed a long Geckho phrase on the ground.

"This is platinum sponge, the product created by chemically processing platinum ore. After this, it is generally purified and smelted into ingots. I'd guess the automatic processer has amassed around six hundred fifty pounds of platinum. We still need to figure out who this treasure belongs to, though."

After finishing, I got worried that the Geckho lady wouldn't understand how much a pound was. Although... the game algorithms had automatically translated measurement units for me many times before. Maybe it would be translated for Uline as well? The Trader lowered a glove into the heavy powder and thoughtfully let the precious metal slip between her fingers. After that, she asked for my laser rifle and engraved a response:

"Gnat, what difference does it make who it belongs to? I know our captain well and am sure that Uraz Tukhsh will not be bothered by such technicalities. In fact, I bet he'll ask me to find a market where we can sell it all under the table. As for you, now is the time to take your share. As much platinum as you can carry."

Seeing me looking closely and predatorily at the filled containers, Uline Tar hurried to clarify, scribbling another line:

"Keep in mind that your contract with the captain assumes normal gravitation, not local. So, don't be a thief. After all, I know you. That's a big backpack and, on this asteroid, you could carry out all the platinum by yourself, especially if you turn off the artificial gravity."

After some thought, Uline Tar lowered the barrel and carved another couple sentences:

"Gnat, I've got an offer. I agree to temporarily hold some of your things, but only if we can split the extra platinum two ways."

Astrolinguistics skill increased to level forty-two!

I met gazes with my friend and gave a distinct nod of agreement. And while I set all my things out of my inventory and handed them to her, Uline Tar quickly erased our writing with her foot, activated her radio and said:

"Captain, I have two pieces of news: one good and one bad. The bad: we broke the levitator. It's shattered and cannot be repaired. The good: we found something, and you should come see it firsthand. I know you're gonna like this!"

THE CAPTAIN CAME by heavy loader and brought his senior engineer with him. As I guessed, they had quite a jubilant reaction. Uraz Tukhsh walked around the whole area, sticking his nose everywhere and jumping with such joy that, at one point, he accidentally left the artificial gravity, jumped off the asteroid and nearly flew into open space. The safety tether pulled him back, though.

The Supercargo was called off the shuttle, and the captain asked him to bring the radio jammer. Their conversations were not intended for the rest of the crew. Still, the Trader and I were right next to the automatic processer the whole time. No one chased us off, and we heard everything they said. We were already aware of the valuable finding, so the captain simply saw no need to hide anything from us.

Uline guessed the captain's reaction spot on. The question of whether to take the platinum or not was not even up for discussion. However, the captain and his helpers had a concern I didn't expect. They wanted to take not only the ore, but also the Meleyephatian processer, drill, enricher, loader, gravity generator and distortion generator. The Supercargo was opposed, saying it would not fit in the Shiamiru's cargo hold, especially given that our automatic processer already took up more than two-thirds of the space. All the same, the captain was taken with the idea and couldn't be stopped:

"The equipment is worth too much to leave! That processer alone will get go for seven hundred thousand crystals, and the whole setup must be worth a million! Could we unload our stuff temporarily on a neighboring asteroid, hide it and cart this off to sell?"

"We shouldn't hide it nearby..." the main engineer said dubiously. "Whoever owns this processer is not gonna be happy when they notice it's gone. The first thing they'll do is look for tracks here on the asteroid, then scan everything nearby. And who knows how good their search equipment is?"

Uline cut in to answer the seemingly rhetorical question:

"If they could afford this processer and the rest, they aren't exactly poor. And seeing they found such a great deposit, they must have high-quality search equipment."

"Looks that way," the main engineer agreed. "A functioning processer can be detected practically from across a star system with good scanners. Sure, that may not apply if it's well hidden, but you never know. Also, it would be a huge shame if we go off to hide our processer, and the owners of this one come back before we do. After all, who knows what kind of security systems they have here? You never know, maybe a signal has already been sent out and they know we're here."

After that, the arguments stopped for some time. The Geckho went silent, exchanging somewhat frightened glances. I even guessed the captain might be rethinking it and would leave the equipment. But I was wrong. The threat of exposure just steeled Uraz Tukhsh's determination:

"So, here's my decision! The equipment will be packed up and loaded into the cargo hold, then our processer will be tied down to the external fasteners..." The captain intercepted the main engineer and Supercargo's objections with a gesture. "Yes, I am aware that we will not be able to land on a planet like that and would burn up in any atmosphere. I also understand that, if we try to dock at any normal station, we'll be stopped, and the rumors about this incident will spread farther than we can allow. So, we're going to a place that won't care if our cargo is abnormal, and it won't matter who we are or what we brought to sell."

"I hope you are not referring to the pirate station Medu-Ro IV!" Uline Tar declared with clear alarm.

"That's exactly right," the captain answered. "And don't turn your nose up, Uline. It isn't a pirate station, it just belongs to captains who think more independently than most. Geckho laws don't hold sway there, nor do those of any other spacefaring race. The owners just couldn't bear the constraint! Sure, last time we ran into trouble, but that doesn't mean this time will be the same. Medu-Ro IV is the largest independent trade hub in this part of the galaxy, and we can unload both the platinum and this whole drilling setup no problem. Also, we don't have proper registration documents, so that's just what we need. Think for yourselves, in a mere four ummi, we'll all be rich! And not a word about the platinum when we get to the Shiamiru! The rest of our crew should be led to believe we found just an abandoned automatic processor. We have the legal right to take that. The equipment is of Meleyephatian origin, which means they should never have been in Geckho space in the first place!"

BACK IN THE SHUTTLE, I asked a burly Uline about the past problems on Medu-Ro IV. My bunkmate, even gloomier and less talkative than usual, first refused to answer. I figured it wasn't worth pushing, and just got to my own business. But suddenly, the Trader had a change of heart and decided to bring me up to speed:

"It's a nasty story that might come back to bite us in the ass... As you know, Uraz Tukhsh is from a well-known family of Geckho aristocrats. And his origins sometimes guide his behavior more than they should. In fact, believe it or not, the captain used to be even more arrogant. Anyway, the inhabitants of Medu-Ro IV don't take kindly to such behavior. The station belongs to freebooters, and the majority are of Miyelonian origin. That means Miyelonian is the common tongue on the station, and all payments are made in the Miyelonian currency, crypto. To be honest, I was not aware of that and, in many ways, it was my fault we came to Medu-Ro IV for repair in the first place. It may be hard to believe, but Uraz Tukhsh used to be an even worse pilot and the ship had to be repaired on a regular basis. Anyway... the captain didn't have any of their currency, even though he had more than enough crystals... Perhaps, if Uraz Tukhsh had been on better behavior with the Miyelonians, we could have come to an arrangement. But the captain's noble instincts took over and he just couldn't bring himself to act decent..."

Uline went silent midsentence, as if considering whether the story was worth continuing. But then she made up her mind:

"They accused him of bad faith, and Uraz Tukhsh threw a fit, even challenging the freebooting captains to a duel. But Miyelonians are famed for their skill in hand-to-hand combat. Our captain got his ass handed to him two times. His opponents weren't even trying to kill him, they were just having fun, maiming him with their bare hands for all to see... Then, Uraz Tukhsh was thrown in prison and the Shiamiru was impounded until our captain's influential relative Leng Waid Shishish came in and smoothed things over."

Hmm... Quite the unpleasant story. The captain's decision to come to Medu-Ro IV seemed even stranger now. I for one would have been ashamed to show my face there again. They made him look so pathetic! But I was no Aristocrat and perhaps I just didn't understand what it was like to play that class. Maybe Uraz Tukhsh wanted to improve his Authority or something and was trying to prove he had become a respected and successful captain. Who could say? But another part of Uline's story caught my interest:

"Say, what is the exchange rate from Geckho crystals to... what did you call the Miyelonian currency... cryptos or something?"

My bunkmate lowered the curtain to our room and bared her teeth predatorily... actually no, it was just a smile.

"Gnat, your question shows just how little experience you have. You could only ask something like that after just finding out about the spacefaring races. You see, any great civilization eventually reaches a point where they can easily exist on their market alone, without any outside investment or resources. For such a self-sufficient civilization, alien or foreign money is not only unnecessary, it's a liability. Considering the huge size of the Universe, a financial system can only be stable with extreme protectionism."

I did not understand and asked for a better explanation. Uline did her best to clear it up:

"If a free flow of cross-border investments were allowed, what would stop the Miyelonians from buying up strategically important resources and industries from the Geckho, and just closing them all down? It would be easy. At any time, they could just mint an infinite amount of their money, exchange it for crystals and, before the Geckho got wise, they'd legally own everything! Get it, Gnat? So, currency exchange is done centrally on the level of state banks, under the watchful eye of financial inspectors on both sides and in a very limited amount. Unauthorized currency exchange is a serious crime. The absolute minimum punishment is confiscation of property!" Here, Uline Tar lowered her voice to a whisper and continued. "Well, that's the official story. In reality, the exchange rate on Medu-Ro IV is seven crystals to one crypto, and almost every trader offers the service, even though it isn't discussed openly. But first-time buyers and other potentially unreliable merchants are almost sure to be refused. Trust must first be earned."

"So Uline, are you in good standing on this station?" I asked. The Trader snarled, baring her sharp teeth:

"What a provocative question! Have I broken the law? No, Gnat, I haven't. And it isn't because of any deep respect for the institution, they just don't know me, so they don't trust me. But there's nothing to stop traders from buying goods from one race and selling them to another. It's hard to detect such trade, and no one really sees the point. As long as the volume stays relatively small, they prefer to close their eyes. Sure, I *could* exchange currency, but the rate would not be optimal. For those who have earned a trustworthy reputation, there are other ways as well: contraband, black-market currency traders, fictitious deals, money laundering and millions of other options... That is exactly what the freebooting captains engage in, and the Medu-Ro IV station is the largest trade hub in this sector of the galaxy where deals can be made between members of different races. Also, all kinds of fortune hunters unload their spoils there, and you can see really freaky ships from all corners of the Universe, including some belonging to space pirates wanted throughout the galaxy!"

What could I say? After this detailed explanation, I more or less understood what had drawn our captain to the station. I had one question left. I asked the experienced trader what the value of platinum was.

"Purified, in ingots with a stamp from a respectable trading houses — sixty-eight hundred crystals per pound. But in this cruder form, it's about half that. By the way, I told Uraz Tukhsh that you took your share. He didn't mind."

As she said these words, I was watching the furry lady's facial muscles carefully and would wager my head on the chopping block that, instead of "pound," Uline had said a different word. It seemed she said a different number, too. And although I was already familiar with the Geckho measurement units, the algorithms of the game that bends reality were still translating them for me.

"I heard the captain doesn't want to lose half the value of the precious metal, so he isn't going to sell the platinum like this. He is going to find a person on the station to purify it, cast it and certify the bars. I suppose I'll do the same. What about you?"

I had thirty-two pounds of metal in my backpack. The potential profit was over one hundred thousand crystals, even if I sold it without any further processing. Of course, I would have liked to purify it and double that, but I doubted Uraz Tukhsh could find honest business partners that wouldn't throw him under the bus. So, I hadn't made up my mind yet.

Chapter Five

Medu-Ro IV

A TWENTY-TWO-HOUR journey... As strange as it seemed, I had no problem keeping busy. First, I helped Dmitry Zheltov learn the control panel, translating the captain's words. After that, I had a Geckho writing lesson, which was again given by the strict and quarrelsome navigator Ayukh. The short elderly Geckho was especially fierce today, giving more and more complicated tasks with more new words and an emphasis on mathematical and spacefaring terminology.

Elliptical plane... Back point traverse... Relative bearing... Sideslip angle... Mainstream speed vector... Ionic and gravitational thruster interlink system... Ship stress tensor... Adaptability of graph theory for the warp beacon system...

But there was a certain sense in how hard he was pushing me. My Astrolinguistics skill was leveling very fast, especially considering the bonuses from his Pedagogy skill. But the pace and volume were just frying my brains! After an hour, I was about to howl and climb up the wall, but I forced myself to concentrate, staring at the loops and broken lines on the tablet screen. At a certain point, Zheltov tried to join our Geckho lesson, but the Starship Pilot left the bunk fairly quickly with a look of traumatized shame and even fear.

By the end of the second hour, when I was about to give up, a double message jumped in:

Intelligence increased to 22.

Intelligence increased to 23.

What? I mean, I wasn't especially surprised the stat had gone up two times. Any added point after twenty gave a bonus, as I'd recently become aware. But I'd heard from my faction that a stat would only increase for the second time after two or three weeks of use! Either I had been misled, or our trainers didn't know, but a stat could grow much faster if it was practiced at extreme intensity. At any rate, that gave me a second wind, and I was again bursting with energy, soaking up new information like a sponge. Another half hour later, I earned another portion of messages:

Astrolinguistics skill increased to level forty-five!

You have reached level forty-two!

You have received three skill points!

Wow, awesome! And although I was willing to keep going, the old navigator was tired and gave up:

"Gnat, you're young. You're like some kind of computer, you could go all day! But I'm a living being... Let's wrap it up, I can barely think..."

Authority increased to negative 5.

Uline was looking on, and her eyes squeezed into barely visible slits, while her breathing grew strained and raspy. When the old Navigator left the bunk, the Trader commented in astonishment:

"I never thought such a thing was possible! You wore out old Ayukh! By the way, Gnat, you missed a very funny scene! While you were studying, your friend was offered Geckho food for the first time. Naturally, our traditional spicy stew was the only thing on the menu. Well, Dmmmitry sat for a long time after the first spoonful, all red with his cheeks puffing out, then he said every curse word he knew in any language. He's seemingly already learned around a dozen phrases in Geckho! But the funniest part was that Dmmmitry finished it all, then asked for seconds!"

I went off to look for Dmitry and discovered him asleep on a bench in the second bunk. Woah! The Starship Pilot, lying there in his armor, had already reached level forty-two just like me! I was reminded that, before the raid behind Dark Faction lines, Dmitry Zheltov was just level thirty-two. It had only been a day since then, but my friend had gained ten levels! What an appetite he had for his profession!!!

My attention was drawn by the senior engineer, Dmitry's bunkmate:

"Gnat, tell Dmmmitry when you get the chance that he shouldn't leave the game in space. This is a red zone and his body froze in a doorway. I dragged him to a cot, so he wouldn't be in anyone's way, but that is not how it should be done. According to the safety protocol, one must never go offline in space because surprises can sneak up on you, and a character stranded in the game is vulnerable and useless to their crewmates. If he wanted to sleep, he should have done it in game. His real body would get all the rest he needs."

Useful information. I'd take it into account! I promised to have a talk with my friend, then decided to follow the senior engineer's sage advice and got some rest in my bunk before we reached the space station.

ULINE WOKE ME up. She was lying on the next cot in her short puffy robe reading something that must have been amusing, because she was rumbling happily through her teeth, like a purring kitten. When she saw me stir, my bunkmate covered the screen of her tablet with a hand, then turned it all the way off. I didn't embarrass the furry lady and pretended I hadn't noticed. I felt very well rested, beyond belief really. Looking at the clock, I discovered that nine hours had passed.

"We won't make it to the Medu-Ro system for another ummi, so you woke up too soon!" Uline said.

I answered something like, "this world is full of so much interesting stuff, I can't just sleep!" Uline rumbled back happily, unfolded the table and started setting up a game of Na-Tikh-U.

"Gnat, how about we play a round or two then? No one else on this ship is any match for me. Some don't even know how to play, and the others are too stupid or unlucky."

Sure, why not? I didn't want to just waste the next few hours on mindless entertainment, though, so I added a condition:

"Before I went to sleep, you said I was a total newbie and sometimes ask stupid and weird questions that betray a deep ignorance. And you were right. I've got a million questions about this world, alien races, and the rules of the game that bends reality. But who can I ask without opening myself up to mockery? Heck, some of my questions could even cause trouble. I need someone I can trust! So, let's do this: as we play Na-Tikh-U, you fill me in on things I don't know. Sound good?"

The Trader agreed, and while she opened the game box and generated a map, I asked my first question:

"There are rumors that a player can change faction. And not just the tag next to the name on their clothing, but completely move their body from one place in the real world to another. Is that true? And how is it physically possible?"

Uline had already finished generating the game and suggested I go first. And while I thought over the placement of my pieces on the map, the Trader started to answer:

"Yes, that is true. I am not an electronics specialist and don't know the finer details, but I can say for sure that, while playing, the physical body is somehow 'cut out' of the world. I read about one case that happened a hundred tongs ago during a war between Geckho clans. One group infiltrated another's base, but found they were hiding in their virt pods. The attackers were pissed off and shot through all the pods, riddling them with holes, then smashed them to pieces in search of bodies. But, other than twisted metal and electronic chips, there was nothing there. Eventually, the Geckho hiding in the game made peace with the other clan, joined it and left the game through one of their former enemy's virt pods. But how that happens, as I already said, I have absolutely no idea."

Very interesting. But that meant the traitor Tyulenev could fully defect, not just joining the Dark Faction in the game, but moving his obese body into their dimension. How could he even get into a pod, the fat bastard!? So, when Minn-O La-Fin praised my blue eyes and said women in her world would like them, she knew that wasn't strictly hypothetical.

Fame increased to 36.

Authority reduced to negative 6.

Authority reduced to negative 7.

What was that??? My game with Uline couldn't have caused all those messages, so it must have been something in another place. It was probably something in the H3 Faction. Most likely, my name was put in a negative light. But what could it have been? I got distracted and made an obviously stupid move in Na-Tikh-U, which Uline immediately jumped on. I looked at the starships that had broken through my defenses and admitted defeat, suggesting we start a new game.

"Uline, why are there magic points in my character stats? What can I use them on and how?"

"Gnat, do you actually have magic points?" she answered with a question.

"That's the thing, I do! One hundred forty-four

magic points. And I don't even know if that's a small or large amount."

Uline thought for a long time before answering.

"There are some game classes that actively use magical abilities from the get-go like Shamans, Psionics, and conjurers of all kinds. There are other classes that are entirely barred from using magic: Traders, Mechanics, Scientists, Soldiers. But there are also classes in neither category, who can gain magic points under certain circumstances. One such example is Healers. They can heal with skills or medicine from first aid kits and get along without magic just fine. But some Healers do have magic and use it in their work. As far as I know, other than mana you need a skill to actually use magic. But you'd better talk to our ship's healer. He knows much better than me and might actually be able to help."

This game of Na-Tikh-U was still going and, at points, it seemed I might win. But eventually Uline came out on top due to her greater experience and extensive knowledge of winning strategies. I suggested we play again.

"One more question, Uline. How long can a player stay inside a virt pod? Basically, how long will a real body last, with only virtual rest, sleep and nourishment?"

"Those are dangerous questions," the hairy lady responded. "I really hope you aren't planning to test that! I do not recommend it! Anyway, a body can stay in the game perfectly well for a short time, three or four days at least. When our crew was under arrest on Medu-Ro IV, I spent four days in the game with no break. The prison cell there was a yellow zone, and I was with a bunch of suspicious guys, so I was wary of being robbed and stripped bare while my character was helpless and vulnerable. I've heard some mention of an eight-day maximum. But every race has a different physiology, so it can vary. At any rate, sooner or later, you hit a wall, and your body will die. And you really should not try to find out where it is!"

I won the next two rounds, and the last was a crushing defeat. Then Uline, clearly roused by my double victory, suggested we play one more for keeps. And this time, she wanted to bet something serious:

"Gnat, I bet my Annihilator! You have to bet something just as valuable, your Listener bracelet or some platinum!"

I really wanted the Annihilator, and I figured the odds were in my favor. I knew the rules of Na-Tikh-U now, and my high luck modifier gave me a leg-up. But still I refused.

"No matter who wins, the other will be upset. Uline, I really value our friendship and couldn't stand to lose it, no matter how bad I want your Annihilator. But if its burning a hole in your inventory, name your price. Maybe I'll have enough to buy it."

Authority increased to negative 6.

Was it just me, or was Uline embarrassed? No, it was clearly embarrassment. The Geckho lady lowered her semi-transparent eyelids and pointed her snout at the floor.

"I was wrong, sorry... You guessed it, Gnat. I cannot use the Annihilator, because I don't have the Rifles skill. Also, I've never engaged in combat before and don't plan to, so the Relict weapon is worthless to me. What can I say? My price is one hundred thousand crystals. I'll also take platinum at a fair rate."

I set out sixteen large crystals on the table in silence, then poured out a handful of metal powder. It was half the platinum I had. I looked at Uline inquisitively, and the Trader mutely set the Annihilator on the table. After that, she waited a few seconds and... added her Na-Tikh-U box and a little remote control.

"This is a roll manipulator. It lets you fix a roll however you like," my bunkmate told me. "You can figure out how it works on your own. Gnat, I have something to confess. I purposely lost to you in the last two rounds. I wanted to make you bet big. But I changed my mind after what you said. Just one more time, I was wrong. I'm sorry."

Just then, Dmitry Zheltov walked in and stopped our chat. The copilot looked startled and, from the doorway, said that the faction was displeased with my prolonged absence and expected me to exit soon and give a report.

"Did something bad happen? Or is leadership just tugging on my leash to test its strength?"

"Both. Something bad happened and they're mad you're acting so independent," my friend admitted. "Radugin has a new deputy, and it looks like he's FSB[1]. He wants to talk to you. Radugin and Lozovsky are just as impatient. If I were you, I wouldn't keep annoying the higher-ups. You should leave the game as soon as possible. They aren't mad quite yet, but if you keep

---

[1] The modern-day successor to the KGB.

ignoring their commands, it might blow up in your face."

I promised to leave the game right after the Shiamiru docked at the Medu-Ro IV station and I found a safe green zone. I also told Dmitry that space was a red zone, and the Geckho didn't like him leaving the game here, because it violated their safety protocol. The copilot looked seriously embarrassed. Clearly, he didn't know that. But he quickly came to his senses and said:

"Anyway, we're already in the Medu-Ro system and the captain has set a course for the station. If I understood Uraz-Tukhsh correctly, he will be piloting as we dock, because he needs to talk with the dispatchers and follow their commands."

"How did you understand such complicated Geckho without Astrolinguistics?" I asked in surprise.

With a happy smirk, Dmitry answered that he hadn't. Instead, the captain put on a long and complicated pantomime to communicate. The Geckho aristocrat tapped his clawed fingers many times on his furry chest, then pointed at the control panel and imitated moving the levers. Then he pointed at the microphone and speakers, then his tongue and ears. Even the dumbest person could guess what that meant.

"I'm sad I missed it," I laughed, imagining the amusing spectacle. But then I turned serious and said: "Dmitry, I'm leaving the game at the station as promised, but there is one little nuance. When I went into the virt pod a day ago, my knees were shattered, and my leg was broken. I have a hard time believing regeneration has healed me already and I would feel really stupid if I left the game but couldn't get out of my virt pod. Plus, I'll still have to walk down the corncob!"

"Don't you worry about that, Gnat! I'll leave a bit before you and come help. Plus, I've heard that cameras were added to the corncobs to keep tabs on all the kernels. I'm sure as soon as yours opens, someone will notice!"

Chapter Six

Under the Dome Again

I WANTED DESPERATELY to see the huge space station as we approached! I imagined its miles-long body extending into space and surrounded by swarms of death-dealing starships of every imaginable shape. It sounded unforgettable and fantastic. But the reality was anticlimactic. Nonessential personnel were strictly forbidden from being on the bridge during the difficult landing procedure. That had me crawling out of my skin, but hopefully this was not my last space flight, and I would eventually be able to take in every detail.

Uraz Tukhsh was at the helm and, as usual, his abilities were lacking. In fact, he didn't even have a lot of the skills needed to be a decent pilot. Uline carefully buckled her safety belts and even suited up in full outer-space attire. She just kept moaning and groaning about Uraz Tukhsh's bad piloting. But today, luck was on the captain's side. Sure, the Shiamiru gave us a few jostles and spun around a bit but, in the end, we made it into dock, then got snatched up by the station's gravity claws and placed gently in our hangar.

"I'll lose my hair with all this stress!" Uline moaned in dismay. She then unbuckled, tossed a long attentive gaze over me and commented: "My advice to you, Gnat: change out that Energy Armor for something more basic. It'll draw attention, and that is not what you want on a pirate station. The locals here are not exactly welcoming. In the blink of an eye, they'll knock you out, strip you down, and rob you blind! And only leave the space port zone with a large group... even that's no guarantee you'll be safe, though."

As if confirming Uline's words, the captain's voice thundered down the corridor:

"Attention! We have arrived at the Medu-Ro IV station. Let me remind you that this place is not exactly friendly. So, external hatches are to be kept closed at all times! An enhanced security force must always be keeping watch over the main airlock! Do not leave the space port zone unless absolutely necessary. The rest of the station is crawling with trouble, and there's nothing to do there. Few of the locals understand Geckho, and they do not accept our crystals. But even in the space port zone, stay on guard! I don't think I need to tell you about space pirates. Just keep your distance. Do not get into any scuffles! And anyone who plans on leaving the Shiamiru must set their respawn point in a safe area near our docking point. I will not be flying back through the galaxy to come get you! I understand that these rules may inconvenience you, but please try to be understanding. We'll only spend a few days on Medu-Ro IV, no more, just enough time to arrange our trades."

It was no surprise that, after such an unequivocal warning, almost all crew members opted to remain on the Shiamiru. Just Uraz Tukhsh, Uline and a couple big strong Geckho, who were serving as bodyguards, left the ship. I was also preparing to leave the shuttle, but a bit later. I didn't want any crew members to see where I left the game because I was afraid they might take advantage of the brief period of vulnerability after I logged out but before I disappeared. I told Dmitry I was leaving and asked him to meet me under the Dome. He didn't take the same precautions, and simply headed to his bunk, laid down on his cot and went offline. Lucky devil! He didn't have anything valuable in his inventory to worry about. I couldn't say the same...

I wasn't planning to go far from the Shiamiru, but it was still a risk to show off the energy armor on the pirate station. So, following Uline's sage advice, I changed into my old kevlar jacket. But that caused a small issue. There was no longer enough room in my inventory! The Relict suit had a large backpack and additional pockets for storing small items on the side and both legs. Now, I didn't have that and had to store the bulky armor suit as well.

I took my Krechet, its ammo and five of the seven geological analyzers out of my inventory, then stuffed them into a bag under my bed. But every cloud has a silver lining. This meant I wouldn't have to lug an extra fifteen pounds around, which was not bad. I threw all three skill points into Rifles, raising it to forty, then headed out of the starship. The twin brothers Basha and Vasha were armed to the teeth and wearing heavy armor as they kept watch over the airlock. Of course, they didn't stop me, just wished me luck and advised me to be careful on the pirate station.

Then the airlock slid aside, and I took a look around. The ninety-foot long Shiamiru was hovering about three feet over the floor in the brightly lit boxy hangar. Its huge size made our ship look like a midge. Apparently, this place could host starships of much larger classes. Also, I couldn't tell while inside the Shiamiru, but our shuttle was leaning pretty far to the left. Seemingly, our balance was thrown off by the automatic processer awkwardly clamped on the outside.

The gravity on the station was approximately equal to that of earth, so I jumped onto the metal floor without fear. First, I walked to the back wall out of curiosity. It housed a forcefield that shimmered with all the colors of the rainbow, separating our hangar from a colossal vertical shaft. Apparently, that was what we'd come from. Yes, exactly! Right before my eyes, automatic robotic loaders carried a small sleek starship up the seemingly endless tube. The ship had a long needle-shaped body that smoothly transitioned into a mono-wing. Very pretty! I sensed something predatory and dangerous in it. Much to my chagrin, I couldn't identify the ship without my IR Lens. It was quite far away, and the forcefield made it look somewhat blurry. Although... my scanning icon was lit, so I could try that. While on board the Shiamiru, I had stopped using it regularly because, with nothing new to scan, it was not leveling. But here on the station, I had plenty of unfamiliar terrain.

Tiopeo-Myhh II Miyelonian Long-Distance Interceptor.

Eagle Eye skill increased to level forty-two.

Scanning skill increased to level forty.

Long-distance interceptor? It was clearly made for atmospheric flight; otherwise, why would it need such a sleek shape? But meanwhile, another ship came into view. Large and almost ball-shaped, it had no visible portholes, hatches or any other openings in its spherical body. The huge number of antennas (or some kind of stick-shaped objects) made it look like a sea urchin. It passed through the shaft just one hundred fifty feet away so, even without scanning, I managed to see the bulky giant in great detail.

Yaoo-Krom U. Miyelonian light cargo ship.

Eagle Eye skill increased to level forty-three.

Light?! The diameter of the Yaoo-Krom U was no less than three hundred feet. I was afraid to even imagine how huge a medium might be, much less a heavy! Also, my Eagle Eye skill had leveled two times in two minutes! Standing at this force field staring at all the ships passing by on the other side, I'd hit Eagle Eye one hundred in no time!

But as if refuting my optimistic hopes, I didn't see a single starship for the next ten minutes. Oh well... Alright, the time had come to leave the game. There would probably be someone waiting for me under the Dome. After making sure this hangar was a green zone and placing my respawn point as the captain ordered, I chose the menu option "Exit Game."

Would you like to review your statistics for this game session?

Sure, why not? I opened it.

Time in game: 32 hours 42 minutes. Your character leveled up 10 times, gained 11 statistics points and 82 skill levels.

Not bad, not bad at all! I noticed again that this game did have experience, though it wasn't explicit, and that I had earned an earth-shattering 252730 points.

You killed 27 players and 11 NPC's. Your session ended due to: exited game.

Here I thought for a moment. I guess I *had* killed twenty-seven players. That would have been the crew of the *Sio-Mi-Dori* antigrav, and the Dark Faction commandos on board. Add to that the ones I'd shredded with the grenade while defending the comms tower, and it was obvious where I got all that experience! When had I managed to take down eleven mobs, though? I didn't remember killing even one... Maybe there were pests in the fields I torched during the raid, and it was counting that? No other explanation came to mind, and I had no way of checking.

I opened my virt pod and shuddered in fear. There were dark figures looming over me again. Deja vu! Fortunately, my eyes quickly adapted to the change in light and I saw my friends. I was being greeted by Imran, Dmitry and Anya.

"Don't move your right leg!" the medic warned

immediately. "The fracture may not have healed yet, and the damaged meniscus could still be weak. Wait, Gnat, get your hand away from there. Let me take the bandage off your face! Woah! Your nose is good as new! The stitches can come out now, too."

I couldn't hold back and felt my nose, which I couldn't even touch two days ago. There were no painful sensations now, but I could feel a certain tension. Must have been the stitches pulling at the edges of the wound. With my friends' help, I left the virt pod, stood up and very carefully tried to put some weight on my right leg. I felt a pain and immediately decided against trying to walk. No, it was too soon. Whatever the healing effect of the game that bends reality, my broken leg and torn meniscus had not recovered in the past day and a half.

"Kirill, brace yourself on my shoulder!" Imran offered, and Dmitry Zheltov helped me from the other side.

And so, like that, all three of us started slowly down from corncob number fifteen. The guys mostly kept silent, but Anya was babbling away like a motormouth. Before we got to the bottom, she told me about Tyulenev's defection, the widespread destruction in the Eastern Swamp, and Radugin's new deputy. I asked her to tell me more about him.

"His name is Aleksandr Antipov. Some army guy, maybe a cop, that's all I know."

"He's probably FSB," Dmitry cut into the conversation, and Anya easily agreed, saying that she didn't understand the distinction.

"He came under the Dome yesterday but, in one

day, he managed to whip Gerd Tamara into a tizzy along with many other respected players. He talked with Imran and me too, but he obviously didn't suspect us of anything. All his questions were about you."

Anya sharply went silent, because we were already at the bottom of the spiral staircase and had come face to face with a group of players waiting there. I immediately recognized them all. Gerd Tamara, her second-in-command Roman Pavlovich and her two constant companions, a pair of tall muscular brutes.

"Gnat, we need to talk! Not for long, just three minutes. And everyone else, please leave us alone!" Once again, the short frail girl said this with such a surprisingly powerful intonation and boundless confidence in her right to give orders that none of my friends could object. "You too!" Tamara said, turning to the armed soldier guarding the entrance to the corncob, and he walked away unquestioningly.

It was uncomfortable to stand on my one good leg, so I sat down on the bottom step. The dark-haired girl lifted the hem of her long dress and sat down next to me.

"For starters, Gnat, I want to thank you! Your unexpected intervention changed the balance of forces in Karelia and allowed the Second Legion to go on the counterattack. Unfortunately, not everyone in the faction understands that, but I am acutely aware that our victory in Karelia was all thanks to you. And in many ways, we only kept the Eastern Swamp because of your raid as well. So, I wanted to ask: did you read my note?"

I confirmed that I found the sheet of paper in my

radio just in time and read her warning. And that was why I didn't inform the faction leaders about my raid, which kept the traitor Tyulenev from learning my intentions.

"Tell that word for word to Radugin and his underlings, that'll handle two thirds of their concerns right off the bat!" she advised me. Then Anya abruptly shifted the topic: "Gnat, three hours ago, many sources informed us that the Dark Faction is offering a bounty of ten thousand crystals for your head."

I just laughed carelessly and answered that Leng Thumor-Anhu La-Fin placed too high a value on sending me to respawn. For that kind money, I would agree to take a fifteen-minute break all on my own. But my jocular response stood in stark contrast to Tamara's stone-cold face.

"You're not getting it, Gnat. He's offering ten thousand to kill you in the real world, not the game! Either that or kidnap you in the game and bring you alive to Dark Faction territory. Also, Leng Thumor-Anhu La-Fin has officially promised sanctuary to whoever kills or kidnaps you. He will even bring their body into his world!"

Aw hell... The smile crawled off my lips and was replaced by an expression of gloom and worry. This was quite the cause for worry. Two thirds of my allies hated me with a passion, and some of them would kill me even for no reward. What was more, the persistent darksider propaganda and speeches from the Tyulenev were leading many on our team to believe the H3 Faction's days were numbered. Given that, there would surely be a few people to take them up on the offer.

By the way... was that what caused the recent boost of fame and fall in authority? The news about a bounty on my head? What was more, a reduction in authority, as far as I understood, could be caused by allies thinking worse of me. That meant I had gained some enemies, who were probably now willing to kill me for the Dark Faction's reward!

"Gnat, this is more than a serious threat!" Tamara assured me, though I already understood that perfectly. "So, whether you like it or not, I am giving you two of my bodyguards! They will always accompany you under the Dome and subdue any person who even thinks of threatening you. They're battle-tested soldiers and I have no doubt in their loyalty and skill."

I didn't resist or try to refuse. I sincerely thanked Tamara for the concern. Then she turned her head and happened to meet eyes with me. I wasn't wearing dark glasses, and I was afraid I might accidentally read her thoughts as I had done before with Anya. But Tamara held steady, in fact locking gazes, and staring deep into my glowing blue eyes...

"Should I warn Gnat that Antipov is a federal agent? Probably not worth it. Gnat is a grown boy and can figure out how to talk with people like that on his own. In fact, he'd only get angry that some little squirt like me dared give him advice. Gnat clearly thinks I'm too young and inexperienced. Oh well. Should I tell him my seventeenth birthday is in a week? I'm already almost an adult. No, that'll come across like I'm asking for a present. Better let him know but not directly, as if on accident. Then I'll gauge his reaction. Why is Gnat looking at me so weird? Is there something wrong with

my face? Maybe he noticed the scar under my lower lip. Or is my cheek twitching again? Oh! He's smiling!"

Tamara unexpectedly smiled back, but it seemed somehow unconfident and tortured. No, it didn't just seem that way! She told me why:

"I can see by your reaction that it didn't look natural. Yeah, Gnat, I'm not used to smiling... Everyone thinks it's so easy. Babies knows how to smile from birth. They laugh without thinking how to do it. But my facial muscles atrophied while I was in a coma, and I lost the ability to convey emotion. I've been practicing in front of a mirror but, so far, I can only make this predatory scowl, not a warm smile."

"It looks just fine, Tamara. You have a pretty smile. I couldn't see the scar under your lip either, and your cheek wasn't twitching. I'll give you a present next week, too! But don't say a word to anyone about what you just learned! If it is the only way of exposing traitors, no one can know about it!"

Yes, I was taking a serious risk by revealing my ability to read thoughts to the leader of the Second Legion. But, I needed to entrust someone with my secret, and Gerd Tamara was definitely not working for the Dark Faction, so I figured she could be a very useful ally. Leaving the dumbstruck and blushing girl sitting on the step, I stood heavily and called over my friends and the two Second Legion bodyguards she'd assigned to me.

"Take me straight to headquarters! If the leaders are so desperate to see me, it would be wrong to keep them waiting!"

Chapter Seven

Claim to Fame

THEY WERE WAITING for me. All my bosses were gathered in Tyulenev's former office: faction leader Radugin, Diplomat Ivan Lozovsky, and an unfamiliar chubby dark-haired man, clearly the "fed" Aleksandr Antipov, who my faction-mates all seemed to fear. I'm not sure what they found so intimidating about him, but the new deputy leader made no such impression on me. Maybe it was because of the stereotypical spy-hunter or agent from the movies. I was expecting an inconspicuous gray man with an attentive and tenacious gaze, and this plump dark-haired guy in a warm sweater just didn't seem to fit the bill.

Imran and Dmitry helped me get in the seat, then hurried to leave the room.

"Tell me!" Radugin suggested, not even trying to greet me or introduce me to the new faction member.

"What, you don't even offer coffee or a drink to a weary cosmonaut?" I asked, feigning surprise. "Sure, I'd help myself and not bother the mucky-mucks but I've still got this broken leg, so it might be a bit hard to hobble over."

That took them aback. The leaders exchanged glances until Ivan Lozovsky said he'd make me a coffee. He even offered to add a strong infusion of taiga herbs, which he said would perk me up even better. I agreed with gratitude.

"Ah, that's a lot better!" I declared with bliss after the first little sip of burning hot liquid. Beyond coffee, it smelled of wormwood, pine nuts and Saint John's wort. "So, what do you want to know? What should I tell you?"

My bosses wanted to know everything! Why, despite my injuries, had I suddenly decided to enter the game? Who gave me the authority to allow newbies into the game before the introductory lecture and Labyrinth training? What made me think riding into Dark Faction territory would be so easy, and how did I know that there wouldn't be serious resistance in the Golden Plain node? Why didn't I inform leadership? What made us choose the communications tower to hole up in and why did I change artillery targets? How did I know the Geckho would come get me on the Shiamiru and evacuate me? Why had I brought another player into space?

Lots of them were trick questions. It was as if they implied I had committed some sin and were trying to get me to admit to it. But I tried to answer honestly and in detail, because I had nothing to hide. Hell, I considered my actions absolutely correct, and damn near heroic. Sure, I had to tell them about the warning note from Gerd Tamara, and even promise to show it to them when I got back from space. But the leader of the Second Legion had given me permission and even suggested I do it, so I wasn't exactly betraying her.

I was worried leadership would have doubts about the downed Sio-Mi-Dori and the twenty-seven Dark Faction enemies I killed, but that part of my story went unquestioned. Either the upper leadership could see statistics on faction members, or that part of the story had already been told in full detail by Imran, Anya and Dmitry. What surprised and even offended me was that the leadership wasn't interested in the detailed scan of the Dark Faction antigrav.

The questioning was primarily conducted by Ivan Lozovsky. The faction leader just asked a few clarifications, while the fed just kept silent and listened closely. When the first wave of questions was over, I finally heard a reaction from Radugin:

"What can I say? I'm totally satisfied with your answers. Gnat, your only real shortcoming was when you overstepped and sent seven newbies into the game without preparation. And it isn't just that they didn't bring any stuff in from the real world, even though we're hurting for materials and they could have carried two hundred twenty pounds each. It's more that our faction was counting on them and now six of their characters are handicapped, because they didn't get any bonus stat points at the start. Now, we're left with six weak Drivers, Miners and, by the way, another Prospector. In the end, the Prospector didn't have enough stat points to take Eagle Eye and Rifles to copy your path and might even not be able to use the Prospector Scanner! So tell me, Gnat, was all that worth one decent Journalist?"

"A Journalist?! Is there even such a class in the game?" I didn't answer Radugin's provocative question, but still couldn't hide my astonishment.

"As you see, there is. Her name is Lydia Vertyachikh, and she was the only one who got out of the Labyrinth within the allotted time. Also, the game only offered Lydia two professions: Journalist or Prostitute. She makes no secret of that and has told the whole faction. I don't think anyone was surprised that Lydia ended up picking Journalist after hearing that. It seems unlikely that our faction will ever need a Prostitute. I find it even more dubious that she could find enough opportunities to level such a character... But we actually did need a Journalist, because shining a light on our successes will raise our overall morale. And Lydia found her rhythm quickly. Yesterday, she tied your record for day-one leveling!"

"She just got lucky," Ivan Lozovsky said in a dismayed tone. "It just so happened that, on the day she entered the game, we had that epic battle with the Dark Faction. Tons of our players performed acts of heroism that day. All that was of massive interest to our players. They also wanted to know what was happening at different parts of the front, so it was all timing."

I found that interesting but still tried to steer the discussion away from the lucky journalist. First of all, I asked about the scan of the Dark Faction antigrav.

Why was their reaction so subdued and even ambivalent? It was a rare achievement! Was our faction really not interested in the design of enemy tech?!

"What makes you say that? Of course we're interested," Aleksandr Antipov spoke up for the first time. "But it is worth somewhat less than extraterrestrial technology."

Antipov then fell silent, as if ashamed he'd said anything. His thought was finished by Ivan Lozovsky:

"Yes, Gnat. Dark Faction technology is somewhat better than ours. But all the darksider weapons, apparel and transport we've captured is an order of magnitude less impressive than our specimens of Geckho and Miyelonian technology. Dark Faction laser pistols and rifles are just a bit more powerful than our weaponry and are actually worse than our best, made-to-order real-world imports. But our firearms, like the Dark Faction guns, might as well be Christmas crackers in comparison with Geckho blasters and target-seeking pulse pistols."

Well, dang... I lowered my head, feeling chastened. The hard-won model of the Sio-Mi-Dori was nowhere near as valuable as I'd guessed. Here, as if wanting to cheer me up, Ivan Lozovsky continued his speech:

"But that model of the Shiamiru is truly invaluable. In fact, we the curators of the Dome project thanked us officially. They say our rocket scientists shrieked in elation when they saw the highly-detailed model of a working space shuttle! Our scientists are studying away, but there is no certainty modern understanding will be enough to grasp all the technological principles. In any case, though, it is a huge step toward interstellar flight for all mankind!"

Radugin stopped his subordinate's fiery speech, and made a gloomier comment:

"But there's also another side of the coin... Now, the curators are asking us for more 3D models. They think we must have starships growing on trees! Gnat, it looks like you're the only player in our faction who can possibly carry out this critical mission. So, from this minute forward, your main job is to get more blueprints of space technology from the great interstellar races! If you need more scanner supplies, just say the word. The faction can provide whatever you need. If you want anything at all, draw up a list and we'll do our best to either bring it in from the real world or buy it from our suzerains. For every starship of a different model, we'll pay you a five-hundred crystal bonus!"

Radugin spoke of the bonus with such a smug tone that I really had to strain not to break down laughing. How much now? Five hundred??? And that's for a unique blueprint that will allow scientists and engineers to reproduce a genuine alien space ship? Was our faction really that hard up for Geckho currency? After buying the new gun from Uline, I was left with mere pocket change, three or four hundred crystals. I basically considered myself broke.

But I didn't get on my high horse. And I definitely didn't ask for more. I just told them I still had enough Scanner supplies, and the faction didn't have to spend any of their obviously lacking Geckho currency on me.

Radugin nodded, as if he wasn't expecting

anything else, then sharply changed topic:

"So, now that we've covered your new mission, I suggest we discuss the biggest thorn in our side: your reputation in the Faction. Gnat, we regularly receive all sorts of complaints about you from all kinds of players. But that is just the tip of the iceberg. We can work with that. Just explain the situation to the players, and they calm down. It's the underwater part of the iceberg that has me worried — the anger and discontent that are not voiced but end up stewing in players' minds. I have to admit, it scares me. I mean, it doesn't look like simple envy or small issues like missing border patrol shifts or flying off with the faction's expensive stuff. You're becoming something of a pariah!"

Ivan Lozovsky asked for the floor and, with his boss's approval, continued:

"Our Geologist Mikhalych is managing just fine and I don't think he has much need for help. So, sending Gnat there would just mean wasting valuable analyzers. And not showing up for patrols is an even more worthless complaint. Our faction has more than six hundred players that never patrol the border, but none of them have any issues! It's like Gnat is just too big a deal. All anyone sees is you missing training sessions and patrols! And though earlier, the negativity could be chalked up to your conflict with the beloved Gerd Tamara, you two have made up now, so I don't see a logical explanation anymore. But it is a clear problem, and it must be dealt with ASAP."

"In my opinion, this hostility is being stoked and managed craftily by someone outside our faction," said the taciturn agent. "It just stacks too conveniently with the Dark Faction's huge bounty on his head. Seemingly, our enemies see Gnat as a threat. But they cannot touch him, so they're trying to use someone else. What do the darksiders know that we don't? What makes them see Gnat as a threat?"

"Maybe it's just personal?" Lozovsky suggested. "At any rate, Gnat lowered the Authority of their leader Thumor-Anhu La-Fin, put his granddaughter Minn-O La-Fin in a bad light and has basically just been a thorn in their ass ever since he started playing."

"That doesn't add up..." Antipov shook his head with doubt. "I have carefully familiarized myself with the Dark Faction Leng's psychological portrait. Thumor-Anhu La-Fin might allow emotions to slip out sometimes, and in those moments his rage is fearsome. But overall, he's restrained and a very clever player, who has demonstrated an ability to work through scenarios many moves in advance. According to our prisoners, many in the Leng's world wish him harm. And actually... what's stopping us from copying them and announcing a bounty for his head? How about ten thousand crystals just like theirs?"

A silence took hold. The faction leaders spent some time exchanging glances. Finally, Ivan Lozovsky answered:

"It isn't a bad response. It will show our enemies they cannot make such threats against our faction. But we cannot take out the Leng himself. He's a very strong Mage Psionic and would surely uncover the murderer by reading their thoughts before they even got close. But the old Mage has a weak point: we know he truly loves his granddaughter. He has shown it on a number of occasions. If we announce a reward for Minn-O La-Fin's head, that will have a much stronger effect on the Dark Faction leaders."

"Sure, we can announce it..." Radugin said in thought. "But how are we gonna pay?! Our faction coffers have only eighteen thousand crystals, and fifteen hundred of them are already going to rent a ferry to deliver supplies for rebuilding the oil refinery!"

I'll admit, I was somewhat shaken by the breathtaking ease my leaders displayed when discussing paying for a murder. Sure, Minn-O La-Fin and her grandfather were enemies of our faction in the game, but I didn't think it was right to kill them in the real world. However, our enemies had let that genie out of the bottle when they placed a bounty on my head, so it was technically equal retaliation. I kept silent and didn't argue. Anyway, now that our faction's lack of crystals was on the table, I couldn't keep myself from touching the hot-button issue:

"Maybe I'm missing something, but I'm very surprised to hear we're low on crystals! If the game that bends reality is so important to the government, what is stopping us from using the next batch of newbies to bring in something to sell? Like platinum, for example. Fifteen strong lads from the next group of beginners can bring in forty-five pounds each, and that'll get us six hundred seventy-five pounds. In space, pure platinum goes for sixty-eight thousand crystals per pound. Sure we probably won't be able to sell it at that price, and there will be some fees for delivery and certifying the bars with the Geckho marking system, but merchants will buy it for three and a half to five thousand crystals per pound easy! And that's around three million monetary crystals, which would immediately solve all our financial problems! That's a thousand good blasters for our army and two million crystals to spare! And if we use not just fifteen newbies but thirty, the Human-3 faction could buy its own starship! And once we have a starship, we won't have to depend on Geckho middlemen with their ridiculous markups!"

My emotional outburst was met with dead silence. Then Ivan Lozovsky turned to Radugin and said with a smirk:

"So, now we know why Gnat is such a threat to the Dark Faction! What did Geckho Diplomat Kosta Dykhsh tell us about the value of platinoids in the Galaxy? Three hundred twenty crystals for a pound of palladium, three hundred eighty for osmium and two hundred thirty for platinum? And the Dark Faction gets in the way of us selling even at those draconian prices by cutting us off from the space port and thus our source of Geckho currency. Without money, we can't import high-tech equipment, and without that, we can't beat the Dark Faction. Everyone understands that perfectly. And then, Gnat comes on the scene. He speaks Geckho, knows a few of them and has even earned their respect. Hypothetically, he could help us smooth over the trade problem, and even bypass all these greedy middlemen in the space port! That's what the Dark Faction is so afraid of!"

"Gnat, in th-that case there's a new m-mission for you!" The faction leader was excited and even started hiccupping slightly. "Ask the captain if he could maybe serve as a middleman to sell our platinum and other precious metals. Get all the prices and financial conditions, too. If it's all a-go, I'll try and get Gokhran[2] to give up some precious metals for the Dome project. As for the faction having a negative reaction... we'll work on that. First of all, we need all the players to know how much you've done for our whole faction. The most obvious option here is a big interview, because now we have a Journalist! As soon as Lydia leaves the game, I'll send her to find you, so you can agree on a format and schedule a time."

The federal agent took advantage of the faction leader's pause and grabbed the thread of the conversation:

"Now that you're an especially valuable player for our faction, we must assign you increased security. We can provide you with physical protection under the Dome for starters. As a high-profile player, you deserve a separate more comfortable room as well. For security, we'll have you draw up a friends list, and only people on it will be allowed to come visit you without prior approval. We will assign you guards who have no connection with the game or the Dark Faction. And you must be accompanied by them at all times! As for in the game, this issue will be resolved before you return from space."

And at that, the substantive part of the meeting came to an end. I was just asked approximately when I'd be back from space, how Dmitry Zheltov was doing as a pilot, and how he was getting along with the

---

[2] Translator's note: the Russian equivalent of Fort Knox

Geckho crew. Then they issued me a debit card for making purchases under the Dome and said I was free to go.

In the doorway, I asked Imran and Dmitry to wait and turned back around:

"I know there is audio and video surveillance everywhere under the Dome. For security reasons, of course. But I need an actually private room, where I can feel comfortable and relaxed without constantly looking for hidden cameras and microphones. "

Lozovsky and Radugin for some reason looked simultaneously at Antipov and, after a second of thought, the agent nodded:

"Alright, Gnat. Give us five minutes to remove our equipment and the room will be clean. We won't have any kind of surveillance. You have my word as an officer!"

Chapter Eight

Big Interview

I HAD TO ADMIT, talking with the higher-ups left me with more questions than answers. All the measures they discussed looked more like moves of desperation than well-thought-out actions. Putting a bounty on Thumor-Anhu La-Fin and his daughter, spontaneously deciding to sell platinum for millions of crystals through an unvetted Geckho captain, refusing to study the Dark Faction vehicle in favor of more advanced alien designs and betting on buying weaponry rather than producing it ourselves — it just didn't come together as a coherent plan.

I was forming the impression that the leadership was just bewildered and didn't know how to get our faction back on track. Still though, they understood that changes were vitally necessary. The recent battle with the Dark Faction showed just how shaky our positions were and underlined our lack of resources and manpower. Sure, the faction got lucky, and we managed to keep the Eastern Swamp node but, without oil production, its swampy infertile land had no real use. As far as I understood, it was not going to be easy to get our oil extraction and refining facilities back online. After all, the faction had already spent a good chunk of our limited funds on replacement parts. And they were talking about having that transported via Geckho ferry, so there probably wasn't enough gas for the Peresvets to do it. Maybe our vehicles were even seriously damaged and needed repair.

Overall, I was in a state of deep contemplation, even though my particular mission didn't seem all that challenging. Captain Uraz Tukhsh would clearly be interested in reselling the platinum, I had no doubt about that. And starships came through the forcefield tunnel in the pirate station all the time, so getting data on a couple of them on my Prospector Scanner would be easy-peasy. I would just have to warn the Shiamiru crew to turn off our electronics first.

I was in such a deep state of thought I didn't even notice it had grown dark under the Dome. Only the night lighting was still on. A street sweeper drove down an empty park path in the distance. First, my friends led me to the hospital building, where Anya took the brackets off my nose with a pair of tweezers and disinfected the remaining lacerations. The whole operation took two minutes at most, leaving nothing to remind me that, just three days ago, someone broke my nose.

After that, my friends and new bodyguards led me to a separate residential building concealed behind the tennis court and a thicket of trees. There were two buff guardsmen at the entrance, but our group was let inside without question. The pretty night receptionist smiled at me, displaying a row of flawless pearlescent teeth, and pointed at the elevator:

"Ah, Gerd Gnat, go up to the second floor and take the hallway to the right. Your room is the only one there. You won't get lost."

I thanked her for the information, then my friends took me under the arms and led me into the elevator. On the second floor, there was one short hallway to the left and another to the right, both with identical doors. I had no idea who I shared this floor with. Possibly, the other room was just empty.

My brand-new Dome debit card also opened the front door of my apartment. The light automatically turned on as soon as we entered, and I couldn't hold back a whistle of surprise. This was a far cry from the spartan chamber I was originally stuck in with three other expelled students. Ornate furniture, expensive rugs, crystal chandeliers and stucco ceilings... everything around simply screamed luxury. What was more, there was an electric wheelchair and crutches at the door. That level of attention to detail deserved its own thanks!

"Breakfast lunch and dinner can be ordered directly to your room," said the receptionist, who had come up the stairs instead of going up the elevator with the rest. And now, she was showing me around.

What a cool bathroom. The main room had a touch-screen on the wall where I could order whatever I wanted. The bar was stocked with all kinds of alcohol. The in-wall fridge next to it was pretty well filled, too. The bedroom had a bed big enough for ten. There were lots of electronics from a media center and gaming setup to a huge television that took up nearly a whole wall. Overall, I liked my new digs a lot.

The night receptionist drew my attention again and said:

"My name is Yana, by the way. The lady who works day shift is also named Yana, so it's easy to remember. Gerd Gnat, we need your friends list by tomorrow morning to give to the guards. This is a secure building and we won't let in anyone if they're not on it. You can open and close the window blinds with this remote. You'll find new sheets in that cabinet, and you can throw your dirty clothes in that basket. If you need anything else, call any time from the touch-screen."

As soon as the door closed behind Yana, my friends also said goodbye. But why? I was hoping we could sit all together and talk about the game and stuff, maybe even take a peek at the bar and celebrate my housewarming...

Imran just threw up his arms at all my attempts to dissuade him:

"Sorry, Gnat. I don't drink. And I'd love to sit and hang out, but it's already two AM, and Anya and I have second shift in the Yellow Mountains, which is in four hours. Maybe we can celebrate tomorrow? Masha and the other guys could come too then."

I thought Anya was hesitating and even thinking of staying but, in the end, she followed Imran with the excuse that it was late, and she had to work early.

"Gnat, I'm gonna sleep too," Dmitry Zheltov apologized. "I haven't slept for a day and a half because

I spent all my downtime talking with the leadership. Tomorrow evening, I'll come to your party if you're ok with that."

The door shut behind my friends and, much to my surprise, I was left alone. It was a strange feeling. Life had been bubbling up around me for the last few days. Things were happening everywhere I looked. But now, I had some time all to myself, I just didn't know what to do with it.

I tested out the electric wheelchair. I studied the rooms and sampled the hastily made canapes. I turned on some background music just to keep me company. I started to draw a bath but looked at my leg cast and decided against it, limiting myself to a quick wash-up and change of underwear. I didn't even have a moderate desire to sleep, despite the late hour. But what to do?

And then, as if answering my unasked question, a knock came at the door. Who had the deep night brought me? Well, no matter who it was, it would be a welcome distraction. I rolled up perkily to the front door, nearly overturning my wheelchair in a sharp pivot, and undid the lock. There was an unfamiliar lady standing in the doorway. She had a pleasant face, mascaraed eyes, slightly wavy chestnut hair that came to midway down her back, and a lithe figure. The woman was very tall, more than six foot two, and her legs were damn long. Based on her clothing, she'd just come from the tennis court. She was wearing a visor on her head, an athletic bag over her shoulder, a sleeveless vest with number 1555, short shorts, knee high socks and tennis shoes.

"Seeing those glowing blue eyes, I'm guessing I found the right door. You must be Gnat. I mean Kirill," the stranger said instead of greeting me and, without asking permission, she walked around my wheelchair and into the room. "Well, well! I guess high-profile players live pretty well in our faction. Pretty damn well! When I become a Gerd, I'll have to insist on a room no worse than this. By the way, in case you didn't know, I'm Lydia Vertyachikh, the official faction Journalist."

I had already guessed as much, but her introduction finally removed my last shreds of doubt. Lydia tossed off her shoes, fell back exhausted in an armchair and stretched her legs.

"I just got back from our recently-started fort in Karelia. Ten miles on foot each way, because there's no vehicle transport to Karelia right now. And though I got some awesome material, you can't even imagine how sick and tired I am! Today was endless! And as soon as I got out of the virt pod, I was called by leadership with an urgent mission to interview Gerd Gnat! Sure, if I was still in the game and leveling my Journalist skill or leveling my character, but in the real world... I'll admit, I wanted to tell them to go to hell and just get some shut-eye. And if it was anyone other than you, I would've done just that. But you're impossible to pin down. You can't be found in the game, and it's hard to catch you under the Dome as well..."

Lydia finished her exasperated speech, crossed her legs and scanned the room. The journalist's eyes stopped on the mini-bar and refrigerator.

"A vermouth with ice and orange juice, plus a snack like a fruit or pastry and I'll come to..." the lady said, sharply going silent and looking skeptically at my wheelchair and leg cast. "Alright, I'll get it myself. And I can pour you something too, Gnat. What do you say? But before we start, I'd like to take a shower. I was urgently forced into the game today from the tennis court, and I can smell the sweat on me."

So, I guess I wasn't wrong about her sport of choice. I pointed Lydia to the bathroom door and promised to pour the wine and cut the fruit while she cleaned up. She kept me waiting a long time, forty minutes. If not for the sound of falling water and the occasional bout of singing from the bathroom, I'd have thought Lydia fell asleep in there. Finally, the door opened, and my new acquaintance came out wearing a pair of warm slippers, a bathrobe and a towel around her head like a turban.

"Wow, I feel amazing! It's like I was born again! On the way to your door, I could barely crawl. Every muscle was aching."

"I know the feeling," I chuckled. "After my first day in the game, I was practically walking on all fours."

"Oh! You already set the table! Then I suggest we hold the interview over a late dinner. And first let me give a toast — to new friends!"

We had a drink, then Lydia took a notepad, pen and voice recorder out of her bag. She opened the pad, wrote the date then started thinking and... set the pen aside.

"Gnat, I have to admit, I really don't have any incentive to ask questions here in the real world. I don't get anything out of it and, if it weren't for a direct order from above, I'd have set all these questions aside until we met in the game. But you, on the other hand, need this to publicize your achievements and improve your reputation... So, I propose we play a little game. We'll flip a coin. If it's heads, I ask a question and you answer. If it's tails... tails... what can I think up to keep you hooked? Hm, let's say I remove one article of clothing!"

What?! My brows shot up in surprise. I'd been interviewed a few times before, but never under such unusual and intriguing circumstances. Then, before I managed to agree or refuse, Lydia clarified:

"We'll flip the coin ten times, no more. I'm wearing five pieces of clothing now including this towel on my head, so I could easily run out of clothes before we're out of tosses. Well, we're both adults, so I think we'll have an easy time figuring out what to do if it comes to that. Everything seems fair to me. I might get an interesting ten-question interview out of this, but we might also find a way to pass the time more pleasantly."

BY SIX IN THE morning, our second bottle of vermouth was finished. All the juice and even a large box of liquor-filled chocolate candies, which I'd ordered from my touchscreen at three in the morning for urgent delivery, were also gone. The coin tosses stood four to four, and Lydia was blushing and giggling, sitting on my lap in just a pair of thin lacy underwear. The voice recorder and notebook had already been back in her bag for a while, however, the interview was surprisingly still ongoing. She was just asking me about Gnat's adventures and carefully listening. The half-naked woman was not drunk at all and was in complete control of her faculties, even though she was consuming just as much as me. Clearly, she had plenty of experience partying in college. Also, she wasn't exactly diminutive, so it probably took more to get her drunk than me.

"Hey now, don't be naughty! Otherwise I'll go back and sit on the couch! Win another coin toss or two, maybe then you can feel me up!" Lydia said, slapping my wandering hands as they reached for her breasts, which were heaving at eye level. "Don't get it wrong. I'm a free spirit, not a slut!"

This was Lydia's favorite topic, and she had already enlightened me on the difference more than once. According to her, being a free spirit was very useful for a journalist. It allowed her to feel comfortable in any environment. And so, the fact that she was sitting in a man's room half-naked on his lap in the middle of the night didn't seem the least bit shameful, because she wanted me to open up and speak my heart. But she still wasn't going to let me cross a certain line.

All that was interesting and even looked authentic... but a few hours ago, after yet another toast to friendship, I accidentally met gazes with Lydia and read her thoughts, so I knew she was not against getting more intimate. It was actually why she'd come to my room. I also found out that this clever lady had two identical-looking trick coins in her bag, gifted to her by Antipov. One of them always fell tails up, and the other heads.

Naturally, this did not seem like a love story, just pure naked calculation. While carrying out a mission from faction leadership, the Journalist was also making a play for the vacant position of a freshly minted Gerd's girlfriend. She figured that would boost her Fame in the video game and have significant material benefit in the real world. In return then, Gnat would get a whole series of glowing reports about his achievements and a fully loyal Journalist, who could help smooth over the faction's negative opinion of him. Also the leadership, and more specifically Aleksandr Antipov, wanted us to date. He figured it would cement Gnat's connection to the H3 Faction.

I had to admit, that made me very sad. After all, it was one thing to like a woman, try and find ways of spending time with her, pore over every little thing after dates... and another thing entirely to know her thoughts in advance. Totally different emotions. Also, I didn't sense Lydia having any warm feelings toward me and didn't see her as having the right qualities to make a steady girlfriend. But of course, I wasn't going to tell her to leave, either. In any case, I was not some monk upholding a vow of celibacy, and I had never before refused good sex with a pretty woman. So for now, my goals and those of my faction aligned, and I was willing to play along.

"Let's toss the coin again!" the journalist suggested, throwing the small coin into an empty shot glass, shaking it and turning it over on the table.

I didn't even have to look to know the result. I

had foreseen it. For the Journalist to bring her "big interview" to its logical conclusion and get us together once and for all, both of the next two flips would be coming up tails. And in fact, Lydia filled the room with a joyous cry:

"Tails! You're lucky, Gnat! You wanna take off my underwear, or should I do it myself?"

Lydia, flushed red with alcohol, smiled at me with a cunning squint and looked me right in the eyes. She really should not have done that... Now, the feeling of my hands started pulling the last piece of clothing off her seemingly endless legs was relegated to the back of my mind. I was concentrating on something else:

"Alright, the long runup is almost over, and this idiot still hasn't guessed what I'm up to. It all actually came together brilliantly. I shouldn't have worried. I guess I was wrong about him. He's not a psychopath. I almost scared him off. I changed tactics just in time. I'm very lucky things didn't go south. Although, if it really is true that Gnat hasn't been with anyone for ten days, he'll never tell me to leave now. Hell, he'd probably get aroused by a plastic doll! I can even feel how excited he is through his pants. We probably won't be needing a tenth coin toss. I should make my move right now. What if he makes a wish and it's something dumb like 'dance naked on the table.' He's enough of a simpleton to do pull like that. No, I should take the bull by the horns and show Gnat how good I am in bed. Actually, should I even bother dragging him to bed? After all, his leg is broken. Might it be better right here in the wheelchair? The most important thing is that, during sex, I need to get him to agree to let me sleep over. Gnat definitely won't say no.

And in the next few days, I should build on my success a few times, then I can move in here for good. After that, I can tell the whole faction that I am Gerd Gnat's girlfriend. My fame is sure to grow..."

"Hey, neighbor, just what is going on here?!"

A dismayed voice rang out right over my ear, tearing me rudely from my concentrated mindreading. I shuddered in fear and lost concentration. Together with that, I dropped the thin white underwear I had been pulling off my guest and gracefully twirling with the first finger of my right hand. Gerd Tamara?! What was she doing in my room?! How'd she get in? Had Lydia and I forgotten to close the door after the courier brought that chocolates?

Following Murphy's law, the pair of underwear flew right at Tamara's face, and the leader of the Second Legion peeled them off her shoulder using two fingers with a look of extreme disgust, then threw them right at Lydia's face.

"You have fifteen seconds to get dressed and leave this room!" the severe paladin said with her famed bone-shaking voice. After that, she turned to her soldiers in the doorway: "Boys, this Journalist is lost, help her back to her room. If she doesn't get dressed fast enough, just take her as she is, naked!"

Lydia Vertyachikh didn't tempt fate and taunt the fearsome paladin. She wrapped herself in the bathrobe and somehow threw her things in her bag, then ran out barefoot. I had to admit, for some time I lost the gift of speech, so I didn't intervene. It was just all too surreal.

But after the door closed behind Lydia and the

Second Legion soldiers, and only Tamara was left in the room, I threw myself at her with reproach. Why the hell was she giving orders in my apartment?! I was an adult man, and I had the right to bring around whoever I liked whenever I wanted! And really, what was she doing here uninvited?!

I was expecting arguments, shouting and a big scene. But what came next left me completely astonished. The stern Gerd Tamara, a source of so much horror in the enemy ranks... covered her face with her hands and started bawling!

"I... don't know what came over me! I'm sorry, Gnat, you're right... I shouldn't have done that... I lost control. My nerves got to me. I just got back from my night shift in Karelia, and it was hard going! There's no fuel, no vehicles, and not enough people. Also, a giant man-eating constrictor has been attacking at night, abducting and devouring our sentries... The soldiers are losing their minds. I have to constantly be there to smooth over problems. My authority as a leader is splitting at the seams... And then, after I leave the game to relax, I notice that someone has moved into the apartment next to mine and they left the door cracked open. I couldn't hold back and peeked in... And then I saw that vulgarity and it was like a fog came over me... A Gerd isn't supposed to act that way! A Gerd should serve as an example to the players of his faction, envied by all... But you... you..."

Tamara started weeping even harder, wiping the abundant tears off both her cheeks. I slightly cooled my jets. I no longer wanted to strangle Tamara, but I was still very annoyed, so I had no tact:

"This looks more like the hysterics of a jealous underage idiot than genuine concern for a Gerd's reputation. I feel like there's a lot you aren't saying. You ruined my night. I'm very mad at you and have the right to know why you did it! Come closer and look me in the eyes!"

The girl turned her head in fear and refused. But when I raised my voice in anger and even, unable to hold back, shouted rudely, Tamara turned and ran out of my room. What a bad kid! Angry as a devil, I rolled over to my front door and, standing up, picked up the crutches leaning next to it.

Oh, fu...! The sharp pain nearly made me fall when I put too much weight on my right leg. Colorful circles started dancing before my eyes. My mouth filled with the salty taste of blood from my bit-through lower lip. I readjusted the crutches, went out into the corridor and saw the two Second Legion soldiers Tamara had given me as bodyguards. Both of them looked plainly bewildered and stared inquisitively at me in hopes of getting some kind of explanation of what just happened. Clearly, the panicked exits of the Journalist, then the leader of their legion had the soldiers confused.

"I've had it up to here with those girls. They were catfighting in my room now... Help me get to my virt pod, I won't be able to get to the fourteenth floor with a broken leg otherwise. I'm not gonna fall asleep right now anyway, so let me at least get some work done..."

The walk to corncob number fifteen and subsequent climb up it somehow passed by my conscious mind. I was still full of feelings, turning over the recent events in my head again and again and cursing my poorly behaved floormate. Also, my broken leg was in ferocious pain. I could barely hold back a howl. Finally, my kernel!

I thanked the Second Legion soldiers for their help, left the crutches on the floor, then got into my virt pod and closed the lid. I needed to get into the game right away! To the calm and predictable Geckho, to the starships and voyages to the distant cosmos. The real world and its people were driving me crazy!

But this was not my lucky day. I loaded up the game and immediately recognized the room I'd recently exited from. The hangar was a huge dim space. The only light was the dull pulsing forcefield at the far wall dividing this bay from the vertical shaft of the space station. I took a closer look. I was soon left with no doubt that this was that very same hangar I had been in before, watching starships through the forcefield. But the Shiamiru was nowhere to be found! The Geckho had flown off without me!

Chapter Nine

Playing Solo

THE TRAGEDY OF THE SITUATION didn't reach me right away. For some time, I tried to raise my crew via radio, hoping that the Geckho had simply moved the shuttle to a different hangar, but the only answer I received was buzzing distortion. Seemingly, Captain Uraz Tukhsh and the rest of the crew had simply forgotten about me and had to flee the unfriendly station in a bit of haste.

I quickly checked the only obvious door and found it locked. There was no keyhole or other way to get it open on this side. The door was adorned with a set of intersecting glowing orange rectangles, which clearly meant something. But I didn't know a single world of Miyelonian, and certainly didn't understand their written language. I spent ten minutes pounding on the closed door with my hands and feet, hoping to attract attention to my miserable position, but it seemed no one could hear.

Other than the door, there was an inactive cargo

conveyor belt that led gradually down into a tunnel blocked by a thick metal door. But the massive weight of the door and lack of control panel or communications devices of any kind meant the barrier could not be moved from this side. Seemingly, the owners of the station hadn't considered that a living creature might be inside a locked empty hangar. Well now I'd done it... Even death couldn't solve my problem, because my respawn point was in here as well.

I walked the perimeter of the hangar with a flashlight, trying to find a service hatch or other path to freedom I might have missed. I even tried knocking on the walls and floor in search of empty cavities. No dice. The walls were thick, and the floor was uniform and all-encompassing. Running a Prospector scan confirmed these observations. There was a small difference, though. With scanning, I could see through the wall into the neighboring hangar. Based on the markings on my mini-map, there was a large spaceship there. I could only partially see it and couldn't tell its name or class, but I still understood that the hangar to my right was not empty. I started pounding on the wall, hoping to attract attention. I almost broke my hand on the porous stone, but it still didn't help.

Was this a dead end? Would I really have to just sit here and hope for another starship to enter the hangar? What were the chances? How many hangars did this station have? I walked over to the force field and looked into the blurry distance. The far wall of the huge shaft was very indistinct. I had to change into my Listener energy armor because of +2 Perception bonus from the IR lens I'd recently had transferred into its helmet.

Eagle Eye skill increased to level forty-four!

It did help me see the opposite wall of the round vertical shaft, but that just made me more despondent. None of the five hangars I could see that way had starships in them either. The situation was coming together very poorly. The chance that any dispatchers would send the next arriving starship here was miniscule at best. Seemingly, sitting here like an idiot and hoping for rescue was the wrong option...

I turned back to the locked door and looked even closer, shining my bright helmet-mounted flashlight on it. The glowing orange symbols on the door were not made with glow-in-the-dark ink as I first thought. It looked something like little light bulbs. I wondered where their power source was. What kind of lock did this door have? Seemingly it was electromechanical. If that was so, maybe I could break it with a powerful EMP?

Before checking, I decided to wait for my Scanning ability to reload so I could see the details of the locking mechanism. The magnets, arrangement of wires inside the wall and so on. At the very beginning of the game, I didn't even dream of such detail but, as my Scanning skill improved, I had been able to see the small details clearer and clearer, including ones hidden behind barriers and walls. So, the scanning icon changed color and my ability reloaded. Let's go!

Scanning skill increased to level forty-one!
Electronics skill increased to level thirty-three!

I had to zoom in the mini-map as much as

possible to see any details but, even then, I didn't gain total confidence. Sure, there were power cables inside the wall going up, and rectangular things that reminded me of magnetic clamps. So, should I check to see if I could short the electronics with a geological analyzer? The risk was very great. I was seriously afraid that the locals might be upset by a powerful EMP frying their electronics. I might earn a swift beating for sabotage...

On the other hand, the Miyelonians would definitely notice me, so I'd get out of the locked hangar at least. And the diagram of the starship on the other side of the wall would be useful for my faction. Actually I'd be carrying out an order from Radugin, which was a bonus. So, I made up my mind and, opening my Prospector Scanner, reduced to zero the sliders for protein and nonprotein organic matter, super-heavy metals, radioactivity, movement detection and other crap. Then, I turned up neutrinos, echolocation, cavity scan and structural analysis to max. Here goes nothing! I activated an analyzer.

Scanning skill increased to level forty-two!
Break-in skill increased to level sixteen!
Break-in skill increased to level seventeen!
You have reached level forty-three!
You have received three skill points!

The orange lights went out, and I managed to open the heavy metal door with a good strong push. It worked!!! Hooray!!! However, I wasn't celebrating for long. The floor underfoot shook palpably and, even through the wall, I could hear a loud hum, crack and scrape. Seemingly, along with the door I meant to deactivate, all the gravity cranes in the neighboring hangar had turned off and the many-ton starship had fallen to the hard floor. Oops... I guess I wasn't considering that. I hope my neighbors' ship hadn't broken too badly. In any case, I now needed to get my ass as far from this place as possible, so no one would connect the accident with my presence in the neighboring hangar. But before I closed the scanner, I checked the diagram of the starship in the neighboring hangar.

Gerd Setis-Vir. Tiopeo-Myhh III class Miyelonian Long-Distance Interceptor

Almost as soon as I saw the name of the ship, a system message jumped before my eyes:

ATTENTION!!! The captain of this ship, Gerd Setis-Vir, is one of the Galaxy's most wanted space pirates. Danger rating: 4.

Yikes... I had no idea what a danger rating was, and whether four was a high number or a low one but, in any case, I didn't want to find out. Seemingly, I had just dinged up the ship of a dangerous pirate, so I became even more convinced I needed to move my butt. I did feel pity for the damaged ship, though. I had seen a Tiopeo-Myhh interceptor of the second series earlier through the forcefield and I found that the height of perfection. And although it was hard to make anything out from the confusing image on my scanner, the third series starship was probably even prettier, more dangerous and technologically advanced. And probably it cost more to repair. Like so much my faction wouldn't earn enough to pay it off in a century! Anyway, the last thing I wanted was to meet with this enraged pirate captain after that.

I just took a quick peek at the bit of the space station on my scanner. A bunch of floors, bulkheads, corridors, rooms... The layered three-dimensional diagram was about as clear as mud. I had no time to figure out the confusing intersecting lines on my screen, so I just put my scanner back into my backpack and walked forward.

Past the open door, I discovered a gradually curving corridor that extended a long way in both directions. The stone walls held incomprehensible inscriptions, the floor had bright lights in it at even distance, and the ceiling was around twelve feet high. To the right, I heard agitated shouting. Most likely, it was the crew of the damaged pirate interceptor commenting on the fall and looking for someone to blame. I guess I should avoid that. I could easily be downed by a hot-tempered pirate, so I quickly changed out of my Listener suit into my old jacket, turned left and quickened my pace.

Cartography skill increased to level forty-four!

The corridor was turning gradually to the left, and all the doors on the left were identical and locked. And they looked exactly like the one I'd recently forced open. It soon dawned on me that this corridor must have gone in a huge circle around the shaft and hangars, which my mini-map confirmed. I walked almost half the circle before I found a fork and turned to the right. There were a bunch of bright words and arrows there. Among them, I could even find a couple in Geckho, both pointing right:

"Document check. Registration service."

Documents? I didn't have any documents that proved my identity. And I really didn't see any need for them. After all, this was a game, and a person's information could be checked digitally. Nevertheless, some kind of documents were being checked at the other end of this corridor, and that could be a problem.

I turned right and walked just ninety feet before seeing yet another door beyond a turn in the hallway. Fortunately, it was not locked and opened automatically when I got near. And that was when I first saw a Miyelonian.

Can you imagine a huge emaciated cat with pierced ears, standing on its hind legs and absolutely laden with leather straps, holsters and sheathes? That was approximately how it looked. Five feet tall and all covered with fur, it had a long bushy tail like a fancy breed of cat. The only real clothing this "cat" had on were fingerless gloves on its clawed hands, and something like a loincloth. However, the Miyelonian had more than enough bladed weapons, holstered pistols and other implements of destruction. And I was also immediately drawn to a hat with ear slits, more like a bandanna, which had four puffy tails clipped to it. Those must have been trophies from defeated rivals.

Aik Ur Miyeau. Miyelonian. Pride of the Comet's Tail. Level-64 Gladiator.

When I approached, the gladiator peeled himself off the wall he was leaning on and said something from afar, perhaps asking a question, as he seemed to expect an answer:

"Ah-sahntee maye-uu-u rezsh shashash-u?"

I didn't understand a thing and didn't react, so

the furry gladiator repeated himself and pointed at the laser rifle on my back with his clawed finger. Was he asking me to put away my weapon? Most likely, it was not allowed to be armed on the station. I stopped, smiled in a friendly manner and nodded, stashing the weapon in my inventory.

That was my final move, though, because the overgrown cat was suddenly behind me giving a backhanded swing with a sparkling curved blade.

Your character has died. Respawn will be possible in fifteen minutes.

Would you like to review your statistics for this game session?

What statistics...? I had played an hour and a half at most, and I didn't really do anything in that time. I cracked open the virt pod lid and just lay there, thinking over my recent death and difficult position. I didn't want to leave all the way to explain myself to the leadership. It was a stupid situation, after all. So, I just waited fifteen minutes and went back into the game.

Death is never nice but, in this case, it just zeroed out my progress bar, because it wasn't empty. I definitely remembered that, after reaching level forty-three, Cartography had gone up. That calmed me down.

Also, the Miyelonian killed me instantly, so he couldn't have stolen anything of value from my inventory. There was a low chance that my kevlar jacket or other old clothing items might have fallen as loot. I also had the Paralyzer in a holster on my side, so it was at risk. But none of that was too bad. I could survive these losses. Now I'd like to know why the

Gladiator attacked me at all. Maybe he had taken my toothy smile as a threat? And why hadn't Danger Sense kicked in?

"Gerd Gnat, do you need any help?" Next to my pod, the guard of corncob fifteen appeared, along with an unfamiliar ally in a First Legion uniform.

The surveillance cameras probably detected the opening of my virt pod, as well as the fact that Gnat hadn't left the bed, so the nearest guards had been sent to figure things out.

"No, I just died in the game and I'm waiting fifteen minutes to respawn," I admitted honestly, not wanting to totally fill them in. "Actually... wait! Yes, I do need help! Find Dmitry Zheltov. He's probably sleeping off the long game session. Order him to immediately enter the game and tell the Shiamiru crew that Gnat is still at the dock on Medu-Ro IV. It's critical!!!"

"Shiamiru? Medu-Ro IV?" the guardsman repeated the unfamiliar words to secure them in his memory and promised to convey my message.

While the corncob guard called a "Post Four" on his radio, the First Legion player came up, leaned over and asked in a whisper:

"Gnat, did Gerd Tamara and the Journalist really have a fight in your bedroom tonight?"

Boy, rumors sure did spread fast under the Dome! It hadn't even been two hours, but the whole faction was already in the loop! Anyway, I didn't try to hide it:

"No. Would you really call that a fight?! Even though Gerd Tamara is shorter than the Journalist by a head and a half, she won right away and pushed Lydia into the hallway."

"Ah, I knew it. Our little Tamara is just super! She could take down a hungry lion! Just awesome! The guys said she chased the Journalist out of your room in her birthday suit!"

"Well, that was a lie! Sure, she didn't have on underwear or shoes, but I distinctly remember a short bathrobe."

The conversation ended, because the corncob guard was back, reporting that my message had been passed on and that the receptionist was going to wake up Dmitry Zheltov. I thanked my ally for the help and closed the lid. The fifteen minutes were already up, so I could go back into the game and try a different tactic.

Chapter Ten

Second Attempt

I APPEARED IN THE dark empty hangar again and first looked at my inventory. Nothing was gone. Seemingly, luck was on my side, and not a single piece of my clothing or weaponry had dropped as loot. That was good news. Unfortunately, though, the door I'd worked so hard to open before was locked again.

Hey, why hadn't I changed my respawn point to that long round corridor?! Now I was going to have to fiddle around with the damned door again! Although... I did have some information about the floor plan now. Before, heading out into the unknown and possibly dangerous pirate station, how was I supposed to know what was out there? What if it was a shitshow, and I died over and over again, just because I changed my respawn point too soon?

Alright, hindsight is twenty-twenty. It was dumb to think about what could have been. I had just one geological analyzer left, so I couldn't afford to mess up now. I didn't change the Scanner sliders, as they'd served me well before. Here goes nothing!

Scanning skill increased to level forty-three!
Break-in skill increased to level eighteen!

Well, not a bad way to quickly level skills. I'd just have to stock up on scanner supplies. The orange lights went out, the metal door gave to my push and opened again. As before, I didn't manage to step over the threshold before the floor shook. The pirate interceptor in the neighboring hangar had been left without its invisible supports again and fallen. The many aliens roaring and yelping incomprehensibly were clearly audible through the wall. I suspected it was all four-letter words in their language. Sorry, pirate dudes. I guess this wasn't your day either!

Going out into the ring corridor, I turned left, quickly ran from the scene of the crime, then changed my respawn point. Jeeze... I hoped I wasn't trapped in an instant death scenario! I glanced at my progress bar and noticed with satisfaction that it was not empty. It was fifteen percent full, in fact, which meant dying again wouldn't be a catastrophe. I quickly gathered confidence and started off boldly, cruising for a seemingly inevitable bruising.

This time, reaching the already familiar turn right, I ignored the door with the aggressive gladiator and went to see what was further down the main corridor. But I was soon forced to stop, because I had almost made a complete circle and come back to the hangar from the other side with all its hysterically screaming pirates. As much as I didn't want to, I'd have to find some way past the overgrown cat.

I turned toward the room and stopped, gathering my thoughts and considering my next move. What would I do if that cat attacked me again? For weaponry, I had the Dark Faction laser pulse rifle, the discharged Annihilator, a totally unremarkable knife and the Paralyzer.

After brief consideration, I decided against the pulse rifle. I couldn't kill a level-64 character in one shot with that, especially a Gladiator. His class meant a greater number of hitpoints. And the six seconds it took to reload were more than enough for the pissed-off overgrown cat to make minced meat out of me with his razor-sharp blades. The knife? Not even funny. All that remained was the Paralyzer, even though it wasn't lethal.

I took the Paralyzer out of the holster and stared at my last remaining hope. It looked most of all like a short paintball marker, and it shot approximately equal-sized balls, but they had thinner walls and glowed slightly. I had just three of them left in the hopper. Not much at all. Although, on the other hand, I wouldn't manage to even use them all if I missed the furry Gladiator with my first shot. That meant I had to shoot point blank before my enemy realized what was happening. And to do that, I'd have to get close to him...

Authority increased to negative 5.
Authority increased to negative 4.
Authority increased to negative 3.

I shuddered, startled. What the heck?! It took some time to realize these system messages had nothing to do with my current actions on the pirate station. Almost no one here had seen me yet, so there was no reason for such a sharp growth in Authority. Most likely, it was Lydia Vertyachikh's journalism endeavors, spreading the facts on Gnat, and how much he was doing for the whole faction. Although there could have been some totally different reason, like the amusing rumors about half-naked girls fighting in my bedroom at night.

Alright, this had nothing to do with my reality now, and was just distracting me from serious business. I placed all three free points into Danger Sense, raising it to 19, took a heavy sigh and went decisively forward to meet the armed Miyelonian. I was still holding the Paralyzer in my inventory, not wanting to show it too early, but I kept the transparent window open, so I could switch it into my hand at a moment's notice.

Aik Ur Miyeau the cat-gladiator was in the same place, still leaning his furry back against the wall. Just like before, still far away, he straightened up when I came nearer and asked the very same question:

"Ah-sahntee maye-uu-u rezsh shashash-u?"

But this time the intonation was a bit different. The Gladiator clearly recognized me. He looked happy and bared his sharp teeth in a predatory grin. And I noticed that he had a new trophy hanging off his belt, a severed human hand:

Hand of Gerd Gnat, level-43 Prospector (trophy)

Eagle Eye skill increased to level forty-five!

"Go to hell, you flea-ridden animal. This means war!" I said in my own language, though keeping my inflammatory declaration in a calm and peaceful tone, making sure not to smile and accidentally show any teeth. I also held out my empty hands, trying to convey a lack of hostile intent.

The gladiator was perplexed. He froze in confusion, blade in hand and made a huge error, allowing me to come near. When I was close enough, I turned over my empty hands and carefully controlled my thoughts as not to trigger a possible Danger Sense skill. No, I didn't wish death on this cat-man. My intentions were peaceful, this was only a game!

When I was just three steps from the Gladiator, the Miyelonian took a step forward, blocking my path, and asked something else. Actually, his tone was more like demanding. What he wanted I couldn't understand. Maybe just to check my documents, given that the sign pointing over here said "Document check," but that didn't matter.

"Yes, yes, of course I have documents! I'll show you right away!" I said and moved the Paralyzer from my inventory to my hand. "Here!!!"

I don't know if the Gladiator cat had Danger Sense or not, but he didn't have time to dodge the point-blank shot. I looked at the twitching body on the floor and shot him again just in case. Who could say how well the Dark Faction paralysis serum would work on a space cat, or whether one ball could down him for long?

The Miyelonian stopped thrashing. His vertical pupils froze. Had I accidentally killed this alien? Did I overdo it? But no, killing an enemy more than twenty levels stronger than me would have given a generous outpouring of experience. That meant this tom-cat was still alive.

I crouched down next to him and unceremoniously rummaged through the Miyelonian's belt pouches. I was looking for documents, so I could see what that even meant. There were plenty of things in the pouches, mostly incomprehensible, but I didn't find anything that even slightly smacked of documentation. However, I did find a triangular metal box, which the game told me was a wallet.

Two hundred forty-three crypto (Miyelonian currency)

I took the wallet and money as compensation for my moral and physical damages, unclipped my severed hand from his strap and, glanced at it, gave a snort and stuck it in my inventory. Now, I just had to find Gnat's heart. Then, if a girl struck my fancy, I could literally give her my hand and heart, as a set.

I also looked at all the paralyzed cat's weaponry and carefully studied it, but I only took the curved blade, which glimmered with electricity once per second. I couldn't use the razor-sharp sickle myself because I lacked the Blades skill and had too little Agility, but my Gladiator friend Imran could find a use for it. I was also interested in the many earrings glinting up from the downed space cat's huge ears. There was lots of jewelry, but almost all of it was useless fakery, except one earring, which was shaped like a green star:

Tantalum earring with emerald inset. Agility +1

Items that gave stat bonuses were a big rarity in

my faction. Crafting them required specialists with magical abilities, so my allies in the H3 Faction couldn't make them even in theory. I vaguely remembered hearing that magic rings and bracelets were sometimes taken off the bodies of Centaurs and Minotaurs on the Antique Beach, but they were extremely rare, and we still didn't know where they were getting them.

I couldn't just leave my prostrate rival with such a rare item so, removing the earring brusquely, I stuck it into my inventory. I would have used it myself, but my ears weren't pierced. Plus, all the colors and stars would look much better on a girl than a boy.

Alright, I was almost finished with the defeated Gladiator. All that remained was the most important part... If it was accepted practice to demonstrate one's lethal capabilities by taking trophies from downed enemies on this pirate station, then I figured I should do the same. I took out my knife and tested the sharpness of the blade with a finger, then sliced off the cat's reddish-brown bushy tail in one confident motion.

Tail of Aik Ur Miyeau, Level-64 Gladiator (trophy)

Fame increased to 37.
Authority increased to negative 2.
Authority increased to negative 1.

Great! Now I just had to figure out how to attach the fluffy thing. I took it in my hands and looked at the tailless cat's bandanna. I discovered that all his trophies were clipped onto special pins. And hey... I remembered seeing something like that in one of the Gladiator's belt pouches. Actually, he had at least forty of them. Apparently, Aik Ur Miyeau was a self-confident and well-prepared optimist! I took a couple of the pins and, while I clipped the trophy tail onto my helmet, a message suddenly jumped before my eyes:

Danger Sense skill increased to level twenty!

I immediately realized what caused it. My paralyzed enemy had come back to his senses but wasn't showing it! Either the paralyzing poison had simply run its course, or the Miyelonian was woken up by the pain of losing his tail, but he was definitely alert now. His eyes were open just a tiny bit, though, like little barely visible hyphens. Aik Ur Miyeau was trying not to give himself away with an accidental or abrupt motion, but his clawed hand was very slowly, inch by inch, reaching for the spare blade in his scabbard. Not this time. I didn't beat you just to lose everything again! I took out the pulse rifle and aimed the barrel at the cat's forehead.

"Stay down, pussy-cat!!!"

Unfortunately, either the enemy didn't understand me or put too much self-assured hope in his agility and speed. The Miyelonian gave a sharp jerk, trying to hop up and grab the barrel of my rifle, and I instantly shot the cat right in the head! It was definitely a crit, no question. The point-blank shot blew my enemy's big-eared fanged head to smithereens. The Miyelonian's decapitated body fell to the floor and went quiet.

Rifles skill increased to level forty-one!
Sharpshooter skill increased to level twenty-one!
Authority increased to 0.
You have reached level forty-four!

You have received three skill points!
You have reached level forty-five!
You have received three skill points! (total points accumulated: six)

Oops... I had to admit, I didn't see anything good in killing him. Just fifteen minutes from now, an enraged and highly dangerous Gladiator would respawn to hunt me through the entire space station like a homing missile. And he'd probably find me, because he knew all the floors, rooms and passageways much better than me. And in a fair fight, I'd be no match. After all, it would be naive to think Aik Ur Miyeau would let me use the same trick again. And the chance of getting off a shot right into the forehead of a lightning-fast bounding enemy also seemed miniscule.

I had no real claim to the Miyelonian Gladiator's trophies, so I didn't take his four differently colored tails. Alright, now I had to run further down the corridor. I had just fifteen minutes head start to try and hide.

Successful Perception check

Basically at the very last moment, when I had already started moving, my attention was drawn by an unusual unprepossessing bracelet that had dropped from the dead body. What was that? I stopped and picked up the strange item. In the thin strap, there was a small metal disk clanging about, covered on both sides with incomprehensible symbols.

Aik Ur Miyeau's identification card.

Well, well! Seemingly, I had figured out how their documents looked. What was more, I now had a functioning specimen! I clipped the bracelet on my wrist and ran further down the corridor.

But I soon stopped in a small room next to a bank of elevators arranged in a thick transparent column. Right before my eyes, inside one of them, a high-speed elevator shot past like a bullet. It was full of strange creatures that looked like short-tailed crocodiles. But I was less drawn by the alien creatures than the huge whole-wall panorama window, and even more the fantastic view it revealed. I walked up closer, and my mind was boggled. Now that's beauty!!!

Medu-Ro IV. Volcanic-type planet.

I saw a huge gloomy planet illuminated by the bluish glow of the local sun. The planet itself was matte black, webbed with cracks thousands of miles long which contained blood-red rivers of magma bubbling up from below. The planet did have an atmosphere but, based on its oddly viscous texture and dirty yellow shade, it was unlikely to be breathable.

Eagle Eye skill increased to level forty-six!

Cartography skill increased to level forty-five!

If I weren't so severely pressed for time, I'd have stood there at least an hour just taking in the spirit of space, admiring the infinitely distant volcanic planet. But I had a desperate lack of time, so I hurried to the wall panel. I could probably call an elevator from here. But how? The panel had the same squares and rectangles, some intersecting and some laid separately. I pressed the first one I saw.

Some blue and green rectangles lit up on one of the transparent doors so, I had seemingly called that one. To be honest though, I had no idea if I'd called it going up or down.

Electronics skill increased to level thirty-four!
Astrolinguistics skill increased to level forty-six!

The elevator appeared very shortly, in just five seconds. But I wasn't prepared for the other passengers. Three six-legged short-tailed crocodiles took up almost all the space inside. Packed into suits of metal armor, they had massive bodies, elongated fanged snouts and tiny independently-moving yellow eyes. Each of their six feet had on a piece of clothing midway between a boot and glove... I froze in indecision and tried to figure out who these creatures were:

Gerd Ussh Veesh Trillian. Trillian. Gray subrace. Level-143 Trader

Level one hundred forty-three?! Holy crap! No wonder this trader was so at ease on the pirate station! He could probably talk smack about anyone! Also, the two other Trillians were Bodyguards by class, both around level one hundred. A reap bunch of bruisers! I'd already decided to just wait for another elevator, but suddenly Ussh Veesh, who had been lying horizontally, scrunched up his body and made the front part of it go vertical, freeing up some room for me. His bodyguards also went into motion, letting me through. I politely thanked the Trillians both in my own language and Geckho, then walked into the elevator.

It blasted off upwards so fast I could barely stay on my feet. Just ten to fifteen seconds later, we stopped on a different floor. A large sign in Geckho informed me where I'd ended up:

Space Port Zone. Residential floor

"Temporary residence permits. Hotel. Cafe. Exit from space-port zone into Medu-Ro IV station"

I was especially glad to see that there was no "document check," which was my greatest fear. Seemingly, the check was meant to be done by Gladiator Aik Ur Miyeau, and I had managed to bypass it, if perhaps by an unorthodox method.

Chapter Eleven

New Friend

THERE WERE THREE hallways leading different directions, and I couldn't see any legible words down any of them, so I stopped in indecision. Where to go? I was also bewildered by the fact that there were around a dozen armed Miyelonians next to the elevator, arguing about something in elevated tones. I had no idea what was happening there. Some kind of shouting match, or perhaps the beginnings of a duel, but the quarreling parties were evenly numbered and holding their clawed paws on their weapons. What was more, members of both groups were looking at me with curiosity. I could not say what sparked their interest. Perhaps they had simply never seen a person before, and maybe they were drawn by the trophy on my helmet, but I really didn't appreciate the heightened attention.

Danger Sense skill increased to level twenty-one!

That bad?! Uh oh! I tried to keep closer to the respected merchant Gerd Ussh Veesh and his bodyguards, so it would look like I was with the Trillians. The Miyelonians immediately stopped paying me any mind. My feeling of alarm and imminent disaster quickly abated. Yikes... Danger averted!

Uline's warning came to mind a bit too late, but I remembered that I should only walk around the pirate station Medu-Ro IV in a large group. So, I decided to keep following the Trillians, though I did trail a bit behind. The Trillians clearly knew their way around and would lead me where I needed to go.

After coming out of the hallway, the "crocodiles" got down on all six legs and tore off with surprising swiftness. I even had to start running not to lose them from view. Ignoring some branches off the main corridor and confidently turning down others that looked just as unremarkable, the Trillians soon reached a small semicircular room containing glass doors that led to a passage.

The only thing of note here was a transparent glass counter with inscriptions in various languages, including Geckho: "Visitor Registration." Behind the counter on a tall round chair there was a Miyelonian lady sitting cross-legged. And it was definitely a lady because, for some reason, the system told me that clearly:

Ayni Uri-Miayuu. Female Miyelonian. Pride of the Comet's Tail. Level-71 Translator.

The Miyelonian woman was a fair bit shorter than the Gladiator Cat and the soldiers near the elevator. She had thick orange fur from her head to the tip of her tail, and a large number of earrings in her pointed ears. The lady cat was only wearing a pair of very short, light-colored shorts with a slit for her long furry tail. It was warm on the Medu-Ro IV station, I would even say hot, so there was no good reason to wear much clothing, especially for creatures with thick fur. I also noticed that the Miyelonians were apparently not mammals, because their bodies had no nipples or breasts, meaning the females had no need for bras or anything like that. The fluffy lady's lack of clothing was easily compensated, though, by an insane amount of jewelry. She had on rings, beads, earrings, necklaces, crowns, and tons of bracelets and anklets.

While the Trillians conversed with Ayni Uri-Miayuu, I stood and watched from afar, thinking over my next move. The Miyelonian was a Translator by class, so maybe she knew Geckho? There was Geckho writing on the counter, so it seemed logical. That would greatly simplify things and allow me to tell her about the sticky situation I'd landed myself in. Maybe she could even help me get in touch with my Shiamiru, or at least give me some advice.

Meanwhile, the Trillians finished talking with the registration service employee and each got a bright yellow ribbon from the fluffy Translator, which the "crocodiles" immediately fastened to their front left legs. The transparent doors flew open, letting the Trillians out. My turn had come. With a deep sigh, I gathered my thoughts and stepped decisively up to the registration desk.

"Kento duho, amiri Ayni Uri-Miayuu!" I said in

Geckho, showing I knew how to communicate, and using an honorific meaning "splendid" before her name, figuring flattery couldn't hurt.

"Kento duho, Gerd Gnat!" the Miyelonian answered mechanically, demonstrating her knowledge of the Geckho language. Then she froze, looking carefully at the trophy on my helmet. "I see that Aik Ur Miyeau challenged a stronger enemy yet again!"

I removed my helmet and turned it over, looking with significant pride at the hard-won fluffy tail. Then I decided to admit my confusion:

"Honestly, I have no idea why, but he attacked me!"

"What? Did Aik Ur Miyeau just attack you without warning?" she asked, surprised and even shocked. "That cannot be, it's illegal! He should have said the traditional phrase to challenge someone to a duel: 'ah-sahntee maye-uu-u rezsh shashash-u,' which means 'may the Great First Female resolve our dispute.' Only after receiving an answer or seeing a gesture toward a weapon may the instigator start the fight!"

Astrolinguistics skill increased to level forty-seven!

"Yes, he did say something like that. But I, unfortunately, do not speak Miyelonian so I didn't understand. I thought he was asking me to put my laser rifle away. I reached for my weapon, and the Gladiator attacked me..."

The Translator called up a transparent holographic screen and, using her manicured claws to quickly move some colored rectangles around on it, shook her head shortly just like a person:

"Just what was Aik Ur Miyeau thinking when he started a scrap with a Gerd?! That rank, after all, is not handed out willy-nilly. He should have chosen an opponent more carefully! Gerd Gnat, your pass to the station is ready, here!" With these words the registration worker extended me a lemon-yellow plastic bracelet with a metal chip. "Passes are generally worn on the front left appendage to make it easier to open doors. This shows your interceptor *Gerd Setis-Vir*, and where it's parked, dock eight, level sixteen."

Seemingly the employee had looked up the floor the Gladiator cat worked on, noticed there was only one ship there and come to the incorrect conclusion that I belonged to the pirate crew of the starship *Gerd Setis-Vir*. Perhaps that was for the best. It got me a bracelet anyhow, so maybe I shouldn't point out her error and risk throwing away my pass. Or should I tell her about the Shiamiru and getting out of the locked hangar? I still hadn't decided what to do when suddenly the Translator froze in worry, studying the contents of the screen closely and raising her gaze to me:

"By the way... here in the database, it says that your ship has been having some technical issues."

Ugh, crap... I immediately realized that admitting I caused these "technical issues" would mean taking the blame, and possibly compensating the consequences, which was not exactly the wisest move. But Ayni Uri-Miayuu was waiting for an answer, so I had to improvise on the fly:

"Yeah, that's true. We don't know why, but the gravity crane in the hangar turned off and our interceptor's tail slammed down on the floor. Our technicians are trying to assess the cause of the accident and the severity of the damage now. So, the captain gave some leave to all crew members who aren't busy with the repair."

Clearly, what I said matched up with the information on the Miyelonian lady's screen, because no questions followed. Ayni wished me a pleasant stay on the station and opened the glass doors to the residential floor:

"Gerd Gnat, you have permission to stay on the residential floor or leave the space port zone and enter the main part of the Medu-Ro IV station. However, you must return to your ship within two of our days, approximately nine ummi, otherwise you'll be declared a criminal with all the consequences that go with it!"

Well, well! I roughly approximated how long I had. All in all, it was just fifty hours of freedom, then there would be big trouble. That was very important information, so I took it into account. I even called up the in-game menu and set a countdown timer, so I could always see how long I had left.

In theory, I had the pass, and nothing was stopping me from going further. But I wasn't in any mood to leave yet, having decided to take advantage of the rare chance to speak with someone who understood me to get the information I so desperately needed.

"Ayni, I know that there was a Shiamiru-class Geckho shuttle in the dock next to number eight. I have a friend who works as a copilot on that starship, and we agreed to meet up and go out to the station together.

But when I got past all the watches and duties, the neighboring hangar was empty. Could you look through your databases to see where that Shiamiru went?"

The Miyelonian lady refused to answer, saying it was confidential. I had to try a different approach:

"Ayni, I don't know the culture or traditions of the Miyelonians very well, so I am afraid of accidentally offending you with my ignorance. However, my people like to be honest and tell pretty girls how crazy beautiful they look and give them a nice little gift. You are the cutest Miyelonian I have ever met, so I cannot hold my tongue! I'd really like to give you ten crypto. And I do have the money, but I don't know how to use your currency yet. I'm used to paying with Geckho crystals, but they aren't in circulation here. And you also have such entrancing emerald green eyes!"

And I stared unabashedly into her green eyes, having accidentally met gazes with the orange-furred bushy-tailed lady, but I didn't turn away. Maybe it was a brutish impulse or more likely just curiosity, but I wanted to know if I could read an alien's thoughts. We spent ten seconds staring into each other's eyes, and Ayni didn't do anything to stop it, as if she was entranced. But after that, I saw a few lines:

Function unavailable. Your character lacks the Psionic skill.

Your Astrolinguistics skill is too low. Minimum level to read the thoughts of an alien: fifty-five.

Action terminated. Magic Points exhausted.

Apparently, it was a lot harder to do in the game than real life... And just then, as if breaking the trance, she gave a sudden shudder and the furry Translator objected:

"Stop, stop, stop! Otherwise, all I'll be able to do is lie on my back and move my legs. As it is, my body temperature has jumped up so high I'm almost fainting. Gerd Gnat, the culture and traditions of the Miyelonians do not allow such blatant compliments and insistent staring. I will not deny that your words are pleasant to the ear, but they have too strong an effect on the psyche, suppressing my will and ability to resist. Compliments like that are only allowed between partners after marriage in a temple of the Great First Female!"

Well, well! Of course, I apologized for my lack of tact, and tried to justify my actions with a complete ignorance of local norms and taboos. Ayni, still not totally calm, gave a nervous chuckle, showing two rows of sharp little teeth:

"That's the first time something like that has happened to me... I wasn't expecting it to feel so strong... My body temperature still hasn't gone back to normal. I believe it was all by accident with no ill intent, so your apology is accepted, Gerd Gnat. And I wouldn't be opposed to a small gift. I could even show you how to use a wallet to transfer crypto. And in return for your present, I will try to find out what happened to your friend!"

I took the wallet I'd stolen off the Gladiator from my inventory and handed it to her. Ayni pressed on the opposite narrow edges of the rectangular block and the surface showed orange symbols:

"Point this edge where you're transferring to, if

you're making a payment to a friend standing nearby. And here you can write the amount with your finger. Do you know Miyelonian numerals?"

I had to admit total ignorance here. The orange cat wasn't bothered at all and showed me all the numbers in the space of a minute. They were rectangles of various proportions like I'd seen before, while zero was a perfect square. If the number contained several tens places, the rectangles were simply interlaced. To my great joy, the Miyelonians also used a base-ten number system, which seriously simplified things. So without Ayni's help, I wrote the number ten and transferred it to her.

Astrolinguistics skill increased to level forty-eight!

"Thank you for the gift, Gerd Gnat! Now let me return the favor!"

Ayni Uri-Miayuu sat back in her chair, and her clawed paws flickered rapidly, moving colored rectangles over a transparent holographic screen.

"Ah, I see! There was a Geckho starship in hangar seven on the sixteenth floor, but it left the station an ummi ago. And, it looks like your friend and the whole crew of the Shiamiru had big problems. The thing is, three pirate interceptors went into space right after the Geckho shuttle! That cannot be a coincidence! I'm really not sure what those Geckho have that's so valuable, but the Free Captains must know, and they never let easy pickings go!"

Just what I needed! I knew perfectly well what the Shiamiru had on it, and why several pirate captains had an interest. The six hundred fifty pounds of platinum plus an automatic Meleyephatian processor with all modules were worth a very respectable sum. Three million crystals, if not a whole four But I couldn't understand why Uraz Tukhsh hadn't sold it right here on the station, even at half price! The captain must have spotted a threat, given how hastily he'd run away. Or had he sold the cargo, drawing everyone's attention, and now the Free Captains wanted to deprive the Shiamiru captain of his glut of local currency?

In any case, it was a very unfavorable outcome for me. I had no cause to hope the Geckho shuttle would return to the Medu-Ro IV station any time soon. Even if my friends were able to escape from the pirates, they'd hardly want to risk coming back into this hornet's nest. And if the pirates did catch them and take their cash and loot, they'd be even less likely to return. Also, that was if I only considered the scenarios where the pirates didn't destroy their starship, which was a distinct possibility...

I was already in a bad mood, then the translator saw something on the screen and told me in a joyful tone that the elevator had just started up from the sixteenth floor.

"Gerd Gnat, your friends from *Gerd Setis-Vir* will be here soon! No matter what, they will come here to get their temporary passes, so you can just wait for them to catch up to you."

Just what I needed, a meeting with "my pirate crew!" And as if just the pirates weren't enough, the fifteen minutes since I'd killed that overgrown cat were up. And the most obvious place for the enraged Gladiator to look was the registration desk, a required stop for any station visitor. It was dangerous to stay here, and just plain dumb. So I made an excuse that I wanted to be alone and was sick of talking with the boisterous pirates. I asked the Translator not to tell them I was here, bid the orange cat farewell and hurried back out the glass doors.

Chapter Twelve

Fox the Space Fox

WHAT TO DO if the Geckho never came back for me? Such an outcome looked highly possible, and I didn't even have a near appreciation of what I would do. Probably, I would have to find a way back to my home planet. First at least, I'd have to get to a Geckho space port, then I would practically be home. After that, I'd get back to Human-3 territory somehow.

It was a good plan, but as usual the devil was in the details. What did they call my home planet, and where was it located? Sure, in the real world it was called Earth, the third planet in the Solar System, which was in the Local Interstellar Cloud of the Local Bubble in the Orion Arm of the Milky Way Galaxy. But in the game that bends reality? Even if the stars in this virtual world were like the real world (which was nowhere near certain; back on my first day in the game, I noticed there wasn't a single familiar constellation in the sky), what were they called in Geckho? And that was to say nothing of Miyelonian, which I didn't know a lick of! I had no idea, even worse, I didn't have a clue who to ask.

After all, it wasn't enough to simply know the "address" of my home world, I needed to somehow get there, into the exclusive zone of the Geckho, where starships of other races were not allowed. And first I had to leave the Medu-Ro IV station, which was under control of the less than law-abiding Free Captains, who were primarily of the Miyelonian race. Now that was a real humdinger...

I had to stop thinking, though because my character's hunger bar, which had been blinking frantically for some time reminding me to have a bite, was now down to twenty percent and had changed to red. At the same time, I got an alarming system message:

ATTENTION!!! Your character is starving!!! While starving, Endurance and Magic points will not be restored, regeneration will be suspended, and positive effects of medicines and antivenoms are only half as powerful. When your hunger bar reaches zero, critical malnutrition is triggered, causing a gradual loss of Health Points.

Just what I needed... Sure, I had two briquettes of dried rations in my inventory, but I decided to hold onto them for a direr circumstance. I was reminded that, when I left the elevators, one of the many arrows pointed to a "Cafe," so there must have been somewhere for a hungry traveler to have a bite around here. I just had to find it.

Well, well! I stopped in indecision, because the hallway led me into a spacious brightly lit room, which was at least as large as a soccer field. Tall glowing columns, decorative stone structures, lots of bright multicolored flickering signs, even a glistening fountain in the middle of a pool of pink water. Pretty! This must have been the main room of the residential floor where the crews of docked starships congregated because there were tons of creatures of all kinds of space races.

Probably, the innumerable inscriptions and information stands with flashing and blinking multicolored rectangles had plenty of information I might find useful, but I didn't understand one iota of Miyelonian...

I stopped, admiring the grandeur and trying to discover something that even distantly resembled a cafe or restaurant among all the wonderment. Or, failing that, I hoped I'd at least see one of these crazy creatures chewing or swallowing. But no, I couldn't see a thing...

Successful Perception check!

Failed Agility check!

Clearly, there were usually idiots standing around with their mouths agape here because the local pickpockets quickly noticed me. I almost missed a small and nimble Miyelonian sticking his clawed hand into my backpack. The lean and disheveled brownish gray cat immediately ran away with a folded bit of paper, stashing it in his belt pouch. How had the thief managed to sneak up to me unnoticed?! And, much more importantly, what exactly had he taken???

The little thief had moved so quickly that there was definitely no reason to run after him, especially because I couldn't jump over obstacles and clamber up vertical stone columns and statues. But I couldn't allow the thief to just make off with my stuff unpunished. So, not giving a hoot about the safety of the many onlookers, some of whom were just talking, while others actively cheered on the nimble pickpocket's escape, I pulled out my Dark Faction pulse rifle.

He was already two hundred feet away. The thief froze for a few seconds on the very top of an abstract stone statue, looking around for a convenient escape route and wanting to see if he was being chased. However, he really shouldn't have stopped, because I took my chance and shot! Wham! Hit!!! A bright beam stitched through the Miyelonian's left leg just below the knee!

Eagle Eye skill increased to level forty-seven!
Rifles skill increased to level forty-two!
Sharpshooter skill increased to level twenty-two!

Now you won't get away! Not dropping the rifle, I unhurriedly and confidently started forward to shouts of admiration from the crowd. The thief was still standing in the same place and didn't react to my beckoning him down. All the worse for him! I'd already reloaded, and it took me just one shot to get the petrified thief down on the ground. The beam sliced through the runaway's right leg this time. The thief stumbled and collapsed right at my feet. I placed my heavy military boot on the cat's neck and pushed the unlucky runaway hard against the floor. The Miyelonian didn't even try to move and only whimpered in fear and pain. So, who did I have here?

Tini Wi-Mauya. Miyelonian. Pride of the Heavenly Warrior. Level-17 Thief.

Just seventeen? I somehow felt offended; this wretched whelp tried to rob me, a respected level forty-five Gerd?! Also, the Miyelonian looked frail. He was small, emaciated and pitiful. Clearly, this wasn't an adult, just an underaged youngling or even a baby. My anger instantly vaporized, so I changed my mind about cutting off his tail. I mean, would that even count as a trophy? The tail of a weaker enemy, and quite a mangy one at that!?

Nevertheless, I had to punish this pickpocket somehow, otherwise he and others might get the idea to test me again. I browsed through the thief's bag at my leisure. Some rags, a small knife, a leather bag, a glass cutter... a heavy bag of platinum powder??? So that's what he pilfered! I wonder if the little thief managed to figure out what it was? Did he have the Intelligence to identify the precious metal or not? The question was of utmost importance. It would be quite the problem for me if the news spread that a human named Gnat had a pack of platinum! I quickly put the stolen item back in my backpack and kept digging.

A crowbar, a throwing knife, an unusual flashlight, gloves for clawed fingers, a roll of plastic bags... a whole set of thief's tools as it turned out, but I didn't take them, not wanting to deprive a poor kid of his only means of providing for himself. I discovered a wallet with thirteen crypto and, as Ayni had just showed me, transferred twelve of them to me. The unfortunate thief didn't have anything else of interest, and I took my boot off his neck. I gave the Miyelonian a good little kick in the butt, sending the cat right into the fountain of pink water, then I turned around and walked away. No one obstructed my exit, and the onlookers actually seemed impressed with my "performance."

Fame increased to 38!
Authority increased to 1!
Authority increased to 2!

ATTENTION!!! You have unlocked the Authority bonus for high-profile players. Positive Authority makes you more likely to succeed in negotiations with neutral or friendly NPC's, and also has a direct effect on any player's opinion of you and the loyalty of your allies.

I had to admit, I didn't understand. Sure, the NPC part made sense. The game algorithms simply took positive Authority into account and made bots more talkative with a Gerd, but how did it work on living players? Could an Authority stat, which players couldn't see, really influence the behavior and word choice of an intelligent being? Strange, to put it lightly...

And then, as if the game was sick of picking on my lost and hungry Gnat, my nose caught the scent of food! The glorious pleasing smell of roasting was coming from a building along the wall of the large room. I sharply changed direction and headed toward it.

THE HARDEST PART was not what you might expect. In fact, I had no trouble finding something edible among the unfamiliar dishes or explaining what I wanted to the monolingual Miyelonian worker. The real struggle was finding a place to sit. The cafeteria was just so packed with space travelers! My cardboard tray laden with bulbs of bright and bubbling victuals, I spent a long time walking down narrow passages between occupied tables. Some hissed at me threateningly, others roared, squeaked, or waved their tentacles, paws or wings, all trying to communicate that a place was taken. Next to some of the tables, there were chairs and even sofas. Other customers were sitting right on the floor. I would have been fine with either option, but there was just no space.

Finally, I got lucky. In a gloomy back corner, a group of Meleyephatians, who looked like huge human-height spiders in helmetless spacesuits, just happened to finish their meal and got up from a knee-high table, throwing their disposable plates in the trash sorter. With my tray in hand, I hurried to take their place, but was a bit too late. Already about to place my tray on the low table, I looked down and discovered that there was a strange furry creature with intelligent and vivacious humanlike eyes sitting on the other side. How did it get in front of me? Very strange. I figured I'd have noticed if something passed me on the way to the table. Maybe it was just sitting there with the huge eight-legged Meleyephatians?

I couldn't read any data about this strange creature, although that didn't mean much. I had already noticed that many of the creatures I came across on the Medu-Ro IV station blocked their information. Perhaps there was a special skill that could hide it, or maybe it came from a suit or other item, but the identity of almost every third inhabitant of the pirate station was a mystery.

The creature at the table looked somewhat like a red fox. Actually... why beat around the bush? That's exactly what it was. An everyday terrestrial fox, even if it was too big and way out here in space. And its eyes... I would put my head on the chopping block to bet that they'd changed! Now they were animalistic yellow eyes that didn't even look remotely human! Yikes, how can that be?!

As the muted scene stretched on, I started speaking Geckho in a peaceable tone, not especially hoping for a response:

"You'll have to excuse me, I didn't notice this table is was already occupied..." I sharply went silent because I noticed that the odd fox didn't have a tray.

What was it doing, if it wasn't going to eat? Was the fox just holding the table for the other members of its crew? Or was this just a silent pet, guarding a table for its master? I turned but didn't see anyone coming with a tray. And overall, this table was in the very farthest dark corner of the dining hall. What happened here wasn't even visible from the main room.

Danger Sense skill increased to level twenty-two!

Not understanding the source of the threat, I adjusted my left hand's grip on the tray. With my right,

I felt for the Dark Faction pulse rifle. But the presentiment of danger, which came over me with a wave of cold, retreated just as quickly without a trace.

"Please sit, Gerd Gnat. It's really no trouble."

That was unexpected. The fox had a pleasant feminine voice and spoke very cleanly-accented Geckho. She had clearly spent some time among them. I was even more surprised to see that I could now read a bit of information:

Name [undetermined]. Morphian. Clan [N/A]. Class [undetermined]. Level [hidden].

I set the tray down and sat right on the floor, crossing my legs. The fox, watching my reaction very carefully, noticed my interest and hurried to explain.

"It seems to me you do not comprehend who I am, and so I had to reveal some of my information. I am a Morphian, one of the few surviving members of an almost extinct race."

"Who... drove your race to extinction? And why?" my voice shuddered treacherously because the question was very important and even, God forbid, relevant to humanity itself.

Before answering, the fox extended a hand and took one of the glass flagons off my tray without asking permission. She took a few big gulps of the thick bubbling substance, which had a consistency and smell very much reminiscent of apple sauce. After half draining the bulb, she froze and looked at me.

"Don't worry, Morphian. Treat yourself to whatever you like. If there isn't enough, I'll go get more."

"Thank you, Gerd Gnat. I've been pained by

hunger for some time." The Morphian set the empty flagon aside and immediately grabbed another full of blood red liquid that smelled of citrus.

I didn't waste any time and followed my new friend's example, gulping down some grub. The Morphian then, very successfully imitating human emotion, gave a heavy sigh and answered my earlier question:

"Our planet was discovered by the Cleopians one hundred fifty tongs ago, and we entered the game that bends reality brimming with vigor, hoping to discover new knowledge and travel through space. But our planet's immunity period came and went, and the Cleopians were just vassals of the even stronger Miyelonians, so they couldn't really help us. The Miyelonians themselves couldn't be bothered. So in the game, we were swept away by the Meleyephatian horde. The battle was short and hopeless. All at once, innumerable invading starships appeared, orbiting my home planet. Events in the game are always reflected in reality, so it was all over very soon... "

The fox stopped her story at the most interesting part and grabbed the last container of food unceremoniously off my tray as I was extending a hand for it. I didn't get mad, just asked the Morphian not to go anywhere and came back shortly with another tray, fully laden with food. This serving cost four crypto, which equated to twenty-eight Geckho crystals. Sure, it was pricy, but the unique intel about space politics and the relationships between space races was worth much more than that. The Morphian gave a favorable nod after seeing the second helping and continued:

"At first, the Meleyephatians treated us bearably, and even included us in their horde of subject races. There, we tried to prove our worth, ruthlessly enslaving and exterminating other races together with the rest of the horde. But one day, our masters decided they didn't like our ability to take any form, and the Morphians were declared dangerous parasites subject to extermination. The few who survived took shelter inside the game that bends reality. They learned to hide and travel illegally on alien starships and eventually taught their children how to do the same. Now, Morphians are little different from NPC's. We cannot leave the game. The real world is lost to us. Morphians were declared outlaws in all Meleyephatian and Trillian space. And here, among the Miyelonians, no one tries to hunt us, but we aren't especially welcome either."

"Wait, wait..." I was very intrigued by a purely technical aspect of the Morphian's tale, "does that mean you have never left the game? Do you even have a material body? As far as I've heard, it degrades fairly quickly. So how do you even know you would be able to leave into the real world?"

"I don't know, I just believe," the fox said, looking embarrassed. Then she lowered her voice and continued. "No Morphians alive today can say for certain what would happen when leaving the game, even though we still do have the option in the menu. Everyone who has tried never came back. Some believe that it is a final end for those who tire of the never-ending cycle of deaths and rebirths. But our whole faith is based in the idea that, one day, we will reenter the real world and obtain a new home planet."

The issue was clearly difficult for her, and the fox was plainly sad. So, I tried to change the topic to something less fraught:

"Say, why is your name displayed as 'undetermined?' Do Morphians not have names?"

"Quite the opposite. We have hundreds and even thousands of them. But, Gerd Gnat, how would you speak to me if my name was, let's say, U-owwuu Oh-ouuu-iu or Shishishash Shsha U-shshsh-shi, or just a set of twenty-seven hexadecimal numbers? So, I always give myself a name and appearance that will be pleasing to my company. Your consciousness told me that humanity would like the look of something inoffensive big eyed and fluffy. So, for you, I look like a sweet little animal, even though I don't know what it's called. Anyway, if a Morphian senses rejection during a conversation, they take it into account and quickly adapt to whoever they're talking to."

By the way, the Morphian was changing shape as we spoke. It was imperceptible and gradual, but now she was no longer a wild animal, but a much more anthropomorphized creature expressing vibrant emotions with its face. I could still easily tell it was based on a red fox, sure. It had pointy ears and some fur, as well as a long tail. But the head changed shape, the eyes and neck became humanlike, and the body took on a shapely feminine aspect. That created a strange animal human hybrid, a made-up race that should probably have been called a "furry." But the anthropomorphic fox didn't inspire disgust or negative emotions. It was actually the opposite. I felt at ease.

But what did that mean? Had she pulled this image from my mind?! Let's check!

"I don't like talking to someone without knowing their name, so I'll call you Fox. That's what you are, after all, so it's what I'll call you."

"Sure, no problem," she snorted. "Fox is no worse than any other name."

And just then, the name Fox appeared in the Morphian's description. Its appearance reacted to my imagination, but with a noticeable delay. I curiously looked on as Fox's shape changed to meet my desires. So, let's get rid of the fox ears. Flatten that snout, make the face more human. Make the waist thinner. Pull in the stomach. Make the breasts bigger, and less furry or, even better, totally hairless. Shorten the front paws and make the fingers longer. No, that's too long. Instead of claws make the nails flat... Ah, crap... That's not it at all. Now this is a real terror, not a person! Try as I might, I just couldn't make the Morphian into a pretty girl!

Fox tore herself from a dish of nourishing broth, then made an offended comment:

"You got what you ordered! This is the first time I've met a person, and I don't know what kind of beauty standards prevail among your kind. Overall, Gerd Gnat, if you are trying to construct a particular female of your race, just show me a full-length picture of her. That will make things much easier."

I got embarrassed and asked Fox to go back to the more pleasant anthropomorphic fox. She changed her appearance back, then gave a totally humanlike yawn, covering her jaws with a clawed paw:

"Thank you. I've eaten so much I could burst. And I also need to rest. My Endurance Points are at zero. You think it's easy to shed fur and grow breasts, then put it all back on a whim?! By the way, do you have a hotel here? Can you get me a room too? It's just thirty crypto per day. As you can see, us Morphians have neither items nor money..."

Thirty crypto was two hundred ten red Geckho crystals. That was a damn high price for a hotel room on a space station! I was reluctant to spend such a huge sum even on myself. And as for this barely familiar animal, no thanks! What the heck did I need her for? She just ate for free on my dime. Let her at least say thank you!

Fox could clearly sense my mood, because she rushed to forward an alternative suggestion:

"Human, I cannot read thoughts, but I can sense emotions very well. You're upset and somewhat afraid. You don't know what to do. But I know Miyelonian well and could serve as your guide, and help you negotiate with the local traders and captains. You don't have to get me my own living capsule. Just register me as your pet. That will only increase the cost by two or three crypto. The two of us will fit in one room just fine!"

It would have been a huge error on my part to just let such an unusual and valuable creature go. Sure, Fox looked strange and maybe was just going to use me for some personal end, but she knew Miyelonian and her way around the station. Maybe she could help me solve all my issues. So, I thought for just a second and agreed with a wave of my hand:

"Alright, Fox. Agreed! I'll give you a place to live

and food to eat, and you will serve me as a guide and translator. So now, show me the way to the hotel!"

I stood up from the table, preparing to exit the cafe, but my new companion was still sitting on the floor. Fox actually looked very upset. What was this?

"Gerd Gnat, I admit. I still do not know if this creature from your imagination should walk on two legs or four. Your mind's eye held a few options, so now I'm confused!"

I laughed happily at the unexpected and amusing problem, then told my fluffy translator how to behave:

"Fox, when you're playing a stupid animal, walk on four legs. You can even wear a leash and collar to make it look more authentic. But when you're intelligent, walk on two legs like a person."

"I see. But now we're going to the hotel, and I am your pet!"

She nodded and, taking the shape of a common red fox, started walking on all fours and shook the dirt off her fur just like a dog. I then looked at the new information that appeared over the Morphian:

Fox. Fox (creature). Pet of Gerd Gnat. Level [hidden by pet owner].

Hidden by pet owner? Well, well... The Morphian was really stubborn about revealing her level, so she was falling back on such tricks. I suspected there was some reason for her secrecy, but what? Either the small and inexperienced Fox was embarrassed to reveal her weakness, or it was the opposite and her level was shockingly high!

Chapter Thirteen

Enemy of Two Prides

THE "HOTEL ROOM" was just a capsule around nine feet by six that closed with a metal curtain. But it was very tall for some reason. I never could have reached the ceiling even by jumping. I didn't know what race these strange dimensions were made for. Perhaps the Miyelonians simply took the maximum sizes of various races — the height of a Geckho, the length of a Trillian, the diameter of a Meleyephatian spider's huge abdomen — and calculated the minimum size of a room that could fit any of them.

And there was no hint of furniture. The springy soft floor was made of a soft synthetic, but couldn't be considered a true bed, while the only other thing in the room was a single ceiling light. Well, there was also a ventilation crack in one of the walls. What was more, I could adjust the power of the fan, but not the air temperature. And that was quite hot, so the room quickly became stuffy. I just closed the ventilation. Mhm... Honestly, I was upset. I mean, for thirty-two crypto I was expecting something more comfortable.

But my companion was expecting these truly spartan conditions. Fox immediately changed to an anthropomorphic fox when I closed the curtain, and her clearly female body had all the tempting curves and intimate details you'd expect. When I noted her provocative appearance and lack of clothing, she remarked that she was just following my fantasies and desires, and not intentionally changing anything.

"Morphians can use clothes, but they seriously complicate our shapeshifting. We can also imitate clothing..." In just five seconds, a camouflage body-armor jacket just like mine appeared over Fox's fur, along with pants and army boots. "Is this better? Your reaction is telling me no," the space fox turned back to her naked form. "Anyway, I'm afraid I have to disappoint you, Gerd Gnat. This is only my appearance, so there's no need to feel ashamed, blush or stare. I don't have any female anatomy, so we cannot be intimate."

"I wasn't even thinking of it! It's just hot in here. That's why I'm all red," I said in embarrassment, making the fox give a happy laugh:

"Who are you trying to fool, Gerd Gnat? Did you forget I can sense emotions? But what do I care? Stare at me all you want, if I tickle your fancy. I'm so exhausted I'm passing out. I really need to sleep."

Just like an animal, Fox curled into a circle,

wrapping herself with her luxuriant tail, closed her eyes and went quiet. I just sat in the other corner of the room and tried to figure out if my companion had really fallen asleep or was just pretending.

The only advantage of this hotel room was that it was a green zone so, after selecting Exit Game in the menu, Gnat would disappear in thirty seconds. That wasn't long at first glance, but it was more than enough to clean out my inventory and slink off without a trace. With such an unusual and suspicious roommate, whose true motives I did not understand, I had to bear that in mind. Finally, I made up my mind and quit.

Again, someone was there to meet me and help me up. But like last time, I didn't want to climb out of the virt pod and tell the leadership about my awkward situation just yet. There was no news from Dmitry Zheltov, which was strange and put me on guard. I just wanted the copilot to leave the game for a minute and tell me what happened to the Shiamiru! What could be easier? If he hadn't been able, Dmitry must have been in trouble.

Anyhow, I wasn't upset and tried to use a different method. I had them tell Ivan Lozovsky to ask Kosta Dykhsh where Earth was located in the game. After all, our suzerains' Diplomat probably knew where he'd been sent and could share that information and more.

I also remembered too late that I hadn't sent my friend list to the receptionist. So I got to work composing it, then invited them all to my housewarming party, which I even scheduled for nine PM today. It was now just after eight in the morning, so I still had plenty of time. I finished all my urgent business and reentered the game that bends reality.

Fox was still lying there balled up and pretending to sleep, but I noticed that the body of the anthropomorphic fox was in a slightly different place. My heart seized, and I checked my inventory, but everything was where I left it. Nothing had disappeared. So, had she dug through my stuff or not? I didn't wake the Morphian up to interrogate her, especially given that I'd never manage to test whether she was answering truthfully. So, setting my jacket on the fairly soft but perhaps somewhat dirty floor of the hotel capsule, I laid down more comfortably and decided to get some good sleep like my roommate.

Danger Sense skill increased to level twenty-three!

You have reached level forty-six!

You have received three skill points! (total points accumulated: nine)

I was awoken sharply, as if a tub of ice water had been poured on my head. I was breathing rapidly, and my heart was pounding in my chest. What just woke me up? And where was I? There was darkness all around. I realized almost immediately that I was still in the space station hotel capsule, and that it had been less than an hour since I entered the game. But why was it so dark?

Trying not to make any sudden movements, I cracked open an eye and took a look around. The light on the ceiling was flickering dully, as if someone had turned the dimmer down to its absolute lowest point. But that ghostly illumination was enough for me to see that Fox was not sleeping and was even sitting up. The huge furry shadow suddenly took a couple careful steps and loomed over me. I saw a pair of burning red predatory eyes and sharp teeth, clearly larger than before.

Successful Perception check.

Eagle Eye skill increased to level forty-eight!

Also, at that tense moment, I realized distinctly what had triggered Danger Sense in the cafe earlier. It was the hungry Morphian in the dark back area, keeping watch for a foolhardy lone traveler. If I hadn't reached for my weapon then, showing that I was prepared to resist, then fed the predator, it would be hard to say how our encounter might have ended.

To my surprise, I felt no fear, but I was annoyed that I had been awoken so rudely. I was also simmering in annoyance at the fact that I might have to use my last ball of paralyzing poison. Maybe, I'd at least be able to cut off a fox tail as compensation... Plus, a trophy would let me see her level. The Morphian froze stock still and looked at me. I could sense with my skin that she was feeling doubts. Fox clearly understood her victim had awoken and was prepared to resist, so she wouldn't have the element of surprise. Maybe I'd be able to avoid a conflict.

"Fox, if you want grub, take the dry rations in my backpack. But you really could just wait it out. We can go down into the cafe together in a bit and have breakfast." I said, casually slipping away from the dangerous beast, as if a set of razor-sharp teeth over my throat was not sufficient cause to disturb my slumber.

Yes, my behavior may have seemed illogical and even thoughtless, but I could sense it was the right move. If the Morphian really was planning to attack me in my sleep from the very beginning, she'd have done it as soon as the chance presented itself. When I exited the game for example. But she hesitated, spending a long time staring at my motionless figure thus allowing me to sense the danger.

"Easy for you to say," the fox snarled in a dismayed tone, nevertheless walking to the far end of the capsule and lying back down. "Gnat, you really have no idea how much energy all these transformations take! You can't even imagine what it's like to be a Morphian. We're constantly being tracked, forced to hide and change shape. We can't stay anywhere for long..."

You have reached level forty-seven!

You have received three skill points! (total points accumulated: twelve)

I didn't know what just happened. But it was clearly something important because the game algorithms rewarded me with a vast amount of experience, enough even to level up again. At the same time, my sense of fear had totally dissipated. I realized that Fox still needed me for some reason and wouldn't hurt me.

"Yes, I don't comprehend all the tribulations of a Morphian's life," I agreed, answering my fluffy companion's stirring monolog. "But I do have some idea what it's like to be alone in space who knows how many parsecs from home, not knowing the local language or customs, and almost without hope to return to my kind..."

Fox spent a long time lying in silence. I could only hear the space fox breathing measuredly. But then, she suddenly spoke:

"Gerd Gnat, I really need to get out of the space port zone to the main station, but there is strict monitoring at the border so, without documents, even a Morphian cannot slip through. And you need to go there too. All the Free Captains live on the station, and if anyone can help you get back to your people, it is them. As your pet, I could pass through with you. There, I can help you talk with the captains, then our paths will diverge, and I will disappear among the hundreds of thousands of locals. For now, I do not know how to organize a meeting with the Free Captains, but I'll definitely think of something. So, go to sleep. Tomorrow is an important day for both of us."

MY DREAMS WERE all over the place and hard to understand. It was like I was back to the simple life, studying at the Geology department, without any online tournaments, betting, prize money or underground Dome. With a bunch of students, I walked through the endless corridors of the Main Building of Moscow State University. All around me, there flickered a procession of unavailable girls, former classmates, mere acquaintances and others I had seen just in passing. The dream wasn't purely erotic, but some of the girls were partially or even entirely naked.

I never interacted with them, though, and was just hurrying down the hall accompanied by their ambivalent or intrigued gazes.

Despite the wild dream, I awoke feeling totally rested and first glanced at the countdown timer. I had forty-two hours left on the pirate station, then I would be declared a criminal. I tried to turn and stand up... and it seemed that my dream still wasn't over. Next to me, her whole body snuggled up close and her right knee over my thigh, there was a girl sleeping in a light semi-transparent peignoir. She had a pretty face, long disheveled red hair, and a silver fox medallion sticking out under her clothes. I was generally pretty quick on my feet, but this had me flummoxed. Only the fox medallion helped me realize this was not just some stranger.

As soon as I guessed it, Fox opened an eye and started smiling:

"You were just a fountain of vibrant images in your sleep. I couldn't pin down just one. But how do you like this?"

I had to admit, I was blown away. The redheaded beauty next to me now was identical to a real human girl. I slowly extended a hand and carefully touched her shoulder with the tips of my fingers. But I immediately removed them, not hiding a disappointed sigh. To the touch, Fox was more reminiscent of the springy floor covering of our hotel box than a warm-blooded living creature.

"Well, Gerd Gnat, I warned you. This is just an appearance. I considered it necessary to practice so that, if need be, I can imitate a member of your race.

After all, if there are any negotiations with the Miyelonians, it would look very strange to have a wild animal as a translator. But before we go anywhere, explain precisely what you want from the Free Captains. I already know that you are completely alone and very far from home. Do you want to go back? And where did you get the Relict artifacts and all that platinum?"

So, Fox was digging through my inventory after all... I checked my backpack and discovered that everything was there except two briquettes of dried rations. The Morphian took my suggestion and had a bite while I was asleep. I didn't get mad. I had given permission.

Skipping over particularly delicate aspects like stealing the automatic processor or using geological analyzers to escape the locked hangar, I told Fox about my journey with the Geckho crew, discovering large platinum deposits and the misadventures on the station. I didn't hide the difficulties with documents or what happened with the Gladiator and Thief, either. The redheaded girl sat and listened extremely carefully, then said thoughtfully:

"You really stepped in it, Gerd Gnat... From what I know of Miyelonian customs, they never rest until they get revenge. Now, the Pride of the Comet's Tail, and the Pride of the Heavenly Warrior will be searching everywhere to kill you time and again until you apologize or pay a penalty for insulting them."

"Come on! After the scuffle with the Gladiator, I met a Miyelonian translator from the Pride of the Comet's Tail, and she reacted just fine to the trophy on my helmet! And lots of Miyelonians watched me punish that little thief. None of them seemed to mind. So, forget those fears. Let's go get you some food. Although... wait a second. I need to leave the game to see if there's been any news."

THERE HAD STILL been no word from Dmitry Zheltov, and that meant my friend must have run into a very serious issue. But there was news from Ivan Lozovsky, and what news it was! A First Legion soldier, clearly bewildered, handed me a landscape-oriented paper with a continuous complicated line and told me:

"Our diplomat said this was important. I hope you can make heads or tails of it. To my eye, it's pure nonsense. A child's scribble."

I didn't merely understand the message, I was ready to jump for joy:

"Ar constellation. Sector 5. Vector 45 -98. Jump distance: 234 units. Third planet from the sun. Space port node coordinates: 57-478. Our Capital node: 57-475. But if they are, let's say, not entirely legal traders, better have them land outside our territory. Confirm the deal, and we'll prepare a shipment and bring it to a safe landing site."

Apparently, the leadership thought I was still on their mission and had already found buyers for their platinum who were willing to circumvent the official space port. I didn't give a spoken message back to Ivan Lozovsky and disappoint the diplomat. But I did ask for a pen or pencil and, on the back side of the paper, invited him to my housewarming party in Geckho, promising to tell him all the details.

Now, I needed to memorize the numbers and coordinates. And I needed to make sure I had it dead on, because whether or not I'd make it home depended on getting this right. I read the text a few times, then repeated it by rote and checked. No errors! Now, quickly into the game to write it down in my diary so I could be sure not to forget or lose this invaluable information!

As soon as I stored the note in the virtual world, the game reacted with an improvement in Cartography:

Cartography skill increased to level forty-six!

Great! Now, before leaving the safe hotel capsule, I should spend up my free skill points. I had a whole twelve. I placed seven into Astrolinguistics, raising it right to fifty-five. I was very interested in the skill requirement at that level for reading the thoughts of aliens. Now, I just had to take the Psionic skill after my character reached level fifty, and that was no longer so far-off. Then, Gnat would be able to read all kinds of thoughts! Mega cool!!! The most obvious application was exposing Dark Faction agents along with other unreliable players and those inclined to working for the enemy, which would immediately make life easier for the H3 Faction.

But as for spending the five remaining points, I thought for a long time and, in the end, all five went into Sharpshooter, raising that handy combat skill to twenty-seven. Alright, now I was ready for new adventures! After I unlocked the door, Fox the fox, already waiting at the door and clearly hungry, said in admonishment:

"Be careful now! If Miyelonians have taken an interest in you, they probably already know where you're staying. So, there might be enemies waiting for you right next to the capsule!"

I used Scanning but didn't detect anything dangerous. Still, just in case, I equipped my Pulse Rifle and waited anxiously for the metal blinds to raise very, very slowly. And when they were open, I took a look down the empty hotel corridor. I shook my head in reproach, called Fox a coward and alarmist, then headed for the exit.

However, Fox knew Miyelonian society much better than me, and I really should not have been mocking my companion. We didn't even manage to make it out of the hotel before it happened. I had to admit, I made a big mistake. At first, I blinked through the attack. I only saw a fast-moving shadow flicker by to my right but didn't manage to react or even register it. My Danger Sense kicked in, but it was too late. I grabbed for my weapon but didn't know how to help. I just stood there like an idiot and watched Fox bite a furry gray figure by the throat as it thrashed, flailing with flashing blades in a vain attempt to strike the Morphian.

You have reached level forty-eight!
You have received three skill points!

I didn't take any part in the uncompromising battle, so I was surprised to get experience. Fox had enlisted herself as my pet, so technically the algorithms were doing the right thing. What difference did it make how you killed an enemy? An animal sicced on an opponent is a weapon just like a blade or blaster, even though the pet also took a share of the experience unlike a rifle or axe. So, who did "my pet and I" just take down?

Only when the toothy fox had unclenched her bloodied fangs and dropped the breathless body at my feet could I see that the remains belonged to a Miyelonian by the name of Ayuk Ukh Miiyauu from the Pride of the Heavenly Warrior, a level-76 Assassin.

Pride of the Heavenly Warrior? I was reminded that the little thief I'd punished was from that very clan. Was this revenge for shooting an underage pickpocket with my Pulse Rifle? Seriously? And actually, there he was. I noticed the level-17 Miyelonian thief watching me from a balcony. Realizing he'd been spotted, the little thief Tini Wi-Mauya hurried to hide.

"Too bad no items dropped. Just the body. You can take the tail, but the rest is mine," the hungry Morphian said. I didn't argue.

Tail of Ayuk Ukh Miiyauu, Level-76 Assassin (trophy)

Fame increased to 39.

Authority increased to 3!

While I attached a second tail to my helmet, I tried to stand with my back to the ghastly feast and ignore the disgusting crunching and chomping behind my back. But it was no small feat to abstract myself from all that. For some reason, it got to me on the deepest level. Maybe it was because I noticed only yesterday that Miyelonian blood was the same red as mine, and that their body structure was quite similar as well. So, there was a primordial disgust in knowing someone was eating a humanlike corpse. I was grossed out to even be nearby, which was to say nothing of watching. I would just be vomiting if I was watching.

"Alright, that's it, I've had my fill!" Fox clearly could sense the whole bouquet of my emotions.

I turned cautiously, expecting to see bones picked clean or streaks of blood on the walls and even ceiling. However, there was nothing of the sort. The only reminder of the bloody meal was a damp spot where the body had just been. There were no remains, nor traces of blood. The Morphian hadn't left a thing. A foolish thought came to mind that Fox had devoured the Miyelonian together with his clothes and shoes. But I immediately corrected myself. No objects had dropped as loot, so there wouldn't have been any footwear for the space fox to chew through.

"Gerd Gnat, I no longer require feeding. I've had my fill. And you, as far as I understand, will be fighting back disgust for a while before your appetite comes back. So let's not waste any time and make straight for the passage to the main station."

I looked again at the wet spot, all that was left of the Miyelonian killer. I glanced dubiously at the fox licking her lips in satisfaction. Her body hadn't even changed although she'd just swallowed a victim the same size as her. Was I bringing a living terror into this space station, and thus becoming the unwilling coauthor of a ghastly and bloody page in its most recent history?

"I think I'm starting to understand why you want to reach the main station! After all, thousands and thousands of creatures live there, and it's a huge area, where a Morphian could live for years, eating only reckless victims as it changes bodies and slips away!"

I felt as if my heart froze in my chest for a few seconds, like a set of icy fingers reached out and touched it. However, the wave of alarm and fear brought on by Danger Sense quickly passed. Fox then, just like a person, turned her head and commented on my accusations:

"Gerd Gnat, what you described would only fit an unintelligent NPC animal. The mind of a Morphian contains somewhat greater dreams and aspirations than simply filling one's belly."

Chapter
Fourteen

Foundling

SOMETHING MUST HAVE happened... Last time, when I walked alone down the huge luxurious hall of the residential floor, there were around one hundred fifty or two hundred creatures of all different races walking at their leisure or talking peacefully. But now, after leaving the hotel, the room was packed tight with Miyelonians. There were thousands of them, if not to say tens of thousands. They were all moving in the same direction, clamoring and fighting amongst themselves. And at that, it was only Miyelonians. I didn't see any members of other races in the crowd.

What was happening? An evacuation? An attack on the station? That was exactly what I suspected, as I watched the crush in the middle of the room. The Morphian stopped too, looking around and perking her fox ears, even taking a sniff. Finally, Fox said with shame:

"Now we've stepped in it... We should have gone through earlier."

"What's going on? Is it war?" I asked in fear. The answer I received was strange:

"Worse! One of the four incarnations of the Great First Female has come to the Medu-Ro IV station, the honorable Priestess, Leng Amiru U-Mayaoo."

I had to admit, I didn't understand one iota. What exactly was bad about this? How did the arrival of one of these four somehow unusual females have any effect on my plans? In fact, it seemed to be the opposite. The large number of arriving ships meant I would have a better chance of finding a captain to bring me where I was going. I kept quiet for a minute, thinking over what my companion had said and watching the river of Miyelonians. Then, I admitted my ignorance:

"And what's so bad about that female visiting? Does the Priestess hate other races? Could this be dangerous for us?"

"Not at all. As far as I know, Amiru is the most peaceable of the four current incarnations of the ancient female, who first lived thousands of tongs ago. The Miyelonians consider her the divine founder of their race. But what you see now, these crowds of religious fanatics, they flew here from hundreds of inhabitable systems just for a peek at a living legend. I am not at all sure you and I will be let through to the hall where Leng Amiru U-Mayaoo will be preaching. Even if there is not an official rule against admitting other races, some fanatic might kill us 'just in case,' so we can't harm their saint."

I was shaken by the unfortunate perspective. Hrmph, rough... Although Fox was completely right. Fanatics behaved just as aggressively in all worlds. What could I say? Even before, I didn't much want to climb into that dense clamoring crowd, but after Fox's words I had changed my mind about going down the Miyelonian-filled corridor to the main station. Although I didn't see why that was so bad. I figured I'd just have to wait for all these religious events to finish, then cross. How long could that possibly take? Actually... I had just a bit more than forty hours left, so maybe there was cause for alarm...

There was nothing to be done, so me and the fox went up the stairs to the second floor and stood on a little balcony, giving us a view of the crowd. In it, there were Miyelonians of various colorings and sizes. More were arriving every minute. The flow had almost come to a complete halt and now the far end of the room was densely packed with newly arrived pilgrims, so the back rows were just squeezing in more and more. Also, many of the newcomers were not feeling patient. I was seeing more and more sparks of conflict using claws, teeth, and sometimes blades. It really was some kind of madness. One could be killed for a place nearer the exit! And some were!

Eagle Eye skill increased to level forty-nine!

Maybe it was because of the danger, but several of the newly arrived pilgrims preferred to hang back, pressing up against the walls and just waiting for the crowd and bloody squabbles to die down. Although their behavior might have had a different motivation.

Fox translated the outcries of several especially vehement and rapturous pilgrims, exclaiming that Leng Amiru U-Mayaoo would surely pass through this room. They wanted to see her, make spiritual contact with her divine mystery, and maybe even touch the great Priestess with a hand.

And then, suddenly, among thousands of unfamiliar Miyelonians, I saw a familiar face! Well, not human face, but the pretty cat face of Ayni Uri-Miayuu, the Translator who issued my pass at the registration desk. The small orange cat, somewhat disheveled in the tight squeeze, also wanted to get back to the wall and was now looking around in confusion, not knowing what to do next. Ayni was not so far away, so I called out to her, inviting her up with a wave. Ayni immediately took me up on that and was standing beside me a minute later.

"Kento duho, Gerd Gnat!" The orange cat said, glancing without particular interest at the fox lying at my feet. She then cautiously approached the railing and looked down from the balcony. "Woah! By the Great First Female, it looks even worse from up here!"

Carefully choosing my words as not to give away my intelligent fox, I said:

"I am very bad at Miyelonian, but I think that disheveled black-furred Cleric just shouted that the majestic Leng Amiru U-Mayaoo would come through this room. Because of that and the crowd, some pilgrims decided to stay in their rooms to wait. To be honest, though, I just wanted to see a rare spectacle, which is why I'm up on this balcony."

"What the heck?!" the fluffy Translator objected.

"I am one hundred percent sure that Leng Amiru and her retinue will be following a different route! The owners of the space station have launched a direct elevator especially for her that bypasses all these floors. Also, if that Cleric was speaking the truth, the First Pride Elite Guard would have this place on lockdown! But do you see even a single soldier in white armor?"

I had no idea what the First Pride even was, or why its soldiers should be dressed in white armor. But Fox, actively listening in on our conversation, seemingly did. The fox quietly stood up and walked to the railing, perking up her ears and looking at the crowd, as if signing off on Ayni's words. And meanwhile, there was another scuffle raging in the middle of the room, this time especially bloody. There was a group of fanatics that had somehow upset another group and glinting blades had come into play. In just one minute, more than thirty Miyelonians went to respawn.

"How horrible!" my roommate said, shocked. "So many deaths, so much anger... That might lead to a war between the prides, which could end very badly indeed. But at my desk, I was told they would soon be suspending document checks at the crossing to the main station. Registration was also put on hold, because we could never manage such a huge number of arrivals."

Ayni was standing with her back to the Morphian so she couldn't see, but I noticed the fox turn around and start trotting boldly to the stairs, growing smaller in size as she did. Then, I saw a few flashes of red fur in the crowd. Fox was moving fairly quickly under the feet of the incoming pilgrims. Then, at the very farthest end of the room... although here I wasn't sure... next to the very exit, a modest orange cat suddenly seemed to appear. And it looked identical to Ayni Uri-Miayuu, who was still standing next to me.

Eagle Eye skill increased to level fifty!

Based on the sudden system message, I wasn't wrong, and that really was Fox. I suspected the headstrong and unpredictable creature had decided to part ways, take advantage of the lack of control and walk into the station as she was initially planning. I couldn't judge a predator for wanting to reach rich hunting grounds, and I didn't tell the orange Translator about "my dangerous pet." Ayni was still standing next to me and staring in horror down at the rampaging crowd below.

It was possible that I would change my decision and tell her about the threat, but I suddenly no longer wanted to. Three dignified Miyelonians walked unhurriedly up to our balcony. And I knew two of them: the level-17 Thief Tini Wi-Mauya and the level-76 Assassin Ayuk Ukh Miiyauu, whose fluffy tail now served as decoration to my helmet (although after respawn, the Assassin's tail had regrown). The third guest's information was hidden, but I suspected he was also a member of the Pride of the Heavenly Warrior. All three Miyelonians were on guard and keeping their hands on the hilts of their weapons.

The Assassin bared his teeth and hissed at the frightened Translator, after which Ayni Uri-Miayuu sharply lowered her eyes and ran away. Anyhow, that very same third and unknown Miyelonian sharply threw his clawed paw forward, catching the runaway by the shoulder, turning her toward him and asking a question. Ayni meowed back, and the stranger let her go, seemingly after receiving an apology.

I thought she would take advantage of this and run away full tilt but, instead, Ayni put on a calm demeanor, turned around and stood next to me, telling me the contents of their brief conversation:

"Gerd Gnat, that guy from the Pride of the Heavenly Warrior just asked if I can communicate with you. And when I said yes, he asked me to stay and translate. The Pride of the Heavenly Warrior guaranteed that I would be unharmed, and they promised to treat you with honor."

Getting off on the right foot! If the Pride of the Heavenly Warrior simply wanted to kill me, they would have done so right off the bat, then they'd have slain the Translator as not to leave a witness. Well, I wanted to know what these three tomcats were after, and what they considered honorable treatment. I'd hear them out.

"U misi-ni lipir-shi mi Fox?" the stranger mewed out ingratiatingly, and I could tell without translation that he wanted to know about my absent fox.

Ayni fully confirmed my guess.

Astrolinguistics skill increased to level fifty-six!

That's what I needed yesterday: simultaneous interpreting from Miyelonian to Geckho! Despite the tension of the moment, I was very glad at the rare chance to study Miyelonian through another alien language I hadn't yet mastered. Overall, I could work things out though, and it had a very positive effect on my Astrolinguistics skill. I decided to draw out this conversation as long as I could. Even if the sullen Miyelonians decided to send Gnat to respawn, I could chalk this up as a win, improving my grasp on the local lingo.

"I mean, who can say where Fox goes? She was just here on the balcony with me, but I guess she ran off. I could call her if you want her so bad! My pet will show up in no time!"

Authority increased to 4!

Authority increased to 5!

Of course, I was bluffing. I couldn't call the predatory creature even if I wanted to. And again, I didn't need translation to understand that these Miyelonians weren't merely here to pet a cute animal. Meanwhile, Ayni translated the following phrases from the Miyelonian stranger:

"I imagine you understand why we're here. You caused serious damage to the Pride of the Heavenly Warrior by robbing an underage player and, more importantly, punishing him in public."

"Punishing?! Robbing?! That's a very strange interpretation of events! I caught a thief who stole something of value from me. I could have punished him by cutting off his tail or shaving his head bare, but I took his young age and low level into account, so I decided to punish him as mildly as I could allow. I just took a small indemnity, not even all his cash. I figure I taught the pickpocket a little lesson: if you're a Thief by class, then you need to be more careful and pick easier targets!"

My logical and seemingly clear answer caused a

long argument among the Miyelonians. Honestly, I had no idea what they were bickering and cursing about for those few minutes, because Ayni didn't translate. But I took advantage of the free moment, opened my skill window and put all three points into Medium Armor, raising it to 43. That, I was hoping, would at least somewhat improve my chances in the seemingly inevitable duel.

Finally, the orange cat waited for the end of their dispute and said:

"Gerd Gnat, let me say again: you really have a poor understanding of our culture and norms. Taking the tail of a nemesis as a trophy is not a punishment, but a sign of honor and respect to a defeated warrior, recognizing his authority and strength. Such trophies are only taken from honorable and dangerous enemies. If you had cut the tail off little Tini, that would of course have seemed strange for a player of your status, but the Pride of the Heavenly Warrior would not have felt insulted. By the way, let me tell you a secret. They're afraid of you. One of them is supposed to challenge you to a one-on-one duel of honor, but they just keep trying to force the obligation on someone else."

Of course, it was nice to hear they were afraid of me, but it didn't make me feel any better. I knew the true order of things perfectly well. Without Fox or a decent weapon, I couldn't even handle the nimble Tini, which was to say nothing of his more dangerous compatriots. As for the tail... well, crap... I mean how could I have known?! If they'd have said earlier, I would have taken not only his tail, but all the frail thief's extremities just to placate his pride-mates!

And meanwhile, the Miyelonian stranger asked a question, which Ayni translated readily:

"And just who are you, Gnat? We can see you are a Gerd, but what is your species and tribe? Who stands behind you?"

That really was a dangerous question. They were clearly probing to see if they could get away with killing me, robbing me, or worse. They wanted to know if any of that could come back on them. Anyhow, I had an answer tucked away for just such a scenario:

"I am from the faction of the respected Geckho Leng Waid Shishish. He is my boss. Maybe you've even seen me in the news. I was among the subjects of Leng Waid Shishish who recently entered an ancient Relict base."

Authority increased to 6!

It quickly became clear that none of the three Miyelonians had seen the news about the discovery of the Relict base. Nevertheless, they had heard of Waid Shishish before, and they had a healthy respect for him. The Geckho military leader's hot temper was widely famed. I could sense an immediate change in the dangerous Miyelonians' opinion of me. Where before they saw me as some jerky nobody, who their rules said deserved punishment, now I was firmly in the category of "not worth the trouble." The Miyelonians exchanged glances again, then the stranger finally changed topic:

"Tini says that your backpack is half full of some kind of powder. Is it drugs? Mental enhancers? Combat boosters?"

I answered honestly that it was pure powdered

platinum. All three Miyelonians immediately looked glum.

"Oh come on! More platinum!? Yesterday, the Geckho dragged in a whole box, now you. No, we don't care about platinum. Rare metals are not our thing. The Pride of the Bushy Shadow handles that stuff."

A dangerous pause arose in the conversation and I tried to fill it quickly, hurrying to unravel the topic:

"The Geckho with the platinum, did they happen to come in a Shiamiru? Is their captain an Aristocrat named Uraz Tukhsh? It's just that I know them. I talked with them about the platinum. The Geckho even offered to help me sell mine, but I refused. That Uraz is a born loser, so I kept him at arm's length."

"Exactly! A loser, there's no other way to call him!" the Assassin confirmed eagerly. "Uraz Tukhsh got gummed up in a whole thing here on the station before. He was bragging and squabbling with the Free Captains, so they had to teach him some manners. Actually, yeah! I remember! Your boss flew in with a crew of Geckho cutthroats to pull that Uraz Tukhsh out of prison! But clearly, he didn't learn his lesson. He raised a big stink here again, refused to sell the platinum to the Pride of the Bushy Shadow, and treated some bigwigs rudely. Then he tried to run. Naive... Who'd let him leave with that cargo! From what I heard, the Free Captain Ami U-Miya from the Pride of the Bushy Shadow intercepted that Geckho loser's platinum. Plus, he got an automatic processor as a bonus."

Astrolinguistics skill increased to level fifty-

seven!

You have reached level forty-nine!

You have received three skill points!

Yikes... What an uncomfortable moment. My progress bar was totally empty, so my character would lose a level and some skills if I died. If the Miyelonians wanted to punish me, they wouldn't be getting a better opportunity. So, did they notice I leveled up or not?

Just then, a pause took hold. After that, the Miyelonian who still hadn't revealed his information said something, and Ayni started to translate:

"Level forty-nine... Congratulations, Gerd Gnat! You're a strong and authoritative player, and here I thought..." Then I tensed up, guessing I would be challenged to a duel. But I quickly noticed my progress bar had started to fill up from the translating, so the real danger had passed. "You showed respect to the Pride of the Heavenly Warrior by taking the tail of our Assassin Ayuk as a trophy, so Tini's punishment can easily be forgotten. According to Miyelonian tradition, an adult may only raise his hand to a youngling if they are master and student, so take Tini as your apprentice! From now on, care for him, Gerd Gnat. Tini will obey and help however you like! The Clan of the Heavenly Warrior has no more quarrel with you!"

Ayni hadn't managed to finish translating before the two fearsome Miyelonians darted away from the balcony, leaving me in complete confusion together with an equally baffled kitten Thief and a bewildered Translator.

Chapter Fifteen

Playing for Keeps

ABOVE ALL, before Ayni went on her way, leaving me without any way of communicating with my new ward, I asked the Translator to explain what it was a "master" was supposed to do for his "student." At the same time, I asked what would happen if I just left the underage kitten here and went back home. After all, I was not going to be able to stay on Medu-Ro IV much longer, and I was not planning to spend the rest of my life among Miyelonians.

Ayni answered a bit latter, first asking what I meant by "kitten." I answered as delicately as possible, trying not to wound the ego of the Miyelonian lady, as I had just accidentally compared her race with a species of house-pet:

"Cats are small predatory creatures from my

home planet covered in thick fur. They often live in homes with people and serve as a source of affection and silliness. People feed them, train them, care for them and pamper them, receiving in return a loyal friend and companion."

"Gerd Gnat, you've just answered your own question about what a master is supposed to do. But as for the second question, the answer is simpler. The Pride has rejected Tini. He is your 'kitten,' now. See, his description has already updated. You could add him to your pride or leave it as is. But if you're going to fly off, you would be required to either take your student with you, or make sure he is provided for until your return. You could abandon him of course, but that would seriously damage your Authority. And as far as I know, that is very important for high-profile players."

I hadn't really grasped the full importance of Authority yet but, overall, I could agree that low Authority deprived a Gerd of some of their bonuses. But what had Ayni said about Tini's description? I opened the info on my foundling and discovered some serious changes:

Tini Wi-Gnat. Miyelonian. Pride [undetermined]. Level-17 Thief.

Wi-Gnat??? What did that mean? Every person Tini robbed from now on would see my name as a calling card. Would that open me up to complaints and demands for compensation? What a stab in the back!!!

And also, I immediately had more questions about the next lines than answers. For example, Pride "undetermined." What did that mean? Where would Tini go when he exited the game, if his Pride had rejected him? And what would happen if I managed to convince the leadership of the Human-3 Faction to let this newbie join our group? I was sure that, at least just as a test, Radugin and his deputies would agree, because the situation was very unusual. But what did that get us? Was I bringing an alien to Earth? After leaving the game, would Tini come out of a virt pod under the Dome?

I imagined that. A real live alien among us! That would cause a furor the likes of which hadn't been seen since Yuri Gagarin's first space flight, or the Americans landing on the Moon! But after that, it was easy to predict that my "kitten" would be taken for study and interrogation by austere bearded academics and gloomy military types that would inevitably flood the Dome. And getting caught in their sticky fingers was a very gloomy perspective for the Miyelonian. He'd probably never be let back into the game.

By the way, maybe I should ask Tini his opinion about all this. What if the level-17 Thief was not overjoyed with becoming the companion of an alien who had hurt him and humiliated him. What if my student was going to flee from his unwanted master at the first opportunity? Through the Translator, I asked that question to the disheveled, agitated Miyelonian.

"I don't know, Gerd Gnat. I still haven't recovered from the shocking news that the Pride of the Heavenly Warrior rejected me so easily! I'll admit, that really hurt. By the way, I don't know what kind of master you are, but I can say one thing for sure: my pride-mates haven't forgotten about the platinum in your inventory. I know them too well. I'm sure the information about the precious metal is being sent where it needs to go, and they will try to pickpocket your valuable property or take it by force."

Ayni, translating this long message for me, added a personal addendum:

"By the way, I'm in complete agreement with Tini. Here on Medu-Ro, there is a very simple rule: if something can be taken without paying, that is exactly what will happen. It's the law of the jungle here. Only power is respected, and no one helps the weak. So, if I were in your place, Gerd Gnat, I would hurry back to my ship and tell the captain everything I know. Gerd Setis-Vir is a very authoritative Free Captain. Very few would risk tangling with him."

Ugh, if only it was so simple... I definitely didn't want to meet Gerd Setis-Vir, whose ship I had accidentally damaged. But I also didn't want to admit that I tricked Ayni and got the pass dishonestly. I had to try something else. It was dumb to expect nobility and honesty from a group of space pirates, so I needed to immediately make useful connections and get support or get rid of this platinum. And at that, I shouldn't get rid of it on the sly, but loudly and obviously, so the dangerous locals would stop bothering me.

I asked the Miyelonians if they happened to know where I could meet a member of the Pride of the Bushy Shadow, which dealt in precious metals. For example, Captain Ami U-Miya, who had taken the platinum from the Geckho.

Ayni did not have that information, but Tini said eagerly that the highest leader of the Pride of the Bushy

Shadow, Gerd Abi Pan-Miay, was known to frequent the local casino. According to my "kitten," Abi was not just one of the most authoritative and successful Free Captains, he was also a gambling man. He had even blown whole fortunes more than once. But sometimes he also won fabulously huge sums, leaving his enemies without cargo, or even starships.

As it turned out, the casino on the station was right on the residential floor not far away at all. We wouldn't even have to go down through the dense crowd of pilgrims to get there. I asked Ayni to accompany me and help in negotiations, promising the orange cat good pay as a Translator. The Miyelonian lady's answer surprised me:

"Gerd Gnat, I'd go for free. Finally, the game is interesting again! If only you knew how bored I am after sitting for days on end at that loathsome registration desk! I would be overjoyed to become your 'kitten,' but my age is already too high to be a student, and who would let me leave the Pride now?!"

We passed through the gloomy forking corridor and stopped thirty steps from a set of doors lit with bright flashing signs. At the entrance to the casino, there were a few very colorful Miyelonian characters standing and chatting. They seemed to be in competition for the most earrings or trophy tails. All of them were looking around in agitation then took turns secretly sipping a bubbling purple liquid from a narrow transparent vessel. But my eye was drawn by something else. One of the cats was twirling a little remote in his paw, exactly the same as the one in my inventory. Hey, that was a roll manipulator, a tool for cheating in Na-Tikh-U!

Tini quietly jerked my sleeve, warning me through Ayni that they were professional players, local hustler, and that I shouldn't tangle with them.

The regulars watched us as we walked inside, sizing us up. Once through the doors, we stopped. The light was very bright and took some getting used to. The sharp smell of plant-based perfumes and constant noise was a bit much as well. The gaming floor was actually not so large, just barely bigger than a basketball court. There were a few short tables with jubilant players sitting right on the floor playing a game I didn't recognize. But around the edge, there were stands for spectators of all kinds of unbelievable races. Also in the bleachers, there were armed security guards on patrol.

"You know, most of the money that changes hands here is actually in bets between spectators, not at the game tables," the underage thief whispered to me. "The gaming floor is divided from the stands with a sound-proof one-way forcefield, so the viewers cannot intervene in the games or give hints, but they can see what's happening at the tables perfectly. There are also little camera drones flying around and sending video to the big screens."

Astrolinguistics skill increased to level fifty-eight!
Eagle Eye skill increased to level fifty-one!

What could I say? It was laudable foresight not to let the viewers meddle in the games. Although, the fact that electromagnetic signals could still go through the force field was a vulnerability. That needed to be thought over well. In fact, I already had one scheme in mind. As always, it was either genius in its simplicity, or completely idiotic. But before I tried it out, I wanted to do what I came here for.

"Tini, you know the leader of the Pride of the Bushy Shadow by face. Point him out."

My ward spent a long time looking around at the players and viewers. I understood his answer even without Ayni's help. He was not here. I told Ayni to ask one of the guards, whose answer she then translated:

"Gerd Abi Pan-Miay is not here. He is a frequent guest of the casino, but today the respected Free Captain went off to hear the sermon of the great Priestess Amiru U-Mayaoo."

Aw crap... Had we come here for nothing? I asked my companions to find out about other members of the Pride of the Bushy Shadow. But soon, a huge tomcat with dyed-gray matted hair, draped head-to-toe in blades and firearms walked up to me. Unfortunately, I couldn't read any information about him, so I had to just trust that he really was an official representative of the pride.

I asked Ayni to relay my message to the leader of the Pride of the Bushy Shadow as literally as possible: I had a large amount of purified platinum, around six hundred seventy-five pounds, already in bullion. The problem was that my cargo was in the exclusive economic zone of the Geckho on a recently-discovered planet. And although there were practically no security forces, just one Sindirovu-class Geckho interceptor for the whole system, I was looking for a courageous captain not afraid to take a stealthy and fast starship to an inhabited planet to buy precious metals from the natives. The preferred form of payment was Geckho crystals, although other options were possible, including barter. If my proposition was of interest to the Pride of the Bushy Shadow, we could discuss a price, landing site and other details. Also, it was easily possible that our partnership could become long-term and regular.

The gray tomcat stroked his nose with a clawed finger in thought and promised that he would convey this information to the pride leader or other highly placed players.

Now, with my main mission complete, nothing was stopping me from enjoying myself in the casino a bit. I also hoped I could sell the platinum on me. I called both of my helpers along and, after buying the herbal smelling drinks the Miyelonians asked for at the bar, took a seat at a spectators' table and started explaining my plan in painstaking detail.

THE SLIPPERIEST MOMENT was somehow exchanging sixteen and a half pounds of powdered platinum for the multicolored many-sided tokens used in the casino. I suspected we wouldn't find a single sane trader willing to pay a member of a little-known alien race that much for something of unknown provenance. And I was first rejected, which didn't really surprise me. But I pitched a fit, stomping my feet, beating my fists on the desk and cursing in all languages I knew. I was playing the role of a dumb rich outworlder, visiting civilized space for the first time. I wanted to create the image of someone intoxicated by new surroundings and desperate to bet all his gold beads on a horse. Ayni looked embarrassed just like a person and put her ears back, translating my juiciest epithets and curses from Geckho. As I raged, I was laughing on the inside and even mentally reassuring my Translator, because she did not understand my most bombastic curses which were all, naturally, from earthbound languages.

The notion that I may not have had any real platinum to sell and might have been just trying to pass off some worthless powder was not a doubt that occurred to the casino workers. One advantage of a video game was that information could be authenticated by just reading a description! It all hinged on the purity and value of the metal I was trying to unload, but the main obstacle was whether I could take payment not in crypto but some other way.

Finally, the casino's greed prevailed. Security came up to the cashiers, whispered something, and finally they accepted my platinum. I suspected that the guardsman had been transmitting an order from the higher ups. If this naïve foreigner wanted so badly to part with his valuables, why not? I was given a handful of colored tokens with a total value of six thousand three hundred fifty crypto for my sixteen and a half pounds of metal powder. Yes, the exchange was far from fair, but I wasn't going to be fussy. Especially because I saw a suspicious number of members of the Pride of the Heavenly Warrior among the spectators, who were not in the casino before. Seemingly, Tini was right, and some enforcers with less than peaceful intentions had already been sent to track me down.

What could I say? My first mission was accomplished, and all the hunters after me knew that Gnat no longer had any platinum. Now, I needed to get to the main part of the plan. Accompanied by the orange Translator, I entered the gaming floor and headed into the Na-Tikh-U area. I stopped next to a table with a Miyelonian player waiting for an opponent and angled my gaze up at a row of spectators. Tini gave me the secret sign that everything was ready, and I took a seat opposite my opponent right on the plastic floor.

The Miyelonian threw a black token on the table with a bored look. It was shaped like a circle with a section cut out. That was his bet for the game: one thousand crypto. I copied that bet, then gave all the rest of my tokens to Ayni, ordering the translator to put it all on me. An inspector walked up to make sure everything was above board, took Ayni to the viewers stands and turned on a force field blocking our table off from the outside world.

Alright, here goes nothing! The "cat" pressed the keyboard, and a randomly generated game field appeared over the table. My opponent got the first move, and he couldn't resist a satisfied predatory grin: twelve-twelve, the highest roll possible! While he placed his ships on the three-dimensional holographic screen, I could barely hold back a smile of my own. Just wait and see what I have in store for you, furry hustler!

Break-in skill increased to level twenty!

Electronics skill increased to level thirty-five!

It was somewhat strange that, although Tini was using the manipulator in the stands, I got the experience. Was that just because he was my ward? Anyway, the fact the Miyelonian was my student was still unknown to the casino regulars. A Thief, as with a few other game classes, could temporarily hide their information, which Tini took advantage of. The little thief was well known here. They even gave him a bite to eat sometimes, so Tini's presence didn't surprise anyone. Anyhow, security thought he was in the Pride of the Heavenly Warrior, which meant they didn't much care what he did. And certainly no one was thinking the adolescent might be conspiring with me. I wondered how long I could keep up that confusion...

But I didn't bust my brains over it, instead concentrating on the game.

My roll was somewhat more modest: two-seven. And you really should have seen my opponent's reaction when he rolled a second twelve-twelve in a row. It was now a somewhat tortured smirk, and the professional was now no longer quite so elated. One important factor was that I had not chosen my opponent at random. This was the very same hustler I had seen with a roll manipulator earlier. Before I sat at the table, I activated Scanning to make sure it was still on his person. And it was, stashed in a case on his belt.

When my opponent rolled yet another twelve-twelve, I was now allowing myself to grumble in dismay, even though it hurt to look at the Miyelonian. The professional sharp clearly didn't understand what was going on. Furtively (or so he thought), he reached for his roll manipulator and took it out, placing it under his bony bottom. I meanwhile was playing badly on purpose, making questionable and even obviously weak moves, giving away the momentum and not even trying to improve my position or control the board. In the eyes of the viewers, I probably looked like some weak newbie, who had just barely learned the ABC's of the game and didn't understand a smidgen of tactics. But winning was not my objective. I was trying to concentrate on defense and stop him from quickly beating in just a few moves. I set a goal to hold out for just ten turns. The inspector would be sure to notice my opponent's rather curious luck.

Break-in skill increased to level twenty-one!
Electronics skill increased to level thirty-six!

The game ended much sooner than I anticipated. Just five turns in, the Miyelonian rolled another twelve-twelve, and the forcefield over us sharply turned off. The inspector walked up with a pair of sullen armed security guards. I saw the Translator hurrying over and didn't miss the chance to complain:

"My opponent is clicking something before every turn, then getting the best roll! I don't know what kind of trick he's using, but he's hiding it right under his butt!"

When Ayni translated my outburst for all to hear, the inspector told the frightened card-sharp to stand up in a harsh tone that would not bear objections. The Miyelonian tried to kick the roll manipulator under the table, but they noticed. The two security guards grabbed my opponent hard by the shoulders, gave him a shake and stood him up straight. The inspector picked up the manipulator and put it in his bag, then he said something full of reproach. I even recognized some of the words:

"Oni U-Muaa... (incomprehensible)... so experienced (incomprehensible)... could get by without cheating in a game against (seemingly something insulting) ... newbie. You know the... rules... (incomprehensible)... You're banned... (a verb coupled with a curse) ... from the casino for ten days!"

Astrolinguistics skill increased to level fifty-nine!

Tini had explained to me that cheaters always lost officially if caught, while all the bets made by players and spectators were still counted. So everything came together just how I hoped. But what came next caught me totally off guard. The inspector took a curved glowing lilac blade from a sheath and cut off my opponent's tail at the very root, then tossed it before me on the table.

Tail of Oni U-Muaa, Level-144 Rogue (trophy)

Fame increased to 40.

Fame increased to 41.

Authority increased to 7!

You have reached level fifty!

You have received three skill points! (total points accumulated: six)

Congratulations! You now have three more skill slots!!!

Chapter Sixteen

Escaping Alive

I HAD TO FIND another clip to attach this trophy to my helmet, because I was out. But it would be foolish and even dangerous to neglect such a fine trophy. I might offend the Pride of the Agile Paw, which the high-level hustler belonged to. Tini asked his former clanmates for a clip, and they charitably agreed. While I was stringing up the trophy tail, Ayni came up to me, radiant, and handed me a whole handful of tokens:

"Gerd Gnat, the odds on you were six and a half to one, so practically no one else bet on you. Your bet of five thousand three hundred fifty crypto netted thirty-four thousand four hundred after casino fees!!!"

Damn!!! That was even more than I was hoping in my boldest estimates. I didn't hold back and, continuing to play the role of a distant and impulsive outworlder, I tried to look wildly happy with my luck and shouted for the whole casino to hear. After all, I still had another two black one-thousand-crypto tokens as well! I gave them to Ayni and Tini as compensation for their loyalty and work. I wasn't expecting such stormy jubilation from my "kitten." Tini, now a level twenty-three Thief, seemed to be trying to compete with my reaction. He jumped and shrieked for joy, rolling on the floor and squeezing out such strange gurgling throaty sounds that I actually became afraid for his health. No less than my apprentice, Ayni was also glad at the generous reward, although the orange cat tried to maintain proper restrained composure.

"Great job! Get yourself whatever you want! It's my treat!" I sent my helpers to the bar. I had also started that direction when I suddenly froze stock still.

There was a woman looking at me from the balcony on the third floor. A human woman! Here on this Miyelonian pirate station, God knows how many millions of miles from Earth!!! She was dark-haired with a perfect oval for a face and huge eyes like some anime character. The stranger was wearing an armored suit of a blue shade with a design and form factor that reminded me of the light spacesuit I used in my first voyage with the Geckho.

Valeri-Urla. Human. Tailax Faction. Level-96 Beast Master.[3]

She was a real person! Tailax Faction? That sounded very strange, not like any countries of Earth, nor the Dark Faction. But the name seemed vaguely

---

[3] *Valeri-Urla* is a character from Michael Atamanov's novel *Quarantine Planet*

familiar. Ah, that was it! I remembered that the Geckho Trader Uline Tar had mentioned a girl from Tailax, who spent some time with the Shiamiru crew. Maybe this was the same person? I forgot everything else, and ran up to the stands, flew up to the third floor and... met face to face with a blond brute standing in my path.

Denni Marko. Human. Gilvar Syndicate Faction. Level-88 Bodyguard.[4]

Another person?! I figured I was the only member of my race in this whole quadrant of space but, here, there was a whole hive of them! And meanwhile, Denni tapped my chest rudely, put on an annoyed tone and said something in a language I did not recognize. Seeing the total incomprehension on my face, he repeated in Geckho, with an accent so strong it was almost impossible to understand:

"Giorl eez no vannt tallking you. Geet out!"

Was I being chased off? Surprisingly, Denni was right about his pretty companion's mood. Valeri-Urla, still sitting at the table and watching our quarrel from afar, turned the opposite direction, proving her complete lack of concern. How? These two people were from a different faction, seeing residents of Earth for the first time, but also didn't want to know who I was or where I came from?!

I tried to speak Geckho with the Bodyguard, explain my peaceful intentions and desire to simply meet people from another world, but as soon as I spoke, Denni pulled a snub-nose rifle from a holster

---

[4]*Denni Marko* is a character from Michael Atamanov's novel *Quarantine Planet*

and stuck it into my chest:

"If savage no sey wordies, he live! Else eez boom and die!"

I felt a sharp pain in my chest. Danger Sense confirmed that Denni was not bluffing and really would shoot if I didn't leave. I had to take a step back. First just one, then another. The Bodyguard wouldn't settle down and was showing a determination to shoot. Ayni then came up to me with a glass of bubbling drink in her clawed paw and immediately tried to figure out what was going on here, and why that other person was poking me with a rifle.

I couldn't do much to explain myself, and the aggressive Bodyguard didn't want to talk with the orange Translator either. But then I felt something touch my knee from behind and sharply turned around. As it turned out, a huge Trillian had crawled up. With some astonishment I recognized him as the merchant Gerd Ussh Veesh, who had helped me avoid problems by the elevators and get to the registration area. The level-144 Trader hissed and bellowed, and my Translator, thinking for a few seconds, said the Trillian was suggesting we go play Na-Tikh-U. I nodded in agreement, because I hadn't been able to start up a conversation with these people, and the merchant started crawling toward a table on all six feet.

I tried to toss Valeri and her aggressively inclined companion out of my head, then went downstairs. On my way to the gaming floor, I realized that the act I'd put on during the first game had paid off. Everyone thought I was a dull and impetuous savage. That couple of strange people probably didn't want to talk with me for that very reason.

And sure, I was a savage. Why not? But now, I had to quickly decide how much to bet on this horse, and whether to play fair or try to manipulate the results. I suspected that the security workers would be paying somewhat more attention to me now, especially with the cat out of the bag on Tini's new affiliations. That meant I could not get away with using the roll manipulator again. So, I gave an order to use it only if absolutely necessary, if I didn't have any chance to win. And only if I gave him a secret sign.

"Gerd Gnat, I know this Trillian. He's a frequent guest at the casino," Tini told me quietly. "In my memory, he has only come down to the gaming floor a few times, but he always loses quickly. He is not a very strong player. Quite weak, actually. Usually Ussh Veesh sits on the upper floor in a VIP box, relaxing with friends, drinking stimulants that are illegal in his homeland and making bets."

It looked very much like playing the part of a primitive outworlder had borne fruit, and this very mediocre player now wanted to score an easy win against a naive savage. Well, I guess I'd try and surprise the merchant. I was not a total newbie, and I had studied most Na-Tikh-U strategies. Meanwhile, I had an Intelligence of 23 and a luck of +3, which gave this "outworlder" decent chances.

My bet was twenty-five thousand crypto, a whole stack of differently colored polygonal tokens. If the merchant was surprised, it probably wasn't by the size of the bet, but that this "outworlder" had put everything on this horse up to his very loincloth. The inspector walked up, turned on the forcefield over us, and the game began.

IT'S RARE THAT this happens, but we were perfectly matched! The game went on for an hour and a half, but I never got bored or antsy. In fact, that time was packed with enough wild emotional swings to last me a few weeks, if not a whole month. At points it looked dire, like my defense was splitting at the seams. But much to my surprise, the Trillian was struggling to fight back my assault, and he found it so stressful he had to swallow some gel-caps to calm his heart. Finally, with my last few ships, I managed to capture the key points of the game board a few turns before my main base fell. Victory!!! And I played fair, which made me doubly celebratory.

Fame increased to 42.

Authority increased to 8!

Gerd Ussh Veesh gave a fearsome roar, raising the front third of his body and pointing a powerful armored hand with sharpened claws at my undefended neck. Was he threatening me? Or demanding something? Or was that just how he expressed anger?

I didn't know how to act. Grab my weapon, run, or call the guards? Fortunately, just in the nick of time, the Translator ran up to smooth over the confusion, explaining that the respected merchant was very happy with the game, so he was offering friendship and a discount on his wares. The outstretched clawed hand, meanwhile, was a gesture of peace and trust. To return the sentiment, I was to touch the claws with a vulnerable part of my body, somewhere unprotected by either artificial or natural armor. After that, I was to extend a claw, spear or blade, and the Trillian would touch it to his exposed neck.

Astrolinguistics skill increased to level sixty!

I bowed to the honorable Trillian, touching his claws to my bare neck and thus accepting his offer of friendship. After that, I thanked him for the entertaining game, then extended my knife blade and the ritual was complete.

The Trillian merchant knew his way around the pirate station and was well acquainted with the local mindset, so he called his Bodyguards and offered to have them escort me to my ship or some other safe location. I had to admit it was not unwarranted. I could still see some sullen brutes from the Pride of the Heavenly Warrior in the stands, along with a few other sketchy characters staring at me sidelong. What was more, I glanced at my watch and gave a shudder. There were just twenty-five minutes before my housewarming party in the real world!

But I wasn't allowed to just leave... I didn't even manage to collect my winnings from the table before a large number of security guards descended on the floor and pushed the Trillian merchant and his two Bodyguards away. What surprised me was that my newfound crocodile friend didn't even try to resist, just obeyed without a word and went up to the stands. Tini also left obediently, not trying to help in any way, or even tell me what was going on.

A short Miyelonian came up to my table and, without asking permission, sat opposite me. Unlike the other cat aliens I'd seen, this one was wrapped head to toe in loose white garments, something of a white robe with a hood or more like a floor length dress with sleeves that ended in fingerless claw-friendly gloves. All that was left uncovered were my opponent's eyes, which I could see through slits in the clothing. They were both emerald green and had vertical pupils that bored into my soul...

Function unavailable. Your character lacks the Psionic skill.

Would you like to take the skill Psionic?

I didn't rush it or take the skill without thinking. I just quickly averted my gaze, because every second of eye contact ate up a tenth of my Magic Points. So, what did this Miyelonian want from me?

"Gerd Gnat, the leader of the Pride of the Agile Paw, who owns this establishment, would like to play you," a clearly nervous Ayni told me, her tail twitching.

The player didn't give a name, just a position, which of course surprised me and put me on guard. What was more, I didn't understand how, but my orange Translator seemed to know this strange individual. After all, none of the security had said a word, and the figure in white was equally secretive.

"And what if I'm not especially keen to play him?" I asked the Translator in Geckho, to which I was immediately answered but not by Ayni, by the "white figure" himself:

"In that case, Gerd Gnat, I'll get upset, and you will not leave my establishment alive. What's more, you'll have no way to exchange your tokens for crypto. Neither you nor your coconspirators. The tokens themselves will be marked as unfair winnings. Yes, human. Are you really naïve enough to think we weren't recording all electromagnetic signals, and that your little sidekick could use a roll manipulator unbeknownst to us?!"

Very threatening! But I was in no hurry to admit to cheating, and even less to get scared.

"Honorable leader of the glorious Pride of the Agile Paw, did I miss something? Did Tini improve my rolls even once? If he did, I apologize for my ward and will surrender my winnings at once. What, did that not happen? Thought so. Then what did I do wrong?!"

"Words, empty words..." the leader of the Pride said in reproach. "Why all this justification? After all, we both know perfectly well that cheating did take place. Why put established fact into doubt?"

Anyhow, I had already realized this matter wasn't going to be solved with words alone. It looked very much like I would have to play the Pride leader. But under what conditions? I voiced a thought:

"I still don't see how I'm being forced to play. After all, I was threatened with all kinds of bad things if I refused. But what is stopping the great Pride leader from punishing me if I do agree to play? Or even in the unbelievable, but hypothetically possible case that I win?"

"Ah, about that... What can I say? I agree, the stick is totally ineffective without the carrot..." said the Miyelonian, demonstrating a Geckho phrase that was very much like one from back home. Or was that the game's translator choosing words that sounded pleasant to my ear? "Well, here are the new conditions, Gerd Gnat. First, no half measures! We will play one game for all the tokens you have, no ifs ands or buts. Second, no matter how the game ends, you and your companions will not be killed and may leave my casino unimpeded. You have my word as a Pride leader! Third, if you win, I will not only give my assent to exchanging your tokens for crypto, I will personally guarantee your safety on the Medu-Ro IV station for the entire duration of your stay! And as an added bonus, if for any reason you cannot reach an agreement on the platinum with the Pride of the Bushy Shadow, I'll find a captain willing to buy!"

Better now, but still not the most ideal conditions. After all, what was the point of promising not to kill someone, if dying didn't have terrible and irreversible consequences? Trading my tokens for crypto and selling the H3 Faction's platinum? Sure, that was intriguing, but first I'd have to beat the owner of the casino, who was the leader of a pride that specialized in gambling and most likely wasn't called "the Agile Paw" for nothing.

I asked for two or three minutes to think, called Tini over and sent him to get me a drink from the bar, his choice. My throat was parched from all this stress and hot air. I was about to give my kitten some crypto to buy the drink, but the pride leader intervened:

"Tell them it's on me! And also, boy, bring me a glass of whatever you get your master."

I didn't bust my brains over the Miyelonian's unexpected move. I had plenty to do with the free minutes I just gained. After all, I really needed time to think. I had to prepare. My chances of winning an honest match were very low, zero most likely, so I needed to do something unexpected. For example, learn how to understand his thoughts or even influence them.

So then, the long beckoning Psionic skill. What did it give?

Psionic. This skill confers the ability to read the thoughts of nearby intelligent beings (whether NPC's or living players) and practice mind control. Minimum statistics: Intelligence 22, Agility 15, Perception 15.

ATTENTION!!! Using Psionic abilities requires Magic Points. If a character has insufficient Magic Points, they cannot use Psionic abilities, and active Psionic effects will be terminated. The total number of Magic Points and their regeneration rate depend on the Mysticism skill. The Mental Fortitude skill determines the power and range of effects, defense against Psionic attacks, and success chance for multiple simultaneous Psionic actions.

ATTENTION!!! Success chance of Psionic actions depends mostly on Psionic skill, but also on the difference in Intelligence between attacker and target. If the attacker is more than 10 Intelligence points above the target, the success chance is 100%. If the target is more than 10 Intelligence points above the attacker, Psionic actions cannot be performed.

Ugh, so complicated... As it turned out, it wasn't enough to simply take Psionic. I needed other skills for mana points and regain speed. Also for spell power and range... I suspected that a professional Mage specialized in Psionic would have, beyond those three skills, a whole set of others that were also a practical necessity. How nice that I was not a Mage, and these complications were not going to define my gameplay!

Alright, I'd start with the one I couldn't do without:

You have taken the skill Psionic level 1.

I immediately dumped all six skill points into it, raising the skill to level 7. But I decided not to rush with the two other free slots. Life didn't revolve around whether I won or lost this specific game, and Gnat might need other skills. What was more, my Scanning ability had just reloaded and, after activating the icon on my mini-map, I saw something interesting. I even zoomed in as far as possible, wanting to see every detail to confirm my initial guesses.

The leader of the Pride of the Agile Paw, beyond all doubt, was a female! What was more, under her free-flowing alabaster garments, she was hiding a big belly, inside of which I could even make out two embryos schematically rendered on my map. Interesting details. I could try to start a conversation with that, no Psionics necessary.

Scanning skill increased to level forty-four!
Cartography skill increased to level forty-seven!
You have reached level fifty-one!
You have received three skill points!

What great timing! I put three more points into Psionic, raising it up to ten! And no less importantly, when I leveled, my Magic Points went up from 172 to 175. It might seem like nothing, but I still chalked it up as a win.

Tini walked up with two identical flasks of a bright orange liquid, which was bubbling and steaming. The leader of the Pride took one first, leaving the second for me. I listened carefully to my feelings but didn't sense any trepidation. Seemingly, it was all on the up and up. No one was trying to poison me. But still, I looked cautiously and took a sniff of the flask. A thick hot syrup with the aroma of valerian and wormwood. The flavor of the drink was sickly sweet, but also pleasant and tonic. I could only drink it in tiny sips. The beverage restored my Endurance Points just as well as the spicy Geckho vegetable soup, and my Magic Points quickly came back to maximum. Great stuff! I wouldn't mind taking a sample back home for our chemists!

I handed the empty vessel back to Tini and told my opponent I was ready to play. The leader of the Pride of the Agile Paw didn't want to spend any time pussyfooting around and told everyone to go, including the Translator and security. At the last second, before the forcefield cut off my vision, I turned to the stands and saw the girl by the name Valeri-Urla. Despite all that time, she hadn't gone anywhere and was now watching me. Seeing my attention, she hurriedly turned away, as if she had no interest.

"I ordered the forcefield to be made opaque on both sides. I don't want potential rivals watching and studying my style of play," my rival told me, activating the table and generating a game field. "You go first."

"Among my kind, it is common to cede that position to ladies who are with child. What's more, you're gonna have twins. They say that's twice as hard for a future mother."

My rival squirmed, as if she had been shocked with electricity, then spent a long time looking at me with her eyes wide either in fear or surprise. Now was the perfect time for a mental attack, but I was in no rush. Our pieces were not yet placed, so an attack would have no real purpose.

"Prospector abilities?" the pride leader guessed, and I readily confirmed.

"That's exactly right. Plus Perception ramped up to the max and a bunch of skills for detecting anything and everything. If I still had analyzers for my Prospector Scanner, I could even tell the sex of your future children, but unfortunately I'm all out."

"And thank the Great First Female you are! According to our beliefs, knowing the sex of a child in advance can only lead to misfortune!"

The game was on with a vengeance. I thought deeply over every move, desperately hoping to win this game of critical importance. But my rival was barely even looking at the game board, knowing all the opening moves and their nuances to the finest detail and moving her pieces on autopilot. Now was my chance!

"I would like to know why a humble Prospector like me caught the interest of such an important and influential individual. After all, any of your pride's hustlers could have been sent to teach me a lesson and take my winnings. It really was not necessary for the head of the Pride of the Agile Paw to handle such a small issue personally. And, forgive me for being direct, but I have to say something. You have amazingly pretty eyes! They're like living emeralds with refined glimmering facets!"

My opponent raised her green eyes to me in surprise, and we met gazes. Now!

"I really shouldn't have been afraid. He doesn't know the game at all. That's immediately apparent. So, there's no reason to draw things out. I need to end the round fast. I could move my battleship right down the middle, Gnat won't notice the threat posed by that pirate base..."

Action terminated. Magic Points exhausted.

No, I wasn't even trying to read the mind of my experienced high-level opponent. I had a different plan: first try to flatter her, as she was not used to praise, then transmit a whole packet of thoughts in one burst, hoping greatly that the lady cat would be thrown off balance by my compliments, and wouldn't notice the ideas didn't belong to her.

Psionic skill increased to level eleven!
Psionic skill increased to level twelve!
Psionic skill increased to level thirteen!

My mana was down to zero. I stumbled in a bout of sudden weakness, sitting down hard but still trying to keep a calm look on my face. Meanwhile, the clawed paw in white gloves, which was reaching for one of the high-level pieces, suddenly changed direction, taking the very largest and most powerful piece in her fleet and placing it in the center of the field.

"Thank you for the nice compliment, Gerd Gnat. Yes, I could have sent any of my subordinates, but I was curious. Helping an opponent win is a very paradoxical move, and I wanted to get to know you better. Crap! I got distracted..."

The bad move was clearly a surprise for the lady cat, and I could see the pupils in her green eyes tense up into tiny little points in fear. Meanwhile I, thinking for around a minute as if considering my obviously strong opponent's strange move and trying to find a hidden sense in it, eventually activated the pirate base and destroyed the strongest piece of my rival's fleet.

And with that, the substantive part of the game came to an end. Losing a battleship in Na-Tikh-U was comparable with losing a queen in chess, and even if you were some triple Kasparov, a handicap like that meant near certain victory for any adequate opponent. Three moves later, my opponent surrendered.

I asked her not to turn off the forcefield yet, and said:

"Honorable leader of the Pride of the Agile Paw, I don't care how much this offends you, but I cannot accept any winnings for this round. You made an obvious mistake, and I don't get any satisfaction from stupid victories. I suggest we wait for better times and play again when your twins aren't distracting you so much."

"A noble act and a courteous speech. Well, Gerd Gnat, I won't insist. As a return gesture, I suggest we settle accounts right now. I'll pay real crypto for all your tokens and, after removing the force field, all the spectators will see me taking the pot. The brutes after you will have to give up, assuming you lost it all. Also, my reputation as an unbeatable Na-Tikh-U player will not suffer, which is quite important as well. But I will uphold my promises. Your safety on the station will be guaranteed, and I can provide a captain willing to buy your platinum."

And we did just that. But when I had already stashed the wallet with fifty-nine thousand five hundred crypto, the pride leader asked unexpectedly:

"Gerd Gnat, please answer, but be honest. I promise that my opinion of you will not fall no matter the answer. My fifth move... the weird one with the battleship... Was that some kind of cheating?"

I kept silent for a bit, but then decided to answer honestly:

"Yes, it was. I mentally suggested it to you while we were making eye contact."

She breathed a sigh of relief and calmed down. She was seemingly very upset that she could have made such a stupid mistake. Then the cat added:

"The Meleyephatians are famed for such abilities, but not humans. What's more, you expect such things from Mages, but never a Prospector. Gerd Gnat, are you sure I couldn't entice you into joining my Pride? You'd have constant work in the casino. You would bathe in glory and money. And there's lots of other interesting work for a talented Prospector. Sure, it isn't always strictly legal, but that doesn't seem to stop you."

I laughed, thanked the Pride leader for her praise and trust, but still refused joining the Miyelonian pride. However, I said that I wouldn't be opposed to working with her clan, just not full membership.

Chapter Seventeen

Housewarming Party

I WAS RUNNING very late to my party, so I hurried my Miyelonian escort along, feeling worried. It would look bad, and my guests might get sick of waiting and leave. But then, finally, I reached my tiny yet safe room in the hotel on the Medu-Ro IV space station. Hurriedly closing the metal curtain and blocking myself off from the rest of the world, I immediately chose "Exit Game."

Would you like to review your statistics for this game session?

No, I had no time for that. I needed to get into the real world right away! I threw back the lid of the virt pod and, with indescribable joy, discovered friends waiting to meet me. And though I was somewhat expecting to see Anya and Imran next to my virt pod,

Dmitry Zheltov was there too. How long had I been waiting to hear from him? What a pleasant surprise!

"Gnat, you're a whole twenty minutes late!" Anya said with reproach, helping me stand up from the soft bed. "The table is already set in your apartment. The guests have arrived, but you just won't show!"

"I'm sorry I'm late, friends. If only you knew about my endless day!"

I set my weight on my left leg extremely gingerly and was pleased to discover it was no longer broken. So, I turned down the crutches and hurried to the stairs.

"Tell me everything!" I demanded of the Starship Pilot. "What happened with the Shiamiru? Where have you been so long?"

Dmitry gave a somehow tortured smile and admitted that he had no idea where he had gone. He didn't know Geckho, so he didn't understand the crew and couldn't read the screens either.

"But where we are now is not that important. What matters more is what happened. We were attacked by space pirates!!! Picture this, I load up the game, and there's a siren wailing on the Shiamiru. The whole crew is armed and wearing spacesuits. I also put on my helmet, take out my gun and run to the captain's bridge. And there, that furry geezer Uraz Tukhsh is howling away, clicking his nails on the monitor and pointing at three bright orange spots following our ship. Then with gestures, he offers me a seat at the control panel, hurries me along and even shoves me into the chair. Picture this, it's my fourth day in space, and the captain wants me to drive!"

"And what came next?" Anya asked, intrigued by the copilot's story.

"Well... I sat at the control panel and tried to gather my thoughts, then remembered my training. I'll admit, the fear made me forget half of it. I just checked the maneuver drives, added power to the mains, and set the monitor display to something a bit more manageable. Then, it was like I'd been flying a starship my whole life. It seemed easy and even intuitive. Also, everything is setup logically, and all the handles are the perfect size for a human hand!"

"Well, they were probably made for Geckho," I corrected my friend, but Zheltov answered that it made no difference. They had one butt, two hands, two legs and the rest didn't matter.

"Then I started feeling confident in my abilities and gunned it!" Clear notes of self-satisfaction slipped through in his voice. "I pushed that rust bucket for all she's worth and headed for the nearest planet. It's a cargo shuttle, of course, and not some racer, so the Miyelonian interceptors eventually caught up, but I fought like a lion! I entered the cloudy brown atmosphere of the gas giant Medu-Ro VII, which is a lot like our Saturn. There, I tried to throw them off my trail in the atmospheric clouds. We had to jettison the strapped-on automatic processor right away because, with it, we would have just crashed. But even without external cargo, it was not exactly a fun ride. I couldn't see a damn thing, and everything was shaking so hard it seemed like the ship was gonna fall apart!"

"But you must have leveled your skills," I threw out, and the pilot laughed:

"Sure, no way around that! Especially Starship Piloting and Maneuvering. There were system messages flickering in almost constantly. But it was all for nothing. The pirates had good locators, so I didn't manage to escape. I had to change tactics and go into the ring of ice dust around the planet. I survived there for half an hour cutting curves so tight that, if it weren't for the gravity compensators, the crew would have ended up splattered on the walls! As it was, it felt like we were hitting around 7 G! My Agility and Constitution went up by one, and I got my character to 48. I made one pirate hit a flying rock. It was great. It didn't wreck him, but it did cause a ton of damage, and I could see bits of debris on the locator. But then the Shiamiru got caught in some electronic thing, and the engine just shut off. What happened next is obvious..."

Without realizing it, Dmitry pressed his palm to his right side, as if checking his body for wounds and bruises. It was clear that he didn't particularly want to talk about what happened next. The pirates must have worked over the shuttle crew pretty well. But after a little while, Zheltov found the strength to continue:

"That was the first time I saw Miyelonians. They're furry creatures as high as a man's shoulder that look something like leopards. They're very strong, fast and mean. When their boarding crew entered our ship, they immediately shot Captain Uraz Tukhsh for disobedience, then another four Geckho resisted and met the same fate. They spent a long time questioning me, but I couldn't understand a damn thing. They beat the crap out of me, and broke my right ribs, and collar bone. They seriously injured my right eye. It was a miracle it didn't fall out... It's nothing though, it should pass... I hope. Either that or I'll have to wait to die and respawn."

"It'll definitely pass but go to the Medic! Many wounds in the game can be healed!" Anya assured our friend, herself a Medic by class.

Dmitry Zheltov nodded to her and continued his story about the pirate attack:

"The other crew members were also beaten up by the Miyelonians and locked in their bunks. They were all searched and scanned with some device. I think they were checking the contents of their inventory. For twenty minutes, the pirates dug through everything. They opened the safe in the captain's chambers and looked at everything in the bunks. They nabbed your geological analyzers and cleaned out half of Uline's bag. They found your Krechet carbine but didn't take it. I put it in my inventory after that. I'll give it back when we meet again... If we ever do, of course..."

Here Dmitry went silent again and looked embarrassed, lowering his eyes. Clearly, he didn't much believe two people could randomly meet in the endless expanse of space. When we'd reached the garden at the entrance to my residential building, the Starship Pilot finally ended his story:

"After the pirates left the Shiamiru, the old Navigator took control. We spent a long time flying somewhere, then docked at a big space station. I do not know what kind of place it is, but there are a lot of big Geckho combat ships there: cruisers, assault ships. I even saw a huge battleship. With my minimal understanding of Geckho, I believe I heard we are now waiting for Uraz Tukhsh and the other crew members to respawn and come rejoin the Shiamiru. I tried to say that you were stranded on the pirate station, and I think they understood. But I really don't know if the Geckho want to bat that hornet's nest again. I have learned Geckho swearing already, so I know the crew was not happy and was calling the captain names after he tried going to Medu-Ro IV in the first place... But enough about me. How are you doing, Gnat? You probably got it worse than me in that pirate lair, huh?"

I didn't even know what to answer. Should I tell him about taking trophy tails, molding a busty fox, selling platinum and gambling in a casino? It all sounded like a frivolous waste of time, especially after his heartrending tale. Sure, Gnat also had enough problems. I really was not sure anyone else from the H3 Faction could have wriggled out of the situation I found myself in, but I still needed to carefully consider what I should and should not say. Fortunately, no one demanded an immediate reply, and we had also arrived.

We didn't call the elevator and went upstairs. The door of my room was cracked open, and there was loud music, clinking glasses and jubilant voices inside.

"Huh, I guess they decided not to wait. I asked them not to start without the birthday boy..." Anya grumbled out unhappily, letting me walk in front.

My arrival was met by elated shouts and applause, while I smiled at the guests, answering their greetings and looking around the room. The couches and chairs were pushed into the table, which was laden with treats, including the whole contents of my mini-bar. The other half of the room was cleared for dancing, and the speaker system had been shoved into the corner. But most important, of course, was not the repositioning of my furniture. The number of guests was impressive!

Deputy leader Ivan Lozovsky had a glass of champagne in his hand and was sprawled out on a little sofa next to Svetlana the fitness trainer, who was gussied up in a glamorous evening dress. Next to them was the modest teacher's pet Masha, graciously serving salad to the man next to her, Kisly, who I was seeing in the real world for the first time. I immediately recognized him by his powerful musculature and characteristic square proportions.

The journalist Lydia Vertyachikh was sitting in a huge armchair, miraculously having made peace with the leader of the Second Legion. When I stopped nearby, Lydia whispered something in my little floor-mate's ear, and the usually serious and gloomy Tamara giggled like a schoolgirl. Based on their casual poses and half emptied glasses of wine, yesterday's quarrel was already in the past, and we didn't have to fear another scene.

On the opposite side of the table was hippie Artur, having changed his normal t-shirt and ratty jeans for a prim suit. He stepped aside and let Dmitry, Imran and Anya sit at the table. All the guests then pointed me to an armchair at the head of the table. As if by magic, just after I plopped down, a full shot glass appeared in my hand.

"So, I suggest we all raise a toast to the man that brought us all together today!" Kisly started loudly, standing up. "I can confidently say that there have never been as many incidents and protocol violations at the Antique Beach as when Gnat was on patrol! He crossed the border just once and look what it landed us! I still do not understand how Gnat didn't get kidnapped by the centaurs! But it ended for the best, and that's what matters! To Gnat!"

Everyone clinked glasses and drank. Imran, refraining because of his faith, gave me a salute with a cup of juice. Kisly then continued:

"By the way, Gnat, the centauress Phylira keeps asking for you. She wants to discuss something one-on-one. And she'll only speak with you. She doesn't trust anyone else. When you get back from outer space, drop by the Antique Beach. It might be worth your while. Phylira became top filly of her herd, so now you might say she's something of an official representative."

Dmitry Zheltov tried to jump in and say it was no longer clear if Gnat would ever return from his trip to space, but I stopped his depressing interjection with a gesture and made a promise:

"Alright, as soon as I'm back I'll drop by Antique Beach and meet with the Centaur elder female."

After that, the feast began. I gave a very condensed retelling of Gnat's story after the Shiamiru fled the station. The locked hangar, problems getting to the station, my two attempts to get past the Miyelonian Gladiator. Meeting the orange-furred Translator. Getting my pass. Shooting the Thief. Meeting the Morphian and prices on the space station. The Miyelonian assassin and the Morphian tearing him to shreds. The pilgrims and incarnation of the great female. The kitten. Searching for platinum buyers, which led me to the casino. The strange girl Valeri and her batty companion. Meeting the Trillian merchant. The head of the casino promising to provide a ship to come buy our platinum.

And although I skipped over many tricky aspects, not wanting to draw attention to how I had come by my platinum, cheated in the casino and my character's psionic abilities, they were all listening with rapt attention. Finally, I finished my tale, and nerdy Masha said her fill:

"I know I couldn't have done that. I would have immediately died of fear when I realized I was abandoned on a pirate station all alone."

"No one else could have," Ivan Lozovsky answered. "Gnat is a unique player. He exhibits a bizarre combination of risk-taking and pure calculation. Geckho Diplomat Kosta Dykhsh asks about his progress every time we meet and never tires of praising his gameplay."

The festivities continued, and I spoke with all the guests. The journalist had recorded my story on her voice recorder and came to ask permission to publish a short summary tomorrow for the faction bulletin, promising a boost of Fame and Authority.

Artur, who had gotten loaded pretty fast, slurred through thanking me for the invitation to the housewarming party and said sorry he had to go. I tried to convince him to stay, but my friend admitted he hadn't gotten good sleep in a while and was very tired. At the Prometheus, there was work to be done day and night, and he was spending practically all his time in the game, like many engineers and mechanics of the H3 Faction.

"We're working to forge the weapon of victory. But it's a big secret," he said mysteriously.

I led Artur to the door and, in the entryway, Tamara came up with two glasses of wine. She handed me one and tightly closed the door to the main room.

"I wouldn't want anyone to eavesdrop. Kirill, I wanted to say sorry for how I acted yesterday. I don't know what came over me. And I have to apologize again because I have to go. Actually, I should have left a while ago. Honestly, I'd be happy to stay at this party until morning, but there are serious problems with the base construction in Karelia, and I need to be there. Here's to your success, Gnat!"

She clinked glasses with me and decisively, in two big gulps, drained hers to the very bottom. Then she asked me to slightly lean in and close my eyes. I could sense the severe paladin cautiously placing her hands on my shoulders and awkwardly touching her wine-scented lips to my cheek. She didn't even object when I extended my hands, embraced her and kissed her back. But as soon as I peeled my eyes open, Tamara freed herself from the embrace, took a step back and started looking at the floor.

"Gnat, don't look me in the eyes! Alright, I gotta go. I really hope to see you at my birthday party!"

When I came back, there was a slow song playing. I was immediately asked to dance by Svetlana, who looked pretty in her deep-neckline emerald dress. She was a wonderful dancer, and her toned shoulders dipped elegantly in time to the music. Compared to her,

I must have looked like I had two left feet.

"Denis refused to come to your party, saying he had important business at the Prometheus," she whispered. "But I don't think he'd have come no matter what. For some reason, he just doesn't like you. It's obvious."

It took me some time to figure out who Svetlana was even talking about. Ah, that was it! Denis was the "gopnik" guy, who had been brought under the Dome with me and the other expelled students. Imran punished him for his rude language. Anya said that, at the Prometheus, the boorish and unsociable Denis was having conflicts with the other Engineers. I had to admit, I'd forgotten about him, because our paths had diverged on day one. But what did Denis have in common with Svetlana, and why was she telling me about him all of a sudden? I asked that with a smirk.

"Well, because Denis is trying to date me. He even came by and asked me out," she said with a happy chuckle, surprised I hadn't heard. "You should have been there, too. It was a riot! He put on a nice suit, got a bouquet, and walked up to me all dressed to the nines. But he couldn't get a word out! I warned Denis first thing that, if I heard even one bad word out of him, I'd slap him in the face with his own bouquet! But I don't think he knew how to express himself without cursing, so he froze up. Somehow, he squeezed out three whole sentences, but I could tell they were sincere. Denis does have brains, though. You can't take that away from him. And he's gifted with his hands, too! To hear him talk, leadership is nearly begging him, saying all the Faction's hopes and prayers are tied up in some 'Project-371,' which he is working to test and get into production. And he needs to get it done in the next six days!"

I had to admit, this was far out of my depth. What was this "project" that the faction leadership was "praying for," and why six days? Anyway, Artur had also mentioned constant serious work at the Prometheus, something about "forging the weapon of victory."

The music had been over for some time. The other couples had left the dance floor, and me and my partner were still standing and carrying on this strange conversation. Finally, I was distracted by Ivan Lozovsky who came up and pointed to two armchairs and a little table in the corner topped with a bottle of brandy, a sliced lemon and two shot glasses. He suggested I join him to "discuss important topics."

Chapter Eighteen

Political Agitation

IRST OF ALL, just after we sat down, I asked the diplomat about the strange six-day timeframe I kept hearing about. Ivan Lozovsky immediately grew more serious, stopped smiling and answered frankly:

"In six days, the ceasefire with the Dark Faction runs out. Our enemies cannot break the understanding and attack us before then. The Geckho are serving as guarantors, so the Dark Faction will just have to wait. But our spies are all saying another attack is inevitable. Their soldiers are training intensively 'round the clock. All their forces are drubbing away at the firing ranges, quickly levelling up and improving skills. The Dark Faction's last attack was a bitter pill for us. We held out mostly because of the tenacity and skill of the First Legion. All of our veterans were worth five enemies on the battlefield. But during this ceasefire, our enemy is trying to level the playing field in terms of soldier quality. And they have nearly triple our numbers!"

"Is it really that hopeless?" I asked, placing an empty glass on the table, which the diplomat refilled. "I mean, our soldiers probably aren't just sitting around doing nothing. They're also training, right? And from what I've heard, at the Prometheus, there are people working constantly to put the finishing touches on something called 'Project-371...'"

Before answering, Ivan Lozovsky took a digital notepad from his inner jacket pocket, opened a file and scrolled through a long table.

"Alriiight... Three hundred seventy-one. That means the leak came through Denis Tormashyov, an Engineer in laboratory eight... Antipov is gonna want to have a chat with that loose-lipped Engineer about the meaning of the words 'top secret.'"

Ivan Lozovsky made a note in his tablet, stashed it and returned to the topic of conversation:

"Of course, we're preparing to repel the attack. All our troops are working to reinforce our defenses in the most vulnerable places. And let me say this: in headquarters, we are constantly monitoring the situation in real time, moving people and vehicles from one sector to another whenever needed. We are practically sure that, by the time the ceasefire ends, our faction will be able to hold out. But the problem is that these preparations are eating up too many resources, and there's practically nothing left to build with. We've had to use almost all the resources that, in times of peace, might have gone to increasing node level by building bunkers, shelters, ammunition and mine fields. And meanwhile, we cannot just sit and wait, because that's not how you win a war!"

Here he led his eyes over the room. The music was roaring, and people were starting to shift to more energetic modern dances. Lozovsky lowered his voice:

"Gnat, given your status, you're entitled to know more than a common faction player. Yes, there are all kinds of projects underway at the Prometheus. But Radugin has the greatest hopes for thermobaric rounds. The firsts tests have obliterated the bloodthirsty beasts in a network of caves under the Capital node."

Ah, I'd heard of these caves. They were planning to send me there as a Prospector, but leadership had a change of heart and I went to the Geckho space port instead, after which my "space saga" began.

"Eventually, we will also have heavy rocket launcher systems like Buratino and Solntsepyok, enhanced bombs, and infantry flamethrowers, even high-caliber thermobaric shells. But that's for later. Our technicians can already make the shells, although they're pretty rough now and too big. But they're more than capable of taking out enemy manpower. There is the delivery problem, though. We don't have any rockets or aircraft. For now, we can use these new weapons only as radio-activated land mines. But when they blow, they destroy everything alive in a six-hundred-foot radius. Well... Try not to laugh, but we also have a catapult mounted on a Peresvet that can launch a barrel of napalm eighteen hundred to twenty thousand feet."

I wasn't even thinking of laughing. Sure it sounded weird, but a range of eighteen hundred feet was a significant improvement on nothing. There was one part that tickled me, though:

"That's all well and good, but the leaders of the Dark Faction are not idiots," I said, interrupting the verbose man who had gotten carried away with his monolog. "Even if we suppose that the existence a cache of large mines does not leak, and our soldiers do not blow themselves up because an enemy mage is controlling their mind, this tactic will only work once. Then the enemies will just respawn and attack through a pass they've already cleared."

The diplomat filled his glass with cognac again, and I immediately warned him it was the last for me. I was not a lover of strong alcohol, and my head was starting to buzz.

"Good choice, Gnat. You have the whole night ahead of you," the deputy smiled mysteriously, then returned to the previous topic. "Well, we don't think they're naive or stupid, either. We see the new weapons as a way of maintaining the status-quo on the front lines while we are weak and vulnerable."

"And what's next?" I cringed, barely having finished asking the short question because the alcohol, as they say, went down the wrong tube.

While I coughed it out, Ivan Lozovsky launched back into his expansive explanation:

"We have decent growth potential. For starters,

our new base in Karelia is practically ready to go. That will give our faction another eighty-seven players. We need people desperately and, believe you me, eighty-seven players will give a serious jolt to our development. Although it isn't all smooth sailing in Karelia. We still haven't gotten our oil production in the Eastern Swamp back online and have run into a fuel deficit plus another few unexpected difficulties. What's more, we can see the Dark Faction preparing to expand into the node neighboring Karelia, the Poppy Fields. The day after tomorrow, their agreement not to station military forces there will expire, and we expect them to start building a base as soon as possible. And much to our chagrin, they will be able to finish building it before the end of the ceasefire, and we have no way to stop them."

I imagined the node map in my head and immediately realized how much worse our position would become after the enemies built that new base:

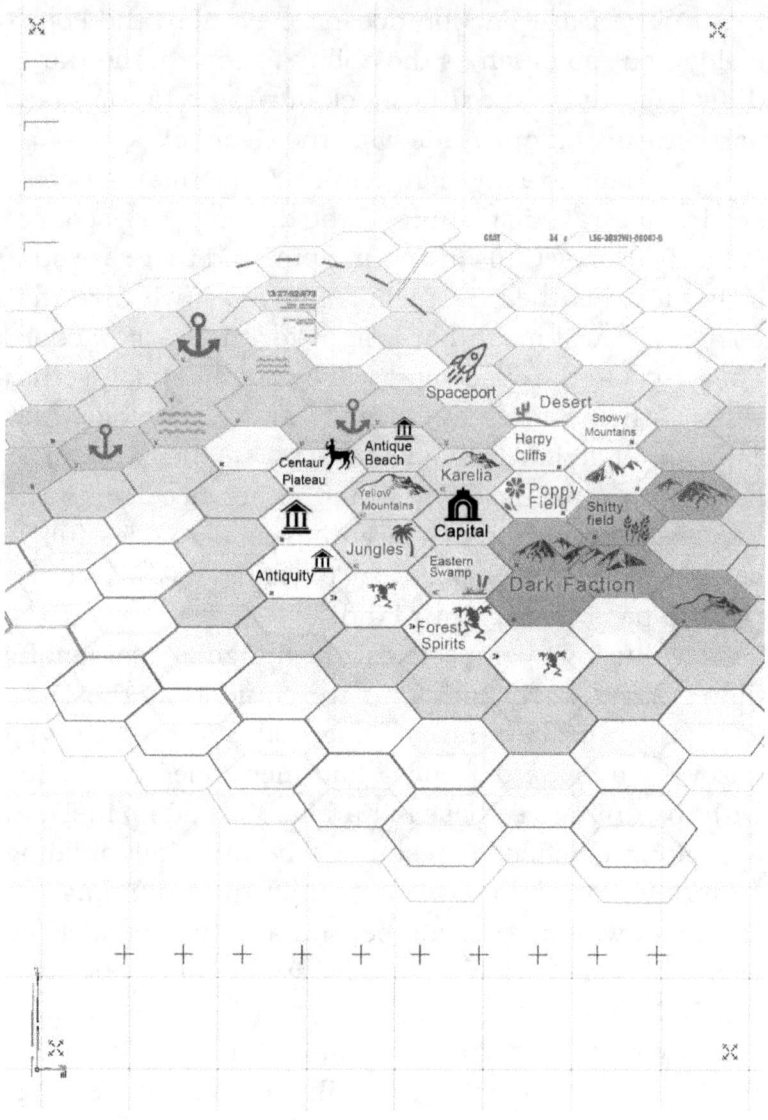

"The Dark Faction doesn't even need the Poppy Fields node so much as the ability to control the Harpy Cliffs from there and fully block our route to the space port, cutting off our trade with the Geckho!"

"That's exactly right, Gnat. You're making great strides in strategic planning," the diplomat praised me. "Yes, the Harpy Cliffs are a linchpin, and there are sure to be fierce battles for them. After all, if we take that territory, it will mean hard times for the Dark Faction. Their road to the space port will be cut off and, together with it, their source of currency and technology. And the Dark Faction has no sea port, so they'd be even harder up than us. They would either need to go the long way through four nearly impassible nodes full of aggressive NPC's or come to us and kowtow for the right to pass through our land."

Alluring perspectives, although I personally didn't have much faith that we could beat the Dark Faction to the key Harpy Cliffs node. Also, both Ivan Lozovsky and Gerd Tamara had mentioned hardships with the unfinished base in Karelia. We had no fuel and a profound deficit of resources because all building materials and manpower were tied up rebuilding the Eastern Swamp. After all, beyond a central citadel, we would also need to build roads, supply lines and a lot of other stuff...

We had a six-day head start on the Dark Faction. That might seem like a serious leg up. However, they had plenty of resources and significantly more people, including many times more noncombat players. Something was telling me the Dark Faction would finish up before us, then be first to expand into the Harpy Cliffs. Ugh, if not for the ceasefire, we could attack the darksider base while it was still vulnerable and unfinished. I'd seen some fortifications of ours that were attacked before completion before. In fact, a group of Centaurs managed to raze it to the ground. And that meant that NPC's could destroy player-built structures...

Actually, speaking of NPC's... I considered it, then asked how much one tank of napalm weighed.

"Different amounts. From around four hundred fifty to eighteen hundred pounds. Why do you ask?"

"We could pay the harpies to throw them down on the enemy base from the sky, hopefully a couple. Naturally, we would give our enemies a couple days to transport in all their materials and begin construction, then blow up all the people and stuff. And it wouldn't come back on us. What do we care what some NPC's get up to in a neutral node?"

He spent some time just blinking in silence, not able to answer. But then he smiled, showing a row of ideally white and even teeth:

"Gnat, that just might work!!! Harpies are strong, and two or three of them together could easily lift one of those bombs. And they wouldn't have to fly very far. It's just two and a half miles from their roost! But then comes the issue of payment. I'm afraid that they'll ask for too much. We might not have the crystals..."

"Ivan, why pay them in crystals?! I'm sure all it would take is a box of dried rations big enough to feed the whole flock. A harpy sold me a laser pistol for three ration briquettes. So for a whole box of tasty human grub, not only will they go, they'll sing songs and recite dirty limericks in the language of the Dark Faction while they do it. But there is one hazard: we need to make sure these wing-armed bastards don't 'accidentally' drop some of the bombs on our unfinished base in Karelia. Those lowdown harpies would just love that!"

"Yes, it really is their style," the diplomat agreed. "The harpies mistrust all humans equally, so they'll definitely try some tricks. But we have just the thing: long-distance detonators. If any part of the harpy flock tries to deviate from the route, we just blast them to smithereens. Then they'll see what happens to those who try and pull a fast one on us!"

But if even we couldn't make a beneficial agreement with the clever and cunning harpies, trying to work with our faction's NPC neighbors was an obvious next step. I suggested the diplomat talk with the Centaurs and other members of the Antiquity Faction. It was entirely possible that our neighbors could help us build, transport materials and guard our lands. And we'd find a way to pay them.

"I already know how we could pay the Centaurs. The whole faction knows. After your attempt to trade went up in flames, Kisly explained Phylira her mistake and started a whole enterprise selling giant condoms to the centaurs. They brought in a big box from the real world, and it'll be enough for many years to come. Plus, they generally appreciate vodka as well as blacksmith services. Otherwise, their unshod hooves quickly wear down on the rocks. At any rate, we can find things to offer them. Payment will not be our issue here. The problem is going to be language and leadership... but I'm sure we'll work things out."

In a burst of unexpected openness, Ivan Lozovsky, already quite drunk, admitted that faction leader Radugin had been asking analysts to predict the outcome of a war with the centaurs. The H3 Faction needed more nodes. But to the west, our territory came up against the sea shore. To the north and northeast we had the abominable Dark Faction. And the east and southeast contained only impenetrable swamps inhabited by vicious forest spirits and kikimora.

There were just two other paths. We could go northwest along the sea to Karelia, the Harpy Cliffs and onward to the Geckho space port, which was the preferred option. Or we could expand south by fighting our way through defended mountain passes into the Antiquity Faction's lands, starting a bloody war of extermination with endless hordes of strong fast centaurs, powerful minotaurs and elusive dryads shooting poison darts. Our analysts did not favor that option. We could not expect a fast victory, while a war on two fronts might lead to our forces being spread thin. And that could weaken our border with the Dark Faction, which would end our faction in no time.

After all, on first glance it seemed that having firearms would give people an indisputable advantage over the NPC Antiquity faction, which was still mired in the epoch of bow and arrow. However, in the game that bends reality, a technological advantage was not the boon you might imagine. Just one minotaur with a bronze axe could crush machine-gunners to dust in close combat. Sure, NPC's didn't respawn after dying, but they leveled and improved skills at least ten times faster, so they could replace a downed comrade with three no less dangerous compatriots in a matter of days.

The more I heard from the diplomat, the more alarmed I felt. Apparently, it was not too smart for us to use force in this case. We would have to find some other way.

"And the other factions from our earth cannot help us? I heard someone mention the Chinese near the Geckho space port. Probably, we could link up with some other ones, too."

The diplomat gave another sad look, this time without returning to a smile:

"No luck for now. We haven't been able to establish contact with any factions from our world inside the game. In the real world, we know from military reconnaissance that Australia has begun demolishing their secret Virtual Corn base near Perth. The Human-11 faction is already totally defeated. As far as we know, their nodes were attacked by enemies that sound an awful lot like the Dark Faction. We also have some info on their coordinates, but it places them thousands of miles from our territory. That means it cannot have been Leng Thumor-Anhu La-Fin's faction."

"What makes you so sure?" I asked. The diplomat responded that they had interrogated some of the Dark Faction soldiers taken prisoner in Karelia, and finally gleaned that they controlled a total of five nodes, with a sixth in the Poppy Fields in the planning stage. Try as they might, our neighbors wouldn't have been able to reach the Australians.

So, a mystery... As it turned out, either the darksiders had multiple factions, or there was some unknown third power. Ivan Lozovsky had nothing definite to say. There was just too little information.

"Our real-world spies have informed us of the coordinates of all seven H4 nodes. That's Japan. Their only neighbors are NPC's. They're doing great and growing fast. They've already managed to get four thousand characters into the game. But the Japanese are also very far away, so we won't be able to meet with them any time soon."

Here we had to stop for a bit. Imran came to say goodbye. He had to patrol the pass between the Yellow Mountains and the lands of the wild centaurs at first shift, which was rapidly approaching. Imran proudly told us that his Gladiator had already reached level thirty and increased Strength and Agility two times each.

The Dagestani athlete gave me a warm hug farewell and said with a note of reproach:

"Gnat, don't forget your old friends! When you get back from space, call me and Anna to join your division. We'll come and help with whatever you want!"

I thanked Imran for the support and trust, then told him I had a special gift for him: a fearsome sickle-shaped Miyelonian blade, specially made for a Gladiator. It was forged of a very light and flexible alloy, razor sharp and every blow hit the target with a powerful electric shock, paralyzing them for a few seconds.

"As far as I know, it requires Agility at twenty

and Blades either forty or forty-three..."

"I've got plenty of Agility, but Blades'll need to be brought up a bit. Now at least I know what to level and where to put my skill points!" With these words, clearly heartened, Imran nearly ran to his Corncob.

As soon as I returned, I was intercepted by Anya and taken off to dance. I tried to refuse, but the blonde beauty made the fair excuse that I was the only man left. Ivan Lozovsky was too embarrassed to dance and claimed he was too drunk for fancy footwork. The other gentlemen were all taken. Kisly had been dancing with Masha all night, and Lydia Vertyachikh had been all over Dmitry Zheltov. She wouldn't let anyone else near him.

I turned to the dancing couple and managed to make out what they were sweet-talking about. I was surprisingly able to make out their words despite the muted voices, loud music and appreciable distance between us. That was very strange, and I was only able to find one explanation: my high Perception in the game that bends reality must have improved my hearing, vision and smell in the real world. Well, that was quite a nice bonus!

Anyway, the Journalist, skillfully alternating praise and feminine wiles, was clearly fishing for a big all-night interview with the heroic starship pilot. I made out some familiar turns of phrase about tossing a coin ten times. Dmitry Zheltov, letting his hands wander and feel up all the tempting curves of her feminine body, clearly was not opposed, promising to tell and show her everything. He even took it a step farther and said he'd like to "give a pretty lady a ride on his rocket ship."

Hmm... I felt awkward prying into their lives and turned to Anya, who was still trying to convince me. I wasn't feeling stubborn and let the pretty blonde pull me onto the dance floor. The music changed again, now a slow dance. Anya placed her hands on my shoulders and squeezed her whole body up against mine, then unexpectedly whispered that she felt really good, and wished she could celebrate with me until sunrise. I wanted that too, which I whispered back.

"Alright, it's decided! We can party and dance until we pass out! But first, I need to go back to my room to grab some... lipstick. Wait here..." Anya smiled and met gazes with me.

In her expanded pupils, I saw a reflection of my own glimmering blue eyes and immediately turned away, not wanting to read her thoughts and spoil all the intrigue.

"Kirill, I've heard you traded something with the Centaurs in the game, would you happen to have any more of them?"

"Don't you worry about that. There are a few packs in the drawer under the mini-bar. So, you don't have to go 'get lipstick,' there is plenty of 'lipstick' here. I've got extra sensitive lipstick, strawberry-scented lipstick and studded lipstick," I chuckled. Then, no longer embarrassed, I pulled her decisively toward me and gave her a big kiss on the lips.

"Great!" Anya laughed after our faces finally came unstuck. "Let's wait for everyone to go home, then we can figure out what kind of 'lipstick' works best."

Chapter Nineteen

Main Suspect

I WOKE UP around midday, which was not too surprising. Anya and I had "tested lipstick" until sunrise, only sometimes taking short breaks from our amorous delights to dance in the nude, horse around throwing pillows at one another and get up to other tomfoolery. I surprised myself. Maybe it was just too long since I'd been with a girl, or maybe Gnat's Constitution had grown enough in the game to have an effect in the real world, but I was simply tireless on that wonderful night. And Anya was a passionate, capable and insatiable lover, so we both had "met our match" as they say. Locked in the most ancient form of one-on-one combat, neither of us was willing to surrender. Only when the day lighting turned did we remember we would have to stop and use the bed and pillows to sleep.

Anya was sleeping sweetly on my bed, and I

didn't wake her up. After taking a shower and quickly snarfing down some leftovers from yesterday's feast, I hurried to leave. By my estimations, the religious ceremony on Medu-Ro IV should have been over already. So, now was the right time to enter the game, meet the Pride of the Bushy Shadow, and come to an agreement on the price of the precious metal and other conditions of our important deal. I was not particularly worried about the negotiations, because the casino owner told me he had his own captain as backup. So, if the Pride of the Bushy Shadow offered less than stellar terms, there was always another option.

At the exit from the secure building, I was joined by an escort provided by faction leadership, and two soldiers supplied by Gerd Tamara. I had no objections, of course, because the Dark Faction bounty was still in place, and the danger was very real. At any rate, I was not planning to hang around in the real world. I wanted to go straight to my virt pod and immediately load up the game, but there were people waiting for me outside.

A strong young boy in an athletic suit stood up when I approached. He was freckled, and his hair was so bright red it looked unnatural. What was more, it was apparently real. I stopped the bodyguards with a gesture, who were trying to chase the stranger off, then allowed him to come closer.

"Greetings, Gerd Gnat!" said the man, extending a strong calloused hand. "I am Eduard Boyko, I'm sure leadership told you about me."

Eduard Boyko? Didn't ring a bell... No, I was definitely hearing this name for the first time, and I honestly admitted that.

"Strange. I am usually held up alongside Dmitry Zheltov as an example of someone who chose the wrong class. I am our faction's Space Commando!"

Everything became clear at once. I even whistled in surprise. Just look what poor Eduard got himself into! Yes, I had heard about this useless faction member from Tyulenev, although the former head of staffing hadn't told me his name. Boyko took in my astonishment and gave a tortured chuckle:

"I can see you're also struck. Yes, my game class is Space Commando! And our faction doesn't have a single starship, landing module, or landing system of any kind. And we don't have any power armor or other crap like that, either..."

"Sure we have power armor!" I objected, referring to Gerd Tamara's suit.

"Yes, our whole faction has one suit of power armor, and it belongs to Gerd Tamara. But she's leader of the Second Legion, a legend and savior, so she has earned it. But no one is going to buy another gizmo like that, it's unimaginably expensive! I cannot use any other types of armor though and, beyond that, without a powered exoskeleton, I cannot wield a heavy weapon... So overall, that leaves me with no armor and no weapon. Now, instead of a combat character, I'm just a grunt. I pick up building debris, clean out irrigation ditches and watch the fields for pests."

"Hrm, that's a shame. And what other class did the game offer you, if it's not a secret?" I asked, just curious. He waved his hand fatedly:

"Sure, I've got nothing to hide... I could have been a Machine Gunner, which would have been great for the faction. I was such a dumbass. I just grabbed for the cool name and picked Space Commando! I've been in the game for six months already. I was actually one of the first people under the Dome. My number is just eighty-four. As a matter of fact, Gerd Tarasov and I entered together. But look where he is now — a real star, a record-setter! But in my six months, I've only managed to crawl along to level thirty-three. That's also a record of sorts, but not the good kind..."

It was all a very sad story, but I didn't understand what it had to do with me. Eduard, pumping his impressive biceps, which were visible through the track suit, answered that question with extreme honesty:

"Well, who else can I turn to if not the player who managed to crawl out of shit just as deep and make it big? I admit, I used to laugh at you. I remember thinking, that's a good one, now we've got a Prospector, too! With no scanner or class junk, he can be my partner clearing muck from the canals. But then I looked again, and Gnat had gotten off that path! After that, you pulled Dmitry Zheltov out of the same hole, and he became another man overnight. Now he's proud, self-confident and even getting interviewed. I gave it some serious thought and figured I'd ask if you can get me power armor and weapons, so I could finally do my job as a player. If you can, you'll never find yourself a more loyal companion! To hell with the faction and all the leadership, I'd follow you to the ends of the Universe!"

With that, Eduard thought he'd said his fill and gave me a shoulder slap goodbye with his heavy hand.

That made my legs slightly buckle, and my bodyguards sharply straightened up. But the muscular man just didn't know his own strength and had no bad intentions.

On the way to the corncob, I was thinking over his offer. As a recently-anointed Gerd, I now needed likeminded companions. It certainly couldn't hurt to have such a powerful warrior as Space Commando Eduard on the newly forming Team Gnat. But I had no idea how to fulfill his request. I wasn't likely to find an exoskeleton power-armor suit for a human on the Medu-Ro IV station. Maybe I could get a Geckho armor suit redone for him? Hard to say. I would need to consult with some experienced mechanics. Also, it was impossible to say how much the raw material would cost. Ugh, I should have asked Gerd Tamara. Most likely, her suit was a "retrofitted" Geckho armor suit, but I couldn't be sure. It would be nice to make sure that was even possible before wasting a ton of my personal savings, though.

SO, THE FOURTEENTH FLOOR of corncob fifteen, my virt pod, loading up the game. My detailed statistics came up:

Gerd Gnat. Human. H3 Faction.	
Level-51 Prospector	
Statistics:	
Strength	13
Agility	16

Intelligence	23
Perception	26
Constitution	15
Luck modifier	+3
Parameters:	
Hitpoints	1464 of 1464
Endurance points	811 of 811
Magic points	175 of 175
Carrying capacity	58 lbs.
Fame	42
Skills:	
Electronics	36
Scanning	44
Cartography	47
Astrolinguistics	60
Break-in	21
Rifles	42
Mineralogy	26
Medium Armor	43
Eagle Eye	51
Sharpshooter	27
Targeting	11
Danger Sense	23
Psionic.	13
Attention! No skill chosen	-
Attention! No skill chosen	-

Yes, I needed to figure out what to do with the two unoccupied slots as soon as possible. As for one of them, I was almost sure. Either Mental Fortitude or Mysticism, because my recently manifested psionic abilities needed to some augmenting, no question. Both options had their advantages and flaws, and I couldn't allow myself both, because it would be wasteful. After all, there were a ton of other useful skills. For example, I was still considering Trade, because knowing prices could be very beneficial.

So, loading up... Why so dark?

Fame increased to 43.

Fame increased to 44.

Fame increased to 45.

Authority increased to 9.

A whole bedsheet of messages ran before my eyes. Plus three Fame?! I simply couldn't believe my eyes. Had all this growth come from the Journalist publishing the story of Gnat's adventures? I wasn't convinced. There was probably some other reason...

Danger Sense skill increased to level twenty-four!

I didn't even have time to feel afraid, much less get my bearings or take any measures before I received a hard blow to the side of my legs and collapsed to the floor. At that, an unknown being next to me thrashed my back with something hard, then grabbed my fallen body by the hair and shoved my face into the floor. My health bar fell by a third, and a new portion of system messages ran by before my eyes:

Failed Agility check!

Failed Constitution check!

Disoriented! Duration: 25 seconds.

Stunned! Duration: 2 minutes 18 seconds.
Paralysis! Duration: 11 seconds.
Bleeding! You will lose 4 health every 3 seconds for 52 seconds.

What an entrance... I still hadn't seen anything, but it seemed there were several attackers. I mean, it couldn't have been just one. Even the fastest enemy wouldn't be able to do all that! And although I had enough Hitpoints not to worry about dying from blood loss, I was dumbfounded and writhing on the floor in vain attempts to move or stand. As if in mockery, at that very tense moment, the game offered me some new abilities:

Would you like to take the skill Dodge?
Would you like to take the skill Hand-to-Hand Combat?
Would you like to take the skill Survival?

Such bad timing! I still couldn't understand what was happening, and these pop-ups were breaking my concentration! Meanwhile, my hands were pulled behind my back, and something like a bag of thick crinkling foil was lowered over my head. Whoever this was, they didn't want to kill me, just take me alive. But what for?

Just then, I realized this might all be to steal my money. I did in fact, have a huge amount of it, almost sixty thousand crypto. And many of the cutthroats that called this station home would have committed just about any crime to get it. But now, immobilized, nothing was stopping the attackers from cleaning out my inventory. I nearly howled in impotence...

I was reminded that the casino owner had

promised to protect me so long as I remained on the Medu-Ro IV station. That meant I could go to her and demand she punish these attackers. But before that, I needed to see who they were!

I still couldn't move my arms or legs, but I could activate Scanning, and the thick bag on my head was no impediment. On the mini-map around me, I saw not just one or two red markers as I assumed, but a grand total of eight! And they all had very similar, and equally astonishing descriptions:

Rani Ust-Amiru. Miyelonian. First Pride. Level-201 Assassin.

Duamii Lei-Amiru. Miyelonian Female. First Pride. Level-211 Warrior.

...

[Information hidden]

Dinaya Stork-Amiru. Miyelonian Female. First Pride. Level-255 Bodyguard.

First Pride??? The white-armored elite guard the orange Translator told me about with gasps of admiration? But this was the cream of the crop on this station! They protected the four incarnations of the Great First Female. Also, based on their names, these eight were part of Priestess Leng Amiru U-Mayaoo's guard team.

I found myself in complete incomprehension. Most likely, the First Pride was not interested in my valuables. I checked and yes, my inventory was still intact, even though there was nothing stopping them from taking everything. Bound by the hands and feet, I was lifted up roughly and dragged off. I quickly lost track of where I was. The bag was obstructing my vision. My mini-map wasn't updating, and my Eagle Eye and Cartography skills weren't growing. All I could do was try and listen to my escorts as they exchanged occasional clipped phrases. I just barely knew Miyelonian, but still I managed to make out the words "main suspect." Also, they were overflowing with rage and itching to tear me to shreds right then and there. Apparently, this was worse than I thought.

Astrolinguistics skill increased to level sixty-one!

Well, that's positive at least... Meanwhile, based on the sounds and sensations, our group seemed to be entering an elevator, which quickly shot off upward. Up??? Strange. The space port zone and docked ships were below the residential floor. But above... What was even up there? Well, perhaps the main station, but you couldn't take an elevator there. You had to walk down many long halls and pass careful checks. Although I was reminded of something Ayni said: for the great Priestess Leng Amiru U-Mayaoo, they had opened a direct elevator to the station. But was my modest Prospector really worthy of the honor of a mode of transportation inaugurated specifically for the incarnation of the Miyelonians' Great First Female?

More corridors followed, then another elevator, and the opaque bag was finally pulled off my face. A bright light slammed into my eyes and, while I was getting used to it, my handcuffs were removed, and the guards walked away. I blinked and managed to look around.

I found myself on a tiny round platform just two steps in diameter surrounded by a cylindrical forcefield humming and flickering with electricity. What was this? A cage? A prison cell? I raised my head and, at the level of a raised hand, discovered a video camera. I was being observed, which was not too surprising after the strange arrest.

The forcefield was flickering brightly in different colored bursts, preventing me from seeing anything beyond it. But I still tried to look through. I spent a minute just staring in different directions until my eyes hurt. No. I was forced to admit that, even with my high Perception, I couldn't see anything. I could only tell that it was a fairly large room, because I couldn't see any walls. Also, it looked like my cage was not the only one. I could kind of make out another few flickering columns nearby.

What to do? Just keep standing stupidly, playing a caged zoo animal? Exit the game? I saw that this was a red zone and decided against it. My character wouldn't disappear and would only be rendered helpless. So, what to do?

My Scanning ability reloaded, and I immediately used it. My guesses about the size of the room and number of cages were immediately confirmed. Now this was interesting. I managed to read the names of the arrestees in the neighboring cells. I knew them all!!! The bushy-tailed Translator Ayni Uri-Miayuu, the Trillian merchant Gerd Ussh Veesh, that strange girl Valeri-Urla, and her bully companion Denni Marko. What was more, Valeri's cage also contained a large animal, which I saw as:

Little Sister. Shadow Panther (creature). Pet of Valeri-Urla. Level 79.

Clearly, the prisoner selection was not random.

If Fox and Tini were here, we'd have everyone my character had interacted with on the pirate station. Seemingly, the Miyelonians had quickly found Gnat's social circle and rounded them all up. But why?

I tried to speak with Ayni and figure out what was going on. But the orange Translator's reaction was very unexpected:

"Gnat?! How dare you talk to me after what you did?! Because I helped you, I am cursed with eternal shame and have been kicked out of my pride!"

"Are you delirious, Ayni? How could I have even done anything? I haven't been in the game for two ummi! And before that, we were together the whole time I walked through the station, talked with the locals and gambled in the casino. But none of those things can be called illegal, no matter how you slice it!"

"And you have the nerve to try and lie your way out of it?! Your pet killed the Priestess Leng Amiru U-Mayaoo right in the middle of her speech before hundreds of thousands of pilgrims here on the station and billions of viewers throughout the galaxy!"

What?! My heart seized in fear. So, the shit had well and truly hit the fan... My arrest no longer looked like a dumb coincidence and now smelled of the most serious troubles not only for me personally, but humanity as a whole. Those of my world, the Dark Faction, the Gilvar Syndicate, Tailax, it wouldn't matter... Fox had just spit right in the face of billions of Miyelonian religious fanatics, and they would not care about the subtle difference between human factions. They would want revenge on all members of my race, even though an assassination in the game only threatened their holy Priestess with a fifteen-minute break.

"If you're talking about the hungry beast I fed in the cafe, it wasn't my pet!" I said, trying to justify myself. "Ayni, you must remember when you issued me a pass. I was all alone then. The animal joined up with me here on the station and walked with me for some time, pestering me for more food. But then it ran away, and I have no idea where it went!"

"I don't believe a single word! It was definitely your pet. You even insisted that you could call it back at any moment! I was there. Your pet constantly protected you and even killed an Assassin from the Pride of the Heavenly Warrior! So, you won't worm your way out of this by trying to lie and deny knowing your own pet! And before that, you lied to me when getting the pass! Captain Gerd Setis-Vir said that you were never part of his crew! All you do is lie!!!"

Yikes, it had all come together so badly... Very badly... For now, I hadn't lost hope that I could prove my innocence, but how? Above all, I should probably claim that Fox was just a stupid stray animal, who followed me for a short time, and nothing remained to connect us. It was definitely not a good idea to mention that Fox and I had spoken. Otherwise, I was afraid it would be practically impossible to convince my Miyelonian captors that I was not conspiring with the Morphian.

I gathered my thoughts and tried to speak calmly.

"Ayni, I have never lied to you. Sure, I neglected to point out your error when you were filling in my ship info for the pass. Yes, my ship actually was the Shiamiru. But first of all, I noticed the error too late, and second, I didn't think it was a big enough deal to mess with the whole bureaucratic machine. As for when I called it my pet... think back to when that happened. Three pissed off members of the Pride of the Heavenly Warrior had just tracked me down with the worst of intentions, and the only thing stopping them was a dangerous animal they thought belonged to me. Naturally, I tried my best to support their confusion. And... by the way, I can prove that the animal that killed your Priestess was not my pet!"

The proof that came to mind was as simple as it was irrefutable. I was surprised it hadn't come to me earlier. After all, one of the four incarnations of the Great First Female, worshipped by billions of subjects and having achieved the respectable rank of Leng, simply physically could not be low-level. Then, while technically my pet, the creature had killed the level-76 Assassin Ayuk Ukh Miiyauu, whose luxuriant tail now decorated my helmet. That had given me a level up. So, how many levels would I theoretically if my pet had killed the great Priestess? But I was still the same level as when I exited, fifty-one!

Just for curiosity's sake, I asked Ayni what level Amiru U-Mayaoo was. The Translator refused to answer. The Trillian Merchant was more talkative, though. Gerd Ussh Veesh said that Leng Amiru U-Mayaoo had recently reached level two-hundred sixty, a fact he learned from the news.

Mother of my wife! Level two hundred sixty!!! I was afraid to even imagine how long one would need to play to reach such unimaginable heights. I tried to distract myself from these intrusive thoughts and turned toward Beast Master Valeri-Urla.

"Valeri, I need your advice as an expert in animal control..."

But Denni shot out angrily that she did not wish to speak with a primitive outworlder, and especially a bloodthirsty murderer. But then, a soft pleasant female voice sounded out, speaking Geckho with a very clean accent:

"Wait, Denni! I think I know what Gnat wants. Also, I cannot sense evil in him. So, let him speak!"

"Thank you, Valeri!" I said, heartened. Then I continued. "Let's say purely theoretically that your Shadow Panther Little Sister managed to maul a level two-hundred sixty enemy. I understand that would be impossible, but still. How many levels would you gain as the owner of that pet?"

There was no answer to my question for a very long time, and I figured Valeri-Urla was simply refusing to reply. But as it turned out, she just needed time to make an accurate calculation. A minute and a half later, the girl gave a detailed conclusion:

"If using only one pet with my current statistics, I would gain forty-four levels. If *you* had one pet do it and, if I remember correctly from the casino, you were level fifty or fifty-one, you would be around one hundred right now if you really were guilty."

"One hundred and two by my calculations," the Trillian merchant piped up.

A long silence fell, then Ayni timidly asked what level my character was now. I answered honestly that I was just fifty-one, just like when I said goodbye to her and exited the game. I didn't manage to even finish the sentence before the forcefield around my cell turned off along with all the others. From somewhere in the floor, an emotionless mechanical voice prattled out in Geckho:

"Ambiguous situation. A serious error may have been made. Given the gravity of the crime, we must convene the collegium of Truth Seekers. The status of the human Gerd Gnat has been reclassified from 'main suspect,' to 'key witness.' The status of Ayni Uri-Miayuu has been reclassified from 'coconspirator' to 'key witness.' Gerd Gnat and Ayni Uri-Miayuu, please come to the neighboring room to speak with the Truth Seekers. Everyone else is free to go."

Chapter Twenty

Along the Blade of a Knife

THE SITUATION STARTED looking somewhat better, but I understood perfectly that it was not over yet. Talking with the mysterious Truth Seekers could end either in Gnat's exoneration, or the uncovering of trouble spots. And there were plenty of those. The most important thing, beyond all doubt, was how well I actually knew the Morphian. That fact had to be hidden at any cost. But even without that, I had plenty to conceal from the nosy Miyelonians, starting with my invaluable Relict artefacts and ending with my Psionic abilities.

Ayni and I were led down a long hallway. An escort of high-level First Pride soldiers stayed twenty steps behind us. Seemingly, they didn't want to spook us, so we would have time to think over our actions before meeting the Truth Seekers. The orange lady cat walking next to me was quaking in panic. There had been a big breakthrough, though: the bushy-tailed Translator was no longer recoiling from my touch as if I had the plague. Now, she just walked next to me at an arm's length. And I reached out to her, touching her shoulder in a gesture of reassurance:

"Don't you worry, Ayni! Neither you or I are guilty of anything, and we will now explain that to the investigators... or who are we going to see?"

Her reaction to my light amicable touch was very strange. The orange cat suddenly stopped, turned around and buried her snout in my shoulder while mewing softly and piteously like a lost kitten. I froze in indecision, not knowing what to do. I could feel with my whole body that the Miyelonian lady was quaking like an aspen leaf, and I figured she needed consolation. Very carefully, afraid to accidentally break some taboo whether cultural, psychological or otherwise, I embraced the furry lady and squeezed her close. Fortunately, she did not object, and the white-armored soldiers stopped delicately and didn't intervene.

"Gnat, I feel very bad! I'm afraid!" Ayni admitted. She was speaking her native language, but I still managed to understand somewhat. "I... (incomprehensible) cannot return to my Pride... (long phrase I didn't understand any of, she was speaking too fast and unintelligibly) ... shame... (incomprehensible) ... Amiru... (incomprehensible) ... everyone saw ... they will not forgive."

I tried to console her also in Miyelonian.

Choosing my words in the barely familiar language carefully and probably butchering them horribly, I told Ayni not to despair. At the first sounds of my voice, she shuddered and seemingly came to her senses, because she immediately stepped away and switched to Geckho.

"Forgive my weakness, Gnat, I shouldn't let out my emotions like that. It's just that, as you probably already know, I'm filled with desperate sorrow. Just think, billions of my compatriots watched me kill the exulted Priestess Amiru on live television! The horrible scenes were shown on every channel in the galaxy an infinite number of times, showing my face again and again, and savoring every detail of the horrible slaying. And it doesn't even matter that I didn't do the crime. Everyone in the galaxy has seen my face now and will associate it with a gruesome murder!!!"

Hrm... not a great situation, to be honest. Although I could barely stop myself from asking a logical follow-up: if the killer looked like Ayni during the attack, what had led them all back to me? But it was good I didn't ask. Such a phrasing of the question could lead the obviously intelligent Ayni to the idea that I knew Morphians could change shape. What was more, no one had told me the murderer's race, so I'd be giving away too much.

Instead, I asked her a totally neutral question about her plans for the future.

"I don't know yet. I don't want to make any distant plans until after I talk with the Truth Seekers. You see, Gnat, I've spoken with Truth Seekers twice before, and I can tell you that it is a very unpleasant and painful procedure. Not physically painful but... how to put it... emotionally I guess."

"Emotionally?"

"Yes. The Truth Seekers root around in your head and bring your darkest and most dubious actions, thoughts and memories to the fore. They make you relive difficult and painful events, reexperience your hardest and meanest decisions. And all of that is held up for all to see, comment on, savor... They turn you inside out, you see yourself as concentrated nastiness, evil, and filth. And you cannot close yourself off to it, either. It is impossible to lie, that's why they call them Truth Seekers. They can detect falseness. You have to go through the whole procedure from beginning to end and admit every time you've ever broken a law or moral precept, or even considered it. It's very hard to live with that. You start to despise and hate yourself... I very much hope you're right, and you and I can prove that we were not involved in the murder of the great Priestess. Otherwise, I'm afraid I simply will not be able to live with the heavy burden. Only after it all ends for the best will I think about the future."

It should be said that her gloomy description of the upcoming procedure made me even more nervous. Meanwhile, we had already passed the long straight corridor and were now in a small dusky circular room. A blinding white spotlight streamed down from above on only the very middle of the floor, leaving thick shadows along the walls. Nevertheless, I could see fifteen chairs arranged in a semicircle, each occupied by a figure shrouded head to toe in black robes. I couldn't read information on a single one of them...

Eagle Eye skill increased to level fifty-two!
Scanning skill increased to level forty-five!
You have reached level fifty-two!
You have received three skill points!

I activated Scanning, which also gave me no additional information about the mysterious Truth Seekers, leaving me only more confused. Those shadowy characters weren't even on my mini-map! How was that possible?!

Lying on the floor, right in the middle of the bright light, folded up like a donut and covering his head with his hands, Tini Wi-Gnat was sobbing. It seemed like my kitten had just taken a long and hard beating. He looked tormented and pitiful. Then, staring at my foundling with horror, Ayni whispered that this was what she was talking about.

"I'm very scared, Gnat. I could hardly survive a conversation with one Truth Seeker, but here there are many..."

Two fearsome First Pride soldiers walked out into the middle of the room, grabbed the underage level-24 Thief by the arms and pulled him away. He was clearly totally out of it. The very same dispassionate mechanical voice rang out and ordered Ayni Uri-Miayuu to stand in the center of the circle.

THEY WERE SPEAKING in Miyelonian, so I didn't even understand a tenth of what they were asking Ayni, or what she answered. But from my perspective, it looked really abhorrent. Just three minutes in, she was on her knees. Then she got on all fours and howled, as if in sharp pain. This was definitely not for the faint of heart! I had to admit, a few times I even felt like running into the circle to stop the sadistic torture.

I didn't, though. I understood that would only make things worse. But in that onerous moment, I decided I did not want to be tortured like that. I did not want them digging in my head. So, I finally and irreversibly chose a skill. I needed Mental Fortitude!!! After all, that would not only strengthen my psionic attacks, it improved my defenses against that same kind of magic.

You have taken the skill Mental Fortitude level 1.

I didn't even have time to appreciate the new skill before I got a message:

Mental Fortitude skill increased to level two!

What was more, my progress bar was going up very fast, right before my eyes. That meant not all the Truth Seekers were reading Ayni. Some of them were spying on me this whole time! I was being psionically attacked!!!

Mental Fortitude skill increased to level three!

I had no idea at all how to defend against it, other than by leveling the skill. I tried and failed to think about nothing, so I started imagining one of the cheesiest and most annoying pop songs off Russian radio with a large number of senseless repeating couplets. Read away! Let's see how fast it turns your brains to mush! It took a second, but my tactic eventually worked. First, the Mental Fortitude progress bar started going up slower, then it stopped altogether just before reaching level 4. A bit after that, Ayni was dragged out of the room, senseless, and the voice called me to the center of the circle.

I obediently went into the middle of the room and cringed in dismay, blinded by the spotlight. I could no longer even make out the figures sitting in a semicircle around me, and that was despite my high Perception. Apparently, that was all intentional, and the Truth Seekers didn't want to be seen for some reason.

Danger Sense skill increased to level twenty-five!

It started!!! Now I could definitely feel it. It was like a bunch of gross, cold and slimy fingers were rooting around in my skull. It felt so awful, too bad to put into words... Come on, move along! Out of my head! I don't want that, I don't want you digging in my brains!!!

Mental Fortitude skill increased to level four!
Mental Fortitude skill increased to level five!
Mental Fortitude skill increased to level six!
Psionic skill increased to level fourteen!
You have reached level fifty-three!
You have received three skill points! (total points accumulated: six)

I immediately put all six points into improving psionic defense, raising Mental Fortitude to twelve. The nasty squirming sensation in my brain faded away. I was just standing, barely able to conceal the smile of satisfaction trying to burst onto my face. At least, until a Truth Seeker asked the first question:

"Gnat, you abandoned your friends to play the game that bends reality. How do you feel now, having traded such close and loyal companions for vibrant new experiences? Your old buddies don't trouble you?"

Not a trace of my confidence remained. I was instantly stitched through with superstitious fear. How did the Truth Seekers know about Vasily and Petka, my college roommates of three years? After all, I really did not know what became of them and, to my great shame, had barely even thought about my old friends until that very minute. Had they been sent to jail instead of me? Or, as the investigator promised, were they pressured into the army? How to find out?

Stop! I couldn't say exactly what grabbed me in the framing of the question, but it wasn't exactly accurate, so I gave it another spin in my head. "Abandoned my friends to play the game that bends reality?" That would probably fit for practically anyone the question was asked to. After all, everyone regardless of race, gender or age must have had some friends or close relatives in the real world, who they couldn't see as much anymore, possibly not even at all. Almost every individual that played this game would have had the same guilt baring down on them. Well, everyone except me!!! I didn't abandon anyone! I was forced into this, placed under arrest and basically blackmailed into accepting an offer to "work in an institute in the Moscow Oblast."

So I... laughed instead of answering, because I suddenly realized how the Truth Seekers worked. A series of trick questions like that would force the interrogee to feel doubt, shame, fear and remorse. That killed two birds with one stone: not only were they breaking down the mental defenses of the bewildered victim, forcing them to justify themselves, which would allow the experienced psionics to take advantage of their weakness and gain access to their memory, the prisoner would actually tell them their weakest and most vulnerable points without being asked. They would give names, dates, and circumstances, enumerate all their transgressions. And each answer enriched their arsenal. After all, no one knows you better than you know yourself. If they want a complete dossier, who better to turn to? What have you done wrong, when and why? If properly tuned, you will always be your harshest judge.

"Honorable Truth Seekers, my conscious is clean, I didn't abandon or betray anyone in the real world. And because I know your time is valuable, I suggest we skip this part of the torture. No need to worm out my past. I'm more than willing to tell you my life story if you want to know."

Fame increased to 46.

A long silence came over the room, approximately forty seconds. After that, a green symbol lit up in the shape of a snaking line inside a square, something of a corkscrew in a box. I guessed that might mean "truth," and was elated. Just like my first encounter with Thumor-Anhu La-Fin, I managed to deflect the mental attack!!!

However, I wasn't exultant for too long, just until the mysterious hidden investigator's next sentence:

"I doubt your old friends Vasily Sokolov and Pyotr Zhukov, who are now working off your shared crimes, would share the conviction that Kirill Ignatiev did not abandon them. But you're right about the second part. Our time really is too valuable to waste it teasing out your biography prior to entering the game that bends reality."

Damn, they really got me... If this was not an interrogation, but a boxing match, I would have at least taken a knockdown... While I was coming to my senses, shocked and bewildered at the detailed information they fished out of my brain, the Truth Seekers hit me with another question:

"Gerd Gnat, you are not a Diplomat by class, but your mind is closed off and cannot be read. Were you afraid of this interrogation and thus prepared for it? Do you have something to hide?"

Now the questions were on topic and getting off to a bad start. I remembered Ayni saying that lying to Truth Seekers was pointless and dangerous, so I answered the pure truth and nothing but.

I told them about my character's high Intelligence and said I had just taken the skill Mental Fortitude. Then I admitted that I was afraid of this interrogation, so I had tried to mount a psychic defense of some kind. Also, I did have something to hide, but my secrets were first and foremost my faction's plans, business dealings and financial information. I had none connected with the incarnation of the Great First Female. Perhaps it came across as rude and even blasphemous to the Truth Seekers, but I had to admit that I only found out about their universally famed Priestess Amiru after I saw crowds of pilgrims filling the space station. I had never seen the Priestess on a screen, and certainly not in person. I assured them I didn't have any reason to wish ill on the great Miyelonian.

A somewhat different symbol appeared in the air. A green corkscrew, only without a square. But most importantly, there was a bright orange pulsing spot next to it. Something in my mostly truthful answer was not to the Truth Seekers' satisfaction. I even guessed what it was: my claim that I had no secrets related to their holy priestess. Crap. Crap! Crap!!! I should have just left that out, then everything would have been fine. I had to be proactive before the Truth Seekers said anything:

"Let me tell you about my animal. As far as I understand, that is what you'd like to hear most."

No reaction followed from the Truth Seekers, so I hurried to take advantage of their silent assent and continued:

"It all started when I was walking with a tray of food, looking for a seat in the café. I saw a group of Meleyephatians that were just leaving. I walked over to sit down but, when I got there, some little animal beat me to it. It looked very much like a species native to my home world so of course I was surprised, especially because I didn't see it walking to the table. I am almost one hundred percent certain it was sitting with the Meleyephatians before I came. Anyway, the creature looked very hungry, so I fed it. After that, something strange happened: its information changed to say it was my pet. I didn't see anything wrong with that and didn't pay it much mind. It followed me for some time, I led it to my hotel and it even came into my capsule. At night, it ate all my rations..."

At that point in my story, I was interrupted. A Truth Seeker was demanding I explain why I didn't leave the game in the hotel green zone. They assumed I was waiting for a signal or afraid to miss a meeting.

But here I was somewhat braver, because I had nothing to hide. I answered sincerely that I had broken my leg in the real world, so I was trying to spend as much time as possible in the game for medical purposes. My honesty was rewarded with a green corkscrew inside a square but... before I could celebrate the small victory, they asked the trickiest question of all:

"Gerd Gnat, have you ever heard of the Morphian race?"

Trying to hide my panic, I immediately started answering, again with the pure truth:

"Yes, I have. Just yesterday, I had a long talk with a Diplomat of my faction about the various races inhabiting the cosmos and the topic of Morphians did come up. As far as I understand, they died off in the real world eons ago, and were once part of the Meleyephatian horde. Some Morphians remained in the game as NPC's, though, and are renowned for their ability to change appearance."

I anxiously awaited their verdict. Green corkscrew! Truth!!! Everything was coming together so well! Yesterday at my housewarming party, Ivan Lozovsky and I had actually discussed the Morphians among other topics. Sure, I was doing the telling, and the Diplomat was just listening and asking follow-ups, but I just got away with implying the diplomat told it to me without actually lying. How fortunate!

Mental Fortitude skill increased to level thirteen!
Mental Fortitude skill increased to level fourteen!

I celebrated too soon, though. The investigators found the truthful answer sign insufficient, and asked me to explain more:

"Gerd Gnat, for some reason you experienced anxiety when answering that question, which was absent previously. Your heartbeat sped up, your body temperature increased, and your breathing became uneven. Explain."

So I did, improvising on the fly:

"Well, of course I was worried. I mean, I can put two and two together! I know that someone disguised as my Miyelonian friend Ayni attacked your great Priestess. What's more, the attack took place when the real Ayni was in a different part of the station. Add to that your stubborn interest in my one-time 'pet,' and the allegation that it killed Amiru, then mix that with the question about the Morphian race. It isn't hard to follow the logic. The animal I met must have been a Morphian, who later changed form and attacked the Priestess Amiru!"

Instead of an answer, a holographic screen lit up in the air before me. I saw a huge room packed to the brim with Miyelonian pilgrims. In the middle of the bustling rapturous crowd, there was a tall stage. On it, illuminated by many spotlights, there was a short figure dressed head to toe in free-flowing white clothing. First, I thought it was the head of the casino, but I quickly noticed the clothing and body proportions were different. Also, the Priestess was a bit shorter.

And then came the murder itself! Standing in the very first row was Ayni's frail, easily recognizable frame. In the blink of an eye, she climbed up onto the shoulders of a First Pride bodyguard next to her and took one long bound onto the stage. Immediately, the claws of her right paw extended and pierced the Priestess's stomach, tearing through both the sheer fabric and living flesh. She twisted her bloodied paw in the wound, at the same time sinking her teeth into the Priestess's neck. Amiru looked paralyzed in pain and fear. A fountain of blood erupted, instantly staining her white robe, then she fell to the floor breathless.

The whole attack lasted two seconds at most. Afterward, the killer managed to cut the luxurious cream-white tail off her victim, hold it up triumphantly in her bloodied right hand, then slit her own throat with a claw and disappear without a trace.

Unbelievable! Such speed! Miyelonians were thought to be unsurpassed melee fighters capable of truly remarkable agility but none of the many worshippers or guards had even realized what was happening yet much less tried to stop the Morphian. God forbid I ever have an enemy like that!

I was simply astonished and did not know what to say, just opening and closing my mouth like a fish out of water. Meanwhile, on the screen, the security footage played sped-up in reverse. Walking backward into the thick crowd, the short orange translator flickered through various corridors on the space station, and finally I saw what I was expecting. One of the cameras in the large room caught the Miyelonian lady in the dense crowd of pilgrims as she changed shape to a four-legged fox, then got down on all fours and trotted tail-first through the whole room to a stairway, which led to a balcony where she calmly lay down between me and the real Ayni.

Well that was that. My connection with the ghastly fox had been conclusively proven. Good thing I hadn't tried to deny it, or this all could have been worse. But now, in light of my evidence, I wondered what verdict the Truth Seekers would give.

I felt the nasty sensation of fingers squirming in my head again. It quickly ended, then a metallic voice came down from the ceiling and said:

"Unfortunately, the security cameras in the hotel and cafe were out of order, so we were not able to track the Morphian prior to this. But your evidence has been checked and fully corroborated. It allowed us to establish who was behind the murder. However, before we rule on your guilt or innocence, we need to see everything on your Prospector Scanner. The other items in your inventory, even the unusual ones like Relict artifacts, are not related to the case, so we make no claim to them."

Give them my scanner? But that had a diagram of a Miyelonian interceptor, which my faction needed badly! If I showed them, they would also get a clear, unambiguous answer of who caused the crane malfunctions and damage to the pirate ship. Also, beyond that, the scanner memory had plenty of other valuable data: the nodes of my home planet, the coordinates of the platinum asteroid and, most importantly, the Relict base. So, I was insistent:

"Impossible! I assure you that there is no material on the scanner related to the murder of the great Priestess, and you can easily check my words for sincerity. But it has lots of information of value.

Geckho Leng Waid Shishish paid six million just for the coordinates of the Relict base. And my captain thought he was getting cheated for that. Now you want that information for free? Nope, sorry, I can't have that!"

In the air, instead of a green corkscrew, I saw five red squares interlaced inside a vertical rectangle. At first, I stared stupidly at the geometric construction, trying to understand what it meant. But then I realized I was seeing the Miyelonian numeral for "one hundred thousand."

"I hope that will be sufficient? At any rate, the Relict base is located in Geckho space, which makes it hard for Miyelonians to access. Also the most valuable items are probably already gone."

My chest was pierced with worry. The Miyelonians were offering me one hundred thousand crystals! That was just beyond imagination for information that no longer had any real value... It took a titanic amount of willpower not to think about the explosion of the Relict base. I changed topic:

"Money-wise, that'll do. But I'd also like to know who is behind the whole scheme to kill your Priestess. Who ordered it? You said you knew."

Mental Fortitude skill increased to level fifteen!
Mental Fortitude skill increased to level sixteen!
Psionic skill increased to level fifteen!

Seemingly, I managed to deflect a psionic attack. Good. Hopefully I managed to keep some of my secrets! I was afraid about the additional demand, that the Truth Seekers would act obstinate, or even object to my brazenness, but they agreed almost instantly:

"Deal!"

Chapter
Twenty-One

Ticket Home

A MIYELONIAN IN WHITE First Pride armor came up to me and extended his hand demandingly. I obediently handed him my Prospector Scanner. I understood perfectly that I wouldn't be getting it back, so I couldn't sell the information to some other interested party. But I was losing lots of important data with that, above all the diagram of the Miyelonian interceptor. However, one hundred thousand crystals was more than enough to compensate all my losses. I could buy myself a new scanner right away, and there would always be other starships to scan!

My wallet vibrated, and I took it out of my inventory. Account balance: one hundred fifty-nine thousand five hundred crypto. What?! I checked it again. There could be no doubt. I had not been transferred the local equivalent of one hundred thousand red Geckho crystals, but one hundred thousand crypto. That was about seven times more than what I was expecting!

My enthrallment was interrupted by the metallic voice:

"Listen closely, Gerd Gnat. Four Meleyephatians entered the cafe, but just three left. The station didn't get any missing crew notices, which means the Meleyephatians knew their friend would not be coming back on board. We carefully searched all parts of the station and couldn't find any trace of the fourth crewman. The starship used by these Meleyephatians left the Medu-Ro IV station immediately before Leng Amiru U-Mayaoo's speech."

"So the fourth one was the Morphian?" I asked, more confirming a guess than actually curious.

"Yes, it was the Morphian. But the Morphian is just an NPC. It doesn't have its own will or objectives. It is merely a tool in the hands of nefarious masters. A very dangerous tool that is rarely used for good, and is more often used for the vilest ends, such as this recent provocation. Murdering an incarnation of the Great First Female is equivalent to declaring war on the Miyelonians. And this Morphian's masters tried to make it all trace back to you. They were trying to turn the great Geckho and Miyelonian races against one another."

Geckho? Well, sure. After all, Earth was officially under Geckho suzerainty and, by all interstellar laws, our masters were obliged to defend their weak and unintelligent vassals in case of war. Unintelligent indeed! My heart seized in delayed horror. Just to think, my chatting with a space fox might have started a real interstellar war, which might have threatened extremely serious consequences right up to the total extermination of my species! And no matter what you say about her being "merely a tool," what a vile wretch that Fox was!!!

"Gerd Gnat, you have been told everything required by the terms of our deal." The circle of light went out, the metallic voice said the interrogation was over, and that the Prospector Gerd Gnat had been found innocent unanimously by all fifteen Truth Seekers in the murder of the Priestess Leng Amiru U-Mayaoo.

Now, the light no longer blinding me, I could see each of the Truth Seekers dissolve into semi-dark and disappear. It was clear that this was all just a projection or hologram of creatures that were actually very, very far away, perhaps thousands of parsecs from me.

Eagle Eye skill increased to level fifty-three!

After fourteen of the fifteen investigators had dissolved, the last one stayed back, turned to me and said a long phrase in Miyelonian.

A voice, metallic and lacking all emotion, came down instantly from the ceiling and translated it into the more familiar Geckho:

"Gnat, I am Leng Amiru U-Mayaoo, and it was my death you saw on screen just now. I'd like to say that your efforts to hide speaking with the Morphian and even giving it a name were entirely in vain. They only slowed us down. Everyone in the galaxy already knows that Morphians are intelligent and capable of speech."

I suddenly realized I was blushing. I naively thought I was playing a clever game, hiding my thoughts and leading the investigators where I wanted with my great cunning. But they, as it turned out, knew everything the whole time, and simply allowed me to deceive myself.

I hesitated for a second then, like a medieval knight in the presence of royals, got down on one knee in a sign of respect and homage to the powerful individual. Then, before Amiru U-Mayaoo disappeared, I asked her to tell me more about the Morphians, because I was just baffled.

"In their time, the Morphians were vassals of the Meleyephatians. But one day, they tried to become masters of the horde, killing and replacing the most powerful and influential members of Meleyephatian society with their kind. When a minor discrepancy revealed their plot, it was discovered with horror that two thirds of Meleyephatian rulers, military leaders and famous figures, as well as leaders of their massive horde's many subject races, were already dead and had been substituted with Morphian impostors. For that monstrous villainy, which knows no equal in audacity or scale in the history of the Galaxy, the Morphian race was exterminated in the real world. The few players who hid in the virtual world became something like NPC's, with no home planet or structured society of any kind. That is the official story. But I don't believe it one bit. Common sense tells me that, with their ability to change appearance, nothing was stopping the Morphians from joining all kinds of different Prides, Factions and Clans of other races and just calmly exiting into the real world disguised as another creature."

Astrolinguistics skill increased to level sixty-two!

I noted the skill growth just for a moment, then thought over Amiru's words. She was right! How hadn't I considered that?! The fairy tale Fox told me about her race's miserable position instantly crumbled. In a sign of gratitude for the detailed answer, I gave a deep bow to the Miyelonian Leng. Then, giving in to a sudden urge, I decided to state my own conclusions:

"Leng Amiru U-Mayaoo, you are very wise and shrewd, know practically everything about the Morphian race and have an astonishing aptitude for finding the truth. So, I have no doubt that the true ringleaders of this murder were already known before I was arrested by you and your team of Truth Seekers. It must have only taken the initial data. But then why this whole spectacle with the arrest and interrogation? Just to get the data from my scanner?"

A green corkscrew in a box sign unexpectedly appeared in front of me. As it turned out, I had told the pure truth!

A second later, I heard a groan and cough from the dark figure, and the mechanical translator readily conveyed their meaning:

"I'm such a ditz, I forgot to turn off the instruments... Argh!"

I apparently managed to embarrass the incarnation of the Great First Female.

Anyhow, Leng Amiru U-Mayaoo instantly came to her senses:

"Your intuitive abilities are impressive, Gerd

Gnat. Yes, there was no other reason for your arrest than reading the information about the base of the ancient Relict race. But it quickly became clear that you have no idea where the base is located. So, we needed your Prospector tool as well, as it would have the coordinates. But after the deal was done, I managed to read that the base exploded. My other colleagues are still in a state of blissful ignorance."

Authority increased to 10.

"Well, Gnat, let me congratulate you. You're an astonishingly lucky man, given you managed to hide such valuable information from my Truth Seeker colleagues! Don't worry about the money. It belongs to you by right. You earned it fair and square. What's more, the coordinates of the Relict outpost alone have quite a high value. They allow us to gain a clearer understanding of the mysterious race's boundaries and the structure of its society, which tells us where to look for other traces of their ancient civilizations."

Leng Amiru made a strange gesture, drawing a horizontal figure eight in the air with her paw, either bidding me farewell or blessing me.

She was clearly planning to follow the example of the other Truth Seekers and disappear, when she froze and said:

"And yes, my advice to you: take your time changing game class. I'll look for information in the Star City archives about Listeners and the other classes used by Relict players. If I find anything, I'll be sure to tell you. But it is easily possible that this ancient profession used some device that is now forever lost and cannot be obtained anywhere in the Universe."

I WAS ACCOMPANIED by two watchful Miyelonians in white First Pride armor. And that was not an excess, given the colossal amount of money currently in my wallet. After all, anything could happen on this pirate station! Uline Tar once said there were plenty of players who would stop at nothing for ten thousand crystals. I now had crypto to the tune of one million one hundred thousand crystals, so I couldn't let my guard down for even a second.

Near the passage from the station to the space port zone, Ayni came out from behind a vending machine and blocked my path. I couldn't even recognize the Translator. Her eyes were sunken, her paws were shaking, her ears were pressed down, and the young orange cat looked to have grown old or fallen seriously ill. Ayni walked up in silence and, just like when we were headed to the interrogation, buried her snout into my shoulder, demanding consolation. I embraced her firmly and even stroked her furry back. In return, the cat lady gave a very soft meow, like a lost kitten:

"Gnat, I'm feeling very bad. After talking with the Truth Seekers, I feel like I've been skinned alive and set out for everyone to laugh at. All Miyelonians recoil from me. When I come near, they go silent and disperse. No one even wants to talk. Please, take me away from this station! I'd be willing to fly to the edge of the known galaxy, even to unexplored space! I know the four main interstellar languages and I'm a quick learner. I could translate at your negotiations!"

"But what about the Pride of the Comet's Tail? I see you've already been let back in."

Ayni's pride membership, which was absent before the interrogation, had returned to her character info.

"Pride?" Ayni looked somewhat confused, having only discovered the change in her social status after I mentioned it. "Those are just empty words to me now! If only you knew, Gerd Gnat, how I wanted the Pride to need me! For them to notice me, respect me and value me. But they just stuck me in a boring job at the registration post then, as soon as I was charged with a crime, they rejected me and left me to fend for myself! So, my pride affiliation is no obstacle!"

It didn't take me long to decide. My level of Miyelonian was still as low as ever, so I really did need a translator to negotiate the platinum sale. Fate had just provided me one and refusing such a gift would simply be improper. Of course, I agreed!

"Now, I just need to find Tini. Did you see where he went after the interrogation?"

"Tini?" she froze up for a few seconds, as if trying to figure out who I was talking about. "No, I didn't see... don't give me that judgmental look! Yeah, I'm still pretty out of it. But that's how it is. It will pass in time. I say we move on, because we're amassing an audience and it's making me uncomfortable."

"*Inspection zone. Have your documents ready.*"

We had to cross the ninety-foot corridor in which every creature passing to the station or space port zone was subjected to a careful check, including scanning both character and bags with all kinds of detectors. But much to my surprise, an exception was made for us. The First Pride soldiers showed the workers their metal badges, saying something I could almost completely understand:

"We're returning prisoners ... (incomprehensible). Successful ... (incomprehensible) by the Truth Seekers. Charges dropped. Completely innocent."

We were led through the service corridors around all the scanning devices, after which the soldiers asked whether to leave me at the hotel or right at my starship. I managed to make that out and, with only a few hints from Ayni, answered that I needed to go to the casino.

AND THAT'S WHERE I found my kitten. Tini was sitting in a far-off back corner of the stands right on the cold metal floor and shivering hard, still not recovered from the interrogation. I picked him up by the scruff of his neck and dragged him to a table, sitting him up on a bench. I ordered Ayni to hold the underage lad, because he just kept trying to crawl under the table or fall onto his side. Meanwhile, I went to the bar. With a heavy sigh, because ordering without a Translator was hard, I spoke in Miyelonian, substituting unknown words with gestures or Geckho:

"Two of the strongest drinks you've got. I need to bring my friends back to life. They've just been interrogated by fifteen Truth Seekers. And give me the same cocktail I ordered before. I really liked it."

Shockingly, they understood me. A few minutes later, there were two identical flagons on the bar, with a bubbling and pulsating substance of a toxic green color. They handed me a tall wine glass with a layered cocktail that smelled of valerian and herbs. I reached for my wallet, preparing to pay for the drinks, but the lean and tall Miyelonian bartender gave a very humanlike wave and said:

"On the house. Too well ... (incomprehensible) ... Pride of the Agile Paw knows the pain of interrogation. All that rooting around in your brains..."

Authority increased to 11.

Astrolinguistics skill increased to level sixty-three!

You have reached level fifty-four!

You have received three skill points!

I returned to the table and damn near ordered Tini and Ayni to drink down their flagons and, hopefully, get over the recent nightmare as quickly as possible. But although the Translator sucked the thick pulsating drink through the tube with surprising composure, Tini put on a real show. First the kitten meekly and even mechanically shook the green jelly out of the flask right into his open toothy mouth and swallowed, then the fur bristled all over the young Miyelonian's body, making him look twice as large. Next, his ears stood on end, and something tore out of his jaws that was midway between a scream and a groan:

"Yughghgh! What was that crap?! I can feel it

moving, and it burns! Waaaaaater!!!"

His eyes bulging, Tini noticed the drink in my hand, grabbed it without asking and drained it in two big gulps.

"Oohh!!! That's the ticket!!! Exactly what I needed! Master Gnat, please excuse me for taking it without asking, but I felt like I might die..." after these words, Tini started giving a stupid smile, showing all his sharp teeth and... fell face-first on the table unconscious.

"Don't worry, he'll come to in no time," Ayni assured me, having noticed my discomfort. "Our race has a fast metabolism and as long as a poison doesn't kill a Miyelonian right away, the body will quickly neutralize it."

Useful information. I made a mental note of it: don't use slow-acting poisons against Miyelonians. It would also be dumb to take part in anything like a drinking contest with one. Then, as our conversation had turned to Miyelonian abilities and traditions, I decided to ask a question:

"Ayni, what does that gesture mean?" I made a figure eight horizontally with my right hand.

The orange cat was clearly surprised and asked where I might have seen such a thing. After hearing about my talk with the incarnation of the Great First Female, Ayni said respectfully:

"Gerd Gnat, you were bestowed with a rare honor. Leng Amiru U-Mayaoo is invested in your fate and has taken you under her protection. That is a very good sign!"

Ayni was forced to stop talking, because a large

severe looking tomcat walked up to our table in a scratched-up matte-black suit of metal armor. He was all laden with weaponry and trophies, both Miyelonian tails and other alien body parts.

Gerd Abi Pan-Miay. Miyelonian. Pride of the Bushy Shadow. Level-145 Starship Pilot.

ATTENTION!!! Captain Gerd Abi Pan-Miay, is one of the Galaxy's most wanted space pirates. Danger rating: 9.

Shooting a curious glance at the bubbles coming out of Tini's nose, the fearsome pirate shouted to the bartender to bring him "what he's having," after which he plopped down on the bench next to my kitten. The Miyelonian stared at my Translator stubbornly for a long time. She was embarrassed by the fearsome pirate, looked away and gave an unhappy snort:

"I've heard that your little clique was found not guilty by Truth Seekers, but I still cannot overcome the hate and disgust I feel when I see your vile mugs. I wanna punch all of you in the head just to settle my nerves."

Danger Sense skill increased to level twenty-six!

I basically understood the Free Captain, but still didn't stop Ayni from translating. Apparently, the pirate didn't like us at first glance, and now he was hesitating about whether to just stand up and walk away or kill us all and get drunk. So, inferring that this space pirate was a godly man, I told Ayni to answer that we not only had been exonerated, the great Priestess Leng Amiru herself promised me protection.

For the pirate captain, as I was hoping, that was a sobering factor:

"Alright, I won't cut off your heads just yet. Human, I was told you wanted to meet with the leader of the Pride of the Bushy Shadow, something about a big payoff. Well, now is your chance to tell me everything about your offer. And pray I don't conclude I was called away from important business for nothing."

Through Ayni, I repeated what I said before. There were six hundred seventy-five pounds of pure platinum ingots (and it was funny to hear the measurement units change in translation) waiting on a distant planet for a buyer unafraid of official Geckho borders or slow-witted customs officials. I also told him our price: three million Geckho crystals for the whole shipment. Next, I transparently hinted that this deal might be the first in a series of profitable transactions. And finally, I asked the Translator to say that the owner of this casino was also interested, and that she could provide us her own captain, but didn't want to step on the Pride of the Bushy Shadow's toes. So, she would take us up on this if they refused.

Would you like to take the skill Trade?
Would you like to take the skill Diplomacy?

I turned down both suggestions. Gerd Abi Pan-Miay asked for details about the location of sale and the characteristics of the planet. Good thing I memorized the coordinates of my home world. It came in very handy! The Free Captain, although he was a Miyelonian by race, understood me perfectly, turned on his palmtop and entered the data.

"There aren't even maps of that system in the star atlas yet... It was discovered very recently, and the

Geckho are in no rush to share that information. Also, such a dangerous voyage promises just two hundred thousand crypto. Subtract fuel and crew pay and you get...” the captain groaned, quickly making some calculations. “It’s not too tempting. Money like that won’t get my ass out of the chair, but someone in my Pride will take it. Two days ago, a young hot-headed Captain named Rikki Pan-Miis broke his interceptor on an asteroid while chasing down a Shiamiru. It wasn’t very serious damage, he lost just a wing and some armor but now he’s pretty hard-up for cash and would be glad to have any work to pay for repairs.”

Two things in that story put me on guard. First, was he seriously going to send me into space on a damaged ship? After all, we would have to land in dense atmosphere on a fairly massive planet and doing that in a spaceship that had lost “just a wing and some armor” was nothing short of suicide. Second, how was this bad-luck captain going to pay if he was desperate for money himself? I boldly voiced both questions.

“I’ll loan him the money for the repair and platinum!” the Free Captain snarled in dismay, lowering his empty drink from the stand. “And Rikki will pay off his debt with this voyage, so everything is fine.”

Danger Sense skill increased to level twenty-seven!

Timely warning! Although I could already sense that something was wrong with this offer, and they were planning to cheat me somehow. I just didn’t understand how. Should I try to find out?

Failed Intelligence check.

Action terminated. Magic Points exhausted.

I couldn't read the thoughts of the dangerous pirate, and that was a shame... In any case, the Pride of the Bushy Shadow's ship seemed to be my only way back to Earth. All that talk about a backup option and a captain from the Pride of the Agile paw was only partially true and just as much bluster. The bartender hadn't seen the casino owner today and had no idea if she'd be coming in any time soon. It was easily possible that the leader of the Pride of the Agile Paw would be gone for a long time, but I had to leave relatively shortly. In fact, I had just twelve hours. So, I didn't have much choice. Either go to Miyelonian prison or take a risk and fly off with the criminal captain.

I chose the second option and answered the Pride leader that I agreed, but I put forward two non-negotiable conditions: the "young and hot-headed" captain would only get his platinum after payment and not a second earlier, and I would be bringing two Miyelonians and lots of baggage.

Gerd Abi Pan-Miay, who was slightly tipsy off the strong drink, turned on his radio and asked his subordinate a question, then conveyed the answer thirty seconds later:

"You cannot bring more than one and a half tons of luggage. Rikki has a small interceptor, not a cargo ship! He sees no obstacles with the rest, though. His ship is a Tiopeo-Myhh II. It is at landing deck number eight, hangar four. They take off in one ummi. By then, the repair will be finished, and we will manage to collect the Geckho crystals."

Chapter Twenty-Two

Project Exodus

THE FIRST THING I did after leaving the Free Captain was ask Ayni and the bartender, who was up collecting our empty glasses, where the nearest green zone was. I was pointed to the casino's VIP box, which was now empty. As far as I understood, it was surrounded by forcefields on all sides, and had a luxurious interior, comfy furniture and its own secure communication terminal for private negotiations, during which anyone could exit to the real world to consult with colleagues or superiors. Exactly what I needed!

For twenty crypto, I was allowed to use the VIP box and immediately left the game. I dismissed the suggestion to familiarize myself with my statistics, hurriedly climbed out of the virt pod and, running down the corn cob, raced to headquarters. I was looking for Ivan Lozovsky, but the diplomat was in the game, so I was received by faction leader Radugin himself.

When I appeared, the slumping, tired and severely sleep-deprived Dome commander looked like a bespectacled scientist running up against a dissertation deadline. He folded up some topographic maps on his desk, and I chuckled. This was clearly Antipov's doing. Leadership didn't used to hide their maps or plans from visitors. In my momentary peek, I made out the six-sided nodes of our faction and those of our neighbors, many colored lines for defensive structures and circles radiating from points the Yellow Mountains. I suspected that, before I arrived, the faction leader was thinking over the optimal placement of artillery batteries, so our long-distance cannons could cover every part of the front during the quickly approaching Dark Faction invasion.

But I was not much interested in military secrets or where our artillery would go. I had come with a different goal. I needed to know exactly where we'd meet the space merchants, so I could give the captain landing coordinates, and also tell the faction approximately when to expect our guests. But the main thing was that I needed to know what the faction wanted me to buy on the space station, where prices for any goods were many times lower than the Geckho space port.

And although the question of where the merchants should land was already settled, there was a clear disconnect with the purchase list. My eyes climbed into my forehead in surprise when I heard the faction leader say that this issue had not yet been considered in detail, only discussed in general terms. Things like, "it would be nice to buy all this stuff in space for cheaper." Beyond that, with unhidden horror I discovered that the faction didn't yet have enough platinum, because they thought it would be a long time before the space merchants came if they ever did.

"Come on, are you all a bunch of morons?!" Yes, I let my emotions get the better of me and started screaming. "The platinum buyer is coming tomorrow. It was a huge effort to convince him to fly to our podunk planet on the edge of the known universe, and now the goods I was hawking aren't even here! None of the great spacefaring races will ever want to do business with us again!"

"Calm down, Kirill. The platinum will be there, I promise! But as for the list, we need to first hold a meeting with the leaders of the main laboratories, both legions and the rest of our military divisions to figure out what they need."

"That's all well and good," I interrupted Radugin's empty and untimely demagoguery, "but I need to place orders right now, because I need everything delivered and loaded onto the starship. Can you even imagine how insanely hard it was to get an advance on the three million crystals to buy weapons and vehicles? I was only given permission to bring one and a half tons of baggage! So, I can only buy things we really need, and I need to know what they are right away!"

I didn't draw his attention to the fact that my

negotiations with the Free Captain had never touched on an advance, and that I was going to pay with my own money, then compensate myself later. I was afraid that, if I told him I had more than a million crystals, he simply wouldn't believe me.

Radugin asked for a minute and made a quick phone call. As far as I understood, it was to the leader of the First Legion. After that, the Dome leader told me their conclusions:

"Buy guns, laser weapons, firearms, or whatever long-distance weaponry. Get ones for Automatic Weapons from level one hundred and up, Machineguns from seventy-five and Sniper from sixty. Buy as much as you can. That is our greatest need. Many of our veterans have long outgrown their weapons in level and skill, so we have a desperate need for quality arms. We need a large number, along with ammunition for whatever you buy. Beyond that, we need something that can short out electronics. EMP grenades, EMP mines, whatever radiation emitters they have. The mission is to stop Dark Faction shock antigravs like the flying *Sio-Mi-Dori*, as well as heavy armored monsters on the ground like the *Sio-Ku-Tati*, which we only know about from recon. Just buy a ton and a half of that, if possible. If there is any room or money left over, buy the rest at your own discretion!"

On the way back to my virt pod, I was in a very pensive mood and was even somewhat despondent. My talk with the faction leader left an unpleasant impression. I naively thought my leaders had their shit together a bit more. "Buy whatever you think we'll need." "Yeah, we didn't think you'd find a buyer for the platinum, so we didn't actually get any." "Just look. Whatever they've got, buy that." Kindergarten, Velcro shoes, not some serious organization! But even that wasn't the biggest nagging issue. It seemed that my Leng was not just tired and sleep-deprived, but emotionally drained and, seemingly, no longer especially believed we could defeat the Dark Faction. There seemed to be a lack of interest, and some kind of gloom, absent-mindedness and strange ambivalence. First, they say they'll get the platinum and bring it into the game as quickly as possible, but then they say they considered the project unfeasible and low-priority...

On my way to the corncob, I was surprised to meet gazes with a jogging Svetlana. She had the hood of her track suit down and didn't notice me right away, but then sharply changed direction and ran up to me, taking out her headphones as she went. I reassured the bodyguards, who were preparing to stop the First Legion Assassin. Svetlana, as I immediately noticed, was running with weight. There were weights on her wrists and ankles, and I could see a broad belt with sheets of lead under her unbuttoned shirt.

"Heya, Gnat. You just get up?" I couldn't tell if the reddened lady was making a quip or really thought I had actually just emerged after last night's raucous merrymaking.

"I wish... Since last night, I've been in Miyelonian prison, gone to court and even met a space pirate in a space casino."

Svetlana whistled in surprise and looked at me with clear respect and even admiration. I then asked why she was exercising under the Dome and not in the game. After all, by running like this in the game that bends reality, she would not only level her stats and skills, she would also improve her body in the real world.

"Yes, I know, Kirill. But you can't only take care of your body in the game. After all, every minute there is regimented. You're always going somewhere, crawling through swamps in camouflage or lying motionless for hours under the burning sun as you watch an enemy post through binoculars. But now I'm totally..." Svetlana looked at the bodyguards accompanying me in hesitation, but still continued. "You talk with faction leadership often enough. Have you heard of Project Exodus?"

I shrugged my shoulders indefinitely. I hadn't heard of it, but I didn't want to reveal my ignorance.

"Well, our guys keep saying the Dark Faction will attack in five days. I'll be honest, not many of our soldiers believe we'll be able to hold out. Last time, after all, we just got lucky and your raid helped get rid of enemy forces. They won't make the same blunders again. Also, their next attack will be fiercer than the last. Our leadership also understands that perfectly so, one after the other, they're sending recon groups to the opposite shore of the bay, past the Geckho space port. And they all have the same mission: find a place for us to build a base there for the so-called Operation Exodus. No one is saying it out loud, of course, but they all understand this is being done in case our capital node falls in the next few days."

I really didn't like hearing about the defeatist attitude held by our soldiers, including the First

Legion. I did not know if it was just Dark Faction propaganda, or skillfully conveyed disinformation, but it was damaging not only the morale of the H3 players. Another negative consequence was that our leadership was getting distracted and wasting valuable resources, reserves and people on cockamamie schemes totally unrelated to reinforcing our defenses.

"That's all crap, we'll hold out!" I assured her, to which Svetlana gave a predatory chuckle:

"Sure, no one is planning to throw their hands up and surrender. We'll fight not for our lives, but to the death, and the enemy will have to pay dearly for every inch of our territory. But will we have the strength? Gnat, I've seen thousands and thousands of Dark Faction soldiers training at the firing ranges with my own eyes. I saw their new high-speed flying antigravs and heavy armored vehicles. They're like our Peresvets but four times bigger, real terrestrial cruisers! There are rumors that our experts concluded we cannot destroy them with our current technology!"

"I wonder how they managed to figure that out, if they haven't seen any in real life, and cannot study real specimens," I quipped.

Svetlana wanted to answer but stumbled and looked at me, smiling in embarrassment. In the meandering stream of her thoughts, primarily revolving around the topic of weight issues and a new diet recommended by a friend, I managed to fish out the name of the person who told her those pernicious rumors. No, it was not Svetlana's panicky fiancée as I assumed, but someone named Gleb Vorshinsky, an Engineer from the Prometheus. I didn't know him, but

I still made a note to check if he was working for the Dark Faction.

I mean, this could easily have been just everyday human stupidity, or the Engineer wanting to look better informed than he really was for a pretty girl. But it also could have been intentional disinformation made to spread chaos and uncertainty in the H3 faction. The whole warped picture of the situation on the front was made up of such small depressing details, and that is what had the soldiers so down, and leadership screwing up.

"Svetlana, that information is out of date," I said, trying to make a confident face with a mysterious smile. "I was just talking to Radugin about that issue, and I'll be bringing weapons from space that can destroy any Dark Faction vehicle, including their *Sio-Ku-Tati* tanks. By the way... Svetlana, you probably know better than our leaders: what do our recon groups need the most?! Weapons, observation equipment, maybe other gear...? Do you know? That's what I thought! Then you have exactly five minutes. I promise that whatever you ask for will be at our base in a day and a half!"

WHEN I CAME BACK into the game, there was a surprise waiting. The merchant Gerd Ussh Veesh was trying to enter my VIP box. The Trillian was up on his hind legs, scraping his claws on the forcefield, causing bright sparks of electricity and clearly trying to get my attention. I quickly put the barrier down and started clearing the room, but it turned out my "crocodile" friend wanted to meet with me. Ussh Veesh spoke passable Geckho, so he asked to leave both of our subordinates outside and talk one on one. As soon as the defensive and sound-proof field had divided us from the outside world, the Trillian hissed:

"I heard you'll be leaving Medu-Ro IV soon and are planning to buy supplies."

I couldn't hide my astonishment. How did he know that?! Anyway... I hadn't exactly made a secret of the fact that I was looking for a starship. Also, I told my assistants and the pirate captains that I would be bringing cargo. Meanwhile, the merchant continued:

"In your place, I would have given the Pride of the Bushy Shadow a wide berth. They are not reliable partners. Also, they're greedy and crafty. But it is your choice, and I won't meddle in your affairs. I came here to make an offer. I want to give you a discount on my wares as a good friend. It's an excellent product, desired by absolutely everyone in the galaxy! And it is of particular interest to races new to the game that bends reality!"

"And what do you trade in, Ussh Veesh?" I had to admit, the merchant had captivated my interest. Even with my vibrant imagination, I couldn't think up anything wanted by everyone, especially new races.

With clear pride, the space crocodile set out a whole range of small decorative items, then waited for my reaction. I glanced over his assortment without particular interest: gold rings with glimmering gemstones, earrings, necklaces, ornate bracelets... So, my friend Ussh Veesh was a jewelry merchant. But what need did I or my faction have for that? I strained to hold back a sigh of disappointment, and... it was good that I did. Just then, I noticed the items had special properties:

Agility +1... Strength +1... Hand-to-Hand combat skill +3... Radiation defense +15%... Bladed weapon damage +6%... Endurance Points +4%...

So all these items were... magic?! Seemingly, I accidentally asked that aloud, because the merchant answered:

"Some call it 'magic,' but we Trillians prefer 'revealing the material essence.' Every player has known a time when they needed just a bit more skill or one more stat point to use a fine little item or weapon. Well, with these, you don't have to say 'no' to nice things or put them off for later. You can have what you want right away. It's especially important for new players because every improved weaponry or armor gives a significant boost to combat abilities, allowing them to catch up to their allies."

"Alright, you have my attention. And how many magic items can a person wear at once?" An image instantly crystalized in my mind of a near demigod with twenty rings on their fingers and toes, bracelets going from wrists to shoulders, and perhaps a couple earrings, necklaces, or body piercings.

"A Human? I have no idea. Trillians and Miyelonians are limited to four, but only two per skill or stat. The Meleyephatians can wear eight. The Geckho just two. But humans... how about you try? I'm interested myself."

Experimentation quickly showed that a person could wear one ring on each hand, two bracelets and an amulet around the neck. I suspected that characters with pierced ears could also wear magic earrings (I had one in my inventory), giving a total maximum of seven jewelry slots. But only two of them could have objects that improved stats, with another two for skills or resists. Overall that gave four pieces of "magical" jewelry. And that was good news, but still Humans were nowhere near the eight-legged Meleyephatians.

A fancy-looking ring jumped out at me, made of fine layers of very skillfully interwoven gold and ruthenium, with a huge dark-purple faceted gem inset. I could not identify it, even though I had a pretty solid understanding of Mineralogy and precious stones. I was drawn by the gem itself sure, but even more by the ring's property:

Intelligence +3

I put the ring on my finger, admiring it and at the same time watching how drastically my Magic Points shot up. Very pretty! Also, useful. I started looking over the treasure on the table in search of another ring like it, but all the others gave a mere +1 to their stat.

"You have great taste, Gerd Gnat! That is the star of my collection. I won that ring from someone who trades in artifacts of the Precursor race. It could be yours for some sixty thousand crypto!"

Sixty thousand crypto?! But that was four hundred twenty thousand Geckho crystals! Pretty steep for just one ring, no matter how ancient... With immense pity, I removed the ring from my finger and returned it to the table. The trader then took the ring in his clawed fingers and started looking through the stone at the light with clear satisfaction:

"What a beaut'! The secret of how to craft items with plus three or more has not survived to the modern era. These days, we mostly make plus-ones. Only the very best master jewelers can make plus-twos, but even then it's rare. By the way, I have a new plus-two Intelligence ring. Want it?"

"You bet I do!" I nearly shouted, because a plan instantly formed in my head.

That old bronze bracelet had been collecting dust in my inventory ever since the Relict base. The item was interesting just for its age of course but, in order to reveal its properties, I needed Intelligence of at least twenty-eight. With the +2 Intelligence ring on my left hand, I asked the Trillian for the ancient ring back and pretended I was comparing them. In fact, though, I hurriedly opened my inventory and looked at the bracelet:

Small Control Bracelet (Listener armor suit accessory)

+15% armor suit forcefield capacity.

+1 controllable drone.

Statistic requirements: Intelligence 26, Perception 26.

Skill requirements: Electronics 40, Machine Control 11.

Attention! Your character's Electronics skill is too low to wear this item.

Attention! Your character lacks the Machine

Control skill, which is required to use this object.

Attention! This object is for the Relict race and cannot be used by Humans.

There were lots of reasons why not, but none of them were insurmountable. I could get past the racial limitation with an experienced Mechanic, and I could easily take the Machine Control skill, then quickly level it to eleven. By the way, what did that skill do?

Obligingly, the information popped right up:

Machine Control. This skill confers the ability to control nearby computerized mechanical devices whether mentally, vocally, gesturally or via remote control. It also allows a character to attempt to hijack machines controlled by others. Leveling this skill allows a player to control more advanced machinery and more devices at once. Minimum statistics: Intelligence 22, Perception 22.

It seemed very useful, especially in combination with the ancient artifact. I immediately decided I was going to level up to this bracelet. Increasing the forcefield capacity alone was worth it, which was to say nothing of the extra drone. I could not tell what exact kinds of drone I could have from the description, but I was reminded of the deadly Relict guard drone that took down the Shiamiru crew. Most likely, the Small Control Bracelet was used to pilot things like that robot sentry. The idea of owning one of those deadly Relict drones was very tempting, so I made up my mind:

You have taken the skill Machine Control level 1!

Was I taking a risk? Without a doubt. But even if there were no more bases of the ancient Relict race in the galaxy, and all their fearsome guards had gone the way of the dodo, the skill description gave me reason to believe I could control other drones and robots, which was also very, very tempting.

Something else threw me though. The ancient bracelet required at least twenty-six Intelligence, which I only had with the outrageously expensive ancient ring, or if I filled two slots with objects that improved that statistic. I really did not want to waste a slot if I didn't have to.

Although, with time, I was hoping to raise my Intelligence by one point the "natural" way. Also, I could save up the money for the +3 Precursor ring or even become a Leng and earn more stat points that way, so the "wasted" slot would free up sooner or later. Overall, there were many ways to skin this cat, so I just needed to be patient. I carefully asked the Trillian merchant how much the new +2 Intelligence ring would cost.

"Three and a half thousand crypto, and only for you as a friend. But I sell the one-point stat rings or bracelets for basically nothing, just eighty-six crypto. Well, except the +1 Constitution ones. They're in the greatest demand so they go for one hundred fifty. And for rings that improve skills, damage or resists, I'd need to have a look. They all have different prices."

In the end, I got two Intelligence rings for three thousand five hundred eighty crypto. My Intelligence instantly went up to twenty-six, while my Magic Points jumped from 186 to 210. Not bad, not bad at all. I also took a silver chain that gave a useful +3% crit chance and a bracelet conferring +6 Mineralogy. All that, as well as a pair of +1 Agility rings for each of my

Miyelonian companions, I considered separate from the faction's expenses.

And so, my personal purchases over, the time had come to tend to faction acquisitions:

"Gerd Ussh Veesh, my friend, I'm gonna need you to dig deep for this one. I want around fifty plus-one stat rings. Can you make that happen?"

The merchant responded with utter calm, activated a device strapped to his front left arm, then confirmed that he could do that, and even provide delivery right to my ship.

"Now that's great!" I pressed the screen of my wallet to transfer him twenty-four thousand crypto, which was the total with discounting and wholesale prices. "And hold onto that plus-three-Intelligence Precursor ring for me. I'll buy it as soon as I have the money."

Chapter Twenty-Three

Way Home

THE GUNS I BOUGHT, primarily of Miyelonian design, took up ten containers. Laser and plasma assault rifles, electric-pulse snipers, a few high-speed heavy machine guns and one rocket system that could attach to heavy armor, a birthday gift for the leader of the Second Legion. I also got distance measurers, IR lenses, targeting systems and a whole box of some medicine that instantly restored Endurance Points... I didn't forget the "special delivery," either: two containers packed with weaponry for taking out heavy vehicles. All told, I got some unimaginably huge armor-piercing mobile railguns, laser-homing rockets with powerful EMP blasts, and fifty EMP grenades.

I didn't buy myself any long-distance weaponry, even though there were plenty of items in the electronic catalog for high Rifles skill. The Dark Faction pulse rifle

I already had was plenty for me now, and I wasn't even close skill-wise to more advanced weaponry. However, I did find nuclear batteries compatible with Relict equipment in the rare equipment section. I ordered myself three despite the fifteen-hundred-crypto price tag. They'd do fine for the Annihilator and my energy armor. I ordered rounds for my Paralyzer as well. At the very least, I was greatly hoping the contact poison balls would be the right size for my gun. I got two kinds, too: lethal and stun.

Another five containers were occupied by a huge mechanized Geckho Space Commando suit in disassembled form. Eduard Boyko's power armor weighed nine hundred ninety pounds on its own, and its weaponry, ammo, replacement batteries, extra filters, pumps and maintenance equipment ate up one hundred fifty pounds more.

I had no doubt that this armor could be refitted for a person, because Gerd Tamara had absolutely the same model. Also, it didn't cost an insane amount. Four thousand crypto or twenty-eight thousand crystals in a more familiar currency. In the space station shop, there were more advanced and expensive models too, but I figured that would be an unjustified waste of money. For one thing, I wasn't sure people could even use them. The only function I didn't see in the suit was cloaking, and the catalogue didn't have any accessories for that either. Clearly, that unique functionality had been added to Gerd Tamara's suit by our mechanics.

That was basically all. I rubbed my tired eyes, put down the VIP forcefield and headed for the exit where my companions were waiting. In the three hours I spent scanning the catalog, I raised my Astrolinguistics skill by two points to 65. And that was at the fact that I could change the language in the settings, and I almost instantly set it to the more familiar Geckho. I just had to ponder a few unfamiliar terms. Those three hours gave another two pleasant bonuses as well. My Electronics went to 37, and Medium Armor to 44.

Ayni and Tini were patiently waiting for me at a table in the stands. Before that, I paid for their lunches and asked them to wait outside and buy everything they'd need for the road, say goodbye to their friends and finish up any business on the space station, because we would soon be leaving and might never return. In fact, I had an ulterior motive for sending them away. I just didn't want to show the Miyelonians the huge fortune Gnat had in his wallet.

I sat at the table, tore a layered rainbow cocktail from the paws of my still tipsy kitten without asking and, after a cautious sniff, gulped down the strong herbal-honey concoction and said in dismay:

"An eye for an eye, as they say. Also Tini, what are you doing? We're leaving in a quarter ummi, and you're still drinking to calm your nerves."

"Yeah, but I'm in my right mind now," the little thief objected, pressing his ears to his head. Then, he boasted that he used the thousand crypto I'd given him to buy real "adult" combat blades and a light armor vest.

Naturally, Tini was speaking Miyelonian, but I understood him just fine. And when I spun back what

I said just half a minute earlier, I was astonished to realize I was also speaking Miyelonian and doing so with ease. Clearly, this was evidence of improved Astrolinguistics and higher Intelligence.

I praised my student for the wise purchases, then gave Tini and Ayni each a pair of +1 Agility rings. My kitten was overjoyed at the gift. Ayni less so. Although she put hers on, the Translator lost her nerve and lowered her eyes to the floor. First, I didn't understand what had her so upset, but then the bushy-tailed Translator made an admission. As it turned out, after the Truth Seeker interrogation, Ayni was feeling very guilty and had donated all her crypto to a fund for Miyelonian orphans.

"Don't worry, I'll pay."

I asked what kind of weapon she wanted. The Translator's reply came as no surprise: she needed a pair of close-combat blades. Ayni even said that every character of the Miyelonian race, regardless of gender or class, had the Blades and Fast Jump skills from their first day in the game. Many Miyelonian players had never used any other weapon, in fact.

"Given that every second enemy has Danger Sense, Stealth, Camouflage or Dodge, shooting long-distance is often pointless. The Miyelonian style is to get right up to the enemy and, using speed and mobility to our advantage, dice them to bits."

I didn't argue with the lady cat and, returning to the VIP box, ordered the Translator some decent curved blades. I was about to turn off the terminal when I suddenly slapped my palm on my forehead. I had almost forgotten to buy a new Prospector Scanner! I was nearly left without the tool of my trade. Now that would be an issue! In the end, I bought the most powerful and advanced model available, with a scanning radius of up to 7000 feet instead of the 5000 my previous scanner could do. I also ordered a set of single-use geological analyzers. Here on the Medu-Ro IV station, they sold for just two crypto a piece.

I looked at my remaining balance with sorrow. Just seven thousand two hundred crypto. I finally ordered my team to head for the elevator. The time had come to go meet the captain and crew, pick up my cargo and load it into the starship.

I MAY HAVE SLIGHTLY exceeded the ton and a half baggage limit. The quarrelsome, hungover Supercargo balked, refusing point blank to accept my five hundred thirty pounds of "overage" even for extra money. I do not know where I made such a serious miscalculation. I was doing my best to add everything up, but I was off by more than five hundred pounds. Either I wasn't considering the packaging of the seventeen large metal and plastic containers, or I had made a mistake.

It looked like I'd hit a dead end. I could get ninety pounds of items stuffed into the inventories of Gnat, Tini and Ayni, but where to put the other four hundred sixty?! I could not just leave the valuable cargo here on the pirate station, and I had no time to quickly sell the excess, even at a third the value. I almost made an extreme move and ordered all the containers unpacked, thus shedding the packaging weight, but suddenly Captain Rikki Pan-Miis came over and solved everything.

I was still holding my horses, though. The captain's flexibility was not necessarily a good thing. And soon after, I heard him say something quietly but distinctly to his crew members. I even understood:

"Come on, what's the damn difference?! We aren't really planning to go anywhere, much less land on that stupid planet, so I don't give a shit how much we're over capacity. All the better, I say. The more these dumbasses load, the more we end up with."

The pirates were going rob me! Probably, someone with good sense would have just turned around and left right then. And I would have done the same, if this voyage was with the deadly Pride leader, Gerd Abi Pan-Miay, a grizzled level-143 tomcat. But this was Captain Rikki Pan-Miis, a somewhat less fearsome opponent.

Rikki Pan-Miis. Miyelonian. Pride of the Bushy Shadow. Level-82 Navigator.

ATTENTION!!! Captain Rikki Pan-Miis is one of the Galaxy's most wanted space pirates. Danger rating: 2.

So, a big enough difference? I'd say so! The Pride leader was so dangerous you could smell it when he walked in the room. When he threatened to tear off my head, I knew he could and felt like he might. But Rikki, from what I could sense, was somewhat afraid of me. After all, I was a Gerd, which carried pretty decent authority. So, I was hoping I could reach an agreement with this pirate, or at the very least pressure him and scare him.

But in the very worst case... the crew of the nimble interceptor, as I immediately realized, had just six members, including the captain himself. And only three of them were even remotely formidable: Captain Rikki, a level-86 Geckho Shocktroop named Wen Shu, and a level-60 Miyelonian Gunner named Avi Wi-Rikki. If my understanding of Miyelonian naming conventions was right, that third one was being mentored or tutored by the captain and, most likely, would be fanatically loyal to him. So those three had me somewhat afraid.

The other three had noncombat professions: the cantankerous level-67 Supercargo was old as dino shit and just as useful in a serious scuffle; the level-42 Engineer had the slow contemplative mannerisms of a pothead and finally, the level-48 cat Prostitute with white-striped gray fur was too weighed down with jewelry. As far as I understood, she was the captain's girlfriend. And although I remembered Ayni saying that every Miyelonian had the Blades skill and high movement speed, I found it hard to take these three seriously as enemies.

What did that give me in the end? I had to get rid of the three dangerous crew members either temporarily or permanently, then I could negotiate with the other three from a position of power...

Wait, wait! I sharply cut off my fantasizing. I mean, I was seriously considering hijacking a pirate interceptor! What would I even do, if I found myself on a starship drifting through the vastness of space, and no one on board could steer it? Fortunately, it didn't come to that, though. And that wasn't my mission. I was supposed to bring platinum buyers to Earth and that was exactly what I was going to do. Although...

"Wait, I need to get something from that box!" I said, stopping the quarrelsome old Supercargo, who was using his robot loader to move my containers into the cargo hold. I threw back the lid and placed a nuclear battery into Gnat's inventory alongside a clip of stun balls and one geological analyzer. "Alright, you can put the rest away!"

I WAS HOPING to resolve matters peacefully. And sure, it may not have turned out that way, but it really wasn't my fault...

Just after our starship left dock, the pirates crowded up suspiciously next to Captain Rikki in the pilot's seat and... wait, yes, they were looking at me and my companions. That was the problem with small ships. All crew members were constantly in view of one another, and hiding conversations or plans was simply impossible. In fact, even the cramped Shiamiru cargo shuttle seemed like a luxury liner in comparison with the tiny Tiopeo-Myhh II. It didn't even have a captain's bridge, just three chairs in the front, one for the captain (who was also the Pilot and Navigator) and two for the Gunners (who were also in charge of Communications, Electronics, Mechanics and a whole bunch of other stuff). The three crew members not involved in steering the starship were supposed to squeeze into a tiny closet, which was boldly identified as a bunk. For me and my companions, they simply unfolded some stools on the metal floor in the tail next to the sealed door to the cargo hold.

The small distance and my high Perception allowed me to hear the crew's conversations fairly well:

"Let's not show our weapons yet, just act cool... (incomprehensible) ... now, let's go away from the station, speed up and pretend we're preparing for a long hyperjump... Gnat's companions we take out right away, but we need him alive. And tie him up... No, you cannot kill him! ... (incomprehensible) ... we are very interested in some ancient items in his inventory... Yeah, and what about... (incomprehensible) ... wants to know where he got such nice Relict stuff... Yes, we'll hand him over to the boss... all the cargo is ours, we can sell it to the Meleyephatians... enough to repair our ship!"

Astrolinguistics skill increased to level sixty-six!

Danger Sense skill increased to level twenty-seven!

You have reached level fifty-five!

You have received three skill points! (total points accumulated: six)

I took my leveling up as a good sign. It was a tense moment, but was I afraid? This may come as a surprise, but no. Not one bit. What was there to fear or worry about here? After all, I knew what I was getting into when I got on the ship. All that remained was to warn my companions. I poked the snoozing kitten and quietly enquired:

"Tini, when I searched you after you robbed me, you had long straps of strong leather in your inventory.

You still got 'em?"

"Yes, Master Gnat. And I have steel wire as well. What do we need to tie up?"

With a slight nod, I pointed at the pirates huddled up around their captain:

"They're going to attack us any time now. They plan to kill you and Ayni right away, then rob me. Naive... I can stun them all, but what will we do after that? Tini, do you know how to tie up prisoners?"

The kitten froze with his mouth agape, but Ayni answered for him, her voice lowered to a whisper:

"I do! But I'm not sure about the Geckho. I haven't had many encounters with that race, and that Shocktroop is especially big, and probably very strong."

I didn't think it was the right time to ask where or when the inoffensive-looking minute Translator had learned to tie up prisoners. Instead, I put forth a radical suggestion:

"Then we won't tie up the Geckho, we'll just stick a knife to his throat and send him to respawn! That'll bring the ship to a better weight, too. Look at that big old brute. I haven't heard of Clan Veesh Ameesh before, so it shouldn't stir the pot too much... Alright, everyone turn around quickly and don't look at him!"

The Shocktroop clearly sensed something was amiss because he stopped talking with his comrades and turned toward us in surprise. But all three of us pretended to be busy conversing and totally uninterested in the pirates. Finally, the alarmed giant calmed down and turned back around.

"Tini, I'd like it to be you who does it. You could really use the experience, and this will get you a couple levels. Ayni, you get ready too. You need to tie down the stunned prisoners. As soon as the lights go out, we begin! Ah crap, I didn't think to get infrared lenses from the cargo boxes. They'd come in very handy..."

Ayni asked barely audibly what made me so sure the light would be going out. I didn't answer, because I needed to get ready. After making sure the ammo I bought was the right size, I loaded the Paralyzer and moved it into my main weapons slot. I used my alternative slot for the charged-up Annihilator. Overall, I was hoping to get by without it but, "just to be on the safe side," I was keeping it at hand.

Now the time had come to spend my skill points. I had six saved up... Where could I put them to get the most benefit in the upcoming scuffle? The obvious options were Rifles and Sharpshooter, so I would hit the six enemies as quickly and accurately as possible. On the one hand, it seemed fine, but how would my helpers be able to distinguish the row of bodies in the dark and tie them up, given it all had to be done surgically, before any of them came back to their senses? Maybe Targeting was best then, to place clearly visible markers on all the enemies? After all, after the fight, we would need to interrogate the captain, and it would be nice to level up Psionic and Mental Fortitude before that... Basically, I needed to level everything!

Not having determined a clear priority, I placed two points each in Rifles, Targeting and Psionic. Almost ready. After making sure Tini had handed the wire and leather straps to the courageous Translator, I took out my Scanner and a metal tripod. Begin!

The light went out as predicted. At the same

time, the interceptor gave a sharp jostle and, seemingly, started spinning on its lengthwise axis. At that second, I clapped the Scanner closed, immersing the ship in darkness and put on my Relict armor.

Scanning skill increased to level forty-six!
Electronics skill increased to level thirty-eight!
Break-in skill increased to level twenty-two!
Break-in skill increased to level twenty-three!

Not busting my brains over what I had just broken into, I lowered my IR lens and grabbed my Paralyzer.

There they were, the bastards! My screen showed a single bright spot. My enemies had clustered together, forming a single tangled mass. Blam! Blam! Blam... Over a couple seconds, I emptied a whole clip of stun balls, but they were still moving! What was more, a nimble bright-red silhouette labeled "level-48 Prostitute" was dashing in my direction with two curved blades!

What happened next felt condensed into a single prolonged action and I would have a very hard time separating the individual parts. Something flickered, someone shouted in pain, then I was hit with a blinding purple flash and saw a message:

1280 damage absorbed by armor suit forcefield

Then I saw the Prostitute's cloven body, her razor-sharp blade a mere sixteen inches from my throat. At that moment, my back poked the heavy door to the cargo hold. So, I opened it with a powerful EMP. The wounded Tini howled. Ayni had locked blades with the Engineer. And then... with a rumble, the divider between the pilot area and the rest of the ship slammed down, and silence took hold.

"Gnat, what are you doing?!" the captain's voice rang out, dampened by the armored barrier.

"What am I doing?! Rikki, you should have discussed your attack plans a bit quieter!"

"Is that right...? So, you overheard..."

A long silence descended. Eventually, the captain shouted that I must have had great armor if I could survive two shots from a heavy blaster. I didn't answer, not wanting to reveal any of the Relict suit's secrets, or that he had missed the second time. Actually, had he? Maybe he hit Tini. After all, something had caused my kitten to shout in pain! But then, I saw Tini turn on a flashlight and go help Ayni tie up the prisoners. His health bar was almost full. Clearly, the shot had missed the Miyelonian teen as well.

Meanwhile, Rikki asked who of his crew was left alive. Before answering, I looked around and glanced at the mini-map:

"Your girlfriend and the Engineer are dead. The Supercargo and Geckho Shocktroop are stunned and tied up. I cannot see your ward Avi Wi-Rikki. I suspect he is with you in the front part of the ship. And let me warn you, Rikki: I will not allow you to activate your electronics or communications. I can easily short them out many times. I will not allow myself to be brought to your boss, and I certainly will not allow you to call for reinforcements or take any of my property. So, I suggest that we cool our heads and calmly discuss what happens next. To my eye, it would be most proper to return to our initial understanding and fly off for the platinum. That way, you can make a profit, and I can finally go home!"

"It'll be hard for me to go anywhere without an Engineer. And it'll be even harder to land on a large planet with all this extra weight..."

"We can get the weight down no problem..." I said, commanding Tini to end the Geckho's life.

But for some reason, the little thief lost his nerve and, holding the blade in his shaking hand at the helpless Shocktroop's throat, could not bring himself to commit murder in cold blood. He removed the weapon. He didn't have the grit. But Ayni did what was necessary. One sharp slash and the furball's fanged head was separated from his body.

"Alright, the weight problem has been solved. There's nothing to stop us from landing on the planet now," I shouted to the pirate captain. "Make your choice, Rikki. Will you fly off for the platinum, or should I blow a hole in the barricade with my Annihilator, capture your starship and, as its captain, find myself a more agreeable pilot?"

I had to wait a decent amount of time for an answer, but then the captain relented:

"Alright, Gnat. I'll take you up! Let's return to our initial understanding! I promise that I will not do anything stupid again. We'll go and land where we initially agreed. But I'll need the Supercargo in the copilot's seat and, for that, I will need to briefly raise the metal divider. However, I would prefer to spend the next five ummi separated from you. I don't want any more surprises."

ATTENTION!!! Captain Rikki Pan-Miis's danger

rating has fallen to one.

Fame increased to 47.

Authority increased to 12!

Authority increased to 13!

Authority increased to 14!

You have reached level fifty-six!

You have received three skill points!

It worked! Victory! I was almost home free! I could bear the thirty hours in transit, especially given that the hold was open, giving me access to the endurance-restoring potions. All that remained was to check whether I managed to complete my official mission. As long as I had a diagram of this ship, I could simply rest and enjoy the trip.

I turned on my computer and looked at the screen. Yes, there it was, a highly-detailed diagram of a Tiopeo-Myhh II Miyelonian long-distance interceptor with all the bolts and rivets. But my attention was drawn by a different aspect. Among all the partitions, thrusters and power sources, there were markers for living creatures, including one that caught my eye:

Morphian. Level 279.

Chapter Twenty-Four

Free Time

I WAS IN NO HURRY and didn't want to do anything rash. The last thing I needed was to piss off the Morphian and instantly respawn back on Medu-Ro IV. Instead, unhurriedly and with a calm look, I changed into my more comfortable jacket with kevlar inserts and fell back on the only bed in the bunk, placing my hands behind my head and trying to get some shut-eye.

Tini came up quickly and said that the enemies had practically dropped no trophies, just an unremarkable utility belt from the Engineer, with all the pouches empty. I waved it off and told my foundling to keep the belt. But the kitten wouldn't leave and stood there, his tail twitching nervously:

"Sorry, Master Gnat, I goofed up. I've never had to kill anybody before, and I... couldn't carry out the order."

"Don't worry, Ayni took care of it." I got up on the bed, extended a hand and turned the furry Miyelonian's left cheek toward me. There was blood flowing down it, and the teenager's ear was split in two lengthwise. "When did you get that?"

"I don't even know," Tini said, now more disheartened. "I was confused and didn't notice anyone. I just felt a sharp pain and saw Ayni pulling a blade away from my head at the very last second."

"It was Avi Wi-Rikki, the Gunner," the Translator threw out, walking up and sitting right on my knee. "Unfortunately, he got away and hid behind the barrier, because I was distracted with the Prostitute..."

I remembered the Miyelonian lady being split in half seconds before her blade reached my throat and nodded in silence. Ayni had come just in time... Also, apparently Miyelonians weren't deterred by darkness. They could see and fight in it just fine. A bit later, I asked my companions about that. Tini looked surprised:

"I've heard that some races have problems in the dark. The Geckho, and I think... is it the Trillians? I don't remember. Do people have that too? Miyelonians have no trouble seeing in almost pitch blackness. Did you really not know that, Gerd Gnat?"

Well, crap... I really did not know that, so my idea to turn off the lights and take advantage of the ensuing chaos was obviously misguided. That's what gummed up my plans. And that error could have been fatal, if not for the phenomenal speed of the deadly Ayni... By the way, now I knew Morphians could also see just fine in the dark.

And another thing... I turned and looked for a trace of the second blaster shot but couldn't find it. Had the Morphian taken it for me?! Ayni's life bar was almost totally full, ninety-five percent, if not more. Considering that my armor blocked one thousand two hundred hitpoints of damage from an identical round, I quickly estimated that the Morphian must have had around twenty-five or thirty thousand Health Points. That was practically twenty times more than Gnat!

"Something wrong?" the Translator asked in Geckho, looking at me closely. "Gnat, your face looks different. You just don't look like yourself after that scuffle."

I took a bit to answer, but then I decided not to hide anything, and say it directly:

"Lots of things are wrong. I don't even know where to start... First, Fox, I'd like to know where the real Ayni is."

I was very worried when asking that question, and was paying close attention to my feelings, but Danger Sense never piped up. Either the Morphian didn't have bad intentions, or it was hiding them carefully. And meanwhile, the orange cat narrowed her eyes and started grinning predatorily, demonstrating her sharp teeth:

"You really are smart and observant, Gerd Gnat. I see why Leng Amiru U-Mayaoo praised you so highly."

"What?! Were you there for that?!" I shouted, unable to restrain my emotions. And Tini, not understanding a word of our conversation, but fully sensing the intonations and mood, perked up his ears and put his hand on the hilt of his blade.

Ayni chuckled happily and, placing her hand on the kitten's forehead, told him to go take a rest. Tini nodded in silence, shuffled off to the nearest chair submissively and, just a few seconds later, had drifted off without a care, having forgotten all his fears and troubles. After that, Ayni removed the rings from her fingers and set them on the pull-out table next to her two sharp blades, then quickly changed into a busty anthropomorphic fox:

"I am reminded, Gerd Gnat, that you found this form more agreeable, so take note: I'm doing my best for you. Now, I'll try to answer your questions. Yes, I was present for your conversation with the Miyelonian Priestess. At that time, I was in the form of a First Pride soldier. I was also one of the guards that arrested you in the hotel, and I took you to the interrogation as well. Maybe you'd like to know that, if you had tried to run right away, I would have helped you. As for Ayni, the last time I saw her, she was wandering toward the residential area of the space station. She was in a very dejected state after the Truth Seeker interrogation, and I attempted to convey that when we met. But it has been almost two ummi since then, so Ayni has probably gotten some rest and recovered. She is most likely just fine."

I couldn't check the Morphian's words, but I didn't see a particular reason for Fox to lie. Most likely, that was true, and the Morphian had not killed her. Well, at least that was a bright side...

"And what next?" I asked a somewhat vague question. But the Morphian understood just fine:

"Next? We fly to your home world. That's what I

want, and that's what you want. The pirates are very scared. I can feel it clearly, so they will not try to open the armored barrier until the very moment we land. So get some rest. You can even sleep. But I don't recommend that you leave the game until the flight is over. Sorry, Gnat, but then I might be forced to kill you for my own safety, which I would very much prefer not to do. Then, as far as I understand, we'll land on your planet. If you like, I'll leave the ship with you and spend some time with your faction. If not, I'll fly back with the pirates. I'm not going to impose on you with my company, but I wouldn't say no to sitting around for a dozen or so on the edge of the galaxy, either."

Well, Fox was speaking very candidly about what might come next. That is, if I could trust the Morphian at all. But I still decided to clarify a couple of strange aspects:

"You said you wanted to spend some time with my faction. What would that entail? Would you take human form? Are you going to eat one of my allies and take their place?"

The creature sat back and laughed just like a person:

"I'll be as honest as I can. If there were more Humans out there, that's exactly what I would do: get lost in the crowd. But you just started the game that bends reality, and your faction has a few thousand players at most, if not just a couple hundred. You know each other well, and your virt pods are probably concentrated in one place in the real world, so a death would be impossible to cover up. Given that, you have to agree that it would be stupid for me to hunt people or take their form. What's more, you know that I cannot imitate people very well. You could tell I was fake from one touch. So, if you aren't opposed, I'll be the Miyelonian Ayni Uri-Miayuu, a modest quiet Translator. Don't worry, I won't harm your faction, but I could be a great help!"

I was prepared to agree with her there. Fox had a massive amount of extremely high-value information about space, alien races, politics, history, weapons and technologies. If I let our scientists interview her, technological breakthroughs of all kinds were a virtual certainty! What was more, she knew all the main languages of the galaxy and could help anyone who wanted to study them. And that was to say nothing of the most obvious application. Having a combat character over level 279 on our side would be very, very helpful in fighting back the Dark Faction! And though that didn't guarantee victory in the skirmish, it was a significant leg up!

I didn't have to say anything. Fox could sense my choice, and she smiled happily:

"You won't regret that, Gerd Gnat. I have lots to offer in return for a ticket to your planet and temporary sanctuary."

"Fox, was that baggage overage your doing?"

"Yes." She didn't deny it. "I needed to add some personal items: equipment for special missions, my weapon, various pharmaceuticals..."

"The tail of the incarnation of the Great First Female..." I added, and the smile instantly crawled off Fox's face.

Danger Sense skill increased to level twenty-

eight!

"Yes, the tail as well," Fox confirmed, now extremely serious and agitated. She extended the razor-sharp claws of her front paws as if in passing. "Alright, I'll tell you about my mission, then we'll never speak of it again, cool?"

I nodded in silence, knowing that I didn't have much of a choice.

"Alright then. Now listen. The background of all this is so confusing that I don't even know who's really behind it myself. But let me assure you that you and your race were never at risk. Every truly influential political player could see clearly that this was too high-level for you, at the very least at this stage in your society's development. Everything the Truth Seekers allowed you to know during the conversation was the truth. Four Meleyephatians entered the cafe, but just three came out. The Miyelonians missed one fairly significant detail, though. Only three Meleyephatians left the starship in the first place! As ordered, I met up with them on the station, made friends and shared a meal in the cafe. There we talked for a bit and parted ways. They went back to their trading, and I got back to my mission, which is when I saw you..."

"So, Fox, you're saying it was not a failed Meleyephatian plot to frame the Geckho, but that the Meleyephatians were also framed?! By who?"

"Now that I do not know. And even if I had that information, I wouldn't admit it. But the tail... well, that was a personal touch. I was only ordered to publicly murder the incarnation of the Great First Female. But now, whoever this trophy turns up with will be automatically declared an enemy of the Miyelonians, and that is sure to start a great war!!!"

THE FUNNIEST THING was that I did manage to fall asleep. Heck, despite the three space pirates just behind the barricade and the deadly monster at arm's length, I woke up decently rested. Clearly, the last day had left me physically and emotionally sapped. The arrest, interrogation, psionic probing, all the stress of making purchases and finagling the pirate starship...

After opening my eyes, I discovered that Fox, in the form of the orange Miyelonian Translator, was asleep in my bed spooning me, while Tini was keeping watch with the plasma assault rifle, already having slept off his distemper. I wondered where the kitten got that weapon. Actually, it was a familiar model. I had bought basically that same kind of rifle for my faction. One glance through the open door into the cargo hold was enough to line these facts up.

"Tini, you'll have to put the gun back into the box before we land, along with whatever else you pilfered. It would be fine if they were my things, but my faction has a list and they're going to check to see it's all there."

The Miyelonian teenager took some time to answer, standing for some time with his mouth slightly open, about to disagree with my order or clarify some aspect, but eventually he just relented:

"As you wish, Gerd Gnat. It's not like I have the

skills to use this thing well anyway."

I sat up on the cot, carefully running my hand over the sleeping Ayni's smooth well-groomed fur (she could faithfully imitate textures when she wanted to!). Then I put my legs on the metal floor and checked my inventory. With the Thief around, I had to always be cautious and keep one eye on my bags. But everything was in the right place, which reflected positively on my companion. I had a dried ration for breakfast and fed my kitten to his satisfaction, then suggested that we put our free time to good use:

"Where we're going, the average level is about double yours. So you'll have to train and study hard to catch up if you want to survive. Does that scare you?"

"Of course it does," said the Miyelonian teen, "but it will still be more fun than collecting specks of experience on the space station by stealing and constantly getting slapped around. In my first twenty days in the game, I leveled up just seventeen times and died four times a day. With you, I've grown eleven levels in two days without dying once! So, Master Gnat, for now I am very happy with my change in fortune!"

We spent the next few hours training. In the small cramped room, Tini was trying to dodge the robot loader, which I was controlling with a remote left by the Supercargo. I was trying to catch the nimble Thief, but he was so quick he could walk on walls.

"Master Gnat, my Agility just grew to twenty!" To say that, the panting level-thirty Thief stopped for just half a second, his claws latched into a ventilation grate on the ceiling. Unfortunately for him, the spry adolescent stopped long enough to catch him in the loader claw.

"Got you! Caught again!"

Agility increased to 17.

Machine Control skill increased to level seven!

Electronics skill increased to level thirty-nine!

Finally, Agility went up by one, the last of my stats to do so. And that was somewhat strange because I always used to prefer classes with high Agility — archers, rangers, assassins, thieves and so forth. Here though, the Prospector class and my gameplay style required Perception and Intelligence more, so my Agility was lagging.

The kitten, after flailing in the robot loader's claw and quickly realizing it was no use, asked me to let him go and at the same time begged for a break. To be honest, I was also tired after two hours driving the loader, so I threw the control away with satisfaction and plopped back on the bed, accidentally hitting the sleeping Translator's leg, which I couldn't see under the covers.

"Let me sleep, you fiends! I've been awake for almost two ummi because of you!" Ayni grumbled unhappily, turning toward the wall.

I mumbled a few words of apology and started looking for something quiet to do, for example level Psionic. But who to train it on? Tini's Intelligence, as he himself told me, was just fifteen. That was the minimum for the Thief class and Break-in skill. With my twenty-six, I had a 100% chance of reading the juvenile's thoughts and taking the kitten under my control. I even tried during our two-hour practice and realized it didn't level the skill at all, just wasted Magic

Points. But who else was there? The sleeping Morphian?

Trying to relax and abstract myself from the world, I sat and looked at the sleeping bushy-tailed Translator. Nothing happened for a long time. Was it because we weren't making eye contact? But I managed to read Tini's thoughts regardless of whether I could see his eyes or not. I tried a number of times before I was suddenly washed over with a flood of alien thoughts:

"I haven't seen Qitir for a long time... Eighteen years have passed since our last encounter, if not more... And Amiray won't answer my requests. But she grew tired of this life long ago and was on the verge of a breakdown. Maybe she took a risk and went into the real world? Most likely... And the clutch on Oruvan III was destroyed... Who could have known about it? Maybe it was an inside job... If we allow the blackmailers to destroy our offspring on the captured starship, it would seem wise old Vaa and I are two of the last of us in the Universe... Also, I don't know if Vaa will even wake up after such a long nap. I mean, two hundred years in suspended animation... Although, the planet we're flying to should be good enough to get her back to normal..."

Action terminated. Magic Points exhausted.
Psionic skill increased to level eighteen!
Psionic skill increased to level nineteen!

An endless wave of impenetrable sorrow and impending doom rolled over me. I fell back and could barely remain sitting on the cot. Then, I sat up more comfortably and... met with the cold attentive eyes of the Morphian who had clearly finished getting her beauty sleep.

"Gnat, do you grow tired of living?" Fox asked in Miyelonian, clearly flustered. And the curious Tini instantly jumped in asking what Gnat had done to make Ayni so mad?

I had to squirm out of it, inventing a believable story:

"I thought Ayni was asleep and looked into her inventory just out of curiosity. But I know I shouldn't..."

"Exactly, you shouldn't do that! And if you do anything like it again, I'll bite your head off! I'm not joking!"

I apologized again and, for some reason, Tini started looking embarrassed, or seemingly even afraid.

We spent the next few hours between intensive training and breaks. Ayni taught Tini mastery of blades, while I tried to fix the now broken robot loader, leveling my Electronics and Machine Control skills. The repair took me an ummi and a half. A few times, I was ready to say to hell with it and give up, but then I realized that, without it, unloading the containers and exchanging the platinum would take far too long, maybe even long enough to kill the deal. And I eventually succeeded. The robot came back to life and, as a pleasant bonus, I got two new levels in Electronics and three in Machine Control!

Just an hour before we landed, when Captain Rikki told us from behind the armored barrier that he could see my planet, I asked about payment. I really did not want to have to hassle the faction for my share of the crystals later or put up with untrusting allies questioning my very right to the money. So, I made what I thought was a reasonable suggestion: he would pay me a million crystals before landing — i.e. approximately the amount I spent on faction supplies.

But that seemingly trifling request was met with unexpectedly serious resistance. Captain Rikki refused outright, referring to the fact that we had not agreed to do so in advance. He also repeated that he would not open the barrier before landing due to safety concerns, and that he had not yet seen the platinum firsthand.

"Perfect time for you to practice Psionic," Ayni whispered to me in Geckho, and I realized I had no other way to change the stubborn captain's mind.

My Magic Points had replenished, so there was just one small thing missing. I needed to see my target in some way. I activated Scanning and saw three markers. On the mini-map, I determined which pirate was which. I wanted the captain. There he was, in the middle seat.

No one had ever taught me this, but for some incomprehensible reason, I planted my feet at shoulder width apart, put my left hand behind my back, clenched my right hand into a fist and aimed it at Rikki. Come on, work!

"I really don't want more problems with these passengers. Gnat has connections with influential Pride leaders and even Truth Seekers. I'd better pay up right now and give him the down payment of one million crystals, or I might have to pay for it later. His cargo can serve as a guarantee. About a million is what it's worth, so I don't stand to lose a thing."

No luck! For some reason, the pirate captain either didn't want to or couldn't even bring himself to do what I suggested. I immediately realized that some part of it was impossible. But I couldn't tell what. Was he afraid to open the divider? Did he not have enough crystals? Close, but no cigar...

My Magic Points were quickly running out, but I still didn't have what I wanted. So, I made one last desperate attempt, slightly adjusting my suggestion:

"I hope Gnat agrees to be paid in crypto. That is safe and reliable, and I could make the payment without raising the divider."

Action terminated. Magic Points exhausted.

I heard the captain's muffled voice on the other side of the barrier:

"Gerd Gnat, what if I pay you in crypto? That'd be one hundred forty-three thousand, according to the exchange rate!"

Score! It worked!!!

Psionic skill increased to level twenty!

Psionic skill increased to level twenty-one!

Mental Fortitude skill increased to level seventeen!

My wallet vibrated, confirming a change in balance. Just then, Captain Rikki said we were coming in for a landing.

Chapter Twenty-Five

Rendezvous on Centaur Plateau

I WAS FEELING like garbage when we landed! I had never had any problems with motion-sickness before, neither in the real world or any virtual one. Here in the game, of course, there were fairly light G forces when the Shiamiru took off, or Captain Uraz Tukhsh made harsh landings, but that was easy to tolerate, and had a sensible explanation. When landing at our space port, the heavy Geckho cargo shuttle simply fell from the atmosphere like a brick to the bottom of a pond. Sure we lost speed a bit faster than recommended, but it was all fairly smooth...

Now, though, I was feeling the joy of entering the atmosphere in a small delicate interceptor for the first time. The unsteady ship was shaking and spinning so much that, at times, it seemed it might break into pieces. But worst of all was a maddening whistling sound that made me clench my teeth so hard I heard crunching. It was as if someone was peeling the armor off the exterior with a huge cheese grater. I had never experienced anything like that before. Maybe, the Shiamiru's forcefield muffled these sounds, or maybe it simply had thicker walls.

I clenched my white fingers into the seat and only barely held back the urge to vomit. No matter how I tried to steel my nerves, I found it physically impossible to get used to! I started to think that, after another minute or two, I would lose some Authority by spilling the contents of my stomach all over the ship.

The kitten was nauseated too. He was doing just as bad as me. Ayni was the only one of us that looked okay. She was smiling and even trying to cheer us up. I only then realized why the constantly hungry Morphian refused to eat with us earlier. It probably had Constitution as a main stat as well, though, so it was having an easier time... Wait! If I needed more Constitution, I could fix that!

To the surprised gazes of my companions, I stood up on my shaky legs and headed into the cargo hold. Which one of these containers had the "magical" rings? Fortunately, I didn't have to look for long. I set the Intelligence rings in my inventory, and instead put on two +1 Constitution bands. And it worked! Everything became much easier, and soon the torture was over. The shaking gradually stopped, and the speed of the starship fell to bearable. What was more, the mind-melting squealing finally finished. We had no portholes in the back, so the only signs we had landed were a barely perceptible bump and the thrusters going quiet.

"There are some people waiting here," Captain Rikki's voice rang out. "Gnat, I think they're your faction. Go out and look. Are those your friends?"

The central part of the starship floor lowered with a light hiss, turning into an angled gangway. The cold, overly filtered and sterilized air rushed out and the ship was flooded with fresh, floral and vaguely salty aromas. I only then realized how badly I missed that the last few days! With my companions, I went down the gangway and saw diplomat Ivan Lozovsky accompanied by Imran and the vigilant armed guards of the First Legion. My people!

And they recognized me, too. Not ashamed at the outburst of emotion, my allies ran up to embrace me and shake my hand. Anya was among them and, with a joyful cry, she threw herself around my neck and sank into my lips with a passionate kiss. Based on the flood of elated remarks and fragmentary sentences, I realized the whole faction already knew about my misadventures on the pirate station. As it turned out, our Journalist had written a bulletin about it. Prospector Gnat, not understanding a single word of Miyelonian, was left totally alone in a treacherous and far-away place teeming with malicious and bloodthirsty pirates! Seemingly, up to the very last moment, my allies didn't believe I could get out of this scrape and return home. The big First Legion guys slapped me on the shoulder and couldn't hide their tears of joy.

Mental Fortitude skill increased to level eighteen!

A mental attack?! But from where??? Not stopping my kiss with Anya, I tried to figure out what just happened. Maybe the Morphian had scanned my feelings to better understand humans? Or was the game system alerting me to the blonde beauty's secret desire to make me her own? It was probably that, because her next words were in that vein.

"Say what you want, Gnat, but tonight I'm gonna swing by your room," she stated matter-of-factly, utterly not embarrassed that others might hear.

Authority increased to 15!

Finally, the greetings came to an end, and we got to business.

"What about the platinum?" I asked Lozovsky with alarm, and the deputy director assured me it was ready.

"But I have to admit that we barely managed! The last bars were brought into the game literally an hour ago. We had one newbie who, despite all the instructions and practice, was dumb enough to get lost in the Labyrinth! It took him two and a half hours to get out! He's a Priest by profession. He says he spent too much time thinking about his place in the game world and lost track of time."

"A Priest??? How'd we get someone like that in our faction?!" I chuckled, to which the diplomat told me it was Radugin's idea. The faction leader figured that since our Paladin, in essence half warrior and half priest, was capable of defending against enemy magic, we needed to try and bring a few people into our faction from the spiritual realm. So the last batch of newbie had two of them come through the Labyrinth. One was an old imam from Kazan who enjoyed great respect in the Muslim world. And the other was an Orthodox monk from the Solovetsky Monastery. And both of them chose the same class: Priest. In the next few days, they would be leveled quickly in order to bless our soldiers before the Dark Faction attack and defend against enemy mages.

Cool! I wanted to know more about our Leng's new project, but our conversation was interrupted by Captain Rikki Pan-Miis emerging on the gangway with his ward Avi Wi-Rikki. Both Miyelonians were armed and on guard. Rikki found me with his gaze and shouted that he wanted to finish this up and get out of Geckho space quickly. I translated for my allies, and Lozovsky gave a wave to the soldiers around him. They started carrying heavy boxes from the nearby Peresvets and stacking them up next to the gangway.

The Miyelonian Gunner clicked open the lock on the nearest box and, using a device reminiscent of a soapbox camera, started checking the bars one after the next. I heard him tell the captain:

"All good. They're solid bars, made of platinum. And the purity is impeccable!"

The captain purred in satisfaction and commanded the Supercargo to turn on the robot loader and bring my goods out of the hold while his assistant checked the rest of the bars. While the many boxes were taken out of the starship, I introduced my new companions to the faction. And I let them all know that these two Miyelonians would be staying with me, not going back home.

As expected, my announcement had Lozovsky flustered. The diplomat was silent but looked agitated, probably imagining the potential consequences. Hopefully, he wouldn't forbid the Miyelonians to stay out of fear for our suzerains' reaction...

"Kento duho, Ivan!" Ayni greeted Ivan Lozovsky politely in Geckho, and he answered mechanically. That automatically conferred the fluffy Translator the status of "friend of the faction," though, which had some privileges, such as the right of abode and guaranteed protection.

"Aw hell..." the Diplomat cursed, realizing what he'd just done. Now, he'd have to bust his brains over the most delicate way of informing our suzerains that members of a competing race were now guests of our faction.

"I'll talk with Kosta Dykhsh myself. I promise there won't be any problems!" I assured the Diplomat, and Ivan Lozovsky immediately calmed down and even started smiling.

Meanwhile, the exchange of goods had finished, and payment time had come. I warned my boss that it would only be two million crystals, while the other million had been paid to me as an advance, which I used to buy all the supplies. I do not know why but, at the last moment, the Diplomat asked me to go elsewhere and let him talk with the trader one-to-one or, more accurately, through the Miyelonian Translator.

Was Ivan Lozovsky ashamed to accept the

money in my presence, or did he want to discuss something in secret with the merchants? I had no idea, but I didn't stop him. Especially given that Ayni would tell me what they said, if I asked. I helped the First Legion soldiers load our stuff into a Peresvet, spoke with now the level-30 Gladiator Imran and reassured my kitten, who was scared to be in an unfamiliar atmosphere. Then, I returned to the Diplomat.

"Everything is great. They agreed to buy more platinum, and we discussed trading other goods as well!" Lozovsky said, clearly satisfied with himself. He then waved farewell to the Miyelonians, who were already on the rising gangway. Then the hatch closed.

The Tiopeo-Myhh II roared its thrusters, started hovering, stowed its landing supports, then bumped its nose on the ground and loudly took off vertically into the heavy black clouds. A half a minute later, there were no reminders of the smuggler's ship on the stony plateau.

"Done deal! Let's get into the ATV's and go back home!" Ivan Lozovsky ordered, himself heading to a Peresvet.

Mental Fortitude skill increased to level nineteen!

Another mental attack! I instantly turned to the Morphian, but Ayni was talking with Tini and seemingly had not triggered it. And Anya had already climbed into an armored vehicle and was now holding the door open for other soldiers, ruling her out as well. So, what was happening?

Most likely, if I had another few seconds, I would have thought to run a scan and figured it all out. But I didn't. Events started unfolding at once.

On the mini-map among the blue ally markers, I immediately saw a few red enemies ones!!! At the same time, Ivan Lozovsky tripped on smooth rock, and a gray Dark Faction Saboteur silhouette appeared next to him, holding our Diplomat's falling body. I saw the enemy stash a bag of crystals in his own inventory, then give everyone a middle finger. But next, he put his laser pistol to his temple and pulled the trigger. Damn!!! He was headed to respawn, taking with him all the money my faction had just earned trading with the Miyelonians! I wanted to howl in impotent rage. All that struggle down the drain! At the very last minute, our reward had been stolen!

I was confounded and spent a few seconds blinking helplessly, just watching. But while I stood there in shock, a slaughter began. People were firing on the First Legion soldiers from all sides. We lost two in the very first seconds. Finally, my consternation passed, and I could think and move again.

"Fight back! Attack the people in the gray suits!" I shouted in Miyelonian, throwing the Listener suit into my armor slot, and the Annihilator into main weapon.

Blam! Blam! The two Dark Faction Assassins nearest to me, seemingly trying to grab me, went to respawn with huge holes in their chests.

Sharpshooter skill increased to level twenty-eight!

Rifles skill increased to level forty-five!

You have reached level fifty-seven!

You have received three skill points! (total points accumulated: six)

I dismissed the messages. Sure they were nice,

but this was not the time. I rolled behind a big boulder and tried to get a clearer picture of the battle. Seemingly, the enemies had us surrounded and were firing from all sides, but... my Danger Sense was silent! Strange. That must have meant they weren't shooting at me! And that could only mean the enemy intended to take me alive.

Then before my eyes, after several precision blows, Ivan Lozovsky fell just as he was beginning to return to his senses. Not good! We were dropping like flies! The enemy fire had also fallen in intensity, though, so they were also taking losses. Then I noticed the Miyelonians, bounding around the battlefield and cutting enemies down one by one. By the way...

"Imran, catch!" I said, tossing the Miyelonian blade to him as he crouched between the wheels of an armored vehicle, trying to shoot his laser pistol.

The Dagestani athlete caught the weapon in midair, putting the nearly useless pistol into his inventory. Then he equipped his old curved blade in his left hand, and the new Miyelonian one in his right, glimmering with electric sparks. An instant later, my friend was a hundred feet away, slicing the head clean off an enemy gunman. At the same time, one of the Peresvets' high-speed cannons thundered into action, raining down molten lead on an enemy firing point. Now we'll see who gets the upper hand!

The battle entered the next phase. There were no more enemies nearby, but the snipers crouching in the distance were making sure we didn't stick our noses out. Then I saw a First Legion soldier take out his automatic and hide behind a rock, hissing in pain and trying to tie off his bleeding arm above the elbow. Anya instantly ran over to help, jumping out of the secure Peresvet and taking out her first aid kit. But... she didn't make it. Our courageous Medic was bowled over by the flicker of a bright beam. An enemy sniper. Not good! Not good at all!

And what was I doing just sitting here?! After all, this was the perfect time for a Prospector! I activated Scanning and saw enemies hiding on the mini-map. There actually weren't many of them, just eight.

"Hey you, on the Peresvet! Put me in your group! I'll set targets!" I shouted. And a few seconds later, the game system confirmed it.

At the left edge of my field of vision, I could now see three semi-transparent First Legion soldier icons. One of them was seriously wounded. I also got some accuracy and armor bonuses, but that didn't matter. One after the other, I marked the enemies, revealing them to every group member. Eight targets, eight markers.

Targeting skill increased to level fourteen!
Targeting skill increased to level fifteen!

The Peresvet tower pivoted instantly, and the cannon spit fire, bringing the enemy-count down to seven. Another sniper accidentally revealed himself and was seen and killed by Ayni. Then, another enemy got up and tried to find better cover, but our gunman took him down as well.

Targeting skill increased to level sixteen!
Eagle Eye skill increased to level fifty-four!
You have reached level fifty-eight!
You have received three skill points! (total points

accumulated: nine)

The battle was clearly already over, and we had won. The surviving enemies, held down tight by our fire, were hiding and couldn't afford to move a muscle. After all the stress and grief, a wave of composed confidence and power rolled over me. I stood up and walked straight toward the enemy, changing out my Constitution rings for Intelligence ones as I went. No, I hadn't lost my mind or fallen victim to shell shock. I simply calculated that one or two shots from the Dark Faction snipers couldn't get through my force field, and they wouldn't have the time to get off any more.

Also, I needed to take risks and push forward. I didn't believe this reinforced Dark Faction sabotage group had just happened to be here. So, it was very important to grab one alive, interrogate the crap out of them and figure out who told them the secret time and location of our meeting with the alien merchants.

Anyhow, I could now see two enemies. They were crouching behind the same boulder and, apparently, preparing to leave the battle by shooting themselves. No such luck! I chose one of them at random. This one had already stuck his pistol in his mouth. I sharply extended my fist and... Bam! Got you, little birdie!!!

Just then, someone shot me and seemingly even threw a grenade, but I didn't let it get to me. Danger Sense would warn me and give me plenty of time to take cover. The main thing now was not to let the enemy escape my mental control!

Before, I had only ever used this ability when training with Tini, but this was a work of art. As soon as I issued the mental command, the soldier threw his pistol aside, and knocked the grenade out of his ally's hand before he could blow himself up.

Psionic skill increased to level twenty-one!
Psionic skill increased to level twenty-two!
Mental Fortitude skill increased to level twenty!

A pitched battle started between the two Dark Faction soldiers, and "my" guy was losing, taking a knife to the chest. But their fight was of little concern to me now, because I had spotted a much more interesting target: Minn-O La-Fin! The Dark Faction Leng's very own granddaughter!!! Most likely, she was the ringleader of this operation, and would have a lot to tell us.

In order not to waste my valuable, quickly diminishing Magic Points, I relinquished mental control over the enemy soldier. It wasn't even necessary anymore, either. Each of the two grappling soldiers thought the other a traitor and was rabidly trying to kill their opponent using knives, fists and even teeth. I meanwhile was concentrating on the more interesting target...

Minn-O La-Fin, without wanting to, played right into my hand and met gazes with me. I didn't even know if I had the strength remaining to take her under my control. At any rate, the granddaughter of the great mage had decent Intelligence. So then... work! Obeying my command, the enemy cartographer threw a grenade away before pulling the pin.

Psionic skill increased to level twenty-three!

"Ayni, tie up that prisoner!" I pointed the Translator toward Minn-O, and the bushy-tailed Miyelonian dashed off.

That was it. The granddaughter of the Dark Faction coruler was the last enemy left. Victory! I put my Annihilator away and changed back into my unprepossessing jacket.

At that moment, I thought I felt a light mental touch, as if someone was trying very cautiously to probe my thoughts. However, after looking around carefully, I couldn't see anything suspicious.

Chapter Twenty-Six

Distant War

WHAT A CATASTROPHE! There was just no other way to call it. Shortly afterward, the faction started reviewing every detail in the Dome administration building in the real world. Seeing the unique gravity of the events, the investigation was entrusted not to players, but the project curators or, to be more accurate, investigators they brought in. I saw a group of people with military bearing led into the headquarters by the "fed" Aleksandr Antipov, who was treating the new arrivals with obvious deference. All three faction leaders were forced to attend, as well as the leaders of both legions and everyone who knew anything about the deal with the merchants before it happened.

The building was surrounded by men with automatics, shooing the curious Dome residents. What happened behind those closed doors I could only guess because... I was not allowed in! Yes, believe it or not, it was true! I figured I counted as a person who knew in advance but, when I tried to get into the building, Antipov stopped me on the stoop. He told me that, together with the outside investigators, he had closely studied all security footage from the last few days. From those recordings it was concluded that, right after Radugin told me the coordinates to land the starship, I went straight to my virt pod and into the game, which I did not exit until after I landed. The only person I had talked with on the way was Svetlana from the First Legion, who was on a run. A recording of that conversation had been made, as far as I knew, by one of my bodyguards and the fed already had it. I hadn't disclosed any secret information, so there was no way I could have been the source of the leak. So, the investigators had already crossed me off the list of suspects, and the deputy director advised me to get some rest after my two days of uninterrupted gaming.

And that is exactly what I did. I was totally burned out, and not even so much physically as mentally. I really was falling off my feet. I can barely remember walking to my room or getting undressed and falling into bed, because I was fully on autopilot.

I felt like I'd just fallen asleep when someone came to bother me. With a groan of dismay, I peeked open one eye to see the foolhardy suicidal who dared disturb my sleep. As it turned out, it was Anya. Oh yeah, she did promise to come visit me. Well, that was a different matter. Wake me up any time for that! I immediately lit up and extended my hands, preparing to embrace Anya and pull her to bed, but she wriggled away and took a step back:

"Not now, Kirill, I'm on business! I was sent to wake you up and say that Geckho Diplomat Kosta Dykhsh is asking for you. They wanted me to tell you he is angry and wants to see you as soon as possible. From what I gathered, the Geckho Diplomat had never acted like this before, so Ivan Lozovsky is alarmed and wants you in the game at our central base. He said he would go with you to Kosta Dykhsh's hut and provide support."

Crap, the last thing I needed was to piss off our suzerains... The last shreds of sleep instantly flew out of my head and I sat up. The lighting in the Dome was still in night mode. The clock was showing just past four. As it turned out, I'd managed to sleep seven hours, which was not bad. While I got dressed and put myself in order, Anya gave me a brief recap of recent events.

According to her, a group of heavy-handed outside investigators had arrived yesterday. They then interrogated a bunch of people: the director and deputies, the leaders of both legions, all the recon guys who scoped out the stony plateau, everyone who made deals with the Centaurs, anyone who came to meet the starship, the heads of our three laboratories, and the players who stored and transported the platinum. Also, Antipov quickly regained spirit and was not ashamed to curse, shouting that far too many people knew about this operation, which he thought should have been top secret.

Yes, Antipov had been struck from the suspects list as well. First, he didn't have all the information about the deal, neither the meeting place, nor the time. Second, he didn't even have a character in the game, so he could not make direct contact with the Dark Faction. The theory that he was revealing secret information through a middleman was also quickly refuted. Antipov had prepared well for the meeting and asked the non-player guards now keeping watch over the Dome to give him a copy of every video and audio recording he was part of for the last 72 hours. After that, he convincingly proved that he hadn't discussed this matter with anyone.

However, even without Antipov, there were plenty of suspects. Thankfully, most suspects had only partial information. That was the only thing we'd done right and even then, it wasn't much. Some knew the place but didn't know why the faction leadership was looking for a starship landing platform. Some knew we could suddenly order rare goods from space and that a merchant starship would be arriving, but they didn't know where or when. Some knew that platinum was being brought into the game and stockpiled but didn't know why. Those who truly knew everything could be counted on one hand: the level-86 Administrator, Faction Leader Leng Radugin, the level-83 Diplomat Ivan Lozovsky, the Leader of the First Legion level-92 Sniper Gerd Tarasov, his deputy and trusted aid level-80 Scout Shoot_to_Kill, and my level-58 Prospector, who looked quite meek compared with these high-level bruisers. But Gnat was already proven innocent, so the remaining four were now the main suspects.

Nearer to nightfall, a lie detector was brought in. Some specialists had to come set it up, too. One of them was carrying a case of hypodermic needles and injection ampules. Faction leader Radugin was called into the office first and twenty minutes later carried out by the arms. The tired and stress-addled man was no spring chicken. As could have been expected, he had a heart attack.

"It was gruesome!" Anya admitted, having seen this all firsthand. "Our director looked ten years older. He was convulsing, clutching his chest and muttering the same thing over and over again, barely intelligibly: "Checkmate... The Dark Faction has us in checkmate... maybe not in three days but still... they have us in checkmate.""

I didn't have time for the end of the story because Anya and I had already reached the foot of corncob fifteen, and I had to go up to my virt pod. Anya refused to go up with me, so I said goodbye and scrambled up.

ALRIGHT, LOADING... As usual, before playing, I took a peek at my information:

Gerd Gnat. Human. H3 Faction.	
Level-58 Prospector	
Statistics:	
Strength	13
Agility	17
Intelligence	23
Perception	26

Constitution	15
Luck modifier	+3
Parameters:	
Hitpoints	1632 of 1632
Endurance points	918 of 918
Magic points	226 of 226
Carrying capacity	58 lbs.
Fame	47
Skills:	
Electronics	41
Scanning	46
Cartography	48
Astrolinguistics	66
Break-in	23
Rifles	45
Mineralogy	26
Medium Armor	44
Eagle Eye	54
Sharpshooter	28
Targeting	16
Danger Sense	28
Psionic	23
Mental Fortitude	20
Machine Control	10
Attention!!! You have ten unused skill points	

Yes, I needed to find something to do with those

skill points right away. It had already been more than twenty-four hours since I got the first of them, and that meant I would lose them if I died. After a moment of consideration, I placed seven into Psionic, which I thought was a handy and promising skill, raising it to thirty. Reading thoughts and controlling creatures was my unique ability. Also, no one was expecting a Prospector to have psionic abilities, so they wouldn't take precautions. I needed to take advantage of that and improve the skill.

I placed the remaining two into Targeting. All my combat experience showed that, at medium and especially long distances, Gnat was weak all alone, practically worthless. Yes, he could shoot the Pulse rifle and even sometimes hit, but any Gunner, Machine-Gunner or Sniper would be able to do so far more effectively than my Prospector. But I had very high Perception and, with my present skills, I could detect and mark enemies from very far away, which was a much greater help.

Well, time to enter the game. I appeared just were I exited — a square in my central base, a mere three steps from Vasiliadi's warehouses. Yesterday, I wanted to get some more grenades, and ask for another battery for my Pulse rifle, but he wasn't there. But now, despite the late hour, the stock keeper was in the game and noticed me right away:

"Ah Gnat old boy! I haven't seen you in a dog's age! What's it been, five days... or has it been six?"

"It's been eight days, eight. But I'm happy to see you, too!"

The giant stock keeper embraced me warmly

and, without the slightest hesitation, gave me everything I asked for. He even rustled up a battery for the Dark Faction rifle, which he had squirreled away somewhere even though, as far as I knew, we had a serious deficit of ammunition for captured weaponry. I then, in my turn, parted with the Laser Pistol and the two Dark Faction chameleon cloaks. Then, after some thought, I returned my kevlar jacket and the rest of the standard uniform, putting on my Listener Suit.

The fact that I had the ancient Relict armor was already known both to my allies and the Dark Faction, so hiding it would be foolish. What was more, the standard medium armor took up lots of space in my inventory and was also pretty heavy, seriously limiting my ability to carry other items. In the end, I needed to move on and part with it.

But I did unclip the three trophy tails from the helmet first, putting them in my inventory so I could put them on my black Relict helmet when I had the chance.

"Look at you! That's what I'm talking about!" Vasiliadi admired, seeing the energy armor for the first time. "I heard you got some weird cool armor, but this..."

Authority increased to 16!

Our conversation was interrupted by the loud arrival of a high-speed two-person buggy, which was being piloted by Lozovsky himself. Seeing my armor, the Diplomat just clicked his tongue, but didn't say anything out loud, instead suggesting we go see Kosta Dykhsh as quickly as possible.

Keeping him waiting would only make him

madder.

WE WERE NOT ABLE to talk on the way. The Diplomat was tired and annoyed and driving over the rough terrain at night required extreme concentration. The only question he answered was about the bottles I heard clinking around in the back.

"Yes, it *is* vodka. It's a gift. Geckho love it, so it might come in handy to placate Kosta."

Despite the early hour, Dykhsh was already awake and, on hearing the buggy approach, came out of his semicircular metal dwelling. He gave me a dry greeting, just raising a hand, but even embraced Ivan Lozovsky in a sign of deep friendship.

"What happened with Radugin yesterday? Why the fall in status?" the huge furry Geckho asked first. And I glanced in surprise at our Diplomat because this was all news to me.

That topic, based on the grimace of dismay that ran over the deputy's face, was not too fun for him, but Ivan Lozovsky was open nevertheless:

"Radugin had a break-down... He couldn't deal with all the stress and burned out psychologically. Instead of preparing for the Dark Faction attack, he gave up and raised his hands without a fight. And that was in public, with one hundred and fifty allied players watching, which of course seriously damaged him in the eyes of his subordinates. That made his Authority fall hard. At the same time, his rank switched from Leng back to Gerd. I'm afraid that when the rest of the faction finds out in the morning, it may go beyond that, and Radugin may fall back to a regular player..."

"Radugin was never a fighter by nature. I've told you that before, Ivan. But he can't become a mere normal player. The game algorithms won't allow it. Fame cannot fall which means that, even if his Authority is deep in the negative, Radugin will always be a Gerd," Kosta Dykhsh said pensively. Then he asked what would happen to the former leader now, and who would take his place.

"Radugin is in the game as we speak. He's relaxing and recovering after he just about died of a heart attack. He's a talented economic manager, and he knows all our supply chains like the back of his hand. I personally can't make heads or tails of them. I think our new leader will stick him in charge of production or procurement. But as for who the new leader will be... I have a promising option in mind, but it's too early to say out loud. We need to first talk carefully with all our high-profile players, so we don't step on any toes."

Kosta Dykhsh and Ivan Lozovsky spent a bit of time in thoughtful silence, then the furball turned to me:

"Last night, the diplomatic channels were abuzz with alarming news about the start of a war between the Union of Miyelonian Prides and the Meleyephatian Horde. Meanwhile, I got a very unexpected request from Kung Waid Shishish: 'Find out when the Human Gerd Gnat returns to our space and immediately interrogate him to find out why he started a war between two great spacefaring races. Report your results immediately.'"

Authority increased to 17!

Ivan Lozovsky gave a whistle of surprise and immediately asked what I'd stepped in this time. Before answering, I turned my attention on a different matter:

"So, the political and military protector of humanity Waid Shishish has become a Kung?"

"Yes, he was promoted just the day before last," the Geckho Diplomat confirmed and, after lowering his voice, added: "The Geckho have no doubt that Waid Shishish, famed for his warlike nature and bloodthirstiness, will want to take part in this conflict. Especially now that he's a Kung, which means 'leader of many divisions,' in the ancient protolanguage. He will want to use it to cement his new status. But I cannot figure out whose side the Geckho will join. Or why Kung Waid Shishish is so certain the Human Gnat could tell him what started this war."

Well, I did know. Both the official story and the version the Morphian told me. But I could not tell the Morphian's tale, where the Meleyephatians themselves had been set up by some unknown client. That would mean mentioning Gnat's deep conversations with Fox, which would cause many uncomfortable questions. Also, the Geckho might perceive my Miyelonian companions negatively in that case, which could bring a different kind of problem.

So, trying to avoid the sharp edges in the story of Gnat's adventure on Medu-Ro IV, I told the story as I heard it from the great Priestess Amiru.

Yes, I knew where my conversation with the Geckho Diplomat would lead. Right after hearing all this, Kung Waid Shishish, not known for his long temper, would accuse the Meleyephatians of attempting to turn the Geckho and Miyelonians against one another. After that, the Geckho would band together with the Union of Miyelonian Prides and go to war. Did I feel any pangs of conscience over that? Well, why now? The war was inevitable, and my answers would only change whose side we fought for.

When I brought up Leng Amiru U-Mayaoo, I was interrupted for the first time:

"So you spoke personally with the incarnation of the Great Female?!" It was funny to compare expressions of astonishment on the faces of different races, and I had a hard time holding back a smile.

Authority increased to 18!

I confirmed my encounter with the great Priestess and carried on. In the end, I finished with Gnat being released along with my Miyelonian friends under guard of the First Pride. Both Diplomats remained jumpy for some time, vying with each other to clarify various details. I was worried about the Geckho diplomat's possible reaction to the two Miyelonians now on Earth, but the furball took this news with utter calm and even ambivalence, just asking their levels and classes. Finally, Kosta Dykhsh thought he'd heard enough and sharply changed topic.

Screwing his furry face up into a frightening expression, he took a red crystal the size of a pinky finger from a large pouch on his belt:

"Yesterday evening, Geckho vassals from what you call the Dark Faction placed a huge order for equipment and materials at our space port. They tried to pay for the goods with counterfeit crystals. Of course, they have been severely punished for the fraud. But that led to questions. They fingered you two as the source of the false currency. And ugh, I should of course interrogate you both and really work you over, so you won't do it again but, as far as I can see, your faction has already been punished for the attempted trade with a dishonest merchant..."

Ivan Lozovsky and I nodded in syncopation, lowering our heads and doing everything we could to demonstrate repentance and humility.

"How much platinum did you sell for all those crystals?" Kosta Dykhsh asked, and Ivan Lozovsky, interrupting me, said we sold six hundred seventy-five pounds and for that the smugglers gave us two million crystals.

"Well, well..." the Geckho shook his head in reproach. "A whole six hundred seventy-five pounds! If you were selling it at my rate, Ivan, you'd have gotten an honest one hundred fifty thousand crystals. And that would be real, unlike what you got stuck with. Maybe, for such a large shipment, my friends would have given you one hundred fifty-five thousand, if the quality was excellent. So take this as a lesson for the future and don't get into any more sticky business with illegal smugglers. That is all, you are both free to go! But before you leave, take that box off your vehicle and bring it over..."

Chapter Twenty-Seven

Race Against the Clock

THE DIPLOMAT AND I were sitting on the bank of a small babbling brook and watching a beautiful sunrise. The sun had not yet come up over the horizon, but it was already shading the clouds pink. The world was waking up. There were ducks dabbling in the rocks, little fish splashing in the river, a myriad of dayflies and butterflies spinning in an infinite dance and hurrying to make the most of their one day of life. We stayed silent. We just didn't want to talk, because we both understood how lucky we were to have found the official Geckho representative in a good mood. We could have easily been punished just then, and quite severely.

Finally, I broke the long silence and asked Lozovsky, who was lying back on the grass with his eyes half open, who would be the new faction leader. The Diplomat spit out a worn-down piece of grass he had been twirling in his teeth and turned to me:

"What do you think?"

I just shrugged my shoulders indefinitely. I didn't know much about faction politics, so I had a poor idea of who might become our new leader. Without waiting for me to give an answer, Lozovsky started speaking:

"Obviously, it must be a famous and authoritative faction member, so the people will consent to be led by them. So clearly, it has to be a Gerd. Tamara, right? Sure, she's the most popular player in our faction, and the soldiers of the Second Legion are basically all willing to die for her. All that said, it's easy to imagine her leading a battle charge, but try to think of her sitting inside behind a stack of paper!"

Here I was in complete agreement with the Diplomat. Tamara could never lead our faction. The Paladin's place was in battle or wherever we needed to resist enemy magic, never on the far back lines taking reports from production managers and shuffling resources between laboratories.

"Gerd Tarasov?" Lozovsky continued forwarding candidates. "A great option, the highest level and most respected player. He was the first one I went to, but Igor refused. 'Not for me,' he said. He is prepared to take on some of the functions of a leader, like commanding and planning combat operations, but nothing more. So, he'll be something of a defense minister, subordinate to the head of state."

And again I agreed. Tarasov was a professional soldier, and no one could better handle issues of defense than him and his First Legion.

"We have another Gerd, a scientist, who I also seriously considered for faction leader. Gerd Ustinov is fanatically devoted to his laboratory, and he just sits in there all day. His calling is to bring technology from the game into the real world, and for that, he is willing to experiment for days on end. Ustinov is the one that provides our curators what they expect from the Dome project, so he is where he needs to be."

But then who? I had to admit, I was totally lost because, other than the previously mentioned players, there was only one other Gerd in the faction: me. Was Ivan Lozovsky really leading the conversation there? No, I was not ready for that! Not for me!!! Fortunately, the diplomat thought so as well:

"That leaves you, Gnat. But I don't think you want to lead. Also the faction, I'll be frank, still mistrusts you. They aren't as negative as before, after our explanatory operation, though. Also, your work for the faction is obvious even to the most obstinate skeptics. But you're still pretty far from being lauded."

"Well who do you suggest then?" I asked, understanding that he wouldn't be starting this conversation for nothing. "Just stick with Radugin?"

"No, of course not. A leader who doesn't believe in himself will never enjoy the respect of his subjects. And that is why my suggestion for faction leader is myself," Lozovsky answered with a slight grin and, before I managed to object, he continued. "My fame is already near thirty, so I'll become a Gerd any time now.

Maybe even today, after the secret operation you helped plan. But if not, it will happen in the next few weeks or even days."

Of course, I asked about the secret operation he mentioned. I couldn't remember what that was about. The Diplomat first declined to share, then admitted:

"As you suggested, we managed to come to an agreement with the Harpy. Not for one box of food, of course, but their services were quite affordable. The sneak attack on the unfinished Dark Faction base in the Poppy Fields will be made today at midday when most of their workers are on site. Our Meteorologist is predicting thick cloud cover, so there is a decent chance the Harpies won't even be seen. The Journalist Lydia Vertyachikh will immediately inform the faction of the grand success, so my Fame and recognition will surely grow. And as I am officially the mastermind of this whole operation well... you understand... if we pull it off, I'll be a Gerd."

Excuse me? Ivan Lozovsky wanted to take all the glory for himself?! Sure, he was the one who negotiated with the Harpies, military and production facilities, but the idea itself was mine! As if sensing my anger, the Diplomat tried to calm me:

"Don't worry, Gnat. I didn't forget your contribution. I know how to show gratitude. Help me become the new faction leader today, and I'll appoint you head of your very own Third Legion. Then you can command two hundred players of your choosing. But if the life of a military leader doesn't tempt you, I'll allow you to create 'Team Gnat.' You can take seven to ten players, and you will all be guaranteed complete freedom. No need to ask permission from leadership for anything!"

What was going on? Was Lozovsky plainly trying to buy my vote without any roundabout turns of phrase? I had to admit that somewhat shook me. However, I was no naive idealist and understood that politics in any form was a dirty thing, so I didn't object. What was more, I had already come to the conclusion that the Diplomat really was the best candidate, so I was going to vote for him anyway. But if my vote could be traded for favors, why not? Being leader of a Third Legion didn't tempt me one bit. But as for leading a team at my own discretion... That was a clever move. He really knew how to hook me!

I asked him to tell me more about "Team Gnat," and Ivan Lozovsky started eagerly explaining:

"I have to admit, it wasn't my idea. It came from our staff psychologist. After all, you're a Gerd in status, and such visible players usually have a crew of companions and like-minded individuals. Both Tamara and Igor Tarasov, for example, have trusted players, adjutants, advisors and assistants. Although there is a small nuance. All their underlings stay within faction territory. But your unique path means you will often be gone for days at a time and thus cannot always be observed. Radugin was not willing to take a group of players away and let them go off wherever, even if it would mean new technologies and knowledge for the faction. But I am not so conservative."

As for a Gerd having companions, I had already heard about that from Anya and Imran, so it came as no surprise. But what was this about being gone for many days at a time? After all, I was back on Earth after my journey with the Geckho, and I didn't have any more space trips planned. Did the Diplomat know something I didn't? Unfortunately, I didn't have time to figure that out. Lozovsky activated his radio, and an unfamiliar female voice said:

"The prisoner Minn-O La-Fin has just entered the game in her prison cell. She is calm and wants to speak with Gnat. She says that she will not talk to any other player from the H3 Faction."

Authority increased to 19!

It was clear that the Diplomat was surprised, and I understood that perfectly. During her last two prison terms, the proud and haughty granddaughter of the old mage had not uttered a word. But now she was asking to talk. The Diplomat took out his radio and looked at me:

"I think the Dark Faction Leng wants to tell us something through his granddaughter. Gnat, go speak with Minn-O and find out what her grandfather's offer is. And I have a massive request from me and the whole faction. Try to chat about other topics like the weather, or nature then, as if in passing, ask about yesterday's battle. If possible, try to figure out whether Minn-O knew when the merchant ship would arrive. It is very important, because it could give our investigators the missing puzzle piece needed to identify the traitor."

I DIDN'T GO to the meeting with Minn-O La-Fin alone.

By radio, the Capital citadel guard post had told me the Miyelonian Translator had been up for a while, had left her room a few times and had even left the fortress, deftly slipping away from her observers. The orange lady cat was considered a guest, so she was allowed to move freely, and they tried to treat her with delicacy. But the guards still didn't like having an alien gallivanting around a strictly controlled site. So they told me to look after her and, in the future, try not to leave my guest by herself.

I found Ayni in the residential building the Miyelonians had been put up in yesterday. The cat had found a page of the faction bulletin and was lying in bed trying hard to study our unknown alphabet. I could not say how much progress she made but, when I appeared, Ayni immediately jumped up and said she had to get out of this camera- and microphone-packed building.

Was that so? I activated Scanning, then had to agree with Ayni. There were microphones and cameras in every corner, ventilation grate and light switch. For the Morphian, who was trying not to advertise its nature, such intrusive surveillance must have been a huge annoyance. I promised to speak with the people responsible for building security and ask them to stop spying on our guests.

I didn't find my second companion. The kitten's room was empty. I was told by my allies that Tini immediately left the game after getting into the room and had yet to return.

The prison block was deep under the capital citadel. Just like faction headquarters, the only way to get down there was an elevator.

"She's with me!" I declared presumptuously to the Second Legion soldiers guarding the prison. They did not object.

Authority increased to 20!

How nice it was to be a Gerd! Before, I would have had to explain myself for a long time, negotiate with the leader of the guards and placate a bunch of other players. But now, I just said the Miyelonian was a friend, and lesser faction members, even of a higher level, respectfully made way, not daring to object. Just as they'd told me when I started playing: "A Gerd never has to explain themselves." And now, I could take advantage of that privilege.

After passing the guard post and going down into the underground dungeon, I walked down the long cold corridor and stopped before the only locked cell. The guard was an unfamiliar lady of middling years with her hair cut short, a level-34 Bodyguard. When she saw me, she sharply shot up from the chair and, embarrassed at the bushy-tailed Miyelonian and somewhat hiccupping, gave a report:

"N-no incidents. P-prisoner has been f-fed and is now exercising."

I didn't embarrass the lady, who was clearly already uncomfortable, although my tongue was itching to tell her that I imagined the Bodyguard class was meant for something other than keeping watch over prisoners. Instead, I asked her to open the cell door, but the prison guard was moving slow and, glancing at the Miyelonian Translator with mistrust again, lowered her voice to a whisper:

"Gerd Gnat, here's th-the thing. Wh-when we were examining the detainee's clothing, on the inner side of her shirt near the collar, we f-found this."

She pulled out a drawer from her little desk, unfolded a thick paper packet and showed me a small object that looked like a pill alongside a tiny circuit board with a battery and antenna. The board had a little fiber stuck to it and a piece of dark colored fabric, which led me to believe it had been forcibly ripped off Minn-O's clothing.

Ampule of contact poison.
Long-distance activator.

"Curious little thing," Ayni commented in Miyelonian, also looking over the object. "It's triggered by a secret word or signal, which breaks the ampule, releasing the poison. It's a reliable guarantee that a high-value player won't be taken captive."

Very interesting... So what did this mean? As soon as Minn-O came to her senses in the Peresvet on its way back to base and before she was put into prison, the granddaughter of the great Mage could easily have killed herself and gone to respawn? But why hadn't she done it? I figured I should lead with that question.

The lock clanked, and the heavy door opened. I entered the prison cell accompanied by Ayni.

Minn-O was tall, standing on a rug next to the far wall and holding her left leg almost vertical, nearly touching the low ceiling with the tips of her bare toes. She was stretching. And when I entered, she didn't stop, allowing me to take in her flawless vertical leg spit and the seductive curves of her feminine body, temptingly emphasized by the form-fitting athletic suit.

"Gnat, I can tell you like her. I sense the background emotion," Ayni chuckled but I, also in Miyelonian, asked the Translator to keep the inappropriate comments to herself, especially those of a sensitive nature, because this prisoner had the Astrolinguistics skill and could quickly pick up new languages.

"Look at you, Gnat! So embarrassed!" The Morphian, clearly enjoying this situation, wouldn't back down. "She feels a certain inclination to you as well and is trying her hardest to make you like her. That is exactly why she hasn't stopped her exercises, even though normally she can't stand them. She is showing off her body and offering to be your female."

I strictly admonished the Translator, saying one more inappropriate comment and she would have to wait on the other side of a locked door until I was done. Ayni seemed to understand that I was not joking and promised to keep quiet. I then, politely bowing, started speaking with the Dark Faction girl:

"Princess Minn-O La-Fin, I've been told you called for me. I suspect that your ruling grandfather Thumor-Anhu La-Fin would like to tell me something through you. Is that right?"

Instead answering, Minn-O asked a question:

"Is seem this orange cat to insult I. What she is say?"

I translated the answer, although quite differently from its original form:

"Ayni was saying that Miyelonian females perform such exercises in order to attract a mate. In her opinion, you purposely didn't kill yourself with the poison ampule hidden in your suit and allowed yourself to be brought to prison because you want to be with me."

Minn-O clearly grew embarrassed, lowered her sore leg, adjusted her clothes and sat on the very edge of the cot, modestly placing a hand on her knee.

"No dying is not this reason as catgirl think. I just no know about poison!!! So, I wanting use grenade for respawn. But then you Gnat in armor give me choice: either tie I proud princess like simple prisoner naked, or promise no to run. I choose second and no try get away, because I have noble honor and no is break oath."

I assured Minn-O that I didn't share the Miyelonian's point of view and valued the princess's ability to stay true to her word. Also, I said if I had wounded her noble feelings, I would apologize for my lack of tact and change topic.

"No, this topic good!" Minn-O did not want to stop discussing the details of her imprisonment. "Ampule poison is many, many explaining one strange thing I no understand. Leng Thumor-Anhu see I losing battle and going prisoner, can to help with strong team and beat all you. But no he do!"

Everything inside me turned cold. The great Mage Thumor-Anhu La-Fin had been present at the scene of our skirmish?! News to me! So, that was whose cautious mental probing I sensed! But why didn't he do anything? A level 100+ Psionic Mage could have tipped the scales even alone and provided his faction a victory. But with a retinue of elite mages and Dark Faction soldiers, he could have easily suppressed our entire small squadron. But then why didn't the fearsome Mage interfere?

Furthermore, I found it very hard to imagine the respected elder sitting for days on end in ambush, waiting for a starship to arrive. Such discomforts could not be tolerated at his advanced age. So that meant the old geezer knew the precise landing time! I quickly tried to get her to admit that clearly:

"Your Grandfather Thumor-Anhu came to support your squadron? So, did he know the exact time the space merchants would arrive?"

"Not only he, all we is know when. But I with squadron take many days for trudge through all you territory, then to sit night in ambush and wait. But grandpa is fly on antigrav just before."

Very valuable information!!! Seemingly, I'd distracted Minn-O into giving away somewhat more information than she was planning on. The Dark Faction not only knew the exact time and place the starship would land, but also had that top-secret information at least one and a half days before the merchants arrived!

So, rough estimation. I told Radugin when the starship would arrive, then made my purchases and loaded for around six hours. The space flight lasted about thirty-six hours. So that gave just forty-two hours between the arrival of the starship and my conversation with Radugin. And of that time, for thirty-six hours at the very least, the Dark Faction was in possession of that secret information, preparing for the encounter. That meant the leak had happened in the first six hours. And more likely that could be narrowed further, because the darksider spies would have needed to prepare and pack before the long voyage.

"But then why didn't the great Mage save you? Or at the very least, why didn't he activate the poison ampule in your suit?" I had to admit, these anomalies had me very worried.

Minn-O looked at me thoughtfully, as if sizing me up, then answered:

"When I is ask grandpa why he no save, he give very strange answer that I no understand right away. He is say that I should to be..." here Minn-O faltered and, not able to find an analogue in my language, used a word from hers, "wayedda. Also Thumor-Anhu is say that is fate decide, he no can contradict high power, and this necessary for saving dynasty La-Fin."

"Wayedda? What does that mean?" I asked.

"How is I explain..." I noticed that Minn-O was very embarrassed, and her ashen gray cheeks even turned a bit red, "is old tradition my people. Wayedda mean 'lawful plunder.' Strong warrior can, when victory, take girl from defeated family, if he like she. No is of violence, no! Take as junior wife or travelling mistress, promise wayedda care, defense and love. And this girl no can refuse, otherwise very insult victor and lose protection, become like common lady."

Yikes... What a surprising twist in the story of my conflict with Minn-O. I didn't even know what to think. The ghastly old Mage, Dark Faction Leng and coruler of his world was insisting and almost violently forcing his beloved granddaughter into my arms, meanwhile talking about "fate," "higher power" and "ancient traditions." But did I want this?! Minn-O was indisputably a woman of remarkable beauty, but how could I explain having a Dark Faction "junior wife" to my allies?

"My people do not have such a tradition of 'lawful plunder,'" I answered as neutrally and delicately as possible. But even without using the Psionic skill, I could tell that my answer pained her. "And among my people, the 'strong warrior' would have to start things or, at the very least the 'girl of a defeated family,' never someone else."

"My grandpa Thumor-Anhu is no else!" the prisoner burst out, raising her voice, but immediately got herself together and continued in a normal tone. "But you're right, Gerd Gnat. Strong warrior is supposed to starting. If he not to want, no one is to force. And now, I want change topic!"

Then, it became entirely impossible not to notice her upset state. Minn-O started periodically sobbing. Her eyes grew damp and she was having a hard time holding back tears. I really didn't think that refusing to discuss the wayedda would have such an effect on the princess. Nevertheless, despite the bawling, Minn-O continued, and notes of resolve appeared in her voice:

"I is give message from ruling grandpa Leng Thumor-Anhu La-Fin. Not just one, but three. First: my strong faction offer you weak faction to give tribute. Twenty-thousand red crystals in day. If yes, we no destroy you hexagon and will be peace and trade. Second is offer: we agree no shoot no base with long cannon or rocket. We know where all you base, and you also know us. Destroying these is bad for every side.

Both no grow and very stupid. Defend Earth after one tong is us common mission, so both need develop and strong. And three message: Thumor-Anhu discuss plan of counterfeit crystal and say that respecting you after this clever move. For my faction, is very pain from Geckho. My grandpa say you wise and crafty, can to join my side and be right hand of Leng. And that is he promise!"

Yikes... even without using the scanning ability I could be sure this cell was packed with microphones. Every word of this conversation was being recorded and would soon be sent to the fed and a whole bunch of other people. Many in the faction already mistrusted me and, after such a flagrant attempt to convert me, they might think I was interested if I didn't respond forcefully enough. I needed to answer immediately in a way that left no questions:

"Minn-O, I will send your first offer to my leadership, but I doubt it will be seriously considered. I will send your second as well. I hope I'll have an answer by evening. But as for the third so-called 'offer,' I told you before and I repeat that you will never defeat us! I will stop at nothing until my faction wins this war!"

The cartographer gave a slight bow, then turned away, letting me know the conversation was over. I was already heading for the exit when I suddenly realized that I had not heard one important thing from the prisoner:

"By the way, Minn-O, what did your grandfather say about a ransom? How many crystals is he willing to part with for his beloved granddaughter's freedom?"

The Princess turned very slowly and met eyes with me. In her teary gaze, I could read sadness and lack of hope:

"Thumor-Anhu is very annoy with last I failure and, in front of many courtier, he is swear that no more is he pay even one crystal for ransom! Grandpa say that only way for me not hurting honor of house La-Fin, it is become Wayedda of Gnat and be honorable junior wife. Otherwise aristocrat and courtier no is approve, and big fall in honor of me."

While saying this, the Princess had her eyes glued on me, although she knew for certain about my psionic abilities. It would have been fairly easy for her to turn away or lower her eyes, so I couldn't read her thoughts, but Minn-O did not do that. It was as if she was inviting me into her mind... And so, bowling over all the guidelines of good conduct, I used my Psionic abilities to dig around a bit:

"Will he guess or no? I will not mention his magical abilities, so the guards listening won't know, even though it's the topic I'd most like to discuss. After all, it is thought that there is no magic in his world. But what was that during the battle on the Centaur Plateau? Did none of Gnat's allies even notice? No, he clearly does not understand my hints. Seemingly, I overestimated his brainpower. And too bad..."

What did she want from me? And what was I supposed to be figuring out? Did she want me to confirm my ability to converse mentally? Most likely. So, I concentrated and sent a message:

"I just learned Psionic abilities, so don't judge me so harshly. And I have very little time, my Magic Points

run out fast. So, if you have something to say this way, make it quick."

A whole wave of her feelings cascaded over me. There was joy, elation, relief, some embarrassment, and a lot of hope. After that, a distinctly formulated thought appeared:

"Gnat, my grandpa is willing to give very, very much for me to become your official wife or wayedda. To him, it is a matter of the survival of house La-Fin, which is an ancient dynasty of magical rulers. So, if you like me even one bit, let me know any way you can. Then ask for whatever you want either personally or for your faction: political favors, a large number of crystals, or even..."

My eyes suddenly went dark and I stepped back. I probably would have fallen on the cold stone floor if Ayni had not run forward to grab my falling body.

Action terminated. Magic Points exhausted.
Endurance Points exhausted.
Psionic skill increased to level thirty-one!
Psionic skill increased to level thirty-two!
Mental Fortitude skill increased to level twenty-one!

You have reached level fifty-nine!
You have received three skill points!

I quickly came to my senses and thanked the bushy-tailed Miyelonian Translator. I straightened up, led the back side of my hand under my nose and saw blood. Just what I needed! I guess using magic doesn't always end well. Apparently, you can overstrain and lose consciousness if you accidentally spend all your Magic and Endurance Points...

Minn-O was least surprised by what happened. I suspected that, in her magic-saturated world, such things were business as usual. The captive extended me a towel in silence to clean up my still-bleeding nose. I had already accepted the towel and thanked her when I suddenly made up my mind to take the "Hand of Gerd Gnat" on a metal chain from my inventory:

"Minn-O, I've thought about the wayedda and am willing to accept you as a travelling mistress, but only after this upcoming battle is over. My people often promise a girl their hand and their heart. Well, I'll give you my hand as an advance, and you can have my heart after Thumor-Anhu La-Fin gives me what I want. I imagine cancelling the ransom on me and returning the traitor Tyulenev would be an entirely acceptable price to save your honor as a Princess and keep up the ancient La-Fin dynasty."

Chapter Twenty-Eight

New Neighbors

WHEN I CAME BACK onto the surface from the prison complex, I was awaited by a small test of my nerves. The elevator doors had just opened when a nine-foot-high robot came out from them and dashed in my direction. In surprise, I stumbled back, squatting down and grabbing my Annihilator.

"Gnat, what was that?! Scared?" The power armor suit's visor slid up, and I saw Space Commando Eduard Boyko's face smiling from ear to ear. "There you are. I wanted to find you, say thanks and show off my new getup! Lefty, the best Mechanic in our faction plodded along all night refitting the armor. He says he got two level-ups before he managed to set and calibrate everything."

"Lefty?" I asked, intrigued to make the new acquaintance. "Could you tell me where to find him?"

As it turned out, he was close at hand, in the neighboring workshop. I turned where he pointed and saw a dark-haired disheveled guy in a smock heading for the canteen.

Lefty. Human. H3 Faction. Level-81 Mechanic

I called out to Lefty and hurried to catch up. The Mechanic had a fairly tepid reaction to my greeting, although he did raise his hand and wave. But it was clear he was trying to hide an unfriendly opinion. I don't know for sure what caused such a strong negative opinion and in large part didn't care. I just wanted a specialist to do a job. I pulled out the Small Control Bracelet, and Lefty twirled it in his hands for some time, then asked in annoyance:

"What does this have to do with me? Bring it to a Jeweler or something."

I had to explain that the value of the old bronze bracelet was not in the metal and read off all the stats of the Relict artifact, because Lefty didn't have the Intelligence to determine its properties.

"Well... I could try to remove the racial limitation," Lefty said, looking closer at the ancient Small Control Bracelet. He turned it over a few times, then squeezed out: "Five thousand crystals!"

What a damn ask! Seemingly, the craftsman had judged by my swanky Listener suit and Annihilator, so he figured I must have money coming out of my ears. Yes, I had enough, but it was in crypto, which were useless here, so I had to negotiate. But first, I dumbfounded the Mechanic with an alternate viewpoint:

"Five thousand? Do you even have that kind of money?"

"What?" Lefty clearly didn't understand, so I had to chew it over for the surly worker:

"Any artisan in the Universe would give their right arm... or tentacle... or whatever appendage... for the ability to work with ancient items! After all, it gives unique experience, which means guaranteed growth in skill and level! Eventually, most craftsmen hit a levelling ceiling, and this is the only way to keep moving forward. Now I am giving you the rare chance to gain experience. So, let's forget about your accidental offer. I want to hear a clear answer. Will you take the job, or should I take it to the Second Legion's Mechanic?"

Lefty clipped a monocle-like device over his eye, spent a long time playing with the settings, turning little wheels, then muttered thoughtfully:

"Yurik from the Second Legion couldn't handle this... it is a really hard job... It'll be two long hard days at least... and there will be expenses for materials..."

"Will three hundred crystals be enough?" I asked, pouring out a handful of red sparkling gems.

Our best Mechanic removed the monocle, looked at the wealth on the table and gave a short nod. We shook hands, cementing the deal.

Mental Fortitude skill increased to level twenty-two!

Mental Fortitude? Not Psionic?! That was very unusual and even made me think. Did that mean I didn't make the craftsman agree by psionic suggestion, but overcame someone else's magical block? Seemed like it!

The craftsman was in such a hurry to eat I didn't even have time to say goodbye. Then, Ivan Lozovsky walked up with Tini, who had finally turned up. The Diplomat handed the kitten off to me and asked me to not leave the Miyelonian teen unsupervised again, because Tini couldn't speak Russian or Geckho and immediately got completely and totally lost.

At the same time, taking advantage of the opportunity, Lozovsky commented on my negotiations with the captive Princess:

"I have to admit, Gnat, I'm struck! It was so easy for you to get Minn-O to open up and tell you everything! As for your unexpected move with the 'junior wife,' I will not try to guess how our faction and especially the outside curators will take it. But if the Dark Faction Leng really does give us back the traitor, they won't be able to object! And think what a crushing psychological blow that will be for those who were going to follow Tyulenev and betray us to the Dark Faction. It will completely undermine their peace of mind. At any moment, they could be traded and sent back!"

Authority increased to 21!

"It's too early to speak about that," I said, interrupting the overly optimistic Diplomat, who was getting ahead of himself. "After all, we don't know the Dark Faction Leng's answer yet."

"No matter, we'll find out soon! Later today, right after discussing this at the directors' council, I will call the Dark Faction on a diplomatic channel and give Thumor-Anhu our official response. I have spoken with the great mage before and have some concept of his value system, so I'm sure that, between saving the traitor Tyulenev, who is despised by all, and improving the fate of his beloved granddaughter, the Coruler will choose the latter."

"Oh! I now little-bit understand you language!" the Miyelonian Translator mewed in satisfaction, which clearly embarrassed Lozovsky, who'd just broached a fairly confidential topic in her presence.

The Diplomat apologized to both Miyelonians and Eduard Boyko, who was also there. He took me further away and lowered his voice to a whisper:

"I got an interesting question from Gerd Ustinov's laboratory, where they are now intensively studying the diagram of the Tiopeo-Myhh II. They found a strange marker in the digital model, a level-279 Morphian. Gnat... is that what I think it is? The same Morphian you told Kosta Dykhsh about?"

My heart ran off on its heels. How could I have forgotten??? After all, I had seen it before. It was how I had been able to tell Ayni was actually the Morphian in the first place! Although... what choice did I have, even if I had remembered? I had no way of deleting just the marker, and the diagram of the advanced alien interceptor had too high a value to humanity as a whole to keep it from our scientists.

"You don't have to answer. I can read it on your face..." the Diplomat chuckled in dismay and turned to Ayni, who was talking sweetly with the kitten. "Hrmph, now here's a problem... Clearly, we don't want that information to spread, because people might react skittishly. And we definitely cannot allow the Geckho to find out. So, I'll tell the science guys that our guests have an item that fudges data, giving a random race and level. And we can pretend we don't know any better."

"It won't work. The Morphian can sense the emotional background of anyone nearby and detect any changes in it. Fear, worry, desire to hide something. It probably already knows that you also know its secret. The best move is to just put it all out there and be honest."

I called Ayni over, and the short orange cat walked over eagerly, smiling good-heartedly, wagging her tail and looking inoffensive. Not hiding anything, I spoke to her in Geckho, which all three of us knew. Fox's reaction was surprisingly calm.

"I have to admit, I thought you told everyone right away. But now that it's happened, all the better. Well, Diplomat, I'll repeat what I told Gnat: I cannot copy people believably, I am not planning to sit around on the edge of the galaxy forever and, no matter what, I will leave you in a few days. I will cause no harm and could be very helpful. I'll pay very generously for my stay with information about the nature of the game that bends reality, and my abilities. All my skills are incredibly high-level, perfect for a fitness instructor. In just one session, I can raise Strength, Agility and Constitution by a point in characters who have not yet grown them. And that's saying nothing about my Fast Jump, Survival, Dodge, Parry, Blades, Melee, and all kinds of armor skills. I can improve those a lot for anyone who wishes."

"Can you help us in two days in the battle?" Ivan

Lozovsky asked, wanting to clear up the most important part.

Ayni considered it for second. While thinking, the orange lady's pupils turned into vertical slits, just like a normal cat's. Her fur bristled, and her claws extended. Finally, a carefully calibrated answer followed:

"I have already concluded that the balance of forces in that battle must be disastrous because your soldiers do not believe victory is possible. And no, no one told me that," Ayni hurried to reassure us after the Diplomat's ears perked up, "it's just the general emotional background is very poor: anxiety, despondency and resignation. I cannot do anything about that, but I can cause chaos in the ranks of your enemies or get rid of their leaders. And I don't care one bit whether they are mages or soldiers, or if they try to hide in underground bunkers or wherever else. Nothing can save them. I can do that two times during the battle, maybe three. But I will not serve as a common soldier to kill hundreds and thousands of your foes. You must achieve victory on your own! I am only backup, not a trump card."

"Our faction is more than happy with that!" the Diplomat bowed in respect to the fearsome Morphian, after which he turned to me. "Gnat, for one day or maybe even two I would like to have Ayni level up our science geeks. And I'd like you to go on patrol next shift to the Antique Beach. The centauress Phylira asked for you again. She has become the elder mare and is very respected by the herd. Talk with her and try to sow the right seeds. It would be great to hire them for construction work, and hopefully even the upcoming battle."

Authority increased to 22!

WE WERE RIDING a Peresvet, not the old beat up little bus. Other than that, the trip was very reminiscent of my first and only patrol so far. The newbie trainer Kisly was in the car too, along with Imran and Anya. Even the Driver was the same, the motormouth San-Sanych. But their opinion of me was different. Back then, I was totally green. I didn't understand anything about the game and everything surprised me. But now, my allies were hanging on my every word.

And how! I was a high-profile player with never-before-seen armor, a unique weapon and experience in space. Plus, I was acquainted with famous aliens. I was considered an example to be imitated and damn near a benchmark of proper gameplay. So, when we reached the top of the pass through the Yellow mountains, and I asked San-Sanych to stop for five minutes so I could go up a nearby cliff and get a good view of the area, the driver didn't even think of saying no.

Last time, we were in thick fog, I couldn't see more than fifteen feet, and I didn't set foot outside the little bus. But now, I could see the winding path perfectly and managed to get a great view. This area was full of natural beauty, and the sentry tower could not have been in a better location. I also had a wonderful view of the piercingly blue sea to the west where, at the very horizon, I could see the outline of the opposite bay. Most likely, that was the node with the Geckho space port. I could also see a Geckho ferry making quickly for the south, probably to collect tribute from whoever lived there.

Cartography skill increased to level forty-eight!
Eagle Eye skill increased to level fifty-five!
Eagle Eye skill increased to level fifty-six!

All I could see to the south though, behind the somewhat lower mountain peaks, was an ocean of green that extended to the very horizon. Those impenetrable swampy jungles were inhabited primarily by dryads, minotaurs and centaurs. That area was of particular interest to me because south was apparently the only direction my faction could expand. If of course, we weren't seriously considering the utopian Project Exodus proposed by Radugin, to build a base on the opposite shore of the gulf and resettle there, leaving all our current lands to escape the constant Dark Faction pressure.

"I used to think Swimming was one of the most useless skills in the game," Tini's said with delight. He was my only companion who had the spunk to follow me up. "I always figured: how much water can there really be? Can't you always just walk around it? Why waste the slot? But look how much there is here…"

"Sometimes, there is even more water. Whole open oceans that take dozens of days to cross by ship," I assured the kitten, who was staring with acute fascination. Then I sharply changed topic. "Tini, do you still have the tail of Priestess Amiru U-Mayaoo?"

It would probably be hard to scare the

Miyelonian teen more than I just accidentally had. The kitten's ears instantly pressed down, and his eyes squinted. Tini started shivering rapidly and crouched down, putting his tail between his legs and covering his head with his front paws. If he even pissed himself in fear, I wouldn't have been surprised...

"Come on, look how scared you are!" I said calmly and even peacefully, trying to reassure my underaged companion before he accidentally died of a heart attack. "Practically the whole Universe knows that Ayni had the tail. And I remember you digging in her things on the spaceship. So I'm asking because I know I wouldn't have been able to resist the temptation of a unique trophy. I just couldn't ask earlier, because Ayni was always nearby."

Tini stood and lowered his front paws, although he was still not confident.

"Yes, Master Gnat. Here it is," said the kitten, handing me the icy white fluffy tail, tied in a double knot. "Other than the plastic capsule where I found this, Ayni had nothing of value. The whole box was filled with some sticky gel. I think it was some special filler, so the scanners couldn't detect the organic matter."

"Probably..." I answered distractedly, because all my attention was now wrapped up in the invaluable trophy.

Tail of Leng Amiru U-Mayaoo, Level-260 Priestess (trophy)

"It's so beautiful! Tini, do you know what this is?" I asked with a quavering voice, not strong enough to hold back my anxiety.

"Uhh... a tail?" the level-35 Thief suggested boldly, but I just laughed in reply.

"No, Tini. This is my own starship!!! And despite your young age, I promise you can have your very own bunk once I get it! Now, I just need to find the right buyer. And Priestess Amiru seems like the best candidate!"

I spent two minutes staring into the lustrous fur, smiling stupidly and forming plans for the future. After that, I stored the trophy in my inventory and told Tini to get back to the Peresvet.

THE ELDER CENTAUR mare had been warned I was coming and was stamping her four shod hooves impatiently on the sand next to a fallen post of the barbed wire fence, not wanting to cross the border.

Phylira. Centaur. Antiquity Faction. Level-112 Matriarch.

What?! I remembered Phylira being a young flirtatious filly of level... I couldn't remember, but I was sure it was nothing too noteworthy. But now, that young creature was all gone except the coat: white with black zebra-like stripes. Phylira herself was twice as large, much taller and more imposing. Thick leather armor covered her voluptuous feminine body and human arms, smoothly flowing into a horse body behind. The centauress was also wearing a classical high-ridged bronze helmet on her head. But most importantly, her level was over 100... I had heard that

NPC's progressed an order of magnitude faster than living players but seeing it with my own eyes was still a shock.

Apparently, the Centaur Matriarch also had a hard time recognizing me in the dark Listener suit.

"Gnat, I can't even recognize you. Level fifty-five! And you're a Gerd! You're growing very fast for a person. I still remember back when you were asking about pearls. Well here you go, a gift from me to you!"

Phylira neighed, giving an order to a group of Centaurs in the distance. A young level-twenty stallion instantly bounded over and, with a deep bow, handed me a large black pearl the size of a walnut. Woah! Without the Trading skill, I wouldn't even come close to estimating the value of such a gift. Two hundred crystals? Maybe a thousand? Or ten thousand? In any case, the elder mare was showing me great respect with this treasure. I suspected it was the most valuable thing she owned.

But how could I answer such a show of respect? What could I give Phylira of even remotely equivalent value? The sparking Miyelonian blade I'd given Imran would have served me well here. Or maybe the +1 Agility tantalum earring with emerald inset? Great thought! Although... I was reminded that my faction had found magic rings on dead centaur before. So, a ring with +1 Agility probably wouldn't impress the mare much. My gift would have to get its value somewhere else.

I extended the magical jewelry in my open hand:

"Oh, wise Phylira, accept from me this gift of jewelry from the distant stars! Among a race of cats that fly through the heavens, like that gray-furred Miyelonian, only the wisest and most respected rulers can wear these earrings, which help the wearer move faster beyond just being a beautiful adornment. It is not only a huge rarity and value, but the true mark of a legal ruler! In two journeys to the stars, I managed to find just one such earring, and now I bequeath it to you, Phylira!"

Fame increased to 48.

Authority increased to 23!

The gift worked it's magic, as they say. The Centaur Matriarch was overjoyed like a little girl seeing a new doll. She whinnied, galloped in a circle and boasted aloud. Finally, Phylira settled down and returned to negotiations.

"Gnat, I wanted to speak with you exactly, because I know you. Of all the people I've met, you are the most capable negotiator, and the least likely to fall back on force and threats. Now, your people are building fortifications beyond the Big Woods and refuse to even talk with my Centaurs, killing all our messengers. We are also killing their people, but still. I'm afraid it could lead to a big war. I wanted you to speak with your people and stop the construction on our land."

I had to admit, this had me bewildered. As far as I knew, there had been peace with the Centaurs for a fairly long time. Over the last month, there were only a few minor border scuffles, both here on the Antique Beach and near the pass in the Yellow Mountains. But we hadn't built any new fortifications in either place and, for now at least, we hadn't even attempted to do so on Centaur land.

"Where is the illegal fortification?" I clarified, and she pointed her head confidently to the south.

"There, four of the territories you call nodes away. And here are the heads of the trespassers!!!"

Phylira unclipped a bag strapped to her zebra half and dumped a collection of decapitated human heads at my feet. There were lots of them. And meanwhile, the centaurs accompanying the Matriarch began to bellow out war cries and wave their blades menacingly. However, they kept their distance.

I tried to maintain composure. I bowed down and picked up one of the heads by a shock of long blond hair:

Head of Klaus Schweiger, level-26 Builder (trophy)

Too bad the faction name wasn't shown in the object description but, in any case, the name led me to believe this was most likely not a player from Russia. I quickly skimmed over the other heads at my feet and only confirmed my first impression: these were the remains of players from either the German, Austrian or Swiss faction.

"Phylira, I really need to speak with these people and tell them they are in the wrong. Will you allow me passage through your lands?"

The mare reared and neighed loudly, then repeated in a way I could understand:

"We not only will let you through, we will provide security. No one wants a big war."

Now that was great! I tossed the head aside with disgust and activated my radio:

"San-Sanych, have you made it far from Border Post Eight?"

The driver answered almost instantly:

"Gnat, I haven't gone anywhere yet. We're still unloading barrels of water. Has something happened?"

"There's a very interesting situation brewing here. We need to book it through four nodes to check on something. Is your car in decent shape? It won't fall apart on such a long journey? And do your antigrav pancakes have enough power to get us there and back?"

"Come on, you offend me! My cars are always in excellent condition, ask anyone! My fuel tanks are almost full, and the pancakes have enough charge to last all day. But I need to warn the Capital, so they send someone to replace me. Where are we going?"

"South through Centaur lands. They say they'll allow us to pass. In fact, they will clear the way for us, and get us out of the mud if we're ever stuck. I was just made aware of something that requires immediate action. I think I've found the Germans!"

Chapter Twenty-Nine

Listener

THEY CALLED THE PERESVET an "ATV", an abbreviation for all-terrain vehicle. One might think such a vehicle could thus drive anywhere, on- or off-road. But either this ATV was not up to snuff, or the name was deceptive, because we spent more of the next few hours stuck dead in the mud than going anywhere.

The metal mesh tires, which had amazed me so much when I first encountered the ATV and did have the distinct advantage of never popping, showed their true colors in the thick sticky mud. And they were not all rosy. Each of the eight wheels would fill with a ton of black swamp muck, which then had to be meticulously cleaned out of thick wire mesh. It just seemed impossible. My impression of the engineers who invented the wheels shifted from general admiration to something more exclamatory with a couple four-letter words.

If not for the centaurs, goat-like satyrs, and muscle-bound minotaurs helping us along, we never would have made it even a quarter mile. But even with NPC's eagerly helping to drag our ATV out of each and every mud patch, it was rough going. I didn't know what the nodes to the south of the Centaur Plateau were officially named, but I marked them on my map as "Mud, no roads," "Definitely don't try to drive here," and "Total shit!!!" Meanwhile, I calculated that one minotaur could lift seven to nine hundred pounds, because it took twenty of these powerful giants to lift our Peresvet and drag it to firmer ground.

In the morning, I warned the centaur mare that our mission was purely peaceful, and that we were not going to war with the southern men. Phylira wanted the same outcome, but still was going to get more clans together to show them the full power of the Antiquity Faction. And seemingly, the mare managed. In the depths of the forest, I could see more and more columns of dryads, satyrs and other classical mobs joining us.

Nevertheless, I only managed to appreciate the full scale of Phylira's army in the evening, when we left the swampy tropical forest to an open area and, with the help of the satyrs, started washing off the Peresvet in a shallow stream. Our vehicle looked more like a huge ball of mud than an ATV by then. Anyhow, by then I could see hundreds and even thousands of members of the Antiquity faction flowing through the hilly valley. I simply lost the gift of speech when seeing the huge warband. I estimated their number at around eight or nine thousand.

Eagle Eye skill increased to level fifty-nine!

Cartography skill increased to level fifty-two!

You have reached level sixty!

You have received three skill points! (total points accumulated: six)

My Scanning, Eagle Eye and Cartography skills had been growing periodically all day. Even Astrolinguistics went up by one and, finally, it was enough for a level-up. But I was in no rush to distribute the free points. I had more urgent matters to attend to.

Nine thousand warriors! It seemed even the NPC's should have been losing their minds over such a grandiose spectacle. The chiefs, after all, could just take their power, say to hell with negotiating, and decide to solve the issue by force. That could not be allowed!

I looked around and saw Phylira in the distance on the top of a hill. Leaving Kisly to watch over the satyrs fervently cleaning our ATV, I called the nearest centaur over and, not asking permission, jumped on his back. Tini followed me immediately. The large centaur male first was taken aback at our impudence and started to buck, but he quickly settled down and made peace with it.

Successful Authority check.

Authority increased to 24!

"To Phylira!" I shouted, pointing at the elder mare, who was conversing with the other chiefs on a hill, and the Centaur understood.

After a three-minute gallop, I jumped off next to the chiefs of the Antiquity Faction. Four Centaurs, a huge scarred one-horned Minotaur and two Dryads, whose nakedness was almost totally uncovered. Hrmph... Phylira with her level-121 was the youngest of all the chiefs. None of the others were below one hundred fifty. Despite the modest level of my Gnat in comparison, they all bowed to me, and I replied with an identical gesture of politeness and respect. Tini had opted to hide his information, so the chiefs also bowed to him. After all, who could say how powerful this weird alien was?

"I see that you've brought sufficient forces not just to convince the people to the south, but to blow their fortress to pebbles!" I said, making a wide arc with my hand over the many thousands of mythical warriors.

Phylira was the only chief who understood my language, so she had to serve as translator.

"Exactly right," agreed a huge red-maned Centaur, a level-160 Patriarch. "You are observant and wise, Gerd Gnat. The council of chiefs has changed its mind about conducting negotiations with the human trespassers. Why bother, if we can teach them their lesson once and for all!"

So, I wasn't wrong. Hmm... This wasn't shaping up the way I wanted. But what to do? Trying to convince the warlike NPC chiefs was utterly useless, I could sense that. It would just make me look bad and lose my unique position as a human the centaur leaders and other mobs could talk to. No, this would turn me into someone they wouldn't even let speak. But I also could not allow this massive horde to wipe out several nodes of one of my world's factions, thus weakening the overall position of my Earth.

"Here's what I think..." I started carefully choosing my words, "just killing these border-hoppers is not punishment enough. After all, they'll respawn in a quarter hour without losing anything and will rejoin the battle. And that battle will kill your friends and relatives once and for all. The humans won't even know what happened, and they definitely will not realize it was a punishment for trespassing. That'll just make them think... excuse me for being direct... that Centaurs and Minotaurs are too dumb to negotiate."

"And what do you suggest, Gerd Gnat?" Phylira asked, translating the whinny of a fierce Minotaur, clearly offended at my words, but still understanding that they were sincere.

"I suggest we take your whole army to show them the crushing might of the Antiquity Faction, surround the unfinished fortress and its garrison, but not attack. Before you strike, let me and my group communicate your faction's fair demands. My guess is that they will leave your territory and establish a clear boundary, which they will respect and observe from then on. Also, we could have them hand over the fort to your faction in perfect condition. But if the Centaurs and Minotaurs don't want a fortress, I say let it become a free market where you can all sell your goods to these people and buy what you need from them — hopped grain wine, weapons, unrusting metal, beautiful fabrics and light airy dresses..."

I saw the Dryads begin to smile and wink at one another. The Centaurs were also seemingly not opposed, but the Minotaurs were frowning. I had to hurriedly make some changes:

"Also, this might intrigue you, oh powerful chief of the Minotaurs. People can heal wounds and even grow new horns to replace those lost in battle. As a sign of your victory, I would demand a new horn and lots of strong drink for your army. After all, you brought thousands of warriors through dense forests and stagnant bogs to get here! But if they are unreasonable and refuse, you can grind them all to dust, capture this and the neighboring fortress, then decorate the new border with stakes topped by their foolish heads!"

Psionic skill increased to level thirty-three!

Fame increased to 49.

Authority increased to 25!

The Minotaur finally nodded in agreement, the council of chiefs ended quite abruptly, and Phylira voiced their decision:

"Alright, try, Gerd Gnat! A new horn, a clear border and at least thirty barrels of beer are our minimum demands."

WE RETURNED to H3 lands long after midnight and, just after reaching the first green zone in the Yellow Mountains fort, we hurried to exit the game. We were rushing because we'd been hearing an urgent announcement for the last few hours. The faction was holding an emergency meeting, and everyone was required to attend, except those guarding the borders and working at crucial production facilities. Gerd

Tamara even called me personally a few times. First, she contacted me to tell me about a meeting for directors and advanced players that was supposed to precede the big meeting. Then she asked me to confirm something Ivan Lozovsky said, that I had voted for him as leader.

We were extremely late for the big meeting, at least three hours. But it wasn't over yet, so we tried to join and hear what leadership had to tell the players. Still up on the fourteenth floor of my corncob, I noticed a big group of people next to the athletics fields and saw that lighting under the Dome was still in daytime mode. Next, chasing after each other, Anya, Imran and I ran down the spiral staircase and tried to sneak unnoticed into the huge audience. Unfortunately though, we were spotted. As soon as I got near the crowd, a few voices trumpeted out: "Hey, Gnat's here!" And they demanded I come up on the stage.

And come on stage I did. As they looked for a microphone for me, I whispered to Tamara:

"So, what did you talk about at the directors' council? And what have you been discussing here?"

The serious dark-haired girl whispered back without turning her head:

"The Dark Faction tied up Tyulenev and dropped him off at the border. He's in prison now. Lozovsky became a Gerd, and he also was elected faction head almost unanimously, only one opposed. The Dark Faction base in the Poppy Fields has been destroyed, the harpies did a real number on it. But five hours later, the Dark Faction came back with a little response. Hundreds of forest spirits and kikimoras draped in explosives tried to blow up our base in Karelia. The Second Legion was almost completely laid out. No more than ten soldiers survived. But, by some miracle, we held out and made minced meat of those NPC's. But now, the fort and half the buildings don't have walls. Then, an hour later, a second attack wave arrived, including flying harpies. But we were ready and the two Priests and I managed to remove the control charm from them, so all the mobs dropped their suicide vests and dispersed."

I had to admit that had me very on guard. By hiring the NPC harpies, we'd accidentally opened a Pandora's box. And our enemies were fast learners, who quickly took that painful lesson to heart. From now on, we faced both the threat of direct conflict with the Dark Faction and the risk of random NPC raids, both by hired agents and mind-controlled beasts...

"And now..." not hiding her exhaustion or annoyance, the yawning Tamara led her hand over the audience, which was humming in dismay. "The new leader Lozovsky has decided to prove himself a man of democracy and discuss the Dark Faction's offers. To my eye, that was a big error... We haven't yet come to a consensus and, right before you showed up, we nearly voted to capitulate and accept an offer of vassalization. We've been chewing the fat and pontificating for three hours now, but we still haven't made any real decisions. And the funniest thing is that there is no way back now. Lozovsky assured us he came ready for dialog and would listen to every opinion. Now, we're seeing where that gets us."

"I see. And why was I dragged up on stage?"

The dark-haired girl shot me a tortured smile, giving a clear demonstration that she was still working on her facial expressions, though she was getting better:

"You know, it's the same old song... I was hoping they wouldn't be mad at you anymore. And that was basically true, but as of today their hostility is back out in the open. They're really raging, demanding the leadership explain why they keep indulging you and what makes you so different from everyone else. They're also asking about the captive Princess, the alien merchants, your Miyelonian companions, and the investigators, who many players seem to think you brought down here. Also, instead of working a normal shift on the Antique Beach today, you drove off somewhere else, which didn't go unnoticed and upset a couple players... This is gonna be hard for you, Gnat. Get ready, they're really upset. I can support you if it gets too crazy, though!"

Tamara fell sharply silent, because they found another microphone, and Aleksandr Antipov handed it to me with the words:

"Well, who better to explain Gnat's gameplay than the man himself? Come on, Gnat. Don't be shy! Tell our players what you've been up to!"

As soon as I took the microphone, the crowd started humming in dismay, demonstrating a clearly negative opinion of me. I could hear many hard-hitting invectives. They were demanding I explain myself and damn-near apologize. Did they seriously think I would do that?! Naive! Well, you wanted a memorable explanation, here you go! I smiled predatorily and raised the microphone:

"Many of our players enjoy discussing strategy and politics with an expert eye, especially those with a clouded impression of the true state of affairs. But very few truly understand my role in the faction. And it's no wonder! Such lofty matters as conversing with the leaders of great alien races and obtaining new technologies for humanity are not for those of limited intellect! Yes, you heard me right! My main mission is to get as many starship designs as possible at any cost, along with specimens of high-tech apparel and weaponry. It is not the simplest mission, let me tell you, and there are no easy formulas or rules to guide me. But still, I'm plugging away and I have been quite successful! The designs I already provided have advanced science by decades and brought humanity that much closer to interstellar flight!"

In short, I dumped a stream of inflammatory declarations on the audience. Not expecting such an aggressive charge, the crowd fell silent, listening attentively but not yet having determined how to react. I decided to build on that momentum:

"The leadership thinks Prospector Gnat is unique, and that no one could duplicate my successes. But maybe our directors are wrong. Maybe someone out there could replace me. Who of you could conduct negotiations with an incarnation of the Miyelonian Great First Female, a creature who can easily read thoughts? And could anyone here obtain information for the impatient and bloodthirsty Kung Waid Shishish, the great Geckho military leader and sovereign of our home planet? Or maybe one of you thinks they could survive on a space station teeming with bloodthirsty pirates... Anybody?"

The response was a strained silence, no one in the audience could gather the courage to make such an audacious claim. Good, I could take a breather and fortify before moving on to more pressing and obvious issues. But then, I saw that I was congratulating myself too soon. A lone cry tore out of the crowd:

"If I could study the language of these aliens, I could try too! And maybe I would do just as well as Gnat!"

I instantly picked out the loudmouth from the crowd. So, who do we have here? I easily read his thoughts and even gathered some superficial background information, then prepared a striking reply:

"Well, Viktor Viktorovich Samokhin, born 1980 in the city of Tula, a five-month veteran of the game who plays a level-54 Agrarian, what's stopping you from taking Astrolinguistics and spending at least an hour a day practicing Geckho with Kosta Dykhsh?"

The crowd gave a predictable gasp, some even stumbled back. A few players crossed themselves in fear. Tamara whispered:

"Kirill, have you lost your mind? Why did you reveal your secret?!"

But I did not think it was a mistake. In fact, now was the best opportunity. I not only had the chance, I needed to loudly announce my psionic abilities. That would not only prove my uniqueness, but also show the audience that they could no longer hide their contact with the enemy:

"Yes! That is another aspect that makes me different from the rest. It is one reason the leadership gives me so many special missions. My character has taken and leveled the Psionic skill. And now both in the game and real life, I can root out traitors in our ranks, along with those who have fallen under mental control of Dark Faction mages, and those with the stamp of their magical charms."

"And do many of us carry that 'stamp?'" Aleksandr Antipov immediately shot out, and I assured the agent that there were plenty.

"For example, Gleb Vorshinsky, an Engineer at the Prometheus. Or Lefty, our best Mechanic," I said, pointing at the slobby dude in the first row, who looked identical to his game avatar. "Lefty is an honest player and doesn't even suspect that, while he was a prisoner of the Dark Faction, their mages altered his thinking. Now without knowing it, Lefty carries their magic stamp, spreading distemper, decadence, despondency and a stubborn belief that defeat is inevitable."

Lefty, having unexpectedly become the center of attention, froze in fear. A tall bearded man in a turban came through from the back rows and, with a brief glance at the terrified young man, confirmed:

"This man carries the stamp of magical abomination! Fortunately, it is not difficult to remove. I, the Paladin Gerd Tamara, and our other Priest can all undo the Dark Faction's evil magic."

Just after the audience's shock passed, and the agitated hullaballoo settled, I continued my speech:

"Another facet of my work is obtaining space currency and purchasing goods of extraterrestrial design. After all, you all most likely heard about our faction's recent big success. We managed to sell some platinum for three million crystals and, with that money, we obtained goods and weapons. If anyone here doubts my honesty or thinks that even one crystal was lost to my sticky fingers, let them review the purchase list and compare it with prices in the Geckho space port."

No one dared doubt my honesty, so I held a short pause for order, and moved on to the most difficult part of the tale:

"Now, I strongly suspect you all know this trade was not exactly problem-free. At the very last minute, the Dark Faction attacked us, which is what brought the investigators under the Dome. They are here to determine where and when the leak took place. But still, the main thing is that we managed to fight them off and keep all our things. Plus, all they got for their efforts were some counterfeit crystals, which our negotiator Ivan Lozovsky was holding as bait." I pointed to the new faction head and he gave a slight bow, as if confirming my words and accepting that story as official, for the simple players at least. "What's more, our enemy didn't realize they were fake, and got hit with a very severe penalty from the Geckho after trying to buy items with them in the space port. Yesterday morning, Dark Faction leader Leng Thumor-Anhu La-Fin couldn't even hold back his admiration and congratulated us on the operation, which he said was 'very painful' to his faction."

I heard laughter from the crowd for the first time, along with shouts of approval and even the odd fit of applause. So, I decided not to change topic and build on the effect by speaking about our aggressive neighbors:

"You really can't envy the Dark Faction now! In the last few days, their position has just gotten harder and harder. They couldn't stop us from building a base in Karelia, lost their unfinished base in the Poppy Fields, and angered the Geckho. Then, they failed to intercept our Miyelonian weaponry, some of which can destroy their huge armored tanks! So now, those formerly invulnerable instruments of destruction are nothing more than big lumbering death traps!"

Another volley of elated cries rang out, then confident applause, but I stopped them with a gesture and moved on to the story of my recent journey with the Centaurs:

"And I come bearing even more unpleasant news for our enemies. I know a few people here have asked where Gerd Gnat ran off to today instead of patrolling the Antique Beach. Well, the time has come for you all to know. Today, we signed a military alliance with the Antiquity Faction. Six hundred high-level Centaurs and Minotaurs will be joining us in battle against the Dark Faction. What's more, our NPC neighbors are giving us the Centaur Plateau node and will even help us build a fort there. But that isn't all! Tomorrow... or more like this evening, three hundred fully equipped and heavily armed soldiers from the H6 Faction will be arriving to our dock via Geckho ferry. That's right, friends, I found the Germans. They agreed to aid us against the Dark Faction on the condition that we help them win a heated war with the underwater NPC

Naiads."

My announcement caused a storm of jubilation! They were overjoyed that we had allies and were celebrating as if the war with the darksiders was already won. I understood that this was not even remotely true, but it was still a significant improvement. And so, I figured it was the right time to tell them the slipperiest part of the story:

"And we made another blow to the Dark Faction when we captured the noble Princess Minn-O La-Fin. She is being held in our prison now. This isn't the first time Leng Thumor-Anhu La-Fin's beloved granddaughter has fallen into our hands, and every time I was somehow involved. As such, according to the Dark Faction's laws and traditions, the noble lady has become my wayedda to avoid shame. Now, wayedda translates from their language as 'lawful plunder.' That means that she will not be ransomed, and that the Princess will be released from prison to become my loyal companion. Minn-O is no longer our enemy, although we also cannot demand that she reveal secrets about her homeworld. As a confirmation of the seriousness of this event, the Dark Faction Leng has agreed to our demand and returned the traitor Tyulenev!"

What a harsh and vindictive people I come from! The return of the filthy traitor was celebrated with more vigor than our new alliance. The howls and shouts of joy were deafening. And mixed into all that noise, some of my allies were suggesting ways of torturing Tyulenev that I would not have had either the imagination or the cruelty to come up with.

But not everyone was happy. Gerd Tamara walked off stage showing no emotion, unhurried and with dignity. After she made it away from the crowd, she hid behind some bushes, buried her face in her hands and began to weep. Seemingly, the girl didn't like the news that I would now have the princess for a constant companion.

But there were no questions remaining, so I considered the speech over and followed Gerd Tamara off the stage, ceding the floor. I wanted to catch up to Tamara and explain, but Gerd Lozovsky intercepted me. Not hiding his tense joy, the new faction leader asked me to tell him the details of my negotiations with the Centaurs and the story of meeting the Germans. So I did:

"Everything was simple with the Centaurs. Phylira is much smarter than the other chiefs and negotiating with her is a delight. She was afraid of a serious conflict with humanity, because she understands that a big war would end with the defeat and death of her faction. What's more, those NPC's really couldn't care less about fortresses and fortifications on their lands if we just let them live in peace. The Centaurs aren't much interested in lifeless rocky hills. For them, the only thing of value in that node is the freshwater spring, the only one in the area. As long as we let the Centaurs collect water there and freely move about the Centaur Plateau, Phylira sees no obstacle to us building a fort. The Antiquity Faction is also willing to trade with us. They can provide lumber, clay, fruit and pearls. The Centaurs and Dryads are even willing to work for us directly as long as we give fair pay."

"Now that is what I like to hear!" the new faction leader shot out. "We could use help everywhere, not only in that node. By the way, I'll put Gerd Radugin in charge of developing the Centaur Plateau. He's a talented manager and after all that confusion, he is desperate to prove his worth. Radugin was already considering expansion to the south. He has all the calculations and maps ready."

I shrugged carelessly. Radugin was fine. I had no unkind feelings toward the former faction leader and understood that he had just burned out trying to shoulder too many burdens.

"But if..." here I lowered my voice to a whisper and made sure no one was listening, "we help Matriarch Phylira eliminate the other chiefs, we can have all six nodes of the Antiquity Faction under the same conditions. Phylira herself offered that arrangement, and I promised to think it over. The Centauress refuses to kill her competitors personally, but she would be favorably inclined to our Assassins doing so. The six nodes are not the most inhabitable, mostly just swampy forest, but the new forts would increase our faction's maximum population."

Lozovsky promised to seriously think over the issue, then asked me to return to my meeting with the Germany faction. Here I allowed myself to laugh:

"Oh you should have seen the show we put on! Just imagine the scene: we blew our horns and a huge army poured out from three sides onto a plain where the H6 Faction was building a fort. It was glorious: the Minotaurs, Satyrs and Dryads running, the Centaurs leaping. Their thousands of hooves shook the earth. Dust rose like a pillar. And at the head of this flood, our armored vehicle drives out with the Russian tricolor blowing in the wind! Riding atop the Peresvet, we had a commando group of twenty almost totally nude Dryad Archers over level one hundred. And the fatal beauties were accompanied by our Space Commando Eduard Boyko in his giant exoskeleton armor. It was such a surreal picture I couldn't believe I was really there. It made such an impression on the fort defenders that, even when we entered their building, they didn't fire a single shot!"

"I'm not surprised!" Lozovsky laughed. "I can't imagine how I would behave in a situation like that. But what came next?"

"Well, of course it was all solved quickly, even though only San-Sanych knew German. He used to buy second-hand cars from Germany, so he had a passing knowledge. They agreed not to shoot and called someone from their leadership. A half hour later, H6 Diplomat Gerhard Stern came out and immediately grasped the scale of the problem. The Germans are fast thinkers though, so they ordered fifty barrels of beer rolled out for their 'dear NPC guests.' After that, the Centaurs' and Minotaurs' hostility blew away like the wind. The rest of the negotiations took place in a different node next to a Geckho cargo port. I asked for that because I saw our suzerains' ferry coming into dock. It made a big impression on them, seeing the Geckho crew and their captain recognize me and greet me warmly. The furballs remembered me as the one who stopped their ferry from capsizing. The Germans were watching with eyes wide in astonishment. My Authority immediately took off to unimaginable heights! Of course, after that, they agreed to all my suggestions pretty quick."

I WAS AWOKEN by a cautious but insistent knock on the door. I stood up, trying not to awaken Anya as she slept soundly. I had a hard time finding my pants and shirt. After I finally did, I went to open up. It was Tamara. I found it strange to see her in a dressing gown.

"Kirill, I was asked to come wake you up. You are urgently needed in the game."

"But I only got four hours' sleep... less actually," I said, looking unwittingly at the bedroom door. "What's going on?"

"A Shiamiru-class Geckho starship has just landed in the very center of our capital fortress. Captain Uraz Tukhsh demands to see you. He insists that he has already contracted with you for one more prospecting expedition."

Crap... I didn't even know if that should make me happy or mad. On the one hand, I could expect adventures, new knowledge and unique discoveries. But on the other, tomorrow was the decisive battle with the Dark Faction, and missing that would be swinish behavior bordering on desertion. What was more, my "travelling mistress" was currently in prison (and most likely not in the game, so impossible to find), and my

Miyelonian companions were also probably inactive. I really didn't want to leave anyone behind. Furthermore, I hadn't picked up my bracelet from Lefty yet, and lots of other issues were also still unresolved.

"I wanted you to be at my birthday party tomorrow. We're planning to celebrate it right after the big battle. But I guess it wasn't in the cards," Tamara chuckled glumly. " I was really hoping you'd give me a gift, and one for a girl not a soldier..."

Tamara was transparently hinting at the rocket set I had brought her from the space station. Seemingly, she didn't like it very much. I had to improvise:

"I'll do my best to be at your party in the real world, but I cannot promise. And I have a gift for you not only as a Paladin, but as a pretty girl. It isn't totally finished yet, though. I need time."

Anya walked up wrapped in a blanket, looking out of it. She'd woken up despite my best efforts and wanted to figure out why I was up so early. I noticed that Anya was looking confident and acting like she owned the place. She even dared express dismay to the fearsome Tamara. The Leader of the Second Legion didn't let it go unanswered though, and asked me with unhidden scorn:

"So, haven't you explained to your lover what a wayedda is yet?"

I just shook my head in the negative, not wanting to get into it. Instead, I thanked Tamara for telling me about the starship, apologized for my likely absence from her birthday party the next day and closed the door right in her astonished face.

"You have five minutes to get ready to enter the game," I announced to Anya. "We logged off in the Yellow Mountains fort, and we need to get to the capital node as fast as possible. Do you have the phone number for Imran's room? Great, call him, and have him come too! I'll go look for Eduard's number."

"Hey, what's happening?" Anya didn't understand. "And why the rush?"

"A Geckho starship has come to pick me up. And if Captain Uraz Tukhsh has come this far just for me, he must really need Gnat. I'll see if I can get him to take some friends along."

Anya was naked and decisively threw off the blanket, sat on the bed and crossed her arms over her chest with an unhappy look.

"I'm not going anywhere! There's a very important battle tomorrow, and the survival of our faction depends on it! How will I look my friends in the eye if we lose and I wasn't there?!"

"We won't lose, especially with almost one thousand extra soldiers," I assured the stubborn medic. "What's more... I have an idea for how to force the Dark Faction Leng to delay the attack."

"No, Gnat. I'm not coming this time!" the blonde balked. "Helping you against the Dark Faction is one thing. That was right. But heading off into space instead of helping our faction... that goes too far! So no! No! And no again!"

"You know best. I hope you don't end up regretting your choice!"

I flew out into the corridor and hurried down to the first floor. I asked the sleepy doorwoman Yana to find Eduard and Imran, and tell them both to immediately enter the game, then ran off to corncob fifteen.

FROM THE DISTANCE, I noticed that the Shiamiru had undergone some significant changes. The rear cargo hold was gone. Instead, there was an extra energy shield module. There were also two long cannons in the front and some strange reflectors on its short wings. Had the captain grown disenchanted with mineral extraction and decided to try his hand a pirate?

"Gnat!" A heavily armed figure in a military spacesuit ran at me. They looked short for a Geckho, which was what tipped me off. It was Uline Tar!

The Trader was overwhelmed with emotion and embraced me tightly, lifted me up and spun me around.

"We were so worried about you! I'm so glad you managed to escape those nasty Miyelonians. Oh!"

Only here did Uline notice Tini coming out of the Peresvet after me, and Ayni standing nearby. She held her gaze on the lady cat and probably noticed she was a Translator, because she started looking embarrassed and set me down. Sure, it was awkward, but I tried to distract the Geckho woman, asking what fates had brought them here and wanting to know what had happened to our once peaceful shuttle.

"Well, there's a war on! The Geckho have joined the fight against the Meleyephatians. Our new leader

Kung Waid Shishish is rallying combat starships. Our poor bastard of a captain spent the last of his funds refitting the old Shiamiru for combat, hoping to finally achieve glory. But we ran into a problem. The crew split as soon as they heard what was happening, because no one wants to go to war with a chronic loser. And the remaining crew, including me, constantly reminded Uraz Tukhsh that luck was with us only when Gnat was. Seemingly, the captain believed that and ordered us to immediately fly off to get you, especially given that we already contracted you for one more expedition."

"I agreed to a voyage to the asteroid belt to extract minerals, not to fly half way across the galaxy and fight in some war!" I tried to object, to which Uline Tar mentioned that my contract had no limitations of that sort, and that any judge would find in favor of Uraz Tukhsh.

"But you can try and change the conditions of your contract for the better," she whispered. "If you don't push it too far, Uraz Tukhsh will probably agree."

"Then tell the captain my conditions: the two Miyelonians are coming with me, and it's not up for discussion. They are my companions and I won't go anywhere without them because doing so would violate the norms and laws of their race. I also want to take two human soldiers with me. A Gladiator and a Space Commando. They are my team as a Gerd. Also..." I took a deep sigh, "my travelling mistress is coming."

Authority increased to 28!

I had already managed to speak with Imran and Eduard, so I knew they would join "Team Gnat" and come with me. I hadn't yet spoken with Minn-O, but I also was counting on her assent. Technically, given her position as a "travelling mistress," she would have no choice but to accompany her "strong warrior."

Uline walked away and came on board the ship. She was away for quite some time I even started to worry, but then the Trader came out, nearly jumping for joy:

"The captain agreed! Uraz Tukhsh was actually glad because the humans can fill out our crew. He's ready to take off immediately!"

"Uh, no. I'm not ready yet... This is all too sudden. I need at least one ummi to get everyone together."

Strangely, Uraz Tukhsh also agreed to that. The Shiamiru turned off its thrusters and lowered its ground supports, settling in for a long stay. The Geckho crew, initially nervous to see people surrounding their starship and pointing their weapons at anyone who came close, gradually calmed down. Some of them even risked eating a meal in the human canteen, although I later heard they found our cuisine bland.

The Starship Pilot also emerged. At first, I didn't recognize the huge figure wearing a glimmering armored spacesuit. But it was Dmitry Zheltov, clearly wearing refit Geckho armor. I embraced my friend warmly and he, slightly embarrassed, commented on his new appearance:

"Look at me now. I've been taken on as main pilot. I got a crew-member identity card and all the documents that go with it. And with my first bonus, I bought myself this armor suit at the Oku-III station. I gave all the rest of the money I earned to the faction just now, and that was practically three thousand Geckho crystals!"

My comrade's face was beaming with well-deserved pride because he was bringing the faction a real boon, both new knowledge about the game Universe, and desperately needed space currency. Dmitry didn't hide anything about his plans, either:

"A war has started, so I am leveling skills and preparing to take the official Geckho space-fleet pilot exams. Uraz Tukhsh trusts me completely, and now he just sits in the copilot's seat, very rarely telling me the meaning of unfamiliar terms. Overall, both the captain and the whole crew are glad to see you back, though. They consider you a lucky charm!"

I noticed someone behind me, and Dmitry waved his hand in greeting, hurriedly bid me farewell and rushed over to Lydia Vertyachikh, who was waiting for him. I glanced at their warm embrace and passionate kisses, mentally wished my friends happiness, then headed off to talk with the prison guards about Minn-O.

Sure, my companions were important to me, but they weren't the main reason I wanted the Shiamiru to wait around. Finally though, that had also come around. Lefty walked up to me with clear respect and, dramatically different from his earlier behavior, handed me the bracelet:

"I removed the racial requirement. Now the bracelet will work for a human. What's more, I managed to improve it and add something. Now, the shields recharge faster and have higher capacity."

I thanked the craftsman and studied the new properties of the Relict artifact:

Small Control Bracelet (Listener armor suit accessory)

+25% armor suit forcefield capacity.

+13% forcefield restore rate.

+1 controllable drone.

Statistic requirements: Intelligence 26, Perception 26.

Skill requirements: Electronics 40, Machine Control 11.

My character met all the requirements, so I immediately placed the bracelet in the arm slot of my suit. But I was not expecting what came next. A small wave of unfamiliar symbols ran before my eyes. There were many, many thousands of incomprehensible lines. Finally, the semitransparent bluish pall faded, and one column turned brighter and was translated to Russian:

"Listener, awaiting command."

I had long suspected that my suit contained much more complex functionality than forcefield capacity and radiation resistance and I now had clear confirmation of that. I didn't understand what kind of command it wanted, though, or how I could issue it. How could I answer, or at least get rid of these words, which were taking up room on the internal side of my helmet visor? Mentally? By moving my pupils? Voice?

As I stood and figured out my suit, Minn-O was brought to me under guard, and the proud Princess walked up the gangway before all my other companions. After her, Imran entered the Shiamiru.

But Space Commando Eduard had problems. In his huge exoskeleton armor, he couldn't fit through the door, so he had to remove the armor and change back into street clothes. Vasha Tushihh lifted the heavy armor with the loader claw and put it into a special niche in the back of the shuttle, hermetically sealing it with an armored cap.

The Miyelonians also entered, and I asked Ayni, who was walking forward with only a tiny backpack, where her heavy container of equipment for the special mission was. We had room, if she wanted to bring it. The orange cat looked embarrassed, then slightly afraid and whispered something like: "Gnat, the less you know, the better you'll sleep. Believe me, you should forget about that."

Anyhow, we were about to take off. I was the last thing they were waiting for. And I was just standing there, unable to get the bothersome text out of my field of view. I even tried to remove the bracelet, but it seemed glued to my armored sleeve and refused to go anywhere. But what to do? I couldn't let these illuminated words keep blocking half my view, otherwise I might miss something. I tried everything I could think of to get rid of it or respond. I verbally issued commands, shook my head, spun my pupils and tried to command mentally when suddenly:

"Decision accepted"

ATTENTION!!! Your class will be changed to Listener.

10... 9... 8...

End of Book Two

Want to be the first to know about our latest LitRPG, sci fi and fantasy titles from your favorite authors?

Subscribe to our **New Releases** newsletter:
http://eepurl.com/b7niIL

Thank you for reading *External Threat!*
If you like what you've read, check out other sci-fi, fantasy and LitRPG novels published by Magic Dome Books:

***Reality Benders* LitRPG series by Michael Atamanov:**
Countdown
External Threat
Game Changer
Web of Worlds
A Jump into the Unknown
Aces High

***The Dark Herbalist* LitRPG series
by Michael Atamanov:**
Video Game Plotline Tester
Stay on the Wing
A Trap for the Potentate
Finding a Body

***Perimeter Defense* LitRPG series by Michael Atamanov:**
Sector Eight
Beyond Death
New Contract
A Game with No Rules

***League of Losers* LitRPG Series
by Michael Atamanov:**
A Cat and his Human

***The Way of the Shaman* LitRPG series
by Vasily Mahanenko:**
Survival Quest
The Kartoss Gambit
The Secret of the Dark Forest
The Phantom Castle
The Karmadont Chess Set
Shaman's Revenge
Clans War

***The Alchemist* LiTRPG series by Vasily Mahanenko:**
City of the Dead
Forest of Desire
Tears of Alron

Dark Paladin LitRPG series by Vasily Mahanenko:
The Beginning
The Quest
Restart

Galactogon LitRPG series by Vasily Mahanenko:
Start the Game!
In Search of the Uldans
A Check for a Billion

Invasion LitRPG Series by Vasily Mahanenko:
A Second Chance
An Equation with one Unknown

World of the Changed LitRPG Series by Vasily Mahanenko:
No Mistakes
Pearl of the South

**The Bard from Barliona LitRPG series
by Eugenia Dmitrieva and Vasily Mahanenko:**
The Renegades
A Song of Shadow

Level Up LitRPG series by Dan Sugralinov:
Re-Start
Hero
The Final Trial
Level Up: The Knockout (with Max Lagno)
Level Up. The Knockout: Update (with Max Lagno)

Disgardium LitRPG series by Dan Sugralinov:
Class-A Threat
Apostle of the Sleeping Gods
The Destroying Plague
Resistance
Holy War

World 99 LitRPG Series by Dan Sugralinov:
Blood of Fate

Adam Online LitRPG Leries by Max Lagno:
Absolute Zero
City of Freedom

El Diablo by G.Zotov
(a supernatural thriller)

Mirror World LitRPG series by Alexey Osadchuk:
Project Daily Grind
The Citadel
The Way of the Outcast
The Twilight Obelisk

Underdog LitRPG series by Alexey Osadchuk:
Dungeons of the Crooked Mountains
The Wastes
The Dark Continent
The Otherworld

An NPC's Path LitRPG series by Pavel Kornev:
The Dead Rogue
Kingdom of the Dead
Deadman's Retinue

The Sublime Electricity series by Pavel Kornev:
The Illustrious
The Heartless
The Fallen
The Dormant

Citadel World series by Kir Lukovkin:
The URANUS Code
The Secret of Atlantis

You're in Game!
(LitRPG Stories from Bestselling Authors)

You're in Game-2!
(More LitRPG stories set in your favorite worlds)

The Fairy Code by Kaitlyn Weiss:
Captive of the Shadows
Chosen of the Shadows

More books and series are coming out soon!

In order to have new books of the series translated faster, we need your help and support! Please consider leaving a review or spread the word by recommending *External Threat* to your friends and posting the link on social media. The more people buy the book, the sooner we'll be able to make new translations available.

Thank you!

Till next time!